CROWN CHASERS

CROWN CHASERS

REBECCA COFFINDAFFER

An Imprint of HarperCollinsPublishers

HarperTeen is an imprint of HarperCollins Publishers.

Crownchasers
Copyright © 2020 by Full Fathom Five, LLC

Library of Congress Control Number: 2020937199
ISBN 978-0-06-284516-0

Typography by Chris Kwon
20 21 22 23 24   PC/LSCH   10 9 8 7 6 5 4 3 2 1
❖

First Edition

To Mom and Dad, who patiently read my very first stories.

I promise, this one is much better.

PROLOGUE

THE OTARI CAME HERE TO DIE.

The storm is no place for a living thing. Wind and sleet howl through the ravine, thick greenish clouds tainting what little light reaches the cold planet's surface. The cliff face is bare, just slick black stone eroded by poison rain. The center of the basin has turned to mud a half meter thick, where one misstep would mean a slow suffocation.

And yet a figure moves through the mire.

The otari pauses to get his bearings and leans against an outcropping. The light from his wrist-mounted display is barely visible in the maelstrom. He raises his head, looking back the way he had come. Surely this is deep enough, far enough. Remote enough.

After a moment, the otari trudges on.

His survival suit is standard-issue—airtight and lightly armored, with heavy-duty gloves and boots and the dome of a helmet. But all insignias and labels have been stripped away. The computerized wristband is rudimentary—no geo-pulse or satellite link that might be scanned or tracked. Electronically, magnetically, the suit is invisible.

Its occupant is just as much a ghost. He'd had a name, but he'd left it behind long ago, dedicating himself to serving the throne by joining one of the most secretive, elite forces in the empire. His face exists on no database. His flesh has been scrubbed of any identifying marks.

There is no one who knows him, no one who will miss him, no person or creature left alive who will remember him. He's mastered the art of disappearing, of passing through spaceports like a wraith, another face in the crowd.

This has been his life.

His journey has taken weeks, hopping from planet to planet, following a seemingly random path across the quadrant to confuse any who might be following him. No one can know his task or his final destination. Every precaution has been taken to ensure he cannot be tracked.

And yet he still glances over his shoulder, as if something might be watching him in the dark.

His eyes shift back to the ravine. A little farther.

The wind picks up, buffeting his suit. The howl is deafening, screaming through the canyon. The otari pushes on, wedging himself between two rock faces and shimmying down, down to where no light is visible. Under the rock shelf it's drier, the wind softer, the howling reduced to a low whimper.

This is it. *Here.*

From a secret panel on his suit, the otari extracts the object he's carried with him for so long, the item he's kept hidden until this very moment. It is a small thing to be so important—a flat platinum disc, about the size of his palm. The royal seal.

As his gloved fingertips touch it, the surface ripples, revealing the slightly raised emblem of the United Sovereign Empire: an array of luminous pinpricks representing the allied planets, joined by faint geodesic lines, and on top of that, a crown situated over the crest of the Faroshti family, who currently hold the throne.

Soon—very soon, he imagines—that crest will disappear.

At the back of the small cave is a pile of rocks, almost like an altar. Perfect. He places the seal there.

The otari returns to the mouth of the cave and glances at the sky, wishing for a moment of sunlight. Just a glimmer of reward, after all he's done in service to Solarus, even walking away from the war gods of his childhood.

But the planet is too cold, and the storm too violent.

It's all right. He brought a bit of the Everlasting Light with him anyway.

Keeping his eyes up and open, he unlatches a small panel on the collar of his suit and presses the button underneath. Heat flares against his skin—so bright, so fierce, so much like redemption. He has been drifting in the cold emptiness of space for so very long. A prayer rises, fervent, to his lips, and a ripple of fire and light consumes him. His body crumbles into ash.

The cave goes dark again, and the wind moans.

Though no one knows it yet, the chase is on.

ONE

Stardate: 0.05.09 in the Year 4031, under the rule of Emperor Atar Faroshti, stars and gods bless him and long may he reign
Location: In orbit around Apex on the best damn ship in the universe

SOMETHING CRAWLED UP INTO MY SKULL AND DIED.

I've seen it happen before. Guy named Holder Ocktay. He was the best black-market circuit-hacker in the quadrant until one day all his craft just slipped out of his brain. He got this twitch in his leg he couldn't steady and his eyes started rolling back on the regular. Bright lights made it worse—that was a big red flag. Some Solari came around, talking like old Holder was divinely touched and getting messages direct from Solarus. But I told Holder to wait before he went full prophet and helped him splurge on a medbot instead. The android went up through Holder's nose and fished out this thing, about the size of a hangnail but with pincers and suckers that look terrifying under a microscope. Memory-worm. Little bastard was camped out in Holder's hippocampus. He'd picked it up doing an under-the-table job for a Ygrisl merchants guild on an abandoned planetoid.

This is why I never fly a job without a med plan.

Long story shorter, I bought that specimen off Holder. Turned it over to the Explorers' Society—got a badge for *exotic plasmodium* and a tidy infusion of credits—and have been dealing with low-grade memory-worm paranoia ever since.

This, though . . . This isn't some brain insect. This is thanks to the thirteen (thirteen!—that's our Alyssa Farshot, always breaking records, thank you very much) juniper twists I drank last night. Which means I've got the same splitting headache and sensitivity to light that Holder had, but with an unwelcome coating of sticky sugar and bile gumming up my mouth.

Nice, Alyssa. Real nice.

I roll over on my cot and groan. Feel the cool laminate of my pillow against my cheek.

Wait. Not my pillow. Not my cot. I know that sensation and that burnt-toast smell. I passed out on the galley dining table.

Ugh.

I don't want to open my eyes. Besides the supernova-sized hangover, I know what I'll see: a mess. Last night's celebration got a bit out of hand. I don't want to experience the aftermath.

I could scrap the worldcruiser, take my latest paycheck from the Society, trade up to a newer model. The *Vagabond Quick*—my baby— is several years old, but she has some decent upgrades and is in way better shape than you'd think given the hell I've put her through the past three years.

Like that time we upstreamed a meteor shower on a bet with Nathalia Coyenne. (Lost, but got farther than her, anyway.)

Or when we almost got swallowed up by Sid, the sentient tar pit

I interviewed on Rhydin IV. That was a big one for the Explorers' Society—first contacts always are.

Or when we pulled a slingshot along the rings of Orpheus to outrun a crew of scavengers.

My *Vagabond*. No way I'd toss out a ship this good. Not when we've earned so many of our bruises together.

I peel open one eye, then the other. Streamers hang from the venting. My left boot is somehow up there too. A super-wobbly dartboard has been drawn onto the bulkhead with red sauce. (I think it's sauce. I hope it's sauce.) The galley counter is a disaster zone of bottles and dirty dishes and a pot of what looks like orangey-gray cheese. Did we try to make foarian nachos? Oh hell.

Above it all hangs the banner: "CONGRATS, VAGABOND!"

The "congrats" are for our recent successful circumnavigation of Tinus, an Explorers' Society first. It's been an open challenge for a decade, ever since Tinus was added to the empire. Traversing a planet with a bad case of volcanic acne, which, combined with unpredictable gravity fluctuations, leads to a weather phenomenon best described as "sky avalanches"—yeah, not everyone's idea of a fun weekend. The Explorers' Society had started giving out rewards simply for vids of the planet's surface, just to encourage members to get out there. I did them one better.

Yes, I am that good. Yes, I am that amazing.

Yes, I'm about to be sick.

On the galley control panel, the comms light flashes red. I ignore it.

I take my time sitting up. Continents drift faster. Only the promise of a grease-filled breakfast gets me moving. I work some moisture into my mouth.

"Rose?"

A soothing automated voice answers me from the wall speakers. "Good afternoon, Captain Farshot. Your physiological outputs are suboptimal and indicate you may have engaged in excess. Do you require a BEC?"

"In my hour of need, Rose, you're always there for me."

"Affirmative."

I pull down the banner and wrap it around my shoulders like a robe. Here she is, Queen Alyssa, dauntless pursuer of calorie-rich hangover cures. I roll off my table-bed as the smell of sizzling bacon fills the galley. So good.

The comms are still flashing. No thanks. Not right now.

Go. Away.

The main party, the big event, went pretty late at the Society's ballroom down on Apex—open bar, fancy snacks on silver trays, credit awards for me and the other explorers who earned badges in the last quarter. I was pretty well hammered by the time Hell Monkey and I headed back into orbit. I should have called it a night then, but H.M. had other plans. *Time for the after-party!* he'd said. Bottles for each of us. A card game. Nachos, apparently, and . . . Did I . . . ?

I check under my shirt. Bra's missing.

Dammit. Did I hook up with Hell Monkey? Again? I really need to stop doing that. I mean, he's a buddy and a top-notch world-cruiser engineer, but *he calls himself Hell Monkey.*

The oven pops up with my bacon-egg-and-cheese. Oh yes.

I grab my sandwich and start down the starboard-side corridor to the bridge. The bacon is actually crisp—nice work, Rose—and the bun is soaked in grease. Heavenly. I've ignored the red blinking comms long enough that the alert lights have begun to strobe overhead. Each illumination is like a bolt to my temple. But I know this ship like the back of my hand. I could navigate it with my eyes closed, so that's exactly what I do right now. One hand clutching the last of my breakfast, the other waving in front of me like I'm some sort of undead prowler who's given up brains for eggs and cheese.

My fingers brush the back of my captain's chair, and I sit.

For the second time this morning, I wrench my eyes open.

The comms are still going off, lighting up the whole conn. Someone is hailing my vessel. No identification, no call sign. Just some unmarked liftship. I don't even need to check the viewscreen—I can see the damn thing through the windows that wrap the *Vagabond*'s prow. It hangs there, in synchronous orbit with us above the blue orb of Apex. How long has it been hailing me? An hour? Two? What kind of mad sadist wakes a girl this early in the morning?

I glance at the time readout on the conn. Okay, maybe not quite morning. Maybe more like late afternoon. But still.

Sadist.

I mash the unmute button on the conn's interface and flip on audio communications.

"What?" I say, mouth half-full. "What? What? What? If this is another interview request, I hope you can spacewalk because I'm about to board your scrap-metal liftship and dump you out the airlock. Quote me on that." Silence. "Now, now—don't let my cheery disposition intimidate you. Identify yourself already."

A readout streams across my display, the interstellar equivalent of a calling card. Fancy font. A familiar seal. A very familiar name. In fact, probably the last name I want to see right now.

Shit.

Shit. Shit. Shit.

The name is Charles Viqtorial, my uncle's husband and chief envoy.

The readout says, "Urgent Business."

And the seal? It's the imperial kind.

Yeah, my uncle is the emperor. Sometimes even I forget.

TWO

"H.M., WAKE UP. WE'VE GOT COMPANY."

I nudge Hell Monkey's leg, and my partner in exploring jolts up, hits his head, and crumples back into bed like the loser of an otari bare-knuckle brawl. There's padding bolted to the bulkhead above H.M.'s pillow, because this is not the first time he's had a hangover run-in with it. His face—with his brown hair shaved close to his head and two days' stubble darkening the fair skin of his jawline— is half-obscured by a solar visor, something he usually only dons when dealing with the radiant lights of our engine panels. The rest of him is swaddled in streamers, a flimsy sheet, and not much else.

"Who goes there?" H.M. mumbles, voice rough like radio static. He coughs and lifts up the visor. "Oh. Hey there."

He needs to put that face away. It's too kissable—apparently. According to my inebriated self. But I'm woefully sober right now, so there'd be no excuse for it. No more hooking up with Hell Monkey, Alyssa. Especially not when Uncle Charlie is on his way to our ship.

"Hey, yourself. Get your butt out of bed. We've got a visitor." I nudge him again. "That's an order."

"You should be more careful waking me like that," Hell Monkey says. "You know I sleep armed. My reflexes might take over and—*bam*—you're disintegrated before you can say '*let me get you some coffee, lover.*'"

He reaches into the sheets and yanks out what he expects to be his blaster.

"That's my boot, you idiot."

He blinks at it. "Yeah, well. I could have booted you to death."

I smile and yank up him upright. "Get dressed, ya grunt."

He looks around for his clothes. "Help me."

I start to pick through the piles of dirty shirts and underpants on Hell Monkey's floor. This is the life of a top-tier science jockey and worldcruiser captain. Behold the glamour.

"Do you remember naming me cocaptain last night?" Hell Monkey asks as he tugs on some pants.

"That one hundred percent did not happen."

He grins at me. "Oh, it def—" He's cut off by a hiccup and seems to forget the whole thing when I step in front of him and wipe a bit of lip gloss—my lip gloss—off the corner of his mouth.

I raise my eyebrows, standing just a bit too close to be professional. Like, not even our standard of professional. "You were saying?"

"I . . ." H.M. blinks, drags his shirt on over his head. "I was saying, who the hell is hailing us?"

"You're not going to believe it."

A few minutes later, Charlie's liftship has docked, and the light above the port-side seal turns green. The doors open with a hiss and a rush of coolant, and in steps Charlie. Sash. Glittering ceremonial medals. White, freckled skin. Thinning hair. You don't get to be the chief envoy of an intergalactic empire without going prematurely bald, I guess.

It's a grand entrance, but I'm surprised Charlie's alone. He's usually flanked by two gunned-up otari crownsguards, all stony skin and bad attitudes. The fact he's unaccompanied means this isn't an official, on-the-books visit. This is much worse.

"Hey, Charlie, how's tricks?" I say, trying to sound casual.

Charlie's face pinches. "This is how you greet official guests?"

H.M. and I are seated with our coffee on the floor of the corridor right in front of the docking seal. I'm still wrapped in the "CONGRATS!" banner and H.M.'s all wrinkled clothes and mussed hair. Hardly a royal welcome.

"Sorry," I say. I meant to at least stand up, I really did, but the floor of the ship is super unsteady right now. "Did you want some coffee? It's terrible."

"The worst," mumbles H.M. He's put on his omni-goggles, which make him look half rock star and half android. "Hey, nice to finally meet you in person, Chaz. Your niece here is a hell of a pilot."

Charlie is a full-on small-talk enthusiast. I once clocked him at some ambassadorial event where he made empty conversation with folks for two straight hours. It was master-level work. So I'm shocked as hell when he drops H.M.'s comment like last week's takeout and looks back at me, his jaw set.

"Alyssa, we need to speak."

I don't like this feeling that's starting to grow in my stomach. "Okay."

"Alone."

I shake my head. "Sorry, Charlie. Anything you say to me, you can say to Hell Monkey." I swirl the contents of my mug and make a face. "And our semi-gelatinous coffee."

"It's sludge," Hell Monkey adds. "You sure you don't want some?"

Charlie's Official Chief Envoy mask slips a little, and it hits me how miserable he looks. Like, I know I don't call as often as I should, but the lines on his face are definitely deeper than the last time I spoke to him.

"Don't leave us hanging here," I say. "What's up?"

"Atar is sick."

I frown. Not really what I was expecting to come out of his mouth. "Is that all? Seriously, Charlie, you've been married to him longer than I've been alive. You know what a terrible patient he is. He's mopey and whiny and depressed, but he's not *actually* dying. Not for real."

"I'm sorry, Alyssa," Charlie says, "but this time he is. Dying. For real."

Everything in my chest cavity plummets. Like someone scooped it all out and dropped it in a gravity well. "You're not serious, Charlie. You can't . . . It's not . . ."

His eyebrows lift sky-high. Almost up to his retreating hairline. "Not what? Possible?"

I throw my arms wide, and H.M. barely misses getting a faceful of coffee sludge. "No! It's not possible! He's way too young, by several decades at least! I thought—"

I thought we had so much more time. But I don't say that part out loud.

Charlie steps farther into the corridor and sinks down onto the floor, right across from us. Imperial sash and fancy medals and all. His shoulders sag. I wonder if he ever gets tired of carrying around that official persona. He wears it so well that it's easy to forget it's not all of him. Even for me. And he helped raise me.

"I know," he says wistfully. "I did too. We all did."

Hell Monkey presses his arm against mine, and I let him. I stare down at my hands, wrapped around the now-empty coffee cup in my lap.

"He's the emperor, for god's sake, Charlie." My voice sounds smaller than usual. "They invent a new medical procedure every time he stubs a toe. Where the hell are his doctors?"

"Right where they're supposed to be. All sixteen of them. It's just"—Charlie's face twists as the words hit his tongue—"not working."

I can feel Hell Monkey watching me, and when I don't say anything, he clears his throat. "I'm sorry, Charlie. That's . . . a raw deal, man."

Charlie actually kind of smiles at that. "Thank you, Hell Monkey. It is, indeed, a raw deal, as you put it. For all of us. Atar has been a good emperor, and now"—his eyes fall on me—"we have to think of succession."

"Oh," I say.

So *that's* what this is about.

My uncle unified the quadrant after the Twenty-Five-Year War and brought all the prime families to peace under the banner of Emperor Atar Faroshti. (That's the family name—Faroshti. It got mistyped as Farshot when I registered at the Explorers' Society, and I never bothered to correct them.) But in all the years since then, he's never named an heir. Most emperors just pick their oldest kid and call it good, but Atar and Charlie never got around to having any kids, either. I guess he could pick a successor from one of the other prime families, but if he wanted to choose a Faroshti, he would really only have . . .

My head jerks up. "Oh. Oh shit. Hell no, Charlie. No. Whatever you and Atar are thinking, it's not happening."

"Alyssa—"

"Look at me. Look around. This strike you as regal? Nuh-uh. Done with all that."

"Alyssa," Charlie says evenly. "I'm not here to name you Atar's successor."

I take a deep breath, trying to calm down. There's no way Atar would make me his heir. If he was gonna do that, he would've done it years ago instead of buying me a ship and letting me run off into the stars. Atar is a smart guy. Too smart to hand the throne over to someone like me.

I tell myself that. I almost believe it, even.

"So what, then, Charlie? Why all the cloak-and-dagger?"

Everything is quiet for a moment, save the hum of the ship. There's still something hanging over Charlie, and I've got the sinking feeling it's hanging over me now too.

"He would like to see you. Today."

"Today?"

"Immediately."

I glance at Hell Monkey. He's finally taken off those goggles so I can see his eyes. Big hazel eyes that tell me he's got my back, no matter what.

Run, a little voice in my head calls. Run far. Run fast. Run until you find new stars.

I could just turn tail and let the government sort itself out—governments are good at that, right? I don't need to get involved. We were planning a trip to Drago VIII to hunt down some onyxium samples. Nothing has to change.

But this is Uncle Atar we're talking about. The guy who raised me. The guy who first set my eyes on the stars.

I can't turn my back on him. Can't leave without saying goodbye. Maybe his last wish isn't what I think. Maybe it won't take me too far off course.

"Sure, Charlie," I say. "Sure. Just . . . let me take a shower first."

"That," Charlie says stiffly, "would be advisable."

Godsdamned snobby royals.

THREE

Hell Monkey and I once faced down a flame tsunami, which is exactly what it sounds like. A wall of fire a mile high, rushing at you faster than the orbits of some planets, burning so hot it'll turn your ship to plasma before you see the flash. We rode the solar winds for a dozen parsecs, knowing the whole time that one false move on the controls, one twitch, and we were doomed. And know what I remember most? How we laughed the whole time. We hollered like it was the greatest transcoaster at the largest amusement complex in the galaxy.

I wasn't afraid at all.

But now, sitting in Charlie's cushy liftship as it descends toward Apex, I'm sweating through my suit.

Charlie notices my nails digging into the armrests and raises an eyebrow. I fold my hands in my lap and avoid his look. *Get ahold of yourself, Farshot.*

Exploring the unknown? That's easy. Going back to what you know? Harder.

"Your suit is . . . very nice," Charlie says, just looking for something to say.

I roll my eyes, even though the compliment puts me at ease. I can still look the part when I need to. Back on the *Vagabond Quick*, I'd engaged in a prolonged wardrobe-audition montage, and Hell Monkey had picked out the winner for me. Dark gray and tough, epaulets and gold trim, double-breasted with rows of embellished buttons going down the chest.

Hell Monkey stayed behind on the *Vagabond*, to hold her in orbit and keep the engines warm. I want to be ready to hit a hyperlight lane as soon as everything down here is tied up. It's weird to not have him with me, though. Makes the space feel a little too big. Or maybe I feel too small in it.

Charlie's liftship rumbles as it passes through the upper atmosphere of Apex. The subatmosphere wings unfold with a whir, and then we burst through the cloud line and it's nothing but ocean below. The blue-black Eastern Sea. From this altitude I can just make out breakers large enough to smash a fuel tanker to bits.

Anything looks harmless and pretty if you're far enough away.

I'm struck by a memory that I'm not primed to deal with. Me, barely out of diapers. Uncle Atar, grinning and regal. He holds me up as we look out one of the kingship's towering windows down at the roiling sea. My eyes go wide as I take it all in.

"Amazing, isn't it?" Uncle Atar had asked me back then. "Imagine what's hiding beneath those waves. Would you like to see that, Alyssa?"

Is that when it started? Did the wanderlust creep in right then and there?

It isn't long before the kingship appears on the horizon. It's something to see, and that's coming from someone who's seen a lot. A giant geodesic sphere floats above the ocean, like it's made of air instead of glass, steel, and gold. And trapped inside it is an honest-to-gods fairy-tale castle. The whole thing. I don't know how old it is exactly, but it's ancient. The castle used to be on the ground millennia ago, but no one remembers where. Big sections of the stone facade are still the same as when the castle was built, back when the quadrant was just a bunch of dots on some astronomer's hand-drawn map. They've had to reinforce the structure with new materials here and there. (It's not like there were docking bays for airships on a lot of ancient castle schematics.) And the castle's guts have changed too—state-of-the-art technology, always being upgraded, power of a sun harnessed inside, etc., etc. Hell Monkey is nuts for the kingship. He's got a collection of old blueprints stored on his personal hard drive. Dork.

Charlie's liftship dives for the underbelly of the sphere, and soon we're swinging around one of the three great cables that anchor it to Apex's surface. The kingship can travel interstellar, but Uncle Atar's always preferred to dock on Apex. The anchor cables double as power cords, drawing energy from Apex's enormous waves.

I grew up on the kingship. It was home once, until my uncles gifted me the *Vagabond Quick*. I haven't been back since.

Did they know I'd take off and never visit? Just keep following that starsong from planet to planet? They had to, right?

The eastern hangar hails us in, and we follow the track of landing drones through the bay doors.

"Welcome home," Charlie says after we've touched down.

I grimace. "Not really my home anymore, Charlie."

He sighs. "Are you ready?"

I want to come back with something clever and cavalier, but I've got nothing. So I shoot him a pair of finger guns. Charlie blinks.

Smooth, Farshot.

There's a squad of otari crownsguards waiting at the bottom of the gangplank. Shoot these guys finger guns and they'll probably take it as a threat and vaporize you. Some of the strongest and fastest humanoids in the quadrant. Their wounds heal into craggy scars with the texture and hardness of rocks and minerals found on their planet. Most otari—and the crownsguard in particular—purposely scar their fists and feet, all the better to bash in a head.

Standing out in front of them in bright yellow-and-orange robes, his fingers steepled piously together, is Enkindler Ilysium Wythe. He showed up on the kingship when I was about ten years old, an official ambassador for the Solari religion. I don't know the details, just that the only thing they love more than worshipping their sun, Solarus, is trying to convince everyone else to worship their sun too. Whatever they're doing must be working—Solari temples have been popping up all over the empire the past few years. Wythe here is an enkindler, one of the religion's leadership caste, and we never got along particularly well. I wasn't a big fan of him trying to convert me, and he wasn't a fan of me in general. Too mouthy. Too wild. Not at all useful to him in achieving his political goals.

"What the hell are you doing here?" I blurt out, and Charlie hisses with disapproval just behind me.

Wythe bows, although the guy is like two and a half meters tall so I can still see right up all three of his nostrils. "I'm here to greet you as a representative for the Imperial Council. A pleasure to see you again, Ms. Faroshti."

"Captain Farshot," I correct him. "Since when are you on the council?"

"Since last year," Charlie cuts in smoothly. "There was a push to add someone who might provide a voice for the people outside the prime families, and Enkindler Wythe's name was put forward. All the heads of the prime families voted on it."

I look back at Charlie, and he must see all the questions his explanation definitely didn't answer on my face because he very subtly wraps a hand around my elbow and squeezes. Not hard. Not like I'm in trouble. More of a "we'll talk about it later, Alyssa."

Fine, then. I swing back around to Wythe and smack him on the arm. "Hey, belated congrats, Wythe. Small-town boy really coming up in the world lately, huh?"

He barely manages to turn his sneer into a smile and bows again. "You are as unchanged as ever, Ms. Faroshti. Follow me, please."

What an ass.

We're led across the hangar to a multiperson transport that will whisk us up through the body of the kingship to the emperor's private quarters. Charlie and I sit on one plush bench, facing Enkindler Wythe. He and Charlie stare out the windows as we glide along corridors and up glass-encased lift tubes, climbing toward the upper levels.

"Nice ride," I say, and they look at me.

What? I hate awkward silences.

"You all upgraded since I left. This the Class X model?"

Nothing.

I nod like someone's actually answered. "Expensive. You get good mileage on these—?"

"Alyssa," Charlie mumbles.

I shut up.

I want to *go*. I want to *run*. Not just away from this but *to* something. I want to see more of the quadrant. I want to see *all* of it. I am not like Charlie, polished and respectable. And I'm not like Enkindler Wythe, happily needling his way deeper and deeper into politics. I flew out of here once, trying to shake the weight of the kingship and the throne and everything that came with it.

But I didn't fly far enough.

I sigh and lean back in my seat.

"So," I say after a beat. "Either of you guys ever ridden a flame tsunami?"

FOUR

IT'S BEEN A LONG TIME SINCE I'VE BEEN IN MY uncle's imperial chambers. Back when I lived on the kingship, he'd had family quarters set aside for him and me and Charlie—smaller, less ostentatious. So we could play at being normal, I guess. The few times I wound up in his imperial rooms, I remember them being stupidly beautiful, with vaulted ceilings and jeweled chandeliers and that delicate, gilded type of furniture you never felt you could sit on. The views from the floor-to-ceiling windows were spectacular, all sunlight and sea.

But now the curtains are drawn. It's dark, and the air is close despite the size of the room. The emperor is propped up in his massive bed. Charlie sent almost everyone away to allow us some privacy, so all that's left are the medbots hovering in the shadows, silvery orbs carrying drugs and hypodermic needles. One monitors a respirator; the other massages my uncle's legs with a pair of mitt-like appendages. They don't really have eyes, exactly, but it still feels like they're watching me as I approach his bedside.

Uncle Atar is barely recognizable. He's a full-blooded hallüdraen—most of the Faroshti family are—and as a species, the hallüdrae are something to see. Tall, lithe, ridiculously angular, with hair in these deep jewel tones and the same color contouring their skin. Atar had been all of these things when I left, but now . . . His skin is papery and gray; his cheeks are hollow. He looks smaller somehow. Shriveled.

The only things unchanged are his eyes, as sharp and blue as ever, even under their hooded lids. Faroshti sapphires. I didn't inherit those. I've got the high cheekbones and the Faroshti skin tone—fair with ombre blue shading along the angles and contours of my body. But my eyes are dark brown, and my hair is even darker, a short, choppy mess of layers that I usually keep pulled up off the back of my neck.

When Atar sees me, he smiles, and I feel my heart drop. All I've wanted to do is flee, but now that feeling vanishes. I take his hand and feel tears coming.

"Hey, Uncle Atar."

"Birdie." My chest squeezes at the sound of my old nickname. His little bird, he called me. Because I was always trying to fly away. His voice is thin and whispery, as if there's barely any air in his lungs. "You came."

Oof. That hurts. The way he says it all happy and surprised. Like I'm so bad of a niece that he really thought I might blow him off even on his deathbed.

"Hi," I say again, stupidly. "Are you comfortable? Can I get you anything?"

He chuckles. "These medbots are taking good care of me. I call that one Pokey." He nods to the far medbot, who's preparing another syringe. "And this one giving me the massage is Helga." He winces as the medbot rubs his legs. "She is indelicate."

I laugh. A sense of humor is one thing my uncle and I have always shared.

I sense Charlie standing beside me, and suddenly we aren't emperor, explorer, and envoy, but a weird little family. Charlie's been Atar's husband since before he sat on the throne, and I can't believe how selfish I've been, forgetting how hard this must be for him. I can hear Charlie's breathing, and it sounds feathery. He's on the verge of tears too.

"It is so good to see you," Atar says. "I was worried you wouldn't make it."

"How could I miss this? You know, the Society gives out rewards for observing rare phenomena. I'd say this qualifies."

Beside me, Charlie sighs again. My jokes are a bit lost on him. But Atar laughs, then coughs into his shoulder.

I grip his fingers a little tighter. "I meant to come back sooner. I really did. I just—"

"Got lost up there." His eyes drift up, like he can see the expanse of space through the ceiling. "I know. I remember what it was like. I followed the songs of the universe myself when I was young."

I want to make another joke, tease him about being an old man, but I'm too aware of how young he really is. Especially for a hallüdraen.

It's not fair. The words are right there on my tongue, but he speaks before I can say anything.

"Congratulations on your circumnavigation." He squeezes my hand. "I want to hear all about it. Frankly, I could use a trip myself. I'm sick of this room." He glances at Helga. "Not that you're not great company."

I laugh again. "Soon as you're better, I'll take you on a tour," I say, even though we both know that's never going to happen. "What is it?" I add, unable to keep myself from asking.

My uncle sighs. "Some kind of rare disorder affecting my blood. The physicians tried their best, but they've run out of ideas. All anyone can do now is make me comfortable."

I lose it a little bit, and he reaches up with his free hand and pats my cheek.

"What's this? Tears from a mighty explorer?"

I wipe at my eyes and my nose with the sleeve of my fancy coat. "Yeah, well, don't tell anyone, okay?"

His eyes go serious. "Alyssa, I need you to listen to me."

His use of my real name snaps me out of it.

"I waited as long as I could. Until we were sure all hope of recovery was lost. But it's time now to start thinking about the future—"

I jerk my hand free. I don't mean to, but there's too much dread in me for what he's about to say next.

"No, Uncle. Please. You can't. You can't name me empress."

I'm surprised to hear him laugh. "No, Birdie. I can't name you empress. I wish I could, but I swore—"

"Atar." Charlie sits down on the edge of the bed, pressing a hand to Atar's chest. He flicks his eyes around the room and shakes his head, barely perceptible. I watch my uncles have this whole silent conversation, and then Atar finally nods and looks back at me.

"We must maintain the peace, Alyssa. We need the prime families to accept the next heir to the throne unequivocally. We need the support of the quadrant."

I sit frozen in my chair. I'm amazed I can hear anything over my own pulse pounding in my ears. "So, if not empress, what do you—?"

"Alyssa Faroshti, I name you crownchaser."

And I stop breathing.

A crownchaser. Everyone in the empire knows what that is. Even though there hasn't been a crownchase in—what? Almost seven hundred years? It's got to be the only thing in the quadrant that's got as many musty historical tomes dedicated to it as it does action figures.

It goes like this:

1) A ruler dies without naming an heir.

2) The royal seal—this piece of metal smaller than my hand—is hidden somewhere on the thousand and one planets that make up the empire.

3) The prime families each select their own crownchaser to hunt down the seal.

4) Whichever crownchaser finds the royal seal and returns with it to the kingship gets crowned.

Yeah. This shit really happened. But no one's resorted to this tactic for centuries. And now . . .

Oh hell.

A crownchase would be dangerous and diabolically effective—the victor gains not only the support of the quadrant but the loyalty of the prime families. No one can contest the winner of a crownchase.

To win, you'd need to be cagey, fearless, a brilliant pilot. Speaking two dozen languages wouldn't hurt. Neither would knowing the quadrant like the back of your hand or having friends in every dive, stall, and spaceport from here to the Outer Wastes.

To win the crownchase, basically, you'd have to be someone like me.

Uncle Atar takes my hand again. His bones feel so brittle underneath his skin. "Our family sacrificed everything to bring peace to the empire. But not everyone was glad for it. If a new family were to take the throne, one that thirsted for war . . ." I start to say something, to protest, but my uncle raises his scratchy voice. He can still sound pretty kingly, even on his deathbed. "I know this isn't what you want, Birdie. I always knew it might come to this, but I thought . . . I thought we would both have more time. All I can do now is give you this—the crownchase—one last adventure before you must do your duty."

Uncle Atar's words crash over me. I bring my fist to my mouth and try to hold it back, but I can't. The party, the hangover, the look in Charlie's eyes, my dying uncle, and now this.

I turn my head. Pokey the medbot extends a small receptacle, but not fast enough.

I vomit all over the imperial furniture.

"Birdie, are you all right?" Atar asks.

A crownchaser. A godsdamned crownchaser.

EMPEROR
ATAR FAROSHTI DEAD
**The monarch lost his battle with a mysterious illness
late last night, leaving his throne without an heir**

KINGSHIP ANNOUNCES FIRST
CROWNCHASE IN SEVEN CENTURIES
Imperial envoy Charles Viqtorial releases statement
declaring the contest was Emperor Atar's dying wish

ENKINDLER WYTHE
TO ACT AS STEWARD OF THE EMPIRE
With the crownchase announced, Imperial Council elects
a neutral party to hold the throne until a winner emerges

GAMBLING SURGES ACROSS THE QUADRANT
Bookie networks report overwhelming traffic
as imperial citizens seek to place bets on historical race for the throne

THE VOLES FAMILY HOLDINGS ON THE PLANET HELIX

EDGAR VOLES CAN'T BRING HIMSELF TO GO TO BED.

He knows there isn't really a point to double-checking the numbers on this presentation. He's analyzed them again and again over the past several months, studied the materials he's put together until they haunted his dreams, done everything he could possibly do to prepare. He should go to bed so he can be well rested in the morning.

But he's still awake.

All three large touch screens on the wall of his quarters are filled with design schematics and material lists, efficiency simulations and timetables. His eyes are dry and a little blurry. He knows he's rereading things he's read a thousand times.

But if he misses anything . . . If someone asks a question he's not thoroughly prepared to answer . . .

The door to his room slides open—no knock—and he turns on his heel, thinking for one heart-freezing moment that it might be his father. But instead he sees the efficient movements and sleek alloy lines of NL7, and his shoulders relax.

"Edgar Voles, we expected to find you sleeping," it says. There isn't what one might call "emotion" in the android's voice, but

Edgar has known NL7 all his life, was essentially raised by it. He can hear modulations in its voice mechanics that others can't.

"Are you scolding me, NL7?"

"We are certainly programmed to be capable of scolding, if it is so required."

Edgar doesn't smile. He isn't much of a smiler—he finds it makes his face look more boyish, less likely to command the fear and respect owed to a Voles. But his expression softens as he turns back to the data-filled screens. "I just wanted to go over things one last time. Before I meet with Father in the morning." He waves a hand at the schematics. "What do you think, NL7? I value your thoughts."

The android steps up beside him, making hardly a sound. Edgar doesn't know of any other android that can move so silently. In his opinion, it is a true testament to the superiority of NL7's creation. And the woman who created it. "It is a very effective and efficient design, Edgar Voles."

"Would . . ." He hesitates to ask, but he can't help himself. "Would my mother approve of it, do you think?"

"It is impossible to speak for those who no longer exist." Edgar's face falls, but he nods. He feels NL7 analyzing his expression, his body language. And then it adds, "But we can estimate, based on her known skills and characteristics, and we believe she would approve."

Edgar straightens, a warm feeling filling his chest. That means more than almost anything to him. Almost more than the outcome of the meeting tomorrow.

Only a fool would not see all the benefits in what Edgar plans to present, and William Voles is no fool. Edgar has created the most effective, efficient farming android that has ever been designed, relatively cheap to produce and replace, capable of harvesting and processing an assigned crop in half the time a humanoid could. This will be the answer to all the wage riots and labor protests and welfare lawsuits by the workers on Homestead. So often, his father complains about how the biological farmhands on that planet cost them money, cost the Helix government time and energy and resources.

And now Edgar will hand him the solution. And his father will finally see just how much value Edgar brings to their family.

A corner of the main touch screen flashes red, drawing his eye. An urgent communication.

"Are you expecting news, Edgar Voles?" asks NL7.

He frowns. No, he isn't. Reaching up, he swipes down on the message, expanding it to fill the screen.

It redirects him to a breaking news alert on the *Daily Worlds*. One of their correspondents stands beside a liftship in a hanger bay that Edgar recognizes as belonging to the kingship on Apex. Edgar has been in that hangar many times over the course of his life, but never for very long. His father always hustled him quickly to the guest quarters and left him to stare out at the Eastern Sea until it was time to leave again.

Now the hanger bay appears to be packed with liftships and journalists, all talking urgently into camera drones. Edgar turns the volume up on the screen.

". . . reporting that Emperor Atar Faroshti has passed away at the age of seventy-four, an extremely young age for a hallüdraen. Immediately on the heels of this, Charles Viqtorial, imperial envoy and the emperor's husband of twenty-seven years, announced that a crownchase will now be initiated to determine the emperor's successor . . ."

The screen flashes again, and this time Edgar doesn't hesitate to open it. He knows who the message is from.

William Voles's severe face fills the screen, not a live communication but a video he must've just recorded. "Edgar, it is time to prove your worth. Don't fail us."

Edgar closes the message and swipes the screens clear, dismissing every file, every schematic, every simulation.

None of it matters now.

He has new plans to make.

IMPERIAL SCHOOLROOM, THE KINGSHIP, APEX

". . . Miss Faroshti?"

I drag my eyes away from the big window that overlooks the restless Eastern Sea. My tutor stands over me, arms crossed, frowning. I wonder what his face looks like without that frown. I've never really seen him without it. Mostly because I don't ever give him much reason to smile.

"Have you been paying attention at all, Miss Faroshti?"

I fold my hands on the desk in front of me and sit up straight. "Nope. Sorry, Mr. Odo. Haven't heard a thing."

He rolls his eyes skyward. Like the ceiling might know what to do with me. "I don't know why I even bother to try to teach you on weeks like this."

He means on quarter-council weeks. Once every few months, all the heads of the imperial prime families convene on the kingship to deal with whatever super-important stuff they need to argue about and make decisions on. That's the general gist I've gotten from Uncle Atar, anyway. Dead honest? I don't really care about what the grown-ups do. I care about quarter-council weeks because the prime family heirs get to come on the kingship too.

Which means for one whole week, I'm gonna get to run around with other kids my own age without getting dragged away all the time for lessons or family dinners or serious talks about "the state of the empire" and "my role in society."

Uncle Atar says it's important for all of us to hang out, that it promotes bonding.

Uncle Charlie calls it "sanctioned hooliganism" and walks around angry-sighing more than usual.

He sounds a lot like Mr. Odo does right now.

"I understand that your head isn't really in it at the moment, Miss Faroshti," he says, turning back toward the display screen at the front of the room. "But this is a vital part of imperial history that directly affects—"

There's a beep, and the door to the room whooshes open. Uncle Atar fills the doorway, and a rush of excitement hits me. Because there's only one reason I can think of why he'd be busting up lesson time right now. I jump out of my seat.

"Are they here?"

A wide smile breaks across his face. "Yes, Alyssa. They're here."

FIVE

Stardate: 0.05.15 in the Year 4031, under the stewardship of Enkindler Ilysium Wythe, that prick

Location: A godsdamned hyperlight lane with a side of hangover

I'VE BEEN THIS SIDE OF DRUNK FOR ALMOST A week.

I'm not saying it's bad or anything, but . . . it's definitely not great. Like I'm-getting-looks-from–Hell Monkey kind of not-great, and that guy's never met a shot glass he wasn't interested in seeing the bottom of.

His side-eyes might not be about the booze, though.

Might be about everything else.

Almost definitely about everything else.

Holy sunballs, I should've sobered up before we jumped into hyperlight. What the hell was I thinking? This is some rookie-level bullshit. I should know better.

Don't throw up, don't throw up, don't throw up.

A headache hammers against my skull like a barrage of asteroids, but we're almost at Gloo so I'm trying to hold it together. If I try to make a run for the bathroom or some painkillers, I'm almost positive I'll hork it all over the *Vagabond*'s deck. Better to stay still. Very, very still.

"How you doin' over there, Cap?" Hell Monkey calls from the jump seat to my left.

I shut my eyes. Against the headache. Against the question. Against the question underneath the question.

"Fan-flipping-tastic. Never better. Now shut up."

This is the longest I've had to sit still in days, and I hate it. Haaaaate it. Uncle Atar passed away hours after I got to the king-ship, and the sonofabitch left this enormous, invisible bruise all over me. Asshole.

Gods, I miss him.

Charlie and I were with him. When he died. Had maybe ten whole minutes with our grief, and then reality came pouring in. Officials and assistants with worthless condolences and a bunch of pricks who started yapping about "next steps" and "the good of the empire." I just ran. Nabbed an unattended waveskimmer in one of the hangar bays and took off over the Eastern Sea. Flew around for hours seeing just. how. close. I could get to those massive breakers before I had to pull up.

The next few days were horseshit. Funeral plans, event coordination, fake sympathy . . . And then they took my ship away from me. I couldn't even put hyperdrive lights to that place and blow. Nope, they had to outfit the *Vagabond Quick* for the crownchase. All of us are supposed to start with the same tech in our worldcruisers. AIs, engine upgrades, weapons—it all has to be equal. Evens the playing field or whatever. I thought Hell Monkey was gonna haul off and deck the officials when they started putting their ugly mitts all over everything.

At least they didn't touch Rose. She's apparently already running off the system they're installing in all the other ships, so they let her be.

Me, I just hid at the bottom of a bottle until Charlie found me, peeled me off the floor, and put me back on my ship. As soon as I boarded, they injected a biometric monitor into the back of my neck. (Gotta make sure all of us stay breathing and no one shoves us into a solar flare, right?) Then they put trackers all over the ship, uploaded crownchase rules into our computer, and sent us off to Gloo.

I'm out of booze now. And I'm out of time.

My eyes burn, and I squeeze them tight. *Get it together, Farshot. Don't show up at Gloo in tears or with vomit on your face.*

The *Vagabond Quick* drops out of the hyperlight lane, and my whole body goes soft with relief. Even my headache feels a little better. Hyperlight is a quick way to get around, but damn, it's hell on a hungover person.

Gloo fills the windows, squat and kinda brownish all over. Exactly what the word *Gloo* sounds like? That's how the planet looks. Good people down there, but they got the rough end on planetary aesthetics.

A yellow light flashes on the dash. A broadcast signal from the media feeds. And a text comm from Charlie to go with it.

It is time, Alyssa. I will not be able to communicate with you again until this is all over, but know that I wish you all my best.

Charles Viqtorial

I stare at that last line. *I wish you all my best.* For buttoned-up, tamped-down Charlie, that line is . . . a hug, really. And it's the same thing he said to me three years ago, right before I took off for good on the *Vagabond*.

My eyes burn again. This ship must have a bad air filter somewhere. Or something.

Hell Monkey's hand hovers over a button on the dash, but his eyes are on me. Steady. Loyal. That's Hell Monkey.

"You ready for this?"

No. But not watching the broadcast won't help. "Hit it."

Gloo is replaced on the viewscreen by a live feed of the official throne room on the kingship. One whole wall of the room is windows overlooking the Eastern Sea, and the ship itself rotates so you can see both the sunrise and sunset from there, so it's a pretty killer space if you like a great view—which I do. It's also decked out in the official royal Faroshti colors of ice blue and gold—which I look terrible in and hate.

Standing in front of the dais where Uncle Atar should've been are Charlie and two others I'm far less excited to see: Enkindler Wythe, who's somehow managed to go from ambassador to councilmember to imperial steward in a few short years, and Cheery Coyenne, prime family matriarch and executive in charge of the *Daily Worlds*, which means she controls just about everything that hits the media feeds. Cheery is nice enough, as long as what you want and what she wants line up, but Wythe's smug face up there makes me want to punch something.

Preferably him.

". . . the long and storied history of this contest," Charlie is saying. He's speaking Imperial, the empire's only recognized common tongue, but it looks like they're live translating it into at least a hundred different languages so no one misses anything. "Anyone who attempts to kill or capture a crownchaser will be subjected to immediate execution. Any crownchaser who kills a fellow crownchaser before the seal has been found will be sentenced accordingly, and their entire family line will be disqualified from the contest."

Sounds like we're a few minutes late to the party—Charlie's already done the formal recitations of crownchase history and the rules of the contest. Not that there are that many, besides "don't kill each other" and "first back with the seal wins." If history is anything to go by, it's kind of a free-for-all once the flag goes up, and all the extra stuff they're foisting on us—the cameras, the bots, the drones—is just to help them broadcast the spectacle to trillions of media feeds around the galaxy.

The first crownchase in seven hundred years!

I gotta hand it to Atar—it was pretty smart, really. Not the part where I'm trapped in a contest to win a crown I don't want—that sucks. But the part where the crownchase has given everyone a focus. The netstreams are flooded with people scouring for any rumor or leaked detail about what the chase might entail, and every bookie in the quadrant is living their best life, running odds on everything from who will win to where the seal is gonna be found to how long it'll take. And the *Daily Worlds* and other media sources are fueling it all—every page, every article, every vid dedicated to profiling potential competitors and spinning out rumors. Basically, instead of a grieving populace and a power vacuum, we've got an empire anchored by this—a historic show for the ages. There's even talk of a contest-long cease-fire on Chu'ra. I mean, can you even believe it?

"You're looking a little green over there, Farshot," H.M. says.

I lean out of my jump seat far enough that I can punch him right in his beefy delt. "I swear, if you don't stop giving me those looks, I'm gonna snatch out your eyeballs and throw them out an airlock."

"Then I could get bionic eyeballs. Cool."

Unbelievable.

Charlie is still talking. "Every crownchaser has been given an equivalently outfitted worldcruiser and randomly selected coordinates in the quadrant as their start point. Twenty-four hours from now, all competitors will check in at their start point, and Enkindler Wythe will give the signal for the crownchase to begin."

On the viewscreen, Wythe clears his throat. "As the Church of Solarus's Everlasting Light has no prime family affiliation, it is my honor and privilege to hold the throne in stewardship and announce now those esteemed competitors who will be vying for the royal seal. May they be blessed with the light of Solarus.

"For the Faroshti family, Alyssa Faroshti, niece of Emperor Atar Faroshti, may he rest in the light of the sun."

My face fills the viewscreen—looks like they used my official portrait from the Explorers' Society, which is a damn good one, I gotta say. Much better than how I'm looking right now, which is distinctly pale and sweaty. On the right, there's a column of text that basically lists all the need-to-knows about me and my qualifications.

Almost immediately, the comms on my wristband start flashing, and then the comms on the *Vagabond* do too. I shut them all off. Every line, every channel—I don't need anyone's *Congratulations, I can't believe it!* (neither can I) or *I'm praying for your victory!* (thanks, I guess) or *I hope you die in a gravity well, bitch. Voles forever!* (you seem nice, bud).

Hell Monkey nudges my arm. "Here comes your competition."

"For the Roy family, Setter Roy, son of Radha and Jaya Roy."

Setter's photo pops up on-screen. Gotta be a commissioned family portrait because he's draped in all the official gear, going for that serious, regal look. There's a lot of axeeli blood on the Roys' home planet of Lenos, and you can see it in Setter too. Got the axeeli mood-ring eyes and a dose of their telepathy, but he missed out on some of the more extreme mental abilities, and his skin is a deep brown instead of the usual color-changing. He and I butted heads a lot when we were kids. Not because he's a bad person or anything—he's just so . . . serious. And boring.

I raise an imaginary glass to his image on the viewscreen. "You shall be code-named: Humorless Killjoy."

"For the Mega family, Owyn Mega, son of Jenna Mega and Lorcan Mega."

Owyn's headshot is full-out military glorification. Otari scars on display, dark bronze against his light tan skin; full strategic armor; traditional blades strapped across his back. Typical Megas. Except for the part where if you look close enough at Owyn's eyes, you can see he's straight-up miserable in all his war gear.

Hell Monkey already has this one covered. "Your code name will be: Pretty Sure Your Parents Took All Your Tests for You."

I snort with laughter and immediately regret it when my head gives a painful throb. It feels good, though. To laugh. It's been a bit.

"For the Voles family, Edgar Voles, son of William Voles and Sylva Voles, may she rest in the light of the sun."

Hell Monkey boos loudly and throws a stray stylus as Edgar's pale face pops up on-screen. He's got a big hate for the Voles family, though he's never told me why. He doesn't like to talk about his past, and I don't like to push people to get chatty.

I gotta agree with him on this one. My heart sinks into my stomach. Edgar is kinda worrisome, but his dad is even worse. And the thought of those two taking my uncle's place, after everything he accomplished, everything he sacrificed . . . Shit and hell and damn it to all the stars and gods. "His code name is: Most Definitely Gonna Get Punched in the Dick."

"For the Orso family, Faye Orso, daughter of Sara Orso and Ivar Orso."

I can't help the grin that creeps onto my face as Faye's image fills the viewscreen: tawny skin threaded with bioluminescent lines, gold eyes sharp and shiny as blades, a little curve to her mouth that's more a threat than a smile. It's been a couple years. She looks good. I'm not totally sure what I think of Faye as a prospective empress, but I can say this: whenever she's in the picture, you're ten times more likely to end up in jail, but also twelve times more likely to enjoy the ride.

Hell Monkey snorts. "Code name: Better Keep One Hand on Your Wallet."

"And finally, for the Coyenne family, Nathalia Coyenne, daughter of Cheery Coyenne and Reginald Coyenne."

"Coy!" I shoot forward and just about clothesline myself on my own jump seat harness. Right. Safety first. Oops. I wrench at the buckles, a wave of relief uncoiling the knot of anxiety that's been squirming in my stomach for almost a week now. If I'd taken a sober second to think this through earlier, I would've realized that Coy was the natural choice to be crownchaser for her family. Savvy, charismatic, good with a ship. I'm kicking myself for not seeing this coming days ago. I could've saved myself a ton of existential worry.

And a lot of booze money.

Hell Monkey drums his fingers against the arms of his jump seat as he stares at the viewscreen. He looks over at me, a grin on his face, and I know he's thinking the same thing I'm thinking. "Obviously, we'll call her: Your Official Ticket Out of This Mess."

SIX

"ALYSSA FARSHOT! AS I LIVE AND BREATHE. YOU'RE looking ravishing this morning."

I can practically feel Hell Monkey rolling his eyes behind my back, but I keep my eyes on the viewscreen, which is currently showing me Nathalia Coyenne's grinning face.

"Save it, Coy. This isn't a social call. It's business."

"I like business. Dirty business, risky business—"

"Coy."

She laughs, and it's like a bell calling people to worship. Nathalia's always had this way about her. It's not even a beauty thing, really. It's just like she walks around in a cloud of phero-mones. People are drawn to her, and it would be dangerous as hell if she didn't have such a good heart.

And she does. Have a good heart. She's smart too—smarter than me in a lot of ways. Especially political ways. She loves that say-one-thing-mean-another stuff, and she's good at it. Maybe she hasn't ridden a flame tsunami, but she's definitely coasted a comet's tail or two for the Society in her time. She knows the quadrant, she understands people, and best of all—she isn't me.

Everything I could possibly want in the next ruler.

"It's been a few months. I think we need to catch up in person, Coy."

She raises her eyebrows so high they almost hit her silvery spiraled horns. "Now?"

"No time like the present." I give her a look through the viewscreen. A significant look. Hopefully it translates. "What's your current proximity to Gloo?"

There's a long pause. I can feel her weighing my offer against the timing—the flag goes up in just twenty-three hours. It's a little suspicious that I'm on her doorstep now, trying to get a face-to-face. Or, at least, it would be if she were any other crownchaser. But we have a long history, one I don't think even something as cutthroat as a crownchase can screw up.

Nathalia's eyes flick to the side, checking her nav readout. "Close, actually. Really close. I can be there this afternoon. You want to meet up at the club in Parm?"

I glance back at Hell Monkey, who gives me a little nod, and then I turn to Coy again. "Yeah, let's do it. Bring cred-chips. You're buying."

"What came first here—the name Parm or the cheese smell?"

I stick a foot out, catching Hell Monkey on the ankle as we move through the narrow, claustrophobic streets of one of the biggest cities on Gloo. He trips and almost takes a nosedive. I barely break stride.

"Pretend to be a nice guy. Or nice-ish."

He's not wrong, though. Parm smells about as nice as Gloo looks from orbit. It's squat and a little shabby and not all that much to look at. But you can get a decent lager in a few places, and there's some really great street food if you've got an adventurous stomach.

But that's not why we're here.

The alley dead-ends in a heavy metal door. No handle, no knob, just a touch pad embedded in the center that I slap my palm against. After a second, the lock thuds and the door swings open.

There's a short, dark hallway on the other side, and I tap the big symbol emblazoned in gold on the wall as I walk past. Official sigil of the Explorers' Society. They've got clubs like this all over the quadrant. Exclusive stuff. Dim lounges with big-ass chairs and a well-stocked bar. The bar is key. I haven't met an explorer yet who doesn't need a drink after the stuff we pull.

Coy waves us over. She's already kicked back in a chair, long legs propped up on the short table in front of her. She's foarian, like a lot of the Coyenne prime family, which means horns and sharp nails and big eyes that take up about a third of their faces. For Nathalia, those horns are long, silvery spirals that angle from the top of her head, and those eyes are bright green and set against metal-gray skin and long hair whiter than the caps on the Eastern Sea's waves. Her hands cradle a tumbler of what looks like Solari whiskey. That's nice stuff, allegedly distilled with the essence of the sun. For religious types, the Solari know how to make some good booze.

She gestures to two other chairs close by, which already have drinks waiting at them. "I took the liberty of ordering, since I'm buying and all."

Hell Monkey picks up the glass, his nose wrinkling as he sniffs the iridescent-green concoction inside. "What is this? It smells like piss."

I answer before Coy. "Andujian martini. Widely considered to be one of the worst drinks in the galaxy." I pick up mine, raise it to Coy's grinning face, and down it in one go.

Damn. That is truly terrible.

Coy shakes her head, her smile growing even bigger. "Never underestimate a Farshot."

"Yes, all one of us." I dump myself into the chair, slinging my legs over the arm, and signal to the barkeep for two more of what Nathalia is drinking. Hell Monkey sits as well, setting the martini as far away from him as possible.

"I suppose a proper drink is the least I could do," says Coy, waving a hand benevolently. "After all, very soon I will have a crown and a throne and you'll still be stuck on your rust bucket of a cruiser."

I shoot her a glare. "Hey, hey, easy with the name-calling. That's my baby you're talking about."

The barkeep delivers the Solari whiskey, and this time I raise my glass sincerely, looking Coy right in her bright eyes. "To the new empress of the quadrant. May your reign be long and peaceful."

Coy goes still, assessing my expression, my body language. Realization breaks over her face like a brand-new star. "You're utterly serious."

"Yes," I say, adding in my poshest, most royal accent, "utterly."

"You really have no intention of winning?"

"None whatsoever. I'm not even gonna try." I take a long sip of the whiskey—distilled with the sun, those clever bastards—and set it down on the table.

This makes Nathalia sit up straight, her own drink forgotten.

"Alyssa, you can't be serious. A crownchase is right up your alley. I just bet money on you."

Swinging my feet to the ground, I lean forward, elbows propped on my knees. "I'm not gonna try, Coyenne, because I'm gonna help you."

There's total silence. Coy is completely still, staring at me. Hell Monkey's eyes flick from me to her and back again. I swear I can even hear the sound of cloth on glass as the barkeep dries dishes.

Then she throws her head back and laughs, loud enough that the few other patrons actually pause to look over at us. Hell Monkey shoots them some hard-core glares until they turn away again.

Coy finally stops laughing and stretches her long arms across the table, seizing my hands. "Alyssa Farshot, you've officially made me the luckiest idiot in this quadrant."

My shoulders drop, and I return her grin. "Oh, I know it, Coy. You're lucky I don't want anything to do with ruling a thousand and one planets. And you're mostly lucky that you're the only crownchaser I could stand to see take my uncle's place."

At that, she snorts and sits back. "Yes, quite a crew we're going up against. Owyn? Can you imagine? His family would probably start a war just to try out whatever violent new toy their company developed. And Voles . . ." She shudders. "Emperor Edgar Voles. That would be a nightmare."

I stare down into my glass, picturing Edgar—both the small, round-faced boy he was and the stone-faced guy he grew into. "To be fair, we all bring family baggage with us. The Coyennes like to scheme, the Faroshtis are self-righteous, and the Voles . . . see bottom lines and not people. Personally, it's not exactly an outlook I'd want to see applied at the quadrant level."

H.M. downs most of his drink in one go, a strange edge to his voice as he says, "No . . . no, you really don't."

Coy rolls her half-empty glass between her hands. "Setter would be a bit like putting a crown on the color beige. Empress Faye would be a dangerous ride. It certainly wouldn't be boring with her in charge. But . . ." She flashes a grin at me that's gotten her through more doors and into more beds than I can even count. "I think the crown would look much better on me."

Hell Monkey snorts into his glass. "Your head is certainly big enough."

If that comment bothers Coy, she doesn't show it. She just turns that supernova smile on him and says, "Indeed, sir. Let's go find me a royal seal, shall we?"

A royal seal for her and a wide-open starscape for me. Nothing between me and the rest of the galaxy but time and cruiser fuel. I raise my glass high and drink it all down. That's a toast I can get behind.

SEVEN

Stardate: 0.05.16 in the Year 4031, under the stewardship of Enkindler Ilysium Wythe, may he get bit in the ass by a needleworm
Location: Still orbiting boring-ass Gloo

THE START OF THE CROWNCHASE IS SUPER UNDER-whelming.

I mean, not that I expected fireworks coming out of my ass or anything, but something more than a stupid prerecorded message from Wythe blessing our journeys. Who asked for your blessings, man?

For a minute, it seems like that's that—have fun hand-searching a thousand planets, kiddos!—but then I have the *Vagabond Quick's* AI run a multifractal scan of the message.

Bingo.

An encrypted data package.

Let the games begin.

"What's the play, Captain?" Hell Monkey stands just behind me, and his voice rumbles right down my spine.

"Looks like it's a follow-the-bread-crumbs type of deal. Like when we hunted for that ancient tomb on Ysev." I tilt my head over my shoulder so I can see him out of the corner of my eye. "Last chance, H.M. You don't have to come with me on this. I can drop you off at a spaceport. You're a great engineer—you'd get a job on another ship in no time."

He goes very still. There's a beat. And then: "Fuck you, Farshot."

Never been so happy to hear those words.

I could do this on my own—just me and Rose and the *Vagabond* against the universe—but I really don't want to. I want Hell Monkey at my side. I *need* him at my side.

But don't tell him I said that.

Instead, I say, "Your funeral," and he elbows me in the back.

I tap the nav computer and bring up a three-dimensional projection of the surrounding systems. The level of encryption on Wythe's little package (innuendo bonus point) is pretty intense. Not that the *Vagabond Quick* can't break it—my baby can do anything— but it would take a while. Too long. If I'm going to get Coy that seal and secure a throne-free future for myself, I need to be twelve steps ahead of everyone else.

And to do that, I need a massive computer with much higher processing power. A workhorse. Like a metropolitan database or a central spaceport.

"There." I point to a spot on the outskirts of the Coltigh system. "We're going ghosting. Send—"

I stop and glance toward the back of the bridge at the *Vagabond*'s brand-new passenger. A mediabot. A spindly frame of metal with a camera for a head and two more swiveling lenses on its shoulders. So it can catch all that sweet footage from multiple angles. It had apparently been put in our cargo bay, and about four hours ago, it woke up and started following me around, trying to get me to talk about my *feelings* and *fears* and *expectations*.

It's watching me right now, cameras rolling, so I just give Hell Monkey a significant look and tell him, "Check the comms. Make sure we're all on the same page."

I don't want to mention Coy's name. Or anything about us teaming up. Alliances between crownchasers aren't forbidden, but I don't want to tip my hand until I have to.

Hell Monkey grins and gives me a wink. "Aye, aye, sir."

And suddenly I remember why I hook up with a guy named Hell Monkey. I know. I KNOW. But it's sexy as hell when he follows my orders.

A short hyperlight trip later, we're skirting around the sensor net surrounding Coltigh IV, moving carefully so our signature doesn't ping off any of their orbital probes. Not to treat them like that one person you're desperate to avoid at a party or anything, but we're not here to visit right now. We just need something they left behind, floating at the very edge of their system.

A ghostport.

There's maybe a dozen or so around the quadrant. Old spaceports that got abandoned when a newer, shinier one came along, so they just drift there, all sad-looking.

They're magnets for space pirates, who love to use them as bases, but this one? This one is mine. Won it off one of Ivar Orso's pirate crews two years back in a truly epic card game that nearly cost me my ship and a finger or two.

Hell Monkey drops back into his jump seat as I guide the *Vagabond*

Quick toward an airlock. He scans the ghostport with sensors. Cranes forward to look at her through the viewscreen. Scans her again.

I raise my eyebrows. I can't look straight at him while I'm trying to dock. This is delicate work. "What?"

"What what?"

"What do you mean, what what? What the hell are you doing over there?"

Hell Monkey grumbles and then sits back. "I thought I saw something. . . ."

My hands still on the controls. "Something, like, danger something? Exotic space jellyfish something? What's the something?"

"It's nothing. Scanners are clear. Viewscreen is clear."

I get a flutter in my stomach. It's not a good flutter. It's a bad flutter. It's a danger-danger flutter. But it's too late now. We're only a few meters from the airlock. So I guide her in, seal the bay doors, and push back from the dash.

"Okay, H.M. Get your gear on. Let's do a sweep." I poke the mediabot in its lens face as I walk by it. "Stay put. I don't want to be fined a bunch of credits because you get yourself blown to bits."

The thing about pirates is that, even though they tell you something is yours and they won't touch it anymore—that doesn't really mean anything if it's shiny enough. So every time we come back to this place, we've gotta do a full rundown: survival suits on, sun's-out-guns-out, and walk each deck to make sure we've got no new surprises in store. It takes a little while, but luckily there's the constant threat of walking into the barrel of a blaster to keep you on your toes.

I'm expecting to run into something the whole way, but the

ghostport is empty. A little dark. A little dusty. But we make it to the command and control room at the top without a hitch. Nothing moving in here but the two of us and an official crownchase camera drone that floats, almost silent, near the ceiling.

"She looks good," Hell Monkey says as he pops the helmet of his suit off and slings it into the corner. "Not even a wobbly bulkhead."

I tap the touch screens on the conn, waking up the dormant mainframe. "Can you get her talking to the *Vagabond*? We're gonna need all the juice in that big-ass brain of hers to break this encryption fast. I want to get back on the trail as quickly as possible."

Hell Monkey slides into one of the command chairs. He leans back, all casual, but his hands work fast over the controls. Linking the ship to the port and the port to the ship.

"If it's the kind of trail we're thinking," he says, "we've got a leg up. We've killed it at this kind of thing before."

I shake my head. "Don't underestimate these prime family babies. You don't know them like I do. They may be spoiled, but they've got resources—"

The ice-cold barrel of a blaster touches the back of my neck, killing anything else I was about to say.

And that's when Faye "Better Keep One Hand on Your Wallet" Orso steps into view. Two guns in her hands, shit-eating grin on her face, and a whole world of "you're fucked, Farshot" in her eyes.

Well, then. This oughta be fun.

EIGHT

THE LAST TIME I WAS IN THIS MUCH TROUBLE WITH
Faye Orso, we were fourteen years old, sitting hand in hand in a
Tabarti jail. We'd gotten busted for joyriding in a Tabarti dragon—
military-grade fighter ships worth a hot credit and kept under
heavy guard, which of course made them appealing as hell to steal.
We'd made it an hour, a planetary record, before the redsuits cornered us and hauled us in. I can still picture Faye's face the moment
we got caught, warning lights crisscrossing her skin, her mouth
stretched in a grin that even star devils would be wary of.

Looks a lot like the grin on her face right now.

She's got her eyes on me but a blaster about a foot from Hell
Monkey's face. I can't see who has the gun barrel up against my
neck but I'd bet the *Vagabond* it's her partner, Honor Winger. I put
my hands up—see? so compliant!—and try to match Faye's smile.

"Faye Orso, I was just thinking about how awesome it'd be to
see you again. Been way too long. Those pants and your ass are an
A-plus combination, I gotta say."

She sidesteps her way around the control panel until she's right
up on Hell Monkey, hand on his shoulder, blaster at his temple.

"Straight into flattery. Very Faroshti of you."

My smile drops a little. I try to cover it with a shrug. "It's Farshot now, not Faroshti."

Her expression softens. "You can change the last name, but blood sticks, lovely."

I clap my hands over my eyes, crying out dramatically, "Oh god! I just rolled my eyes so hard I think I broke something! Help! Medic!"

Honor jabs me in the kidney. "Okay, enough of that, *Farshot*."

"I'm serious. I could have sustained a serious injury. Scarred for life. I may never be able to look insolent again."

"Shut it, Alyssa." Faye's voice cuts through the room. "Keep your hands up and stay still."

I throw my arms wide. "Or what? You're not gonna shoot us, Orso, not unless you want to instantly lose the chase. Seriously, can we drop the blasters-and-pirates deal already? Or is that literally the only card you have to play?"

Faye tilts her head to look over my shoulder. "Honor, cuff her. And this one too." She pinches Hell Monkey's cheek. "I'll take them down below while you get to work. And play nice, you two. One of the plasma cannons on my ship has been malfunctioning lately, and we're parked so close to your *Vagabond* . . . I'd hate for anything to happen."

Hell Monkey locks eyes with me as Honor pins my wrists to the small of my back and binds them with compression cuffs. He's tense all over. Waiting to see if I'll give the nod, call Faye's bluff.

Maybe I would've. Back in the day. When she was past-Faye

wand I was past-Alyssa and we were about as close as you could get. But it's been a few years, and I don't really know now-Faye. And I definitely don't know what she's willing to pull for a crown. So I shake my head at him, just a little, and let the compression cuffs seal themselves around my wrists. Honor moves on to bind Hell Monkey too, and then she turns to the control panels while Faye steps over and gestures with her blaster.

Forward march, we go.

She doesn't take us to the lift—smart, I was totally planning on using the small space and the two-on-one odds to try and jump her—and she doesn't take us all the way down to the brig, which is several levels below. No, she just herds us two levels down to where there are a number of walk-in storage compartments. Thick walls, strong sealed doors.

I'm starting to realize just how well Faye seems to know her way around my ghostport.

"You got familiar with the specs on this place real fast," I say as she stops us in front of a door.

She laughs, eyes steady on us. Blaster steady on us. The light's dim in the hallway, so right now she stands out more than ever, the bioluminescent lines looking like lacework across her skin.

"Give me a little more credit for forethought than that. I've been keeping an eye on this port since you won it off my father." She taps a panel on the wall, the door slides open, and she waves Hell Monkey inside. He goes, his eyes on me the whole way.

I move to follow, but she throws out an arm. "Wait your turn, Farshot. No way in hell I'm stupid enough to put both of you in the same room."

Hell Monkey turns, shouts, "Orso, hey, wait, I have a—"

She shuts the door on him. Seals the lock on the panel. Turns that sharp smile to me. "This way, lovely."

I glare at her—*attagirl, Farshot, that'll show her*—but mostly I'm focused on how empty the hallway feels without Hell Monkey in it. How exposed I feel without him at my back.

I don't like that feeling.

But also, when did it get so necessary to have him by my side?

Faye stops at another storage compartment farther down and opens the door for me. "Home, sweet home."

I twist, wiggling my fingers at her. "I'm gonna lose feeling in my hands pretty soon."

"Guess you won't be knitting me a sweater, then. In."

I cast one look back down the hall at Hell Monkey's door. And then I go.

"Hey, Farshot."

I spin around in the small, empty space, and Faye's lingering in the door. Her blaster's still out, but the look on her face isn't smug like I would expect. I mean, in her shoes, I'd be smug as hell. Instead she's got this little crease between her eyebrows.

"Be careful out there. You've been out of the politics game for a while. And just because you stopped paying attention to us doesn't mean we stopped paying attention to you."

She hits the panel. The door closes. And I'm in the dark.

COYENNE JUMPS OUT AS EARLY FAVORITE

The media darling dazzles the public as the crownchase begins

FARSHOT ALREADY SIDELINED

Camera footage shows the explorer
trapped in an abandoned spaceport by Faye Orso

WYTHE: "THE COURSE OF OUR FUTURE IS SUN-BLESSED"

Steward Wythe declares he will push forward with an agenda for
the empire, not wait for the crownchase results

WHO IS EDGAR VOLES?

An inside look at the mysterious crownchaser and heir to an android empire

WORLDCRUISER S576-034, DESIGNATED START COORDINATES

EDGAR VOLES DIDN'T GIVE HIS WORLDCRUISER A name.

The crownchase outfitters told him this was bad luck. They'd even gone so far as to make recommendations.

Call it the Justus Roy, *they'd told him. After the last emperor before the war. Nice, right?*

He hadn't responded. Instead, he'd just stared them down until they'd gotten nervous and hurried back off to work.

He doesn't need their luck or their superstitions or any of those soft, intangible concepts others like to carry around. He's a Voles. And the Voles family believes in only one thing: clear, measurable results.

Edgar kneels on the floor beside an array of robotic parts, neatly separated and organized, and next to them, the half-gutted shell of the mediabot that had been unlucky enough to be assigned to Edgar Voles's ship.

It had wandered around after him as they'd waited at his designated coordinates, squawking questions at him, trying to provoke him into an interview that could be streamed back to the *Daily Worlds* for public consumption. All the other crownchasers submitted at some point, even for just a minute or two. He'd watched them on the media feeds, studied all their familiar-unfamiliar faces. He'd managed not to think of any of them much over the past few years, but now here they are. In a constant parade. It left a hollow ache of sadness in his chest, but he pushed it forcefully aside. Voleses didn't feel sad.

And Edgar had work to do.

When the red light had dropped and the chase started, he'd swept the mediabot into his quarters, where there was privacy from the onboard cameras, and disassembled it in only a few minutes.

And now, with quick, sure fingers, he puts it back together, although not quite the same way. A change in the wiring here. An adjustment to the circuitry there. And a brand-new processing core installed right into its neural network.

He reassembles the mediabot's shell, reenables the power. And waits.

A glow fills the bot's eye sockets. It sits up, metal parts scraping against the floor, and looks down at its spindly, articulated fingers, then up into his face.

"Hello, Edgar Voles."

Edgar almost smiles at the sound of the familiar voice. "NL7. Welcome back."

NL7 stands, swivels its head around, taps the mediabot's feet. "How unusual." It looks over at Edgar again. "We doubt this is within the contest's rules."

He shrugs. "It's not explicitly forbidden anywhere. I just didn't want to bother with the hassle of asking. I'll point out the loophole to them later, after we've won."

NL7 moves around the room, feet ticking along the floor, trying out its new body. "And your competition?"

"Scrambling. Playing exactly the game the crownchase wants them to play."

The android turns to him. "But we have a different plan?"

This time Edgar does smile, tight and strained. Like his face has forgotten how. "Yes, we do."

ALYSSA FAROSHTI'S PERSONAL QUARTERS, THE KINGSHIP, APEX

COY DROPS ONTO MY BED, DUMPING A DOUBLE ARMFUL of decadent sweets and sugar-laden goodies across the rumpled covers.

I push up from the sprawled-in-despair position I'd assumed for several hours now. "Is all of that really necessary?"

"It's your first breakup. Best to just cover all the bases." She snags a package from the middle of the pile—a chocolate-covered pastry—and shoves it into my chest. "Start with your favorite. We'll get weird from there."

I snort like I don't think any of this will help. But I also tear open the package and cram half the pastry in my face. Hey, no harm in trying, right?

"If anyone asks," I mumble with my mouth still mostly full, "I broke up with her."

"Done and done." Coy twists a piece of taffy into a spiral almost as long as one of her horns. "You want me to talk to my mother? She's got a new life-and-society editor. We could plant something. 'Faye Orso spotted in tears after Faroshti heartbreak,' maybe?"

"Gross." I throw my empty wrapper at her, bouncing it off

her nose. "That's gross, Coy. No way I play that dirty, even after being dumped."

"Your funeral. No guarantee she won't."

She won't. Coy's skepticism—and the Orsion family reputation—aside, Faye won't strike that low.

Her face flickers into my mind. Wild. Wicked. Totally enchanting.

Ugh. Where did that other chocolate-covered pastry disappear to?

Coy clambers over to stretch out next to me, snuggling her shoulder into mine. "What happened, anyway? I thought you two were delightedly crashing into love and delinquency."

I jam my hand under her back, extracting a mostly flattened pastry. "That's the problem. I mean, that last part. The delinquency part. Uncle Atar isn't a hard-ass or anything, but I know I'm starting to stress him out a bit with all of this. So after we got bailed out on Tabarti, I told her we should cool it for a bit on the troublemaking—"

Coy raises an eyebrow. "You said that?"

I elbow her. "And she said, 'I'm an Orso. What you call trouble, we call creating our own legacy.' Then she touched my face, told me, 'It was always gonna be a short run with us,' kissed me, and walked off."

Coy whistles. "I know she broke up with you, but be honest. You've got to appreciate her style."

I scowl at her and haul the covers up, dumping her off the bed and onto the floor. "Traitor. These pastries are my only true loves now."

Coy lies there, laughing, pelting me with whatever she can reach, until I finally laugh too.

NINE

Stardate: 0.05.16 in the Year 4031, and from here on out I think we can pretty much just assume that we're all blossoming under the stewardship of His Great Douche-ness, Enkindler Ilysium Wythe
Location: A stupid storage compartment on my own damn ghost-port. Yay.

THIS MAY COME AS A SURPRISE, BUT THIS ISN'T MY first time in compression cuffs.

Total shocker. I know.

It's actually my fifth because I don't count that one time on Divinius IX. (I don't even like to talk about Divinius IX.) The first two times were by actual law enforcement on whatever planet I was on, and I got bailed out anyway, so no big. The last few instances, though, have been run-ins with pirates, and I've had to get a bit more . . . creative when it comes to getting out of them.

I've learned how to dislocate my shoulder.

It hurts like a bitch. It's not pretty. But it works.

I take a few moments to move around the small room, scanning the walls, stamping at the floor, and nudging panels with my boots. Kinda trying to psych myself up. Kinda hoping there's a different option. But this room is exactly what a storage compartment should be. Self-contained, tightly sealed off from temperature or humidity variations. Door locked from the outside. It really is about as good as a brig, and dammit, Faye Orso, for being two steps ahead of me on this one.

We should've waited before we docked, done a more complete scan—like subatomic-level. Something that would've picked up on a mirrormask or whatever modification she used to hide her engine signature. But that would've taken so much extra time, and who else would've even known or cared about a dusty abandoned spaceport that no one paid attention to anymore?

I mean, the obvious answer is Faye. Faye knew. Faye cared.

Just because you stopped paying attention to us doesn't mean we stopped paying attention to you.

How's that for some ominous shit?

I don't want anyone paying attention to me. I just want to get clear of this and get back to being a cruiser jockey for the science nerds at the Explorers' Society.

My fingers are starting to tingle. Compression cuffs—air-inflated synthetic cuffs wrapped in a plastic shell—are generally considered safe if you use them correctly, but I don't think Honor was worried too much about correct sizing when she was slapping them on.

I'm gonna have to suck it up and do it.

I find a handhold on the side wall, just a simple bar used probably for leverage or who-the-hell-knows. I back into it, grab it with my right hand, wrap my left fingers around the opposite wrist . . .

. . . and I pull.

I lean forward, steady, forceful. Ligaments screaming at me

like a Ravakian rattler. I'm grinding my teeth so hard my jaw already aches.

The toughest part is pushing past that point where your brain is like, *This fucking hurts! Stop! Why the hell would you do this to us?* I couldn't do it myself the first time. Hell Monkey had to help me. But it gets easier the more often I have to do it.

That probably isn't a good sign. I should probably see a medic about that.

But right now it means I have to pull for only about twenty seconds before I give one big yank and my arm comes loose from the socket with a gross, thick popping sound. There is just a wholesale stream of obscenities coming out of my mouth—like I could make the worst station merc blush right now—but I've got the space to twist my arms around until they're in front of me instead of behind my back.

More cuss words. Sweat beads on my upper lip and along my temples. Stars and gods, this is painful. And my right arm is worth about nothing. Just hangs there like dead weight. Throbbing, burning dead weight. But at least it's not pinned behind me.

I check the storage compartment door, but it's locked and there's no visible control panel on this side. Guess no one wants sentient cargo getting out and tearing up the place. It sounds absurd, but lemme tell you . . . it happens.

That's okay. I kinda figured that wouldn't be my way out. If I'm gonna get free of this room, the better bet is to squeeze myself into a wall cavity. A complex port like this has a lot of built-in space between all the interior walls to run wiring and vents and cables.

Even better, just about every room except the brig has an access panel to get inside these cavities. Just in case someone needs to make a repair. Or, in my case, make an escape.

I find the access panel at the back of the room, down in the bottom corner. It's a little extra tight from age and lack of use, but nothing that my boot and some desperation can't handle. The cover pops open after the third or fourth kick, leaving a big, dark square in the wall. Just big enough for me to wiggle my way through. My dislocated arm burns the whole way, like, *What the hell are you doing, Farshot?*

Good question, arm.

The space on the other side is a tighter squeeze than I expect. Dark, and barely wide enough to sidestep along because there's a ton of dimly glowing wires roped together and around each other, just oozing heat. Probably not healthy to bask in radiation energy too long. Time to get a move on. I work my way along the wall—grunt, cuss, squeeze, wires in my face, wires around my ankles—until I get to a ladder and climb up into a horizontal crawl space. Not that I can do much crawling with my right arm all messed up, but I get on my back and shove my way along with my legs until I find another access panel, one that I'm guessing is over the hallway.

I slam a boot down on it until it falls open, and then I drop down after it.

I hit hard, legs crumpling beneath me. But I avoid catching myself on my face, which is a feat with no hands.

And I was right. I'm in the hallway.

"Holy shit, that actually worked." I can't wait to tell Coy about this. She's gonna be so pissed she missed it.

Okay, okay, still gotta find Hell Monkey. One step at a time.

I book it down the hallway, pausing to listen, to pick up any sounds. I should've counted doors when Faye dropped me off. I'd been too focused on the blaster at my back.

"Come on, H.M.! Sing out so I know you can hear me!"

There's a thud and a curse and then the muffled sound of Hell Monkey's voice on the other side of a door a few meters away. "Alyssa? Alyssa, in here!"

He pounds at the door so I know which one he's behind, but I'm already at the control panel. A few seconds and then the door slides open and it's such a relief to see him that I want to hug him. I can't—and he can't either. His hands are still cuffed. But judging by the mess on the floor right next to his feet, he'd managed to pry open a section of wall near the door and was trying to rewire the lock from the inside. With his arms literally tied behind his back.

Okay, man. That's sexy.

He steps closer, almost closing all the distance between us, and his eyes drift down to my useless arm. "How's it feeling?"

I'd almost forgotten about it for a second there. "Like hell. But this one's all good." I wiggle my left fingers at him. "Can you talk me through how to disable these cuffs?"

He grins. "My pleasure, Captain."

A lot of people look at tall, broad, muscley Hell Monkey and think: knuckledragger. But I'm careful about who I hire—I'm the only idiot allowed on board my ship. So it doesn't take H.M. long to figure out how to use what we have on hand—and by that I mean the wiring he'd half yanked out of the wall—to short-circuit the cuffs on his wrists. It takes even less time for him to get mine off.

Hands free. Arms free. It feels better right now than a Lenosi massage. Even with one arm still dislocated and aching.

"We should pop that back in," Hell Monkey says.

"You can medic as we walk." I spin around and head toward the lift farther down. "We've gotta get upstairs and take the control room back."

"Are you serious, Farshot? With no weapons and one good arm?"

I give him a wink over my shoulder. "Yup. Sounds about right for me."

TEN

THERE SHOULD BE MUSIC ON THIS LIFT. AREN'T
lifts supposed to have music? Something to fill all this stupid
silence? All I can hear right now is Hell Monkey breathing disapproval next to me. I don't think it's because we're rolling ass-first
into danger—that's kinda our thing. I think it's more because I'm
hurt and he wanted to fix it, but I wouldn't let him. You've gotta be
relaxed to easily pop a shoulder back into a socket, and I've got way
too much adrenaline pumping now. We'd have to go hunt down
some kind of muscle relaxant to help the process along, and we
don't have time for that.

But it's fine. My arm barely even hurts.

Sort of.

The lift doors whoosh open on the control room, and halfway
across the space, Faye Orso and Honor Winger look up from what
they're doing.

Faye locks eyes with me. I lock eyes with Faye.

I grin. "Miss me?"

They pull blasters from their holsters, and I haul Hell Monkey
down by the front of his shirt as laserfire erupts all around us.
We manage to tumble out of the lift and underneath a long, heavy

table. There's probably better cover in here, but it's closer than anything else, and Orso and Winger would have to move from their station to get a better angle on us. I've got bets that they don't want to do that. They still need the ghostport to finish decrypting the data package, and they won't spread out and risk getting cut off from one another.

Blaster shots pepper the walls and floor and tabletop. Hell Monkey is curled up with his knees basically knocking into his chin in the small space. He raises an eyebrow at me.

"Is this going about how you expected?"

"Better, actually. The table is a nice bonus."

Sudden silence. No gunfire. Hell Monkey and I exchange a look, and then we carefully unpeel ourselves and peek out over the table.

Faye is bent over the conn, fingers moving with a fury. Honor still has guns trained in our direction, but her head is angled toward Faye, muttering something.

"They're gonna wipe the whole system," Hell Monkey whispers to me. "It'll take us hours to reboot it and run our own decryption on that message."

"Then we've gotta move." My eyes catch on my blaster, lying on the half wall dividing the command stations from the strategy and communications area. "Can you—"

I don't have to finish the sentence. Hell Monkey roars out from under the table, angling toward the side of the room, and Honor's head snaps around and she opens fire. I move at the same time, scuttle across the floor, and pin myself against that half wall in a crouch.

Hell Monkey has tucked himself into an alcove along the wall, and Honor is just pelting the area around him, pinning him down.

"Don't kill him!" Faye yells over the blaster fire.

I reach up. My fingers curl around warm, familiar alloy, and I pull my blaster down to my chest.

Hell yeah.

I pop my head over the wall, just enough to see. "My turn!"

I send two shots screaming past Faye's ears, making her hit the ground. I wail on the ground around Honor's feet until she jumps back. She returns fire, but I stay up. I just keep at it, lacing the air with bolt after bolt from my gun, until Faye beats a retreat from the command center. She doesn't turn a blaster on me, but Honor does. She and I have a good ol' exchange of how-close-can-I-get-without-inflicting-serious-injuries, and then she makes it to a lift on the other side and—whoosh.

The doors close and they're gone.

I crane my head toward the alcove. "H.M.? You okay?"

He pops his head out. "All good. You?"

My pulse pounds through me. I can feel every vein in my body. And I'm not even lying when I say I don't feel my dislocated shoulder right now. "I'm fan-fucking-tastic."

Hell Monkey makes a dash for the conn, bending over Faye's handiwork. "I was right—she was inputting a system wipe."

I clamber over the half wall to join him. "Can you—"

"On it. Give me a minute."

I wait. It's not my strong suit. I jiggle up and down beside him, too full of everything to hold still. Even when he scowls at me.

"It's been a lot longer than a minute."

"With all due respect, Captain: shut up."

I pace the area and try not to think about how the adrenaline is wearing off and my arm is starting to throb again.

Hell Monkey finally straightens. And grins at me.

"You stopped the system wipe?"

"Oh, sure, yeah, that—" He waves my question away with one hand like it's no big deal and then his other hand holds up the flat, shiny octagon shape of a data card. "But even better: they left before they could clear off the de-encrypted data. And I nabbed it."

I grab him by the face, pull him down, and plant a kiss on his cheek. "Best. Engineer. You're seriously never allowed to quit."

His whole head flushes bright red, and I hear him mutter something, but I'm already heading for the lifts, yelling over my shoulder, "We've gotta get back to the *Vagabond*. Come on!"

I half expect my ship to be blown to pieces by the time we get back, but she's all there, so either Faye was feeling generous or she was bluffing about her cruiser being nearby and snuck in under our scanners using a liftship. Doesn't matter either way. What's important is that my *Vagabond* is here and her AI flickers right to life as we hit the bridge. The front half of this space, closest to the prow, is the navcomm area, with all the basic make-ship-go-now stuff. The back half is strategic operations, which has tons of handy data analysis toys, including a full, three-dimensional display table.

The mediabot materializes almost as soon as we're back on board, but it's a second too slow in following us onto the bridge. I shut the door and swipe my hand over the lockpad, leaving the bot to try to film through the glass. Then I turn and pluck the data card from Hell Monkey's hand and load it into the strategic-ops table. "New project for you, Rose. Analyze this and show me what we got. Full display."

Her smooth voice rings out. "Processing . . . please wait . . ." Half a second later, a 3D projection fills the space above the table. And whatever I was expecting, I gotta tell ya, it wasn't . . . a big mess of lines.

Hell Monkey cocks his head left, then right. "What the hell is it?"

I don't have a good answer. It just looks like a total disarray of jagged lines and squares inside of squares and strange intersecting diagonals. I have Rose switch the projection to manual control and then I start to play with it. With just my uninjured arm, I rotate it, resize it, stretch its dimensions, and then finally spread it all out like it was before, pushing it lower until it's level with my ankles.

Okay, wait . . .

"H.M.—"

He shakes his head at me. "I can tell by your face that you're getting something, but it just looks like a mess to me."

"No! No, it's just—" I clamber into my captain's chair and stand on it for a better vantage point. The jump seat swings and tilts awkwardly at the weird weight distribution. Almost tips me right off, but I get my balance. "Rose, flatten the image." The whole display goes razor thin. "Now reorganize using topographical mapping characteristics. Shade relevant reliefs and elevations."

It takes a minute. Well, it probably takes less than an actual minute because AIs are fast as hell, but time is relative. Or so I've heard. But by the time I've gotten my butt off my chair—without even falling, thank you very much—the image is starting to come together and Hell Monkey's eyebrows are halfway up his forehead.

"A map. Nice. What is it a map of, though?"

"That's the million-credit question." Rose finishes the last touches, and even if you've seen a lot of topographic maps, this would be a weird one for you. Usually they've got a lot of curving lines and squiggly circles, but this is all sharp edges and ninety-degree angles. All the elevations are tall and rectangular, and the slopes form perfect step patterns downward. Through the middle, at the lowest elevation, are two lines zigzagging in perfect unison from one end of the image to the other.

Hell Monkey rocks back on his heels. He doesn't have that furrow in between his eyebrows anymore. "There's only one planet I know of that would have a map that looks like this."

"Agreed. Let's just hope the other crownchasers aren't as familiar with the Peridot system as we are." I check to make sure the mediabot is still out in the corridor where it can't hear us and then start inputting coordinates into the computer. "Rose, gear us up to jump to hyperlight. We're headed to planet AW42."

ELEVEN

AW421979.

The homeworld of a race called blotinzoids. Also the only planet I've ever known in the thousand-plus around here that adopted their numerical designation as their official planetary name.

I've only been there once, but it leaves an impression. Maybe that means we can make up whatever ground we lost thanks to Faye's stunt on my ghostport.

I really need to get better security on that place.

It's gonna take a little while to get there, even riding hyperlight, so as soon as the initial jump is complete, I head for my quarters. Our resident mediabot follows me, its big round lenses glowing. No, actually, not glowing—recording. I can feel it on my back, and I shudder as it spits out questions at me.

"How do you feel things went on the abandoned spaceport, Captain Farshot?"

"Were you expecting to encounter another crownchaser so soon?"

"Do you feel it speaks poorly of your skills in this competition that you were caught off guard so easily?"

I spin around at the door to my quarters. "Why do all of you have the same accent?"

It halts, head twitching this way, then that. The thing must have a dozen audio input sources on its body so it doesn't miss a word I say.

"Seriously, every damn mediabot I've ever met has the exact same Imperial accent like some research group somewhere decided this particular voice combination would make people more inclined to answer questions, but you know what? I don't want to answer questions right now, buddy. I'm tired. I'm taking a break. Shove off."

It can't calculate a response before I turn my back on it and let the door slide shut in its face.

Nice work, Farshot. That's gonna look great for Cheery Coyenne's headlines. Crap.

The only noise in here is the hum of the *Vagabond*'s engines and the clicking of the mediabot's feet as it wanders off somewhere. Good. Get gone, bot. I give it a minute or two after I can't hear it moving anymore before I tap the touch screen on the wall and open up a secure personal channel.

I'm prepared to just send a recorded message, but Coy's face fills the screen in an instant.

"Farshot, your ass better be alive and uninjured or I swear I will—"

"Save the threats, Coyenne." I hold up my left hand and waggle my fingers at the screen. "See? All appendages accounted for."

She sits back a little, one eyebrow raised, giving me a parental kind of look, which is a hoot coming from her. "*Daily Worlds* just had a breaking-news bulletin with camera drone footage of a firefight between you and Orso."

"That was fast. Your mom must have staff working overtime to upload, process, and edit all this."

Coy snorts. "She's nothing if not voracious in her pursuit of entertainment."

There's a very specific cadence of knocks on my door—a code Hell Monkey and I have had for a year or two now. I open the door, and he squeezes in with a med kit in his hand. He doesn't even glance at the screen. Just pulls out a hypo of muscle relaxant and injects it into the tissues around my jacked-up shoulder.

"Well." Coy puts on a kind of bored expression. "I'm glad you're all right. Would hate for our partnership to go up in smoke less than twenty-four hours into things. Terrible inconvenience, that."

Hell Monkey makes an irritated noise, but I give him a little kick to signal him to shut it. You can't take Coy at face value. That's almost never the real Coy. But then again, that's exactly why he doesn't like her. Doesn't like most anyone from all the big, messy webs of prime families, really. Present company excluded of course.

I suck in a breath through my teeth as Hell Monkey starts slowly moving my arm, angling to pop it back into place. "Lucky for you, we're both convenient and *competent*."

Coy jerks upright, almost falling out of her seat. "You cracked the encryption." It's not a question.

"A map. Somewhere on AW421979, the blotinzoid homeworld—AH!" A quick starburst of pain, and then ninety percent of the numbness and throbbing in my arm subsides as the bone settles back into its socket. Thank every god in the empire. Hell Monkey gives me a little wink. "We're having the *Vagabond* run a comparison now to see if we can pin down exactly where on the planet it is."

She swings around, shouting an order at Drinn, her vilkjing engineer. I hear him grunt noncommittally in the background as she looks back at the screen. "We're headed there now. Should be right behind you."

I nod—sure, sure, sounds good—and reach for the display to end the comm, but Coy stops me.

"Farshot." She levels me a look across trillions of kilometers of space. "Let's not make the next round quite so interesting, all right? We don't want to give my mother too much footage to work with. She needs the challenge."

The line goes dark before I can respond with something snarky and winning, and I drop down onto my cot, back against the wall, feet dangling over the edge. Hell Monkey flops down beside me.

I want to sleep. My body feels all hollowed out by the adrenaline and the injury. Exhaustion hits me like one of those three-mile-high tidal waves on Eroth IX, and I sink. Sink against Hell Monkey's shoulder. Sink inside as my brain just kinda drifts. My eyelids close. Hell Monkey says something—I can feel his voice rumble through his body—but I'm only half-there and still going . . . going . . . gone . . .

My feet move across familiar floors. Dark, gilded, so polished and gleaming they're as reflective as a still lake.

Kingship floors.

And then I'm in my uncle's personal quarters. Or, that is, the personal quarters of the emperor. But Uncle Atar isn't emperor anymore. He's gone.

No, he's here. He's moving along the far wall, tall and stately, his hair like a clear waterfall down his back.

Just like he looked when I was little. When no one seemed more invincible than he did.

I thought nothing could touch him. I thought he would always be there.

I step toward him, reach out a hand.

He rips down a curtain covering a window. Sunlight lances into the dark room. I stop short, throwing an arm up against the brightness. By the time I blink it away, he's on to the next one.

"Uncle Atar . . ."

He doesn't respond. He just rips down curtain after curtain until the walls are clear. Until it looks like there's nothing around us but sunlight and rough, vibrant ocean.

He finally turns to me. Points a hand out at the horizon. "Look, Birdie."

"I am, Uncle Atar. I've been out there. I've been looking—"

He's in front of me between heartbeats. Half a head taller than me. He puts his long hands on either side of my face. "No, child. Really look. Really see."

He tilts my head back—

—and there are planets falling out of the sky, obliterating the sun, crashing into each other, and raining . . . raining down on us in a storm of rock and fire . . .

I jolt upright, heartbeat pounding in my ears, lungs working overtime.

"Alyssa. Hey, Aly . . ." A big, calloused hand touches my shoulder, then my cheek, pulling me back into my body. My quarters. My ship.

I look over at Hell Monkey. He must've stayed even after I fell asleep. Of course he did. His hazel eyes are fixed on my face, and I kinda think I'd rather face down a cluster of charging warogs than try to untangle everything that flutters around in my stomach when he looks at me like that.

I'm suddenly hyperaware that his hand is still cupping my neck, his thumb along my jaw. It's like every atom of me zeroes in on that one spot.

"Captain Farshot."

Rose's voice over the comms makes me jump, breaking eye contact. Hell Monkey pulls his hand away, and I shiver at the cold that seeps into that spot.

"Yes, Rose, what is it?"

"We are drawing near the coordinates for AW421979. We will need to drop from our hyperlight lane in five minutes and thirty-seven seconds."

"Thanks, Rose."

I cut a quick glance at Hell Monkey, but he's staring at his boots. I can't tell if I'm disappointed right now or relieved or maybe just hungry, but I don't really have time for any of that. I get to my feet, straightening my jumpsuit collar.

"Let's go see what new hell these people have planned."

H.M. rises and moves for the door, a half smile on his lips but not in his eyes. "I'm ready for trouble if you are, Captain."

TWELVE

Stardate: 0.05.18 in the Year 4031

Location: Dropping into orbit around AW421979 . . . and we're not the only ones, either

"WELL . . . SHIT."

I glare through the viewscreen at the *Wynlari*, the worldcruiser of that gigantic buzzkill Setter Roy. We're still approaching the planet, but he's already settled into orbit, which means he's probably processing the exact map location on the surface.

"Rose, I need the—"

She's way ahead of me: "I am working on it, Captain. Patience, please."

I roll my eyes. Sometimes this AI is like a damn parent.

In the jump seat next to me, Hell Monkey is deftly angling us into AW421979's gravity sphere. Even from hundreds of kilometers up, the planet's unique surface is visible: precise blocks of color, exact angles, and unerringly straight lines. I try to catalog what I might need down there: no survival suit necessary, but a blaster maybe? The blotinzoids are extremely logical but also friendly and open. Almost makes a person think they're simpleminded (though that would be a big mistake). The other crownchasers are a different story. Blaster, for sure. A grappling gun too, maybe.

Hell Monkey pulls up the specs on Setter's ship, frowning at the display. "I don't recognize that name—the *Wynlari*."

"It's Lenosi. It means *True Son*."

He raises his eyebrows at me. "That seems kind of . . . pointed."

"It is, but it isn't from Setter." I swipe at the display, dropping the ship stats for a standard press photo of Setter with his mothers. "Setter's adopted, and I'd bet good money that Radha and Jaya Roy named that ship as a big middle finger to those in the family who question Setter's position as heir."

Rose's voice cuts in. "Proximity alert. Worldcruiser dropping out of hyperlight."

I wipe the display clear. "Identify."

"The *Gilded Gun*."

Coy. Good. She made good time.

"There goes Roy." Hell Monkey points at the viewscreen just in time for me to see the *Wynlari*'s sublight engines flare as she shoots down toward the planet surface. I grab the controls without even thinking and aim the *Vagabond* at her tail, trusting that Coy is sharp enough to follow me.

Setter might be one step ahead right now, but I can make up distance like a champ.

We drop down into the planet's atmosphere, and the whole surface spreads below us like the most precise and orderly quilt ever. No clouds to obscure the vision. Blotinzoids design everything on a schedule, even their weather. We must've hit on a predetermined clear day. Below us, everything from the cities to the landscapes rise and fall in precise shapes. Square skyscrapers. Rectangular mountain ridges. And—this is the part that tends to freak out newcomers—they rearrange sometimes. Nothing on AW421979 is totally static, and the blotinzoids often shift the world around them to optimize efficiency.

It's a trip the first few times you see it. Like, hey, that hill over there just tumbled down into semi-organic blocks that are rebuilding themselves into trees now. No big.

"Captain Farshot, I'm detecting a beacon ahead."

Hell Monkey and I exchange a look. "What kind of beacon, Rose?"

"Unknown. Its signature is quite unique."

"Full manual, Rose. Just give me a visual of the beacon's direction." She puts a bright red point on the viewscreen, and then I feel the *Vagabond* drop fully into my control. It sends a thrill across my chest.

My ship. My hands. Strip away everything else, and I've still got this. I'll always have this.

Hell Monkey tightens the buckles on his jump seat and grins. Obviously not his first time at this show.

I drop us down until we're skimming the planet's surface and jam on the speed, feeling the sublight engines hum underneath my feet. It's the same frequency as my pulse.

"Captain Farshot, if I may—"

"It's quiet time, Rose. Hush."

I push the *Vagabond* faster, zigzagging us along precisely designed irrigation beds. Wrenching her up tight inclines. Slicing along cliffsides.

Hell Monkey laughs out loud as the g-force presses down on us.

A tall ridge starts to fall to pieces as we fly toward it, and I floor it, wrenching the *Vagabond* left, right, up, down. Weaving her body between plummeting blocks, barely avoiding half a dozen collisions that probably would've ended our lives. We skid into a landing near the beacon, and H.M. is laughing and I'm laughing and by all the gods in the empire I haven't felt this fricking good since before . . .

Before Uncle Atar.

We touch down half a second after the *Wynlari* does, and I can see Setter in the cockpit of his ship. I wave and grin at the disapproving expression on his face.

"Coy is a few kilometers back still."

"I'm going," I say as I rip the safety harness off. "Tell her to catch up quick. She's got the legs for it. Rose?"

"Yes, Captain Farshot."

"Send the beacon coordinates to my wristband."

Strapping a blaster to one hip and a grappling gun to another, I make a break for the aft bay doors, skidding down the ramp and onto the planet surface, the whirring sound of one of the crownchase camera drones right in my wake. If you're not a blotinzoid, the ground here is rough terrain, changing elevation by anything from five to twenty-five centimeters every few steps. Makes it tough to pick up the speed I want as I race around to the front of the ship.

Where I almost slam into Setter Roy.

He shoots me a look over his shoulder. Those axeeli mood-ring eyes of his are currently an intense orange. "Careful, Farshot."

"Well, warn a girl next time you're gonna forfeit a race before it even starts."

Setter snorts and waves in front of him. "Go first. Be my guest."

I look down and see that the ground ten centimeters from his feet drops away, into a chasm probably a kilometer deep. Hard to tell, really. There's nothing but darkness at the bottom.

A rush of engines fills the air behind us, and I can hear a feminine voice over Setter's comms. "We've got incoming. Nathalia Coyenne just landed."

I check my wristband. The beacon is still in front of us, blinking at the top of a tall column of ground. Between us and it is a five-meter gap of nothingness and another fifty meters of terrain so rough that it's basically an obstacle course.

Wonderful.

A noise off to our left makes Setter and me turn, hands to our holsters. Six piles of organic and semi-organic blocks rearrange and build upon themselves until they've achieved the vaguely humanoid shape that blotinzoids assume when they choose to.

I don't know anywhere near enough about their culture or how they express themselves to get a read on how they're feeling, but I hope they don't mind too much that a bunch of ships just scorched through their atmosphere and plopped down on their planet. I'm suddenly feeling awkward about our big entrance. Did they know we were coming? Did we land in someone's backyard? Shit . . .

I wave. One of the blotinzoids up front mimics the gesture.

There's a blur of movement out of the corner of my eye, and by the time I whirl around, Setter Roy has dashed back toward the ships and is now sprinting, full throttle, toward the cliff. He times it perfectly (the bastard), toes hitting right at the edge. I freeze, heart hitting the back of my teeth. His body arcs over the empty space, legs and arms pinwheeling . . .

. . . and then he lands on the other side, tucks, rolls, is on his feet again.

"H.M.," I mutter into my wristband. "Did you see that?"

"The buzzkill's got hidden depths. Who knew?"

I run back toward the ships, spotting the long, gangly figure of Coy as she steps onto the planet surface. "I'm going, H.M."

"I figured. I . . ." Something about his pause sounds heavy. I hesitate, dropping my eyes from the chasm edge. "Don't die out there, Farshot."

Oh. Well, yeah, definitely that. Solid advice there.

Digging my toes in, I sprint toward the gap, arms pumping, legs pumping, ground disappearing underneath my feet as I go go go—JUMP—

My foot clears the other side just barely, and then my legs crumple hard and I tumble into a graceless stop. Face pressed into the ground. Scrapes on my legs and elbows.

I pump one fist into the air, triumphantly. Ta-da. Nailed it. Over the comms, I can hear Hell Monkey laughing his ass off. Monster.

I peel my body off the ground (nothing broken, thank the stars) and check left to see Setter Roy disappearing over the first rise. I check right to make sure Coy is catching up and see her sprinting toward the chasm edge, hair streaming behind her, silvery horns glinting in the sun. She jumps, windmilling her arms, reaching for the far edge, reaching . . .

Her hands make it across, smacking into the ground, scrambling for a handhold.

But then gravity takes her and she falls . . .

CROWNCHASERS REPORTED ON AW421979

Coyenne, Roy, and others spotted racing for the surface of the blotinzoid homeworld

EXPECTED FAVORITE
OWYN MEGA TRAILS THE PACK

Pollsters pegged him as one to beat, but the
Mega military heir isn't showing much of an edge

STEWARD WYTHE MAKES
A SURPRISE VISIT TO HELIX

The enkindler is scheduled to meet with the planet's chairman, as
well as multiple provincial boards on the economic powerhouse

ANTI-GOVERNMENT PROTESTS CONTINUE ON TEAR

Despite the ongoing crownchase, protesters march on
local and national government buildings, vandalize public property

PLANET AW421979, FIFTEEN METERS FROM THE CROWNCHASERS' WORLDCRUISERS

EDGAR WAITS UNTIL ALL THE OTHER CROWNCHASERS are there before he lands.

He hates to even look like he's playing the game, like he's as desperate as all the rest of them, but he needs to—just this one time—in order for everything else to work.

And now here they all are, assembled so conveniently. Roy and Faroshti. Coyenne behind them. And Mega and Orso just landed.

NL7 tilts its head, scanning the worldcruisers squatting on the planet surface in front of them. "Are they all present, Edgar Voles?"

He nods. "Yes, meet me in the hangar bay, and we'll proceed."

The android exits the bridge, and Edgar spends a few more moments at the conn, uploading the last of his handiwork. He and NL7 have spent hours cobbling together the footage they need to feed into the surveillance cameras on board. Looping video of him moving about the bridge and the galley, steering the ship, entering and exiting his quarters, pretending to work on the crownchase. They'll add more as they go along, just to switch it up and make it less obvious, but for now they have enough to provide the cover they need for their activities.

He joins NL7 at a release hatch near the aft of the ship. The android has already opened the airlock seal and is standing over a collection of five mechanical creations about the size of Edgar's hand. Each one has a little round body covered in visual sensors and six long articulated legs barely wider than a strand of hair.

His spiders.

He'd designed them a while back to show his father, but his first prototype malfunctioned and William Voles had declared them worthless. Edgar's perfected them since then, made them more intuitive, more connected, and almost undetectable.

NL7 hands Edgar a clear tablet, and he traces precise patterns over its surface, bringing the devices to life. One by one, he sends them slipping out of the hatch and down onto the surface below. They skim across the ground to the other worldcruisers, entering each ship and penetrating behind the paneling into the internal systems.

Edgar leaves NL7 to reseal the hatch and walks back to the bridge, setting himself up at the strategic operations station. He sets the tablet down and watches as the display in front of him starts to fill with live images.

Gear Aluma, companion of Owyn Mega, flitting nervously back and forth on the bridge of their ship, the Godsblade, her fuzzy gold wings tucked tight against her back.

Honor Winger, methodically cleaning her gun in the galley on board Faye Orso's ship, the Deadshot.

Drinn, monitoring his crownchaser's progress from the feeds on board Nathalia Coyenne's Gilded Gun.

Sabela Burga, ship's engineer on Setter Roy's Wynlari, moving down a corridor in her hoverchair, pausing to inspect the power flow on an energy conduit.

And Hell Monkey.

Edgar wrinkles his nose at just having to think the name. He's doing whatever someone who calls himself Hell Monkey would do.

NL7 appears at Edgar's shoulder. "It appears the operation was successful."

"Very successful." He looks back at the android. "Prepare to head out of atmo. We've done all we need to do here."

TWO YEARS AGO . . .

THE *VAGABOND QUICK,* IN ATMO ON THE PLANET DRAKE

I'M SUPER SELF-CONSCIOUS RIGHT NOW.

It's always like this when I have a new crew member. I have to suddenly pay attention to how I move around the ship, the attitude I give off, whether I'm sounding captainy enough. And this is my very first mission with my new engineer—Hell Monkey—so it's pretty damn uncomfortable.

Hell Monkey.

Definitely never heard that one before. But he nailed every test I threw at him, including stripping the nodes on the coolant system in under ten seconds, so who cares what he calls himself, right?

He's sitting in the copilot jump seat, his eyes steady on the conn, monitoring the *Vagabond*'s outer hull as we take another low pass over Drake's Solar Sea.

It's an entire ocean of liquid fire. *Liquid fire.* I remember reading about it when I was a kid, and now I'm actually getting to clap eyes on it. I almost wanna bounce in my seat.

I lean on the controls, swinging the *Vagabond* into a series of wide loops so the cameras and scientific instruments the Explorers' Society set us up with can get a broad range of data. It's a simple assignment overall—go down to the planet and collect as much information as you can without getting burned up—and I'm glad for it. All I have to do right now is fly my ship like a badass, and that's one thing I never have to be self-conscious about. When I'm at the controls, I know exactly who I am.

I check a readout on the conn. "We've gotten quite a bit of data recorded already. How's she doing?"

Hell Monkey grunts. "Pretty good actually. That extra heat shielding is holding up perfect."

"Well, you did an awesome job installing it, so that tracks."

Dead silence from his side of the bridge. I shoot a side glance at him and . . . is he blushing?

Rose's voice cuts through the air. "Emergency alert, Captain Farshot. Sensors detect extreme seismic activity near our current position. Tsunami wave rapidly forming. Projected crest: two kilometers. Estimated time to impact: five seconds."

A flame tsunami. Holy hell, that would be something to see up close. But I shouldn't take the risk, not with a brand-new crew member on board. I've already lost engineers over situations just like this.

Hell Monkey sits back in his chair. "Y'know . . . I bet the science guys at the Society would piss their pants to get data from a real-life flame tsunami." He raises an eyebrow at me, a little smile creeping onto his face.

Delight fizzes through me, and I laugh out loud. "H.M., I think we're gonna be a good pair."

Then I flip the *Vagabond* around and head straight into trouble.

THIRTEEN

Stardate: 0.05.18 in the Year—ARE YOU FUCKING KIDDING ME RIGHT NOW? COY IS FALLING OFF A DAMN CLIFF!

I HAVE BASICALLY THE SPAN OF A HUFFAR'S HEART-beat to make it to the cliff's edge. (Huffars have the fastest natural heart rates in the quadrant, so it's a really short space of time, okay? Trust me on this one.)

Honestly, I don't know how I did it. I heard Coy's name tear out of my throat and felt my body moving, and suddenly I'm hanging over the edge with my butt in the air and one hand wrapped around Coy's wrist. I fumble around with my free hand trying to find something—anything—to lever against, but there's nothing. Just the weight of my own hips and legs to keep us from free-falling.

Reaching down, I wrap my other hand around her arm too, just to make sure I've got a good grip. Coy's face has gone a bit green underneath the gray, and her eyes flick nervously to the empty black underneath her dangling feet. She looks up at me, her immaculate savior, and says . . .

"I knew you were attached to me, Farshot, but this is somewhat next level, don't you think?"

And then she grins.

My arms (one of which was recently dislocated, thanks very much) are shaking, my muscles are starting to burn, and this jerk-off is cracking jokes.

"Nathalia Coyenne, put that stupid smile away and start getting some purchase on this cliff or I swear to every god in the empire that I will drop your ass!"

She keeps grinning, but at least she swings her legs over and uses her toes to find some leverage. It's not much like scaling a regular rock face—it's a lot more sheer—but the building blocks of the blotinzoid homeworld do stick out into little ledges here and there. With her climbing and me pulling, we manage to get both of us clear of danger and onto our feet.

I bend over at the waist, my heart racing, my breath coming fast. Looking up, I catch Coy's gaze, and underneath it I see a flicker of something dark and scared. Like she really thought for a second there that she was a goner.

So did I.

I start to say something, to reach for her arm, but I hear a shout and whip around to see Faye and Owyn Mega racing toward us.

"Time to go," says Coy.

She takes off over the uneven landscape, and I start after her, pausing for half a second at the top of the first rise to look back—

They make the jump. Both of them. Good.

I throw myself into the race, closing the distance to Coy quickly, trying to catch up with Setter, who seems impossibly far ahead. I can see his dark figure jumping over obstacles, skimming up the sides of columns, making it all look easy. This kid is a damn surprise for sure.

My scrambling is a lot less graceful, but it is effective. I manage to stay ahead of Orso and Mega and even have an edge on Coy. I know she and I aren't technically in a competition, but (a) no one else really knows that; and (b) old habits die hard. We spent too much time as kids racing along hallways and up and down access shafts, seeing who could beat whom to whatever random point we'd decided on.

This time it's that bright light of the beacon on the last rise.

I reach the base just as Setter clears the top, touches the light . . . and disappears.

The hell?

"Hell Monkey," I call into my wristband as I start to climb.

"Here, Captain."

"Get the *Vagabond* geared up. I want to be ready to go."

"Less talking, more climbing, Farshot," Coy barks just behind me.

Yeah, yeah, yeah . . .

My fingers find the top, and I haul my body up with a grunt and a curse, rolling onto my feet, just about bonking my head on the stupid camera drone as it sweeps around, trying to get the best angle.

There's a gray metal platform sitting on the ground in front of me, maybe a meter high, and hovering several centimeters above it is a glowing sphere. It's hard to see much more than that because the sphere is so bright that you can't look quite at it, but there's definitely . . . something inside that light. Something moving. Almost like a million tiny somethings.

Coy's head clears the edge as I reach a hand out and touch the light—

—and then I'm on my back, staring up at the lavender sky of AW421979. It feels like all the wind has been knocked out of my lungs, and I gasp in a breath, coughing as I push myself into a sitting position.

I'm by the *Vagabond*. Right by her nose, actually, and when I crane my head back, I see Hell Monkey pressing his face to the window to get a sight line on me. His shoulders visibly relax when he sees me conscious and moving. I check myself over—nothing broken, nothing bloody. But there is something new imprinted on the skin of my palm. It's a replica of the royal seal, and it looks almost like a tattoo, but it's shimmering and metallic and—I look closer, bringing it right up to my nose—shifting very subtly.

From the beacon there's a blinding flash. I scramble to my feet and run around to the back of the *Vagabond* just in time to see Coy appear beside the *Gilded Gun*, coughing and looking disoriented.

The *Wynlari*'s engines hum, and she starts to lift off the surface. Crap.

I nod at Coy and then race up the aft ramp into the *Vagabond*, calling to Hell Monkey over the comms. "I'm in, I'm in. Get her up and follow Roy."

By the time I make it to the bridge, we're taking off into the planet's skies. Doesn't look like the camera drone made it back to the ship in time. That's a shame.

Hell Monkey keeps steady eyes and hands on the controls as I come up behind his chair and take a deep breath, smelling the metallic tang of recycled air and the scents Hell Monkey always carries on him—coolant and conduit oil and the dark, spicy soap he uses.

"Little dicey there for a second," he says, his voice kinda quiet. "I'm not used to you almost kicking it without being right there beside you."

Something about his tone makes me pause. I've never really been scared of death—it's not like I'm gonna feel anything on the other side of that river, right?—but I have a sudden image of Hell Monkey sitting, alone, on the *Vagabond* with nothing but memories to hang on to.

Like me with Uncle Atar.

I clear my throat around the ache that's squeezing at it and punch Hell Monkey in the arm. Keeping it light. Keeping it playful.

"Are you kidding me? We're gonna go down in a blaze of glory together."

He raises his eyebrows. "That a promise?"

"Of course it is."

He smiles just a little as we break atmo out into the sweet darkness of the stars. The *Wynlari* is visible about three kilometers off our bow. I drop into my jump seat, holding my palm up to my face, trying to figure out why we raced all that distance just to get a fancy tattoo.

"Did you get what we needed?" Hell Monkey asks without looking away from the controls.

"I'm not sure. . . ." I glance up and watch as Setter's ship blurs and then jets away, jumping into the hyperlight lane. He must've figured something out. What does he see in this that I don't? "Rose?"

"Yes, Captain Farshot."

"I need you to analyze something." I pull up a scan pad on the conn and press my palm against it, feeling it warm against my skin.

"Of course, Captain Farshot. Scanning now . . ."

I wait, holding my breath.

The lights on board flicker.

And then every system on the *Vagabond Quick* goes completely dead.

FOURTEEN

Stardate: 0.05.18 in the Year 4031
Location: Dead in the water above a stupid planet in the middle of a stupid contest and everything is stupid

))) Greetings, crownchaser. Congratulations on accessing the initial beacon. You were the second person to reach the touchpoint; you must now wait while the winning crownchaser is given a head start. All ship's systems except for emergency air and lighting will be offline for the next one (1) standard imperial hour. Time penalties increase according to crownchaser ranking by one (1) standard imperial hour. In the event of a proximity alert, ship's thrusters will be made available to you. Our apologies for any inconvenience.

I SCOWL AT THE MESSAGE ON-SCREEN AS MY HEAD bumps against the ceiling of the *Vagabond*'s bridge for the thousandth time.

When I was about ten years old, I used to run off with Coy and Faye and sometimes even Owyn and Setter to this dusty meeting room with a really high ceiling. It was on one of the lower levels of the kingship, without some of the soaring views of higher up, so it was empty a lot, and we figured out how to isolate its grav controls so we could float around in there, bumping into each other and doing sweet flips and other stupid stuff until we were caught and lectured and sworn off of doing that anymore.

That was fun and thrilling. When I was ten.

Spinning around in zero grav is *significantly* less fun now because I do not have time for this crap.

Which I guess is kind of the point. Gotta offer some kind of advantage for getting to the beacon ahead of other crownchasers, otherwise how are you gonna get that good footage of us all scrambling over each other? There's a countdown clock on the display right underneath that stupid message and it's currently sitting at 57:38 and ticking away.

Hell Monkey drifts by me, stretched out horizontal, his hands behind his head. "Welp. That didn't really go to plan."

I brace myself against the ceiling and throw a leg out, nudging him hard off course with the toe of my boot. He flails, trying to stabilize, but not before he collides gracelessly against one of the bulkheads.

"All commentary that isn't useful commentary is extremely unwelcome right now."

He rights himself against the wall. "Define *useful*. I mean, I think most of what I say has some use."

"We need to go see if we can get the power back on. Can you go check the engine room? I'll try to get a panel on the navcomm open and see if I spot anything."

Hell Monkey shoots me a side-eye. "Okay, but . . . don't . . . touch anything, okay?"

"Are you kidding me? It's my ship!"

"Oh, I know. I saw how things got fixed around here before I came on board." He pushes off the wall, propelling himself down the corridor toward the engine room. "Just stay on the comms and tell me if you see anything weird."

Grumbling, I maneuver my weightless body down off the ceiling and underneath the navcomm controls. There are half a dozen panels about the size of my face scattered along the bottom of the dash so you can access interior wiring and circuitry when you need to fix something. Which . . . I'm not gonna give Hell Monkey the satisfaction of telling him he's not wrong, but . . . he's not wrong. I cycled through a few engineers before he came on board—not everyone gets my unique sense of adventure—and I've had to jury-rig repairs on my own. Just me and the ship's AI trying to guide me along. It's not that I'm totally terrible, but my work isn't exactly professional grade. That's what I hired Hell Monkey for.

"Hey, Captain."

Speak of the devil. His voice comes over the comms as I'm craning my neck in a painful way to try to get a better angle on the *Vagabond*'s guts.

"You find something?"

"Not exactly."

I let my head fall back on the floor with a thud. "Not exactly? What exactly does 'not exactly' mean?"

"It means that so far I'm not finding anything. Which tells me a lot of something. Does that make sense?"

I snort as I wiggle sideways to get to the next panel. "Complete sense. I'm starting to worry about how much time we spend together, H.M."

His laugh rolls over the comms. "I'm serious, though, Captain. They didn't say anything about this when they prepped you before the chase began?"

I try to think back to those half-blurred days. I don't think so? But gods, I don't remember much about any of it, really. I just remember . . .

. . . Uncle Atar's body being whisked away from me and Charlie before he was even cold . . .

. . . crying, sharp and jagged sobs, in the darkness of my old childhood quarters . . .

. . . the guttural hallüdraen funeral dirges blaring in my ears as I watched the royal oseberg ship arc across the sky on its trek to deliver my uncle's body into the center of Apex's sun . . .

"Alyssa?"

"I'm here." Tears have crawled into my eyes, and I swipe at them and clear my throat. "Yeah, I dunno. I wasn't really present and accounted for at the orientation meeting."

I hear Hell Monkey sigh. "I dunno. Something just seems off about it to me. I saw those crownchase guys work on the *Vagabond*. They got the job done, but they weren't exactly graceful about it. Putting a freeze on our ship? I'd expect to see fingerprints for something that big. Something new installed. It's like . . ."

"Like there's a third party at play," I finish for him.

"Yeah . . . Powerful enough to ghost into our systems like nothing. I gotta be honest—that's enough to twist a guy's underwear."

"Well, there's a visual for you." I put the panel cover back up and wiggle to the next one. I'm not even sure why. I didn't see anything out of place in the last few, and I doubt I will in the others either. But what the hell else am I gonna do for the next half an hour?

And it's a looooooong half hour. I bounce around the bridge, popping panels and checking behind bulkheads. Hell Monkey keeps talking from the engine room, doing this thing where he tries to come up with more and more groan-inducing puns. I tell him he's the worst, but I actually love it and he knows that, the jerk.

I spend the last several minutes of the countdown in my captain's chair, glowering at the clock, feeling itchy all over. I hate feeling stuck, I hate feeling trapped, and I know you're not supposed to speak ill of the dead, but I'm seriously pissed at Uncle Atar right now.

I thunk my head back against the headrest, squeezing my eyes shut against the total lack of anything going on. Why the hell did Uncle Atar even want me to do this so bad anyway? I'd make a terrible empress. I wasn't even good as an emperor's niece, for stars' sake. I hate sitting still, I'm not great with responsibility, I was a horrible, disobedient kid—there's nothing about me that should've made Atar go, *"Yes, she'll be perfect!"*

I shouldn't even be doing this. That illness must've gotten to him at the end.

My mind drifts, pulling at my memories of my uncle.

Of sitting with him in his favorite observatory, looking out over the Eastern Sea while he told me stories of the Faroshti homeworld and my mother and the family he lost in the Twenty-Five-Year War.

Of him pulling me away from my tutors to take me to the

kingship planetarium, how we'd sit there for hours while he displayed one planet after another, reciting everything he knew about the people who lived there.

I want to see them in person, I'd tell him. *Every single one.*

You will, Birdie, he always said. *You will see all their faces, and then you'll know.*

Know what?

He'd turn and take my face in his hands. *How to make something new. Something amazing.*

He never elaborated beyond that. He'd thought there'd be time for that later. We all thought there would be.

I open my eyes again, zeroing in on the countdown clock.

00:03

00:02

00:01

00:00

The lights flicker on.

Go time.

FIFTEEN

As soon as the *Vagabond* powers up, Rose's electronic voice fills the ship, and I've never been so excited to hear her.

"Captain Farshot, all systems are online again."

"Thank all the stars and gods. Rose, you all right?"

"I am functioning as specified."

My mouth twitches with half a smile as I lean forward and program new coordinates into the conn, ones that'll take us to a somewhat central part of the quadrant. I have no idea where we're gonna need to go next, but hell if I'm staying put any longer. The *Vagabond* hums to life, her engines heating up, and then she surges forward—and we're in hyperlight.

Hell Monkey's boots clomp into the room in long, heavy strides as he comes back from the engine room, and in his wake, I can hear the tick-tick-tick of the mediabot following him. It tries to squawk a question at Hell Monkey, but he cuts it off, muttering to it in a low voice, "What did I tell you would happen if you try to interview me right now?"

"That I would spend the rest of the voyage dangling in a net above the cargo bay," it replies in a tinny voice.

"That's a standing offer. Now be quiet." He stomps up behind the captain's chair and leans down low, muttering into my ear. "I'm gonna shove it out an airlock."

I reach back without looking and pat his scruffy cheek. "No, you're not, because you're a good guy who respects life-forms. Even annoying robotic ones."

He grumbles. "I hate being a good guy. . . ."

"Captain Farshot," Rose says, "new information has been input into my computer systems. Would you like me to display it?"

I clench my hand, the one where that beacon's imprint had been. My palm is empty now, the skin clean of any markings. This must be the next clue or bread crumb or whatever the hell it is we're chasing. "Yes, please, Rose. A dynamic projection."

I swing out of my seat and watch the strategic-ops table fill with Rose's three-dimensional display.

A mess. A totally different, brand-new mess from the last mess we untangled that led us here. This one appears to be a bunch of symbols—probably a runic-based language, but I'm not familiar with it. There's gotta be over three hundred of these bastards, and they practically fill the space.

I stick my hands into the middle of it, using gestures to pull one symbol to me, then discard it and bring another. "H.M., what do you make of this?"

"Huh?" He's wandered over to the port-side station, where all the media feeds are currently pulled up, streaming an avalanche of nonsense. "Make of what now?"

"Just the next big puzzle we have to figure out in this ridiculous ride. No big, really." He doesn't even glance back at me, so I stomp over to him, putting on a full huff so he'll get the picture that I'm Not Amused. "What are you even staring at over here?"

He gestures at the screens, shrinking a couple of the feeds smaller so he can expand another one and put it on blast right in the center. "Cheery's latest handiwork."

I stare at it for a second before I process what's on-screen. The *Daily Worlds*, apparently, has put up a crownchaser leaderboard. Except it doesn't seem to be based on our actual performance so far. Instead it has percentages, calculating who the general public *wants* to win.

And my name is at the top.

Granted, my score is only a percentage point higher than Setter's, but still . . .

I blink. And I blink again. I open my mouth. I hesitate. I close it again. Then I lean back and wave the mediabot over. "Get over here."

It clicks across the floor. "Captain Farshot, so glad you—"

"Off the record, buddy. Shut it down."

I didn't know a bot could sag with disappointment like that. "Yes, Captain Farshot," it says, and all its camera lenses go dim.

"What is this?" I wave my hand at the screen. "Whose ass are they pulling these numbers from?"

"No one's, Ms. Farshot. It's a quadrant-wide direct poll that adjusts automatically as people vote or change previous votes."

"Why . . . What . . . *Why?*" I flail a little. Like this is supposed to make up for the gap of actual words.

The droid tilts its camera-shaped head at me. "Historically speaking, a base of public support is very important for a sovereign. Is that not correct?"

Well, yes. Of course it is. Part of the reason why Uncle Atar was so effective was because he was also well liked on so many planets. And having a bright, shiny leaderboard on display like this certainly serves as a good motivator for all of us to put our best faces forward. Play by the rules, jump through all the hoops, smile big for the cameras. After all, prime families love public adoration almost as much as they love power.

But still . . . Why am I in the top spot?

"Makes sense if you think about it," Hell Monkey says with a shrug. Like he read my mind or something.

I round on him, crossing my arms over my chest. "And how is that exactly?"

"Face it, Captain, we make for good TV." He squares off to me, hands in his jumpsuit pockets, a grin on his face that's all mischief. "I mean, I'm obviously bringing the good-looks element—"

I bark out a laugh. "Obviously."

"And you've been doing some action-star-quality stuff—breaking out of a storage closet, saving Coy from falling off a cliff—"

"I *am* excellent at almost getting myself killed."

"We've got everything you want in a vid: comedy, drama, sexual tension—"

I can't even help the grin that's on my face now. This pattern with us—the back-and-forth—is so easy and familiar. "Oh, sexual tension, huh?"

He winks. "Hey, we gotta give the people what they want, right?"

There's a slight hum of machinery behind me, and I glance back at the mediabot. Its cameras are back on, glowing bright blue, recording this whole exchange.

My smile disappears, and I grab the little jerk by its metal shoulders, marching it toward the exit. "Okay, show's over. Go contemplate which net you want to hang from in the cargo bay."

As soon as the doors close behind it, I turn back to the big 3D display and swipe it clean. "Rose, transfer the information to my quarters." She chirps a confirmation as I look over at Hell Monkey. "I'm going to try to sort it out in my room—are you coming?"

He shakes his head, running his hand over his hair. The smile is still half on his face, but it looks different. Irritated, maybe? "Nah, I'm good," he finally says.

"You're good? We're in a race for our freedom and our future, but you're . . . good?" I raise my eyebrows, waiting for him to expand on that. When he doesn't, I throw my arms in the air. "Whatever, man. You do whatever."

Shoving my hands into my pockets, I spin around and storm off the bridge.

SIXTEEN

Location: My quarters. By myself. But hey, y'know, I'm GOOD.

I STARE AT THE UNHOLY MESS OF SYMBOLS FILLING almost my entire quarters for two hours straight without making any headway. My brain and body are wiped. I'm trying to remember the last time I slept for more than, like, an hour. It's been a while. That can't be good, right? No way a body can go that long without crashing eventually.

I eye my cot, calculating how much ground I'll lose if I shut my eyes . . . just . . . for . . . a bit . . .

A loud beeping noise jerks me back to attention.

I recognize that sound. It's an incoming message. Direct to my quarters. On a secure communications channel.

Coy.

I get up and swipe my security authorization into the display, stepping back a bit as her face fills the screen.

"Farshot. You look a little rumpled. I'm not interrupting anything fun, am I?"

"Just me daydreaming of the universe's greatest nap." I hesitate, swallowing hard. "Hey, Coy, about those leaderboards that went up . . ."

It's the length of the pause that tells me there's a sore nerve in there for her. Her face stays carefully nonchalant, her posture doesn't shift, but it takes her just half a second too long to respond.

"Ah yes, that. Well, you know my mother. If you can't gamify entertainment, what good is it?"

"That's not what I'm talking about, Coy, and you know it. I'm talking about me, on top of the public poll. I'm sorry. I wasn't aiming for it—"

She sighs and looks away from me. "It's just optics, Alyssa. Really, it doesn't matter."

"It matters to you. So it matters to me." I chew on the inside of my cheek, turning over the thought that's been sitting on a back burner for the past few hours. "I think we need to go public. With our partnership."

Her eyes widen. "Now? We talked about saving that card until further into the race."

"I know we did. But I want to put it out there now. A public endorsement of you for the throne so everyone can see where I'm placing my bets."

She stares at me for a long minute, her expression growing serious. "You're the one who's going to get blowback on this. From the families and from the public too, probably."

I huff out a laugh. "I've handled a lot worse than a few negative opinions of me. I can take it."

"Fair enough. We'll do it your way, then." She sighs and flicks a hand at the screen. "It won't matter who's partnered with what, though, if we don't sort out our newest puzzle. How have you been doing with it?"

Oh yeah. That. "I've very definitely been staring at it with a lot of . . . intention."

"You too, huh? Seems to be a theme." Her eyes cut to something just to the left of the display. "If I'm judging this right, Faye only came back online just over an hour ago. Owyn is probably still stuck. So we have that going for us."

"That's something at least. You're somewhere private, somewhere secure, right?"

"Of course."

"Gimme a sec. And put your VR set on. I've got an idea." She sits back, grabbing a band of slender tech that stretches across her eyes and curves over her ears like glasses. I tap a few things on the touch screen and pull the big mess of a puzzle up again so it fills the space of my quarters. Then a three-dimensional holographic depiction of Nathalia flickers into existence beside me. She looks around for a second, adjusting, and then moves around the space.

"Your room is smaller than mine."

I shrug. "I took the navigator quarters. Closer to the bridge. Not so far to walk with a hangover."

She shoots me a look over her shoulder—like even holographic Coy can hear the lie behind my reasoning. But all she says is, "Sure . . . sure . . ."

Whatever. I roll my eyes. It's not like it's a major scandal or anything. Just . . . kinda personal.

I was ecstatic when Uncle Atar and Charlie helped me get my

first worldcruiser. Even more thrilled to take off into the stars, ready to do all the things I'd been dreaming about. Discover new planets. Join the Explorers' Society. Make a name for myself outside of empire politics.

But even with all of that, my very first night on my own in the *Vagabond Quick* was . . . lonely. I didn't have anyone else on board yet—no engineer or nothing—and the ship felt big and echoing. It didn't matter that it wasn't nearly as expansive as the kingship. It didn't matter that the designated captain's quarters were smaller than my childhood room. I rattled around in it like a pebble.

So I'd made the ship smaller. Made a nest for myself in the navigator quarters just off the bridge so I had a small little circle to move in most of the time, and I kept it that way even after I acquired a crew member or two. Even after I adapted to life away from the kingship and Uncle Atar and Charlie. Even as the universe got bigger with every planet I visited and every danger I experienced.

But Coy doesn't need that whole song and dance. She can think what she likes, but that story is small and quiet and covered in prickles, so it stays right here in my chest.

"Can you make heads or tails out of this?" I ask, waving at the puzzle.

Coy nods. "It's Tearian."

"Really?" I change my angle on the green, glowing symbols scattered around the air of my room. "I've seen Tearian before. It's never looked like this."

"It's an older form of the language. Three or four centuries old, I think. And it's not in a lot of accessible databases anymore. The Tearian government doesn't like to publicize the native written forms. They're more interested in promoting the imperialized form of their language these days."

That makes sense. Tear has seen a lot of conflict over the past several decades, mainly between the planetary government and the people they're supposed to be representing. The Tearian president reportedly values a lot of the "modern" influences of the empire over the actual developments and progress made by his own people.

I have opinions on this. In case you couldn't tell.

I level a look at Holographic Coy. "I thought you hadn't made any progress on this clue."

She holds her hands up. "Oh, I haven't, personally speaking. My engineer, Drinn, was apparently an archaeologist specializing in the Fyre system in his past life." She means this literally. Vilkjings reincarnate and often retain memories from multiple life cycles. "He recognized it when he came into my quarters to bring me a report on the engine outputs."

Engine output reports. I raise my eyebrows. "Look at you. All official and captainy."

She flicks her hair over her shoulder, all casual like. "Well, you know. I'm going to be empress soon. I thought I'd try my hand at this responsible leader thing. Turns out, I'm a natural, of course."

I laugh, waving my hands. "Okay, okay, tone it down. I haven't slept enough to handle full-throttle Coyenne. Let's focus on this puzzle mess. We know it's old Tearian. Did Drinn have anything more than that?"

Coy shakes her head. "He was able to translate some of it, but it's not like it was spelling out the secrets of the universe or anything. Each symbol is not even a specific word, apparently. It's like a concept, with even more conceptual layers underneath it." Her half-transparent form leans against the far wall, arms crossed. "That's why I called you."

"Okay . . ." I drop onto my bed and pull my legs into my chest so I can rest my chin on my knees. I stare at the puzzle, but I'm not trying to really see it. I'm trying to think of everything, absolutely everything I know about Tear. There haven't been a lot of expeditions out that way since I started flying—mainly because of the unstable political situation. The Tearian government has made a lot of unpopular moves, and the people there have started pushing back. Against them, against the empire, against the Explorers' Society—all of it. So it's been a no-go zone for explorers and Society scientists for a while now.

But still there was something. . . .

I swear to the stars there was something. . . .

An artifact. I remember it now. I saw it at the headquarters on Apex—it'd been so weird to see something Tearian in the research area. It'd been found off-planet and handed over to us to ensure it was safely and securely transported back to Tear. I'd wanted the assignment—I always wanted the assignment—but I'd been pretty brand-new still and the *Vagabond Quick* had gotten mucked all to hell on our last ride through a Nynzeri tectonic mudstorm. So all I'd gotten was the briefest glance at the artifact before it'd gone home.

It'd been this cube shape. No top or bottom—just the four sides.

And each side had had dozens of pieces that you could slide around to make a pattern.

I shoot to my feet. "Rose? What can you find about Tearian puzzle cubes?"

There's a little bleep of acknowledgment, and then I wait, pacing, for her AI to respond. Coy opens her mouth to say something snarky—it's really her only setting—but I shush her.

"Captain Farshot. I have found limited data entries on Tearian puzzle cubes. It seems to be an ancient form of intellectual challenge known for its unique format. It was historically popular over three centuries ago. The objective is to align complementary concepts along vertical and horizontal lines."

"Well, crap," sighs Coy. "That sounds terrible and time consuming as hell."

"Sure does. Go get Drinn. We have work to do."

FARSHOT OFFICIALLY ENDORSES NATHALIA COYENNE

The Faroshti heir puts out a statement announcing that she's supporting Coyenne's bid for the throne

PRIME FAMILIES REACT TO CROWNCHASE SHAKE-UP

"Anyone who blows a shot like this was never fit for the throne anyway," says patriarch William Voles

PUBLIC SPLIT ON THE COYENNE-FARSHOT PARTNERSHIP

Polls show an almost 50-50 division in those who support Farshot's announcement and those angry at their preferred contestant taking herself out of the running

CHANCELLOR ORSED: "IT MIGHT BE TIME FOR A CHANGE"

The primary voice of the Coltigh system floats a radical idea for the future of the empire

WORLDCRUISER S576-034, UNDISCLOSED COORDINATES

EDGAR SITS WHERE HE IS MOST OFTEN FOUND lately: in front of the enormous display of camera feeds hovering above the strategic-operations table on his bridge. He's found it's easier to just set it up as a full, interactive projection. This way he can manipulate and prioritize where his spiders ought to be positioned in a given moment, what needs his immediate focus, and what needs to wait.

Currently his focus is on the personal quarters of the *Vagabond Quick*.

Nathalia Coyenne and Alyssa Faroshti. Working in tandem. News of their partnership hit the media feeds less than an hour ago, roiling half the quadrant and dominating the latest cycle of crownchase news. Edgar had already suspected Alyssa Faroshti would be something other than a straight player in this game, so he isn't shocked, exactly. But it's still strange to watch them in action, teasing and talking and working in a seamless flow.

Just like when they were kids. He remembers seeing them in the kingship hangar, as he stood in the shadow of his ship— and the shadow of his father. How the two of them would crash together in a hug every time they were reunited. How they'd run off, hands clasped, giggling. Inseparable. As close as family, Nathalia always said.

He'd always thought that was an odd way to put it. Family, as far as he could tell, didn't look like that.

Another screen catches his eye and he pulls it up, expanding it to get a better look. It's Owyn Mega's quarters. He'd been working on the current puzzle with his companion, Gear, but now she isn't in the room. Instead the comms display is filled with the faces of Lorcan and Jenna Mega. They seem to be talking earnestly, intensely, to their son. Likely about the crownchase. Likely about Owyn's lack of showing in the race so far. Owyn himself stands stoically, hands behind his back, and nods at certain intervals. Edgar knows exactly what kind of discussion is happening in there right now. He sees it in Owyn's stance and in his expression. He's all too familiar with it.

So much pressure in the Mega family. So much resting on the shoulders of this one beloved heir to finally capture the throne. A throne that none of them have ever sat upon.

"Always the bridesmaid."

He glances over his shoulder as NL7 steps up behind him. "I'm sorry?"

The android gestures at Owyn Mega on-screen. "An antiquated saying to describe individuals who never quite hit the pinnacle of their achievement. It seemed appropriate."

Edgar raises his eyebrows and turns back to the camera feeds. "Very strange to hear you using metaphors."

"Mediabots are programmed to be grossly colloquial. It's very possible the remnants of it have affected our programming."

He shrinks the Mega feed and spins in his seat to face NL7. "Is it done, then?"

"It is, Edgar Voles. All trackers on board have been appropriated and reprogrammed. They will no longer give out our accurate position. Instead they have been set to transmit incorrect coordinates and move in reasonable pattern trajectories."

"Excellent. Thank you, NL7." Let the media and the crown-chase officials chase after his ghost. Let them think he isn't in the running.

He will enter the game when he's good and ready.

A NIGHTCLUB ON THE PLANET YASHA

I'M NOT SURE WHY I AGREED TO COME TO THIS.

I mean, the quick-and-easy answer is Coy. I haven't seen her in close to six months, and she'd begged me to show. And Hell Monkey needed to put the *Vagabond* through some intensive engine work at the Yasha shipyards anyway, so . . . Here I am, in a nightclub covered in glittering lights and even more actual glitter, crowded with a few hundred of Nathalia Coyenne's closest friends.

Including some of my former best friends.

Not Faye, of course. By all accounts, she's thrown herself fully into being the captivating criminal element that imperial media love to see from an Orso. I hear she's been dating her right-hand lady, Honor, for a while now, and it's nice to discover that that info doesn't hurt like it might've a few years ago.

Owyn Mega is in a back corner, talking to an Artacian with soft gold wings folded down her back. Their heads are super close together, and the guy looks the happiest I think I've ever seen him lately. He spots me through the masses and grins, a little sheepish. He raises his drink in salute, and I realize I can't really return the gesture so I just wave awkwardly and edge toward the bar to remedy my drink-less existence.

I almost plow into Setter Roy, standing against the bar, holding a painfully appropriate glass of water. It's too loud in here to hear him sigh when he sees me, but I see it on his face. Gods, he reminds me of Uncle Charlie.

"How's it going, Straight-Laced?" I clap him hard on the back and flag down the bartender. "Still killing it on the party circuit, huh?"

He grimaces. "Not all of us can afford to go gadding about the galaxy."

Now it's my turn to sigh. "I literally just walked in the door, Setter."

"I didn't—"

"No, it's fine. Let's just get this out of the way." I swipe over some cred-chips to pay for my drink and then turn to face him, doing my best impression of his deep voice and Lenosi accent. "'Alyssa, you owe it to your family to be more responsible!'"

"I don't sound like that."

"'Alyssa, your uncle is the emperor! You shouldn't be embarrassing him!'"

"I never said anything of the sort."

"'Alyssa, you really ought to try shoving a steel rod right up your ass! It's so great for the posture!'"

"I'm not—" He slams his water glass on the bar top, slopping liquid all over. "I just don't understand . . . how you can be so *careless* with your legacy."

"Because I don't want to think about my *legacy*, Setter." I reach over the bar, grab a mostly dry towel, and toss it at him. "I have nothing to prove to anybody. And neither do you. Your mothers love you as is. They think you're perfection. And as for everyone else, well . . . I think Owyn kinda likes you sometimes."

I smile a little, so he knows I'm kidding, and he *almost* smiles back. Bonus points for effort. I hand him my drink and pat him on the arm.

"Loosen up, Setter. It's a Nathalia Coyenne party. It'll be good for a show if nothing else."

He looks around, at the chaos of bodies and music, at Coy herself holding court on the far side of the room with a dozen rapt admirers.

"We'll have to let go of all of this someday, you know," he says. "Step into our real roles, our real responsibilities."

"I mean, *you* will probably." I pay for another drink and clink it against his. "But not tonight, Setter Roy."

I leave him at the bar and lose myself in the crowd.

SEVENTEEN

Stardate: 0.05.19 in the Year 4031

Location: A spinning intellectual puzzle box. I mean, I'm not inside it. But I feel like it.

IT'S BEEN SIX STRAIGHT HOURS. HELL MONKEY comes in after about an hour to bring me food and make sure I'm still alive. Whatever words I put together for him must not be very coherent because he comes right back with a cup of coffee the size of my face.

Gods bless him. I could almost kiss him for that.

Coffee's not a long-term fix, but it helps keep my brain from dissolving into a total pile of mush while we sort out the rest of the Tearian puzzle cube.

Drinn's past-life knowledge and the combination of our ships' AIs gave us an edge, and we've got all the symbols translated. It's just been trying to slot everything into the place we think it goes. Every time you place a tile, it has a cascading effect on the rest of the puzzle because it has to go with what's above it, what's below it, and what's on either side. We "solved" it once but nothing happened, so we tore half of it up and started again. But we're almost done, and I've got a good gut feeling. Good enough that I wave Holographic Coy away.

"Get back on your ship. I mean, all the way on your ship. Make sure Drinn has this solution copied in."

Coy leans back, hands on her hips. "You think this is it?"

I swipe the last tile toward me. "If it's not, I'll be right back on your comms."

She nods and reaches for her face to take the VR off, but then she pauses and angles a sharp look over at me. "Try to rest or something, Farshot. You look like hell, and that isn't good for either of my two hearts."

She's gone before I can respond, so I'm left squatting there on the floor of my quarters, mouth half-open.

What a dick move.

I pull the last holographic tile down and slot it into place in the bottom corner of the cube.

A voice comes on over the comms. Not the *Vagabond*'s voice—not Rose.

"Course entered, crownchaser. Preparing to move to hyperlight."

Well. I guess we're off. Hopefully Coy is right behind us.

I should do what Coy said and try to sleep, but I'm in a weird state of exhausted-awake. Not quite coherent, but too artificially stimulated to relax. I step out of my quarters, blinking a little in the comparatively bright light of the corridor. It feels like I've been holed up in there for weeks. I'm rubbing the spots from my eyes when a shadow looms over me, and I look up into Hell Monkey's irate expression.

"We just jumped to hyperlight."

"Yeah . . . Sounds about right." I slip past him, heading for the galley. Maybe sleep isn't the answer. Maybe I just need more coffee. That sounds like a solid plan.

He follows on my heels. "You couldn't have given a guy a heads-up? What happened in there?"

"We completed it—the puzzle cube thing." I turn a corner and flinch as light floods the galley. "How the hell is it even brighter in here? Rose! Dim the lights or I'm gonna smash them!"

The illumination drops at least twenty-five percent, and I sag with relief. Hell Monkey hovers near my right shoulder, one eyebrow raised. "What's the matter with you? You're acting like you're hungover."

"Not true. I have no desire for cheese or fried bread." He's still kinda right, though. Everything seems too bright and too loud and I'm cold and I just want to go to bed.

"Maybe you're getting sick."

I fumble my way around until I've managed to heat up the premixed coffee equivalent we have on board. It's not as good as you can get even at most spaceports, but it'll do the job. I curl half my body around the mug, leaning back against the counter. Hell Monkey watches me with those ridiculous, steady hazel eyes.

"I'm gonna need you to put those away," I say, waving at his face. "I'm fine. You don't have to . . ."

"I don't have to what?"

"Look at me."

He snorts and then tilts his head back, staring at the ceiling. "Sure, Captain. This is a totally normal way of holding a discussion."

"I'm not sick or anything. I'm just . . ." I cast around in my brain, trying to find the right words, but it's basically turned to jelly after the marathon puzzle from hell. I finally give up and settle for ". . . tired."

And I am. That's true. But it's more than that. We've only just started this chase, and I already miss my ship being my ship and my choices being my choices. I miss getting up in the morning and getting to decide—just me—how far and how fast I want to push myself up to the raggedy edge of danger.

And I miss Uncle Atar.

I keep feeling the urge to talk to him. Or thinking "Next time I see Uncle Atar" and then remembering with a horrible sickening drop to my stomach that there's no one to see anymore. The empty echo of him keeps lapping at my heels, and if I stand still too long, it'll swamp me.

Hell Monkey comes over and pours himself some of the terrible coffee mix, drinking it cold because he's a total heathen. I make a disgusted face, and he waggles his eyebrows and makes a big show of taking a long, loud slurp.

"You're a monster."

He hops up onto the counter, dangling his big booted feet next to me. "Maybe. But you knew that when you hired me. So that's on you."

He's got me there. I elbow him in the leg for it, though. He kicks back at me, but I dodge out of the way, laughing. Knowing us, it probably would've devolved from there into a full-out food fight or something equally mature, but then—

Click, click, click. Metal feet mincing over the floor as that ridiculous mediabot comes into the galley, lenses all lit up and recording.

"Captain Farshot! I couldn't help but notice your worldcruiser moved to hyperlight. Is it safe to say you made progress on the latest crownchase development? Can you speak as to where we're headed next?"

I sigh as the mediabot comes right up to me. *Don't be a dick, Farshot. It's just doing its job. Don't be a dick.* My eyes find its designation number stenciled onto a plate on its shoulder: JR426.

"JR—can I call you JR?—I'm gonna be straight and up-front with you here: Do you think there's even the slightest chance at this point that I'm going to answer your questions? Can you calculate the probability on that one?"

It pauses. "Very low, Captain Farshot."

"Correct." I pat its pokey metal arm. "Come on, JR. We're going to go to the bridge and stare at stars and stuff until we get where we're going."

EIGHTEEN

Stardate: 0.05.20 in the Year 4031

Location: I mean, it's a *Tearian* puzzle. You do the math on this one.

IT'S NOT EXACTLY A SURPRISE WHEN WE DROP OUT of hyperlight in the Fyre system, within viewing distance of the planet Tear. I mean, I don't wanna be cocky or anything, but it was kind of obvious, right? Okay, that might've sounded a little cocky. . . . (But c'mon, that's not new. Humility = not my strong point.)

Hell Monkey keeps steady hands on the controls but angles his head back toward me. "You always said you wanted to come here. Today's your lucky day, Farshot."

"That's me. Luckiest girl in the universe." I lean against the back of Hell Monkey's jump seat as he puts in a trajectory to enter planetary orbit. "Anyone else here yet?"

"Nothing in the preliminary scan. Doing a secondary run at it, though. Just in case."

Rose's voice comes on over the comms. "Proximity alert.

Worldcruiser dropping out of hyperlight. Identification: the *Gilded Gun*."

Good. Coyenne right on our tail, as promised, and it looks like we beat everyone else here. That's a break, and I'm damn well ready for it. If we could get through this next challenge without blaster fire or near-death experiences, it'd make for a nice change of pace.

"No other worldcruisers detected, Captain," Hell Monkey says. "But I got something else: a beacon."

"Just like the one on AW421979?"

"The very same. Located on the sun side. We can do a quick burn and then drop through atmo. Should take us under ten minutes."

"I like the sound of that. Get us down there so we can jump through whatever hoops they've set up for us and get on our way."

I tap a quick message to Coy in my wristband but don't wait for her response before I give the go-ahead. Hell Monkey burns us hot for a few seconds to slingshot around to the half of the planet currently lit up gold by the Fyre system's central star. I buckle myself into my jump seat for safety during our atmo drop, but as soon as we're clear of the turbulence and entering the skies above Tear, I snap the buckles off and lean over the conn, trying to get my face closer to the windows along the prow. Like that will somehow give me a better look at the surface below or something. But I'm just so damn curious to see it with my own eyes.

In my (very experienced) opinion, none of the pictures I've seen of Tear do it justice.

It's called the Cobalt Desert, partly for the massive mineral deposits that fuel much of its economy but also because of its color. The planet is a swath of flat ground and outcroppings of jagged rocks, all in various shades of rich, impossible blue, cut through with veins of metallic gray and white. Clumps of plants that look somewhere between a scrub tree and a cactus sprout up out of the ground, and as we speed by, we spot an iridescent river spilling over a cliff. We pass low over expansive cities with some impressive-looking buildings and looping transportation systems weaving around them like snakes. But you can see the strain of conflict if you look closer: smoke rising from streets outside the shiny city center, a neighborhood cordoned off with makeshift fencing, a stream of people gathering in front of a massive building—

—and that's all I can catch before we're past. Still flying. Because that's not where the beacon is leading us.

It's leading us far from Tear's sprawling cityplexes to a small town on the edge of a yawning quarry. Like, a really small town. I don't think it's even half a square kilometer. I shoot Hell Monkey a look as he slows the *Vagabond* down and repositions the engine draft to give us a smooth landing.

"Here?"

He manages a barely there shrug without affecting his concentration on what he's doing. "This is definitely where the beacon is coming from. On the far side by the looks of it. By the edge of the quarry."

Yeah. That's where it would be, wouldn't it. So these people have to watch us stampede like assholes through their whole town to find our next toy. Real nice.

I tell Hell Monkey to hold down the fort, and then I head for the aft bay doors, slamming the button to deploy the loading ramp. He follows me and presses something into my hands.

A blaster.

"Can't be too careful," he says, catching my eye.

He's right. Smart money is on "don't go into the situation unarmed." But we just parked our big-ass worldcruiser next to this place and more ships are on the way. The idea of storming in with a blaster on my hip seems . . . just kind of douchey.

I push it back into his chest and cock a half smile. "Cover me from here, all right? I trust you more than I even trust me." As I clomp down the ramp, I call back, "And enjoy that view as I walk away, buddy!"

His response follows me as I round the corner: "You're the worst, Farshot."

My boots hit cobalt dirt and grit, and damn, I wanna get in on this stuff—pick it up, study it, figure out how it's different from other planets I've been on. But the *Gilded Gun* has already landed and Coy is bounding over to me, her face all lit up with excitement. I'm extra aware of the camera drones hovering above us, recording the first public team outing of Coyenne and Farshot.

"Ahead of the pack and everything!" she crows, slinging an arm around my shoulders. "Did you see where the beacon is?"

I fall into step next to her. "Yup. Far side, near the quarry. What do you bet we have to rappel for it or something ridiculous?"

I scan the town as we approach the outskirts. Little houses and shops, several of them looking in need of repair, and all of them painted in the distinctive fluid style of north Tearian art. I've seen a few isolated examples of this work before, but it was nothing like this—each brightly colored building unique and yet in conversation with the structures around it. They all flow with each other, like a story.

Coy swings onto the main through street, her steps quickening. I follow, but my feet are dragging. It doesn't feel right—us being here. It feels like trespassing. Even the air is saturated with it: *You're not welcome. Get the hell out.*

My eyes catch on three tall, broad-shouldered Tearian women standing near a building, watching me. Their skin is streaked with blue, their arm muscles standing out underneath their clothes. Their hands look rough and worn. And their eyes are angry. And wary.

And why shouldn't they be? I'm betting absolutely no one asked them if they wanted to be a part of this whole mess. A bunch of kingship bureaucrats probably just assumed everyone in the empire would be excited to see the famous crownchasers land on their planet.

I tap on my wristband comms. "H.M., can you get me the name of this town? And any specs you can turn up?"

"One sec, Captain."

I can't see Coy anymore. She's disappeared somewhere ahead, her excitement sweeping her along. I stay right where I stopped, staring back at the Tearian women. I'm not trying to start shit or anything, but I think it would be worse to look away, to act like I can't see them. That's my guess anyway. Fingers crossed.

H.M.'s voice cuts in. "The town is called Beru. Mining settlement for ore. Mainly cobalt, but a few others too. Some big imperial mining corporations pumped a lot of money into the town for a while, got a ton of product out of the quarry, but they all pulled out about a decade ago. There's a small amount of mining business keeping the place afloat these days."

Ah. I'm guessing they're not big empire fans after that. Which means they're probably not big crownchase fans either.

"Thanks, H.M. One more thing. Can you—"

A shout to my right cuts me off. I turn to look—

—just in time for a dark figure to plow into me, sending me crashing to the ground.

NINETEEN

Whatever minerals are in the ground of Tear, they taste bitter as hell, and they're one hundred percent in my mouth right now.

Gross.

I spit and cough, wiping grit away from my eyes and my lips, jamming my elbows down into the ground to try to lever myself up. Whatever knocked me over is scrambling off me now, and I make sure my gaze is clear before looking up.

It's a Tearian child. Young. Maybe three or four turns around their sun. Their face is round as a moon, and I swear to the stars their dark eyes take up half of it.

They're adorable, is what I'm saying, and they look about as alarmed to have run into me as I was to find my face meeting dirt.

"Hey, sorry, kid." I hold out a hand and slow my movements a little so I'm not so scary. "I didn't know this was a high-speed area. My bad."

They blink at me. Tough crowd.

I spot fresh scrapes on their knees, just minor lacerations from hitting the ground too hard probably, but I'm betting they sting a little. I unhook the medkit from my belt and grab two small bandages, holding them out for the kid to see. "Can I help you put these on?"

Heavy footsteps rattle the ground behind me, and I look up as one of the Tearian women sweeps across the street and gathers the child up in her arms. She pinches their chin gently and starts scolding them. I mean, I'm assuming she's scolding them. She's speaking a Tearian dialect, but you can still kind of tell when a parent is laying into a kid. That tone crosses the language barrier. The only thing I catch based on the little modern-day Tearian I know is the kid's name: Thoas.

It's my turn to scramble to my feet now. I put my hands up in front of me, still holding those bandages. Very "I come in peace." I'm going for the harmless visitor vibe.

Not that I think she's worried much about me. I barely hit the top of her shoulder.

"Total accident," I tell her. "I'm not here for any trouble. I'm just here for the—"

"I know what you're here for, crownchaser," she spits in Imperial, slicing a look at me. "The same thing your type is always here for. Take and then go. Take and then go." She turns back to the child, puts on a reassuring smile, wipes at the kid's smudgy face.

"My type?" I laugh a little, going for lighthearted. "You see a lot of crownchasers come through Tear?"

The expression she gives me could flatten a Vaxildan moose.

"You're a prime family. That makes you the highest of imperial shit. And you're an explorer too, yes?"

I think I nod. I don't even know at this point.

"Figured. You look like one of them. The imperials come and strip our minerals. The explorers come and steal our relics. You're the worst of both worlds."

Damn. That hits me right in the stomach. I think I even stagger a little bit.

Alyssa Farshot: the Worst.

My brain catches up with my ears, and I frown up at her. "Explorers stole your relics? When? Who?"

She snorts. "You think they left a calling card? Sat at our tables? Ate with us? I don't know their names. They come when they want and take what they want. Sometimes here, sometimes in the cities."

I swallow hard, and I'm not sure if the bitter taste on my tongue is from the dirt anymore. "No licensed Society explorer is supposed to be doing that. They'd get tossed out on their ass. Did you—?"

"Did we what?" she snaps. The child, Thoas, tips their head forward, snuggling into her chest, and she stares at me over their ruffled hair. "Lodge a formal complaint? Seek restitution? You must not know anything about this planet. No one is stepping in to stop them. No one defends us. Our leaders say, *please come in, what else can we give you.*"

I don't have anything to say to that. I feel like my arms are too long and my hands are too big and I don't know what to do with either of them. It's not like I haven't heard of this happening— explorers working outside of protocols, straight up stealing and claiming it was for science. It was pretty rampant in the early years of the Society. But leadership makes a big deal about how they stamped out those shitty practices decades ago. It isn't still supposed to be happening.

Or maybe we all just try not to see it happening.

My eyes land on Thoas's scraped knees again, and I show the woman the bandages I'm still holding. "Can I . . . ? I mean, do you mind . . . ?"

She laughs a little. It's not happy. It's dark and bitter as hell. But she murmurs something to the kid and then nods me forward. "Sure, crownchaser. The least you could do, I guess."

A horned figure appears farther down the street and starts jumping up and down in my peripheral vision. I flick a quick glance—Coy is dancing around like she's on fire, trying to get my attention. But I ignore her and focus on the Tearians.

"I'm Alyssa, by the way," I say to the woman as I press the first bandage gently onto Thoas's skin. "I know it's probably not worth much, but I'm really sorry. If you want me to, I can ask at the Explorers' Society. About your relics. I can—"

"You can do what? Fix this one small problem so you feel better about yourself? So you sleep well at night?"

Ouch. The truth in her words hits me in the chest, and I feel a twist of shame as I put the second bandage on Thoas and step back. "Okay, that's totally fair. I just . . . I wish I could help."

Coy shouts my name. Like this is a damn playground or something. I wave at her to cut it out, and she responds by taking the hint and waiting patiently and respectfully.

I'm kidding. Of course she doesn't.

She hollers, "ARE YOU KIDDING ME RIGHT NOW, FARSHOT?

WHAT PART OF *CHASE* IS LOST ON YOU?"

I can't look at her right now. I feel like if I look away from this moment, this Tearian woman, I'll fail something big. Something way bigger than this crownchase.

The woman glances down and runs her thumb over the kid's bandaged knee. "You want this to be simple. You come in uninvited, we get hurt, you put a patch on it and leave. All better, yes? But it is not that kind of problem."

"Ione!" one of the other Tearian women calls to her from across the street. She looks over my shoulder at them and shakes her head, and then her eyes cut back to me. Her expression isn't as sharp or unforgiving as it was before, but it's still hard as stone.

"We don't want a savior, crownchaser. We want justice. We want to be heard. That requires more than your bandage."

Then she hoists the child farther up on her shoulder, turns her back on me, and walks away.

TWENTY

I HAVE ABOUT A SECOND TO PROCESS EVERYTHING before Coy appears next to me. She takes my face between her hands, looks into my eyes, and says very low and very seriously:

"Alyssa Farshot, my darling, my truest and bestest friend, move your ridiculous ass right now or I'm going to have Drinn tow you along from our ship."

She takes off again, back down the street.

I cast a look over at Thoas and Ione and the other Tearian women one more time, and then I follow Coy.

She runs hard, so I have to put on a pretty good pace to keep up with her. Drinn's tinny voice comes on over her wristband, and I hear her pant out an answer but I'm not sure what either of them is saying.

We're rapidly approaching the end of town. In another fifty meters or so, the buildings will fall away and all that'll be left is a steep drop into a cobalt quarry.

I call out to Coy. "You found the beacon?"

"Yeah," she hollers over her shoulder. "Almost there."

"And? Then what?"

"Just move, Farshot. Drinn says new worldcruisers just broke atmo."

Ah, hell. I push my speed, following her flying trail of ghost-white hair as she sweeps around a small house and out of sight.

I skid around the corner—and slam into her back.

"Coy, warn a girl!" I bark as we both stumble and right ourselves. She just elbows me in the ribs and nods at what's in front of us.

The beacon. It looks identical to the one on AW42—shiny metal, maybe a meter high, and a bright, glowing sphere several centimeters above it with millions of microscopic *somethings* inside it if you look close enough. Which is hard. Because, y'know, bright.

"What are you waiting for?" I tell her. "Go get it."

She quirks a single eyebrow at me—that's some elegant and dismissive shit right there—and steps forward, reaching out to touch the rotating ball of illumination.

Words appear in the air above the halo of light and a voice rings out:

))) Welcome, crownchaser. Please submit a name.

Coy looks back at me, arms akimbo, but I gotta be honest. I've got no clue.

"Did you try—?"

"My name? Of course I tried my name. Here, watch." She squares her shoulders to the beacon and says, very clearly, "Nathalia Coyenne."

))) Thank you, Nathalia Coyenne. Your name is not the one required. Please return to the town and then submit a name.

She flips a rude gesture at it and then crosses her arms, turning back to me. She's looking at me like the beacon is some kid with a bad attitude and I'm the parent supposed to straighten them out.

Submit a name . . . There are trillions of names in the empire—what kind of name? Is naming babies some kind of unique empress trait I don't know about? Does it mean the name of a person or a place? Or maybe it's an animal—who the hell is even supposed to know?

I realize I'm staring at the message so hard that I'm grinding my teeth, and I work my jaw around, trying to relax. *Relax, Farshot. Relaaaaaax.*

Return to the town. That seems strange. Why would it say return to the town and *then* submit a name? Unless . . .

Coy sidles up to me, her eyes narrowed. "What is it? What's that face? That's a something face."

I hesitate before finally saying, "I think it's a town name. I mean, I think it wants the name of someone who lives in town."

"Really?" She swivels her head around to scan the brightly decorated buildings behind us. "You think so?"

I do. The more I think about it, the more it sits right in my stomach. But I shrug and go, "It's a guess."

"Damn . . . Nobody back there looked particularly chatty."

The roar of ship engines reaches us, and I look above Beru's low, shambly skyline to see two—nope, three—worldcruisers flipping their engines to landing positions and descending.

"Double damn!" Coy rounds on me. "You talked to that townswoman and that child. Did you get any names out of that?"

I did. I have two names, actually. One for each of us to use. But I can't bring myself to open my mouth and spit them out. It feels . . . wrong.

Look, I love Nathalia. We grew up together. She was a sister when I was painfully aware of how little family I had left. And I know she'd be a good empress—clever and rational at working the system but also kind of a softie at heart so that she won't screw us all over for eternity. But for the first time, this deal—me helping her beat everyone else—doesn't feel that great.

Coy should have to go get a name herself. She should have to get back into that town and talk to the people there. Talk and listen. That's the point, right? Connect with some of the people you're going to be ruling? Hear their problems and their pains? And maybe she won't be first. Maybe she'll end up behind the other crownchasers. But wouldn't that still be better for her as a leader?

That's what Uncle Atar would say. He'd say that giving her the names is the easy way out—for her and for me. It'd be the selfish path.

Hell Monkey's voice comes on over my wristband. "Hey, Captain, you're not alone. I've got eyes on Orso, Mega, and Roy, and they're absolutely tearing after you."

I stare into Coy's hopeful eyes. I'll talk to her after this. I'll make sure she understands all of this—the town and the people.

I don't know if I believe it, though.

"Thoas."

She grabs my face, kissing me on both cheeks. Then she spins and jumps back up to the beacon and puts her hand into the light, declaring, "Thoas."

I squeeze my eyes shut, feel the illumination sear across my eyelids. When I open them again, Coy is gone.

The same thing your type is always here for. Take and then go. Take and then go. You're the worst of both worlds.

Ione's words are so loud in my ears that I actually look behind me to make sure she isn't there.

A shout behind me, from back in the middle of town. It sounds like Faye's voice. I drag my feet into position and shove my hand into the light. There's no reason I can think of why this situation should feel bad—it's not cheating exactly—but it sure as hell doesn't feel *good*.

"Ione."

I'm surrounded by a flash like a supernova—and then I'm face-first in blue dirt again.

Lovely.

I can already hear the *Gilded Gun* powering up as I pull my feet underneath me and wrench my body upright. I'm steps away from the edge of town, steps away from the *Vagabond* . . .

. . . and steps away from Setter Roy.

He's not racing toward the beacon like Faye and Owyn. He's stopped just shy of the town limits, and he's crouched low with his arms wrapped around his head. Like he's grieving or in pain or something. Which makes sense. The atmosphere in this place is so intense that even my blundering ass picked up on it, and Roy is a telepath. What's it gotta be like to have a whole town full of anger sitting in your head?

I gotta go. Coy is taking off already. Hell Monkey is waving at me from the *Vagabond*'s cockpit.

But I cross the cobalt-colored earth to Setter Roy's side and wrap my hands around his arm, just above his elbow. I haul him up until his back is straight(ish) and he's looking me in the eye. Setter might not be my favorite person in the quadrant, but he's not a complete jerk, and I'd probably at least piss on him if he were on fire (not that he'd ask me to, but still).

So I clap him on the shoulder and say, "It's not about the beacon. It's about the town. Go listen to the people. It'll be worth it."

And then I haul it fast for where the *Vagabond* is waiting.

COYENNE-FARSHOT TEAM LEADS THE PACK
Public opinion swings in the Coyenne family's favor after a run across Tear

DOES TEAMING UP OFFER FAMILIES AN UNFAIR ADVANTAGE?
Historians look at notable points in crownchase history where prime families chose to combine efforts and how it helped or hurt them

VOLES CONTINUES TO BE MISSING IN ACTION
Poll rankings for the Voles family plummet to only six percent after their heir fails to make an appearance on Tear

RENEWED OUTBREAK OF PROTESTS ON TEAR
Protest leaders release statement deriding the "increasingly invasive imperial presence" on the planet after it's used for the latest leg of the crownchase

WORLDCRUISER S576-034, UNDISCLOSED COORDINATES

"EDGAR VOLES," NL7'S VOICE ECHOES IN THE DEAD silence of their ship. "You have an incoming communication. On a secured channel."

Edgar turns from where he's been monitoring his crownchasers. "I shouldn't have communications from anybody."

"It appears to be from your father."

Oh. Edgar smooths his hands down the front of his shirt. There shouldn't be any wrinkles, but it doesn't hurt to check. Also his palms feel a little cold and clammy quite suddenly.

"I will respond to him in my quarters, NL7. Please monitor the feeds and notify me of anything unusual."

"Of course, Edgar Voles."

He leaves the bridge, moving with sharp, deliberate steps toward the captain's quarters. He can hear his heartbeat inside his ears, feel the frantic uptick of his pulse in the veins of his neck and wrists. His tongue sits heavy and dry in his mouth.

He feels so weak. So vulnerable. Nothing like what a Voles ought to be.

"Worldcruiser S576-034," he calls out as the door to his quarters shuts behind him. "Please transfer the secure communications here."

The face of William Voles fills his display screen—severely angled and exceedingly symmetrical, dark hair streaked with white, blue eyes narrowed with disapproval. Always with disapproval.

Edgar used to try to find himself in his father's face when he was a child, but there was never any sign of it. He's been told he takes after his mother—rounder face, softer angles, brown eyes and honey-blond hair—and he's always hated that. How his mother had imprinted on him so much that was not-Voles, so much that was flawed and sensitive and distasteful to his family. And then she'd died and left him with the consequences of her genetics. The only thing good she'd given him was her last design and creation: NL7. And NL7, in Edgar's mind, is perfect.

Edgar clears his throat, relieved that his hands are out of view. He can't seem to keep them from gripping the sides of his pants, twisting the fabric into bunches. "Father, I did not expect to hear from you."

William Voles raises a sharp eyebrow and snorts. "I find that entirely surprising. You disappeared from the crownchase. There's been hardly a mention of you in any media source. You're last in every poll. Where the hell are you, Edgar?"

"I have plans set in motion—"

"Oh, you have *plans*? You know, this isn't just about logistical strategy, Edgar. It's about perception too. It's about public performance. You can't just lean on that robot—"

"Father, you know I don't appreciate that word—"

"And I don't appreciate you screwing this up!"

Silence over the comms channel. Edgar can feel blood rising

in his cheeks, staining them red. His whole body is tense with adrenaline.

William Voles straightens his collar. "The family didn't want you as our crownchaser. I can't blame them. But to choose anyone but you would've done irreparable damage to my reputation. So here we are."

The door to Edgar's quarters opens, and NL7 appears in the frame. Waiting. Cool and detached.

Edgar detaches too and says, very calmly, "I understand, Father. I will not fail."

"You'd better not. The Voles are the original empire-builders, but we've spent centuries playing second fiddle to idiots like the Faroshti. That time is over. It is time for our family to *rise*."

The screen goes dark. The comms channel goes dead. But Edgar stares at it for a long time until he calms down. Until his breath and his pulse slow so much that he can forget that he has lungs and skin and blood. Until he can forget he has a heart.

IMPERIAL THRONE ROOM, THE KINGSHIP, APEX

IT LOOKS LIKE JUST A CHAIR.

Sure, it's got some extra decorations. Gilding and the seals of the prime families. There are some fancy tech upgrades inside it too.

But outside of all that? It's just a place to put your butt. Shouldn't be worth killing over. You wouldn't think.

"Do you want to try it out?"

I jerk around, but it's just Uncle Atar, standing nearby with his hands folded behind him, wearing casual clothes instead of his fancy imperial robes. Which makes sense because there's no one in here at this time of night except him and me. The long room echoes back the sound of our voices.

"Why?" I ask him. "Plenty of other places to sit around here. Most of them a lot more comfortable."

A ghost of a smile crosses his face, and he shrugs as he moves over to the wall of windows. "It grows on you."

I follow on his heels. "Does it? Really? Because the way you talk about how you used to explore the galaxy, it doesn't sound like this was a trade up."

He sighs, staring out at the absolute darkness of the star-riddled sky and the restless sea. "Bearing this name, Alyssa, brings with it a certain amount of responsibility. When the people needed me, I answered."

I snort, leaning against the glass. "I would've dodged the call."

"No . . . I don't think you will." That ghost smile of his is back. It's completely infuriating. "I think you'll be your mother's daughter in the end."

"Yeah, well, I'll have to take your word on it because I never got the option of knowing her myself. Because of *that*." I make a rude gesture at the imperial throne.

Uncle Atar takes my hands and pulls me around to face him. "You can fixate on the past. Or you can create a better future. Which way is it going to be, Birdie?"

I squirm under all the gentleness and sincerity coming off him. I know what he wants me to say—but I can't say it. I can't even make myself turn around and look at that stupid chair. I can feel it at my back and it feels like a black hole.

"Honestly? Probably the first one." I pull my hands out of his grasp. "I'm sorry, Uncle Atar. I know what you want me to be, but I can't be it. And I'm never sitting on that throne."

I don't look at his face as I walk away.

TWENTY-ONE

Stardate: 0.05.20 in the Year 4031

Location: Orbit drifting with zero gravity. Like you do.

I'M AT LEAST READY FOR IT THIS TIME WHEN THE *Vagabond* goes dead.

I don't like it. But I'm mentally prepared.

Coy uploaded her digital imprint first, so she shot off like a meteor a while ago, and I've been strapped to my jump seat staring out at the planetary curve of Tear against the stars for thirty-three minutes and fifty-five seconds.

Not that I'm counting.

My body feels really heavy for something that's supposedly weightless right now.

I probably should unpack all the junk cluttering my head and my chest as I stare and stare at the big blue shape of Tear on my viewscreen, but I'll be honest: I'm not good at unpacking. It's the whole reason why I travel light.

Thirteen minutes and twenty-six seconds left.

When I started this crownchase—no, when I got thrown into this crownchase—I just wanted to find a way out without totally betraying everything Uncle Atar had accomplished. I wanted to help Coy win because she is one of the closest things to family I have left and because she can do the damn job. And it wasn't really a big deal, even, because it all felt like a game. The clues, the cameras, the highly edited media footage with leaderboards and splashy graphics and people posting odds—it all felt like some kind of new show concept for the reality vid feeds.

Here, kids, take your shiny ships and run around the empire getting into hijinks! It's cutthroat politics but it's also wacky fun!

Five minutes and forty-seven seconds left.

Everything that happened on Tear just threw a weird hyper-focus on this whole mess. There are a thousand and one planets in the empire and trillions of people. Trillions. And whoever sits on that throne is going to affect all of their lives. On Tear. On Coltigh. On Helix and Chu'ra and Otar.

Are we all just assholes for running around and not seeing this? Or maybe the other chasers did already and I'm just the asshole.

The lights around me flicker and then surge to life.

"Captain Farshot," says Rose overhead, "all systems are online again."

Thank all the stars and gods. I turn in my jump seat, letting my eyes drift over every aspect of the bridge. My bridge. My home. I feel . . . listless. I don't know what to do, and I'm not sure I want to do anything.

"Hey, Captain." Hell Monkey leans forward in his seat, elbows on his knees. "You got coordinates you want to head to?"

I shake my head. "Not really. Your call. Just get us out of here, okay?"

"Sure thing." He catches my arm as I unbuckle my safety harness and start to stand. "You didn't do anything bad back there. You did just what we said from the beginning we were gonna do."

I nod, trying to put on my poker face. I'm not sure I get it on right, though. "Yeah, I know. We're . . . right on target."

He lets go as I step away, turning back to the conn while I wander toward the media feeds and scan them. Not even sure what I'm looking for, really. One of the tertiary media companies is running some story about my questionable motives, trying to spin it into a scandal, but no one else seems to be picking it up. The Daily Worlds definitely isn't going to bite on that one, not with Cheery Coyenne at their helm. Trashing your daughter's crownchase partner all over the frequency bands isn't really a good look for anyone. Instead it looks like she's had her staff cut together a fluffy piece called An Enduring Heart, about Nathalia and her touching friendship with me, the poor, orphaned Faroshti child.

Ugh. Gross, Cheery.

I hear the mediabot clinking across the bridge well before it appears in my peripheral vision.

"Congratulations on completing your latest task, Captain Farshot."

I tuck my hands into my jumpsuit pockets, suppressing a snort. "Thanks, JR. It's been a blast."

"Public reactions to your partnership with Nathalia Coyenne have been mixed, and some of the prime families have implied that it applies an unfair advantage to the crownchase. What would your response be to that?"

I'm tempted to say something snarky. To dismiss the whole thing. The words are right there on the tip of my tongue.

But instead, I swallow them down and say, "They're entitled to think that. But the rules are clearly on our side. And I'm doing what I think is best for the people of the empire. I stand by my decision all the way."

"Have you considered—"

Nope. One round of adult responses is enough. I put my hand over its nonexistent mouth. "I'm done for right now, okay? Catch me later."

When I head for my quarters and he doesn't follow, it feels like progress. I'd rather not have a mediabot on my ship, but this isn't bad, right? We can all get through this in one piece. . . .

Safe in my own personal space, I hit the comms display on the wall and set it to record, stepping back a little so my face is fully in frame.

"Hey, Cheery, it's your favorite noncompetitive crownchaser. Seeing as how I'm giving the Coyenne family a big boost in this race-for-the-crown business, I was thinking you could do me a favor. I've got it on good authority that there are licensed explorers out there violating Society laws and stealing indigenous artifacts. I think this sounds like the kind of story the *Daily Worlds* should look into. See how far it goes. Maybe put some pressure on Society leadership to make a formal inquiry of it. Could be a big scoop for your feed too, so you're welcome in advance."

I stop recording, bundle the file up, and send it across the bajillion kilometers of space between here and Apex. Then I flop on my bunk, grabbing my pillow out from behind my head and covering my face. If I know Cheery Coyenne—and I think I do—she'll take the bait. Maybe it'll even help.

Or maybe it's just a bandage.

My stomach churns with dozens of sour emotions, and I press the pillow down harder. I'd scream into it, but I'm worried I'll just throw up.

There's a knock on the door, and then it slides open. I hear Hell Monkey's voice through the foam muffling my whole head.

"This looks like things are going well."

"Fabulous." I pull the pillow away from my face and wiggle ungracefully into a seated position. Hell Monkey's leaning over the threshold, his hands braced against the door frame. When does he have time to build delts like that? "Look, I know I need to upload the clue and start working and stuff, but I just need a minute."

His response is a grimace. Like an "ooh, bad news, boss" grimace. Ugh.

"What is it? What's happening?"

He steps all the way inside and closes the door behind him. "Incoming communication from Coy. Figured you'd want to know." He goes over to the display, presses a few buttons to open a secure channel, and the next thing I know my entire room—my entire skull—is filled with this high-pitched ringing sound. Hell Monkey yanks the hood of his jumpsuit up and slams his hands against the sides of his head. I grab my damn pillow and wrap it around the back of my skull to muffle both ears.

Coy's irritated face appears on the display screen, and I glare at her and yell, "WHAT THE HELL, COYENNE?"

She cocks her head at me. "Welcome to the party, Farshot. This clue officially sucks."

TWENTY-TWO

Stardate: 0.0—I honestly have no idea what my own freaking name is right now because this sound is so loud

"CAN YOU TURN IT OFF?!"

My face is like three inches from the display and I'm yelling over the comms like that's going to make any of this racket any better. But I've got pieces of foam stuffed in my ears to try to make it a little more bearable, so now all of us are reduced to communicating like we're angry as hell.

Which . . . maybe we are a little. Try functioning with a spine-shattering ringing tone filling your entire ship. See how calm and patient you are.

"IF I COULD TURN IT OFF, DON'T YOU THINK I WOULD'VE BY NOW?"

"IT'S JUST BEEN DOING THIS SINCE YOU UPLOADED THE IMPRINT?"

"YES. THE GUN'S AI CAN'T MUTE IT. DRINN'S WORKING ON AN OVERRIDE, BUT SO FAR, NO GO."

"What the hell even is it?" Hell Monkey crouches against the wall, right by my feet, his hood still up and plugs in his ears. "What kind of clue is this supposed to be?"

I shake my head. I can't imagine any good reason for this except to send every crownchaser shooting ourselves into the nearest sun. Which . . . might be a reason.

"IT'S NOT MUSIC," Coy yells.

I see Hell Monkey mouth, "Yeah, no shit," at the exact same time I holler, "YEAH, NO SHIT!" and his mouth curls upward a bit under the shadow of his hood.

"I'M JUST SAYING. OUR AI HAS BEEN RUNNING IT THROUGH THE QUADRANT DATABASE OF KNOWN MUSICAL STYLES AND THERE ARE NO MATCHES."

I start to open my mouth to respond when Hell Monkey reaches up an arm and smacks a button on the display. The screen goes dark. The sound cuts out. I swear I've never been so jazzed to hear the emptiness of silence before. The relief coats my whole body. But . . .

"She needs our help, H.M.," I say as I peel the foam out of my ears. "That was the deal. Combine our resources. Stay a step ahead."

He rolls onto his feet, pulling the hood off his shaved head. "We can't help her if we're being mentally flattened, same as her. You wanna help? Figure out the source of that noise." He glances down at my right hand—the one with the metallic imprint still on it from the beacon on Tear. I never did upload it into the *Vagabond*. His eyes meet mine, and he shakes his head. "Don't go anywhere near our systems until we think we have a solution to this thing."

"No arguments here." I sink down onto my bunk, scrubbing at my face. "This universe is crammed full of noises. How are we supposed to isolate one matching note in all of that chaos?"

Rose's cool voice breaks in. "Incoming message from Nathalia

Coyenne on secure channel, Captain Farshot."

"Ignore it." Hell Monkey paces the room. It's, like, three strides long for him, but whatever makes him feel better. "Focus here. If we can work it out, we can help Coy get clear."

"Okay . . ." My ears are still ringing a little. Like phantom pain but for my eardrums. "It's not music, but a lot of things make music besides people. Maybe it's from the song of a bird or animal of some kind. Rose, send a secured message to the *Gilded Gun*: *Check sound against database of recorded bird, animal, and insect noises.*"

Rose makes a little beep-beep noise of assent.

Hell Monkey drops into a crouch again, right in front of where I'm sitting. He's kind of staring at me, but also kind of staring through me as he processes something. It's not the first time I've seen him do this in order to figure out a problem.

I wait. And wait. And wait some more.

I reach out and boop him on the nose. "Hey, buddy, are you coming back anytime soon? It's borderline awkward."

He blinks at me. "I used to collect a lot of rocks when I was a kid."

I gape at him a little. This is the first time in the two years I've known him that I've heard him mention his childhood. At all. In the slightest. For all I knew, he'd just popped out of a wall panel on the station where we met, fully grown and programmed to snark.

Before I can recover, he plows ahead. "I had a pretty big collection, and most of them were just, like, rocks I could get pretty much anywhere on my planet. But I managed to find some special ones too—crystals that I got off folks I met, usually. They weren't really worth shit, but I thought they were so cool and I used to read all about them."

Part of my brain has already jumped way off track and is just dying to spill out a whole bunch of questions about Hell Monkey's past—what was the planet, where were you born, what about your family. Like this one mention of his about being a kid is a crack in an airlock and if I don't force my way in before it seals, I'll never get through again.

But I don't. I stay on target. I say, "Okay, but what do crystals have to do with The Worst Noise in a Thousand Worlds?"

"A lot of cultures in the empire believe that the structure and properties of crystals give off certain energies, that they actually resonate with frequencies outside our ability to hear them."

I sit back, drumming my fingers along my thighs. "You're saying you think this could be from something inorganic. That maybe there's not even an audio record of it in the databases."

Hell Monkey nods, and I feel this bright little bubble expand in my chest. The excitement of exploration. Of discovery.

"Rose," I say, getting to my feet, "I'm about to input a really terrible audio file into the *Vagabond* database, and I need you to immediately try to identify it by frequency and amplitude and see if there's anything else in our quadrant, like a planet or an asteroid cluster or something, that is giving off the same frequency. Got it?"

"Understood, Captain Farshot. The estimated calculation time for the process you're requesting is two hours and forty-nine minutes."

Hell Monkey looks at me, sighs, and jams his earplugs back in. I do the same thing, and then I take a very deep breath—*brace yourself, Farshot*—and place the palm of my hand against the control panel.

TWENTY-THREE

Stardate: 0.05.21 in the Year 4031

Location: A hyperlight lane and all is quiet, thank the stars

IF YOU THINK ABOUT IT, THE AMOUNT OF CALCU-
lating and scanning and assessing Rose did in under three hours is
pretty amazing.

But that two hours and forty-nine minutes of listening to that
screeching tone without it once missing a beat also felt like two
hundred and forty-nine *years*, so. There's that.

There really was no way to shut it up. We tried. Whatever the
digital imprint did, it embedded itself so far up the *Vagabond*'s ass
that we couldn't find a source point to even try and extract it. So
we just rode it out. Buried ourselves in anything that would help
muffle the noise.

Until Rose saved us. Dear universe, please bless Rose. She's
always been my favorite.

She'd found a source in the Otari system. The Megas' home
system. It was coming from a massive asteroid belt there called the
Ships' Graveyard.

Super promising, right?

I'd called Coy, who was still pretty pissed about being hung up on, but she got a lot less pissed when I gave her some new coordinates. Especially when inputting those coordinates finally turned off that stars-blighted noise. Then Coy was all smiles again.

I tried to talk to her about Tear. About the town and the woman Ione and what she'd said. But we got interrupted by Drinn and then by the mediabot and then I wasn't even sure she was really listening anyway, so I just told her we'd talk about it more later.

Plenty of time to discuss it once she's got the seal, right?

We jumped into a hyperlight lane about an hour ago, but it's going to take a lot longer than that to get to the Otari system. Almost two full days. I know I should catch up on sleep while there's all this downtime—who knows when I'll get to hit the pillow next—but I've been walking the rooms and corridors of the *Vagabond* instead.

I drag my fingers along the wall panels in the starboard corridor, run my eyes along the lines of the *Vagabond*'s frame and the small rectangular windows sitting high up so you can get a peek at the stars. I make my way to the bridge and stand for a while, just inside the door, taking in the blue jump seats, the glowing lights of the navcomm, the streaming colors of the hyperlight lane flowing around us on the viewscreen. Hell Monkey posted up in his jump seat, monitoring our speed and course, making sure we're still on track. I hover there, watching his hands move across the dash, quick and confident.

I love this ship. I love everything about it and the freedom it gives me. I love the life I've built on it.

I just want to hold on to that. I want everything to go back to exactly how it was two and a half weeks ago. Before my uncle was taken from me and replaced with a hijacked future and an infiltrated ship. Where it was just me and Hell Monkey and I was known only for being the best of the best Explorers' Society pilots. Simple, right? That's not such a big ask, is it?

"Captain?"

I refocus. Hell Monkey has swiveled around in his jump seat and is staring at me. "You okay?" he asks.

I straighten up, tugging at my jumpsuit like I suddenly care about the millions of little wrinkles in it. "Yeah, fine. I'm good. Just thinking."

He raises his eyebrow and opens his mouth to speak, but I cut him off. "No, wait! I got this one. How about, 'Don't hurt anything thinking that hard, boss'? Or maybe, 'Are you sure you're cleared for that much mental work?'"

He ducks his head, and his chuckle is a little off, a little sad maybe. But he just says, "Yeah, sure, that covered it."

"See? You don't have to sing me the song, I know it by heart."

I shoot him double finger guns and then slink off the bridge, heading back to my quarters—for real this time. I sit on my cot for a while staring at the far wall, wishing . . .

Wishing I could talk to someone. A grown-up type of someone who might have some decent advice or just be able to say, *Hey, kid, you're gonna be fine.*

I wish I could talk to Uncle Atar, and that hurts like hell.

I go to the comms display anyway. I've got one last family member left in this whole damn universe, and I'm not even supposed to contact him. But I wouldn't exactly be me if I was a stickler about rules.

It's still kind of a surprise when Uncle Charlie appears on-screen. I'd kinda figured he just wouldn't answer. But it's really good to see his face—even if it's pale and tight with nerves and his eyes keep flicking back over his shoulder.

"Alyssa, this is very unexpected." He sounds like he doesn't know whether he's happy or about to freak out. Charlie *is* a rule stickler. "As a royal official, I'm not supposed to contact any of the participating crownchasers—"

"You didn't contact me, I contacted you," I point out. "And you can tell whoever is lurking around in there listening to come on out. I'm not trying to wheedle secret information out of you or anything."

There's a pause and a rustle of clothes and soft footsteps, and then a Solari enkindler appears behind Charlie, looking like an enormous log of cheese in his long yellow robes. This is a new development. I expected some kind of royal enforcer, like an otari crownsguard, but an enkindler? The only one I can ever remember seeing on the kingship growing up is Enkindler Wythe, slithering around and serving as a representative. It's strange as hell to see one babysitting Charles Viqtorial, chief envoy to the former emperor. I raise an eyebrow at him, and then at Charlie, but I see the muscles around Charlie's eyes tighten. Just a little. So I keep my mouth shut.

"I just needed to see a friendly face," I tell Charlie. "Nothing nefarious. I was just . . . sad, I guess."

Charlie's face softens a few millimeters. Which is a lot for Charlie. "I understand what you mean. I have been . . . sad too. I'm glad to see you are well. I've been watching your progress—"

The enkindler clears his throat a little, but when he doesn't say anything, Charlie plows on.

"Atar would've been very proud of you, Alyssa."

"Ahem, a-HEM." It's more pointed this time.

Charlie looks back at him, frowning.

"Uncle Charlie," I say, calling his attention back to the screen. "Can I ask a question? About Uncle Atar—"

"Ahem!"

"—and whether he talked to you much about regretting—"

"Ahem, ahem!"

"—giving up exploring for—"

"AHEM!"

"OH MY GODS, FLAMEOUT, DO YOU NEED A LOZENGE OR SOMETHING?"

There's a pause where all I can hear is the hiss of Charlie sucking in a breath. That's not a particularly nice term for enkindlers. And I shouldn't have used it. I just can hardly see anything right now except the pounding of my own pulse behind my eyeballs.

"I don't appreciate your tone, crownchaser," the enkindler says.

"And I don't appreciate you lurking like a babysitter around Charles Freaking Viqtorial, a highly commended and highly respected representative of the throne!"

The enkindler sweeps forward, filling the screen, blocking any

169

view I have of Uncle Charlie. I hear him object, but the enkindler's eyes are locked on mine. "The throne sits empty, crownchaser. He's a representative of no one now. And this conversation is over."

And then the screen goes dark.

Nice one, Farshot. That went well.

TWENTY-FOUR

Stardate: 0.05.22 in the Year 4031
Location: On our way to the Ships' Graveyard, which is totally normal and not at all ominous, everything is fine

I FALL ASLEEP WORRYING ABOUT UNCLE CHARLIE.

And I wake up worrying about him too. Wondering what the hell is going on over on Apex that there are enkindlers running around the kingship, throwing their weight about like they own the place. It leaves a bad taste in my mouth.

I clean up and head to the bridge, which is empty for the moment. Rose is maintaining our systems, monitoring any small adjustments needed to keep us riding the hyperlight lane, and I'm not going to elbow my way in on that just yet. Instead, I wander over to the media feeds running silently at the port-side station and swipe up from the bottom of the main screen, bringing up a query input. I have it search for every mention of Enkindler Wythe in the *Daily Worlds* or any other news media in the thirteen days since my uncle passed away, and then I start scanning the articles and video clips as they come in.

Steward Wythe declares he will push forward with an agenda for the empire. (Pretty bold declaration for someone who's technically supposed to function as a seat warmer.)

Wythe makes a surprise visit to Helix. (A lot of money and influence flows out of Helix. Homeworld of the Voles too. Very weird. . . .)

Chancellor Orsed floats a radical idea for the future of the empire. (This radical idea apparently is that the empire is lacking "moral leadership" and needs a new form of government to "grow in the right direction.")

There are others too—snippets of him traveling here or there, a brief profile on a brand-new adviser he apparently brought onto the kingship, a report of him being spotted making an appearance at a fund-raising dinner on an orbital yacht owned by William Voles. None of this stuff seems to have made major headlines or been more than a blip across the quadrant-wide feeds, but then again, why would they when there are an eyeball-flattening number of hours of crownchase footage to watch. And analysis of crownchase footage. And predictions of future crownchase footage. And yet more reruns of crownchase footage. All overlaid with polls and predictions and previews of Who Will Win and How It Will Affect the Empire.

And in the meantime . . . I dunno. Maybe we're missing something really big right under our noses.

Hell Monkey's heavy footfalls thud against the deck, and I feel his presence at my back. "What are we looking at?"

"Maybe something. . . . Maybe nothing. . . ."

"Steward Wythe? You think he's got something shifty going on?"

"I think he is shifty. He's always been shifty. The only question is whether he's an empty robe or a blaster in a holster."

Rose's voice breaks across the bridge. "Captain Farshot, we are approaching the selected coordinates. Prepare for deceleration."

We exchange a look and then make a break for our jump seats, strapping in as the multicolored aura of hyperlight falls away and the darkness of space encircles us. The bridge doors whoosh open behind me, and I hear JR, our trusty mediabot, tiptoe its way over to us.

I grab the controls, ready to angle the *Vagabond* toward the asteroid belt, when Rose speaks up again.

"Proximity alert, Captain Farshot. Worldcruiser signature detected. Identification: the *Gilded Gun*."

"Well, that's not really a surpr—"

"Proximity alert. Multiple targets. Warship signatures detected."

Hell Monkey's head whips around. "Wait—what?"

"Classifications: Mega-registered gunners. Mega-registered howlers. Mega-registered destroyers—"

I punch at the dash, calling up every kind of scan we've got. "What the hell is going on? Rose! I need it all on the viewscreen right now!"

There's a beat while the sensors make their sweep, and then everything lights up in front of us. The massive drifting rocks of the Ships' Graveyard asteroid belt. The sleek silhouette of Coy's worldcruiser just ahead and to our starboard.

And between us and the next hoop we need to jump through: a blockade of maybe two dozen warships branded with the Mega family seal, sitting with their front-mounted cannons warmed up like they're ready to start something.

Son. Of. A. Bitch.

Hell Monkey growls. "How the hell did they get here ahead of us? And with a force like that?"

"I'm more interested in what exactly they think they're going to do with all that firepower. Rose? Hail their lead ship. The one that's sitting there like it's got the best hand in poker."

"Yes, Captain Farshot. Comms channel open."

I stand and face the viewscreen. I kind of wish I'd had time for a costume change, something more intimidating, but my wrinkled jumpsuit will have to do.

"This is Captain Alyssa Farshot of the *Vagabond Quick* addressing the commander of this fleet. Identify yourself and explain your presence here."

Hell Monkey gives me an appreciative look over his shoulder, like this is exactly his brand of oh-hell-yeah. Can't really blame him. I impress myself sometimes when I throw on this serious authoritative shit.

The viewscreen flickers and a face appears a second later: otari, with rocky scars very strategically placed along his bone structure. That by itself says a lot because it means he hasn't ever gotten into an unexpected fight. He likely comes from a well-off family and never really had to earn a place.

"This is Commander Hwn of the *Dark Star*," he says, and the sneer underneath his tone makes me square my shoulders and set my jaw a little harder. "You have no jurisdiction here."

I roll my eyes. "Going through an emo phase when you named that ship, were you? We're here as members of the crownchase and are functioning under full diplomatic immunity. We've got jurisdiction pretty much everywhere. So your turn, Hwn. What brings you to this fine abandoned asteroid field first thing in the morning?"

The commander tugs his stiff uniform collar straighter and lifts his chin. "This is a simple fleet exercise, authorized by the admirals' council, and we have every right to be in this space. We weren't aware the crownchase would be in this sector—"

"No? Golly, that is a hell of a coincidence, isn't it?"

He sticks his nose even higher in the air. "Captain Farshot, if you're implying—"

"You're damn right I'm implying. I'm *absolutely* implying. I'll just take a quick second to remind you—and any Mega family members who might be lurking around listening—that if anything happens to me or to Coy, Owyn and everyone related to him are immediately disqualified from the crownchase. So tell your ships to drop formation so we can pass without trouble."

His expression flickers just for a second, and then his eyes narrow. "I am a fleet commander, and we are in the middle of an exercise. You do not give me orders."

I step closer to the viewscreen. "You want to play that way, buddy, that's fine. But one way or another, we're coming through."

I cut the channel and drop into my jump seat. "H.M., warm up our guns and send a message to Coy. Tell her to drop back in our wake and stay close."

He nods, already working. "We're running it?"

"Hell yeah." I crack my knuckles and wrap my fingers around the controls. "We're definitely running it."

MEGA FAMILY EXACERBATES CROWNCHASE TENSIONS WITH BLOCKADE

Mega spokesperson calls it a "prescheduled training exercise" but others decry it as a "full-scale intimidation tactic"

EXPLORERS' SOCIETY LAUNCHES INTERNAL INVESTIGATION

Executive chairwoman Wesley releases statement declaring an investigation will look into accusations of artifact stealing and other violations of Society laws

MARKETS BOOMING IN THE WAKE OF THE CROWNCHASE

Experts say high levels of excitement across the empire are driving big economic growth, even as the chase enters its second week

FOLLOWING THE GALACTIC MONEY

A multipart look at the Orso family's meteoric rise to prime status after centuries of piracy

THE SHIPS' GRAVEYARD, OTARI SYSTEM

WORLDCRUISER S576-034 SITS IN A SENSOR SHADOW on the far side of the asteroid belt. NL7 calculated that this was the perfect position to monitor the activity of the crownchasers and the beacon without being detected by them in return.

Not that he thinks they're going to be worried about him. He wonders if they even remember that he's in the chase or if they've forgotten his existence. They're good at that, after all.

And besides, they have a Mega squadron to deal with at the moment.

It is so very like the Megas to make a move like this. A show of brute force to remind the quadrant what they bring to the table as a family and stir up latent patriotism with a gawdy display of imperial military pageantry. Most likely in an attempt to boost Owyn's standing in the public poll since he's been trailing so much in the actual race. Maybe to rattle the other crownchasers as well and give their heir a leg up. It's not as if nepotism is looked down upon in the prime families, after all. Especially not by Lorcan and Jenna Mega, who never met a problem of Owyn's that they couldn't step in and fix for him.

It's a boorish move. All muscle and posturing. No subtlety or finesse. But it also shows desperation to Edgar, and that is something he could maybe use.

Curious, too, how the Megas knew the crownchasers would be coming to this part of their system. Someone had to have tipped them off. Someone with insider knowledge, with enough influence to convince the Megas to play the power and patriotism card. Edgar can use that too if he can deduce who it was that pulled their strings.

"Edgar Voles." NL7 motions him over to the comms. "We are picking up a ghost signature."

Edgar frowns and moves over to stand with the android. "Put it on the viewscreen."

NL7 taps on the panel, but their current view of the edge of the asteroid belt remains unchanged.

"Nothing seems to be out there," says Edgar. "Could be an error."

"Unlikely. We have picked it up again. Trajectory seems to be toward the asteroid belt. Should we use a more intensive scan?"

Edgar shakes his head. "No. I don't want to give away our position to whomever might be out there. We'll get a clearer picture as they get closer."

In less than a minute, he's proven right. A small, sleek ship comes into view—so to speak. It's been outfitted for stealth with a mirrormask, so Edgar isn't entirely sure he would have seen it if he hadn't been looking so intently for it. It approaches the asteroid belt approximately a parsec away from their current location, close enough that their sensors get a better read of it and produce an outline of its general shape and specs.

Edgar tilts his head as he looks at the readout. "It's a huffar design. That's strange."

"How so?" asks NL7.

"They're not known for being particularly political. They managed to remain neutral during the entirety of the war. At least, publicly they were neutral."

"But now they have a stealth ship headed for the crownchase. Perhaps they are not apolitical anymore?"

"Perhaps."

NL7 swivels its head to look at him. "Would you like to open a communications channel to the other crownchasers? Inform them they are not alone in the asteroid belt?"

Edgar turns this over in his head as he watches the prow of the stealth ship nose past its first asteroid. Handing them information like this would give him no strategic advantage. They might "owe" him, but that could so often be brushed away later when the danger to themselves had passed.

They might . . . like him more.

He wanted that once, a long time ago when he was young and they'd all seemed like bright, vibrant suns that he'd circled endlessly, always at a distance, never allowed to get close enough to discover if he had a light of his own to cast.

But he's not a little kid anymore. And neither are the other crownchasers. They knew the risks when they went into this.

"We stay silent," he says to NL7. "I will not jeopardize our position."

WESTERN HANGAR BAY, THE KINGSHIP, APEX

My NECK HURTS FROM CRANING AT THIS ANGLE FOR so long, but I think I've finally got it. I'd dented the bottom of this waveskimmer my last round out with it—flew a little too close to a big breaker and got clipped—and the hangar supervisor had given me hell for it and grounded me until I fixed it. I hadn't done body work on any of these before, so it was a messy kind of learning curve trying to sort out the best way to handle it. But I've finally managed to bolt everything into place, fix the paint job, put a high polish on the alloy. This is it. The hangar supervisor has gotta let me back into the cockpit now.

I slide out from under the waveskimmer, wiping polish off my hands with an already-dirty rag, and nearly walk right into a column of bright yellow.

"Miss Faroshti, may I have a moment of your time?"

It takes everything I've got not to wrinkle my nose at the sound of that voice. Stepping back, I look up into the face of Enkindler Ilysium Wythe. He looms over me with a placid smile. His eyes are always sharp, though. That's where he gets you.

"I'm actually a little busy right now, Wythe," I say, trying to step around him. I just want to find the supervisor and get cleared. Maybe I can get a quick flight in before they close down the hangar for the day. "Can you come back tomorrow? I'm running a two-for-one special on moments."

Wythe moves very subtly to stay in front of me. "I'm afraid it must be now. I need your assistance. I invited your uncle to a Solari service tonight in my quarters, with a dinner to follow, but he declined, saying he already has plans with you."

I shrug, still scanning for the supervisor. "Yeah, we blocked it off weeks ago. Family bonding stuff."

"Surely it's something that can be postponed in favor of more . . . important things."

Irritation flickers through me, and I snap my head back to him. "Look, my uncle is a grown-ass man. He makes his own schedule. And it sounds like he already decided which event was more important."

I spin around, twisting the polish rag between my fists, but Wythe's voice stops me before I get too far.

"I find young people like you very troubling, Miss Faroshti."

I turn back to him, my eyebrows shooting upward. "Young people like me?"

He nods, his face drawn and grave, his eyes glittering. "Disrespectful. Unfettered. Unguided by any sort of higher power or purpose. It makes me very concerned about the future of our great empire."

Anger squeezes my chest. I can taste the sharpness of it on my tongue as I step into Wythe's space. "Well, good news! Atar Faroshti is the one who has to worry about the future of the empire. Not you. You just have to worry about which shade of yellow makes you look less like a walking condiment bottle."

Wythe smiles, and my stomach sinks a little. I don't like that smile. It's the one people get on their face when they know they're gonna win a game or score on a bet.

"One of these days, Alyssa Faroshti," he says, "you're going to prove that you're more trouble than you're worth. And I look forward to that day."

TWENTY-FIVE

Stardate: 0.05.22 in the Year 4031

Location: Running a blockade of heavily armed warships. Must be a Tuesday.

I DON'T THINK THE MEGA SHIPS WILL ACTUALLY fire on me.

I don't think . . .

But in case anyone has an itchy trigger finger, I make sure Coy and her ship are fully in the *Vagabond*'s shadow before I punch it for the blockade. I'm the one who pissed them off—they'll go for me first if they're feeling feisty, and then Coy can break off and find another way through.

I glance over at Hell Monkey, and there's an edge in his grin and a glint in his eyes. He nods without looking at me.

Full throttle it is, then.

My heart throbs at the back of my throat as I push the *Vagabond Quick* to full sublight speed, racing toward a spot on the blockade where a battleship and gunship are squatting, side by side.

They don't move.

I keep going. Faster . . . faster . . .

Nothing.

I open a comms channel to both ships. "This is Captain Alyssa Farshot, and I will absolutely ram this ship so far up your asses that you will be able to taste my shampoo. Make way."

We're less than a parsec away. They're still not moving.

"H.M.?"

"On it." Hell Monkey brings up the gun controls, the *Vagabond*'s front-mount cannons already primed and ready to go.

I don't want to fire on them. I don't want to start anything big like that.

Move, come on, move . . .

My ears are filled with the whir of the ship's engines and the thud of my own pulse. I'm really wondering about my life choices right now—

—and then it's all clear.

At the last possible second, both ships scramble, engaging thrusters to push up out of our way, leaving a big hole in the blockade. We zoom through it, Coy right on our ass, and nothing is in front of us now but the asteroid belt and the signal of a crown-chaser beacon beckoning to us from the middle of it.

I throw my hands in the air, crowing with triumph.

Forget everything I said. My life choices are amazing. My job is the best damn one in the universe.

I flip open a comms channel to Coy. "You good back there, Coy?"

She's laughing as she answers. "You're killing me, Farshot."

"Exactly the opposite, actually."

"Shut up and let's go get that beacon."

"Roger that," says Hell Monkey. "Approaching Ships' Graveyard."

We enter the shadow of the nearest asteroid, which is twice the size of our worldcruiser, and something about it makes all of us go quiet. Even the mediabot. Judging by our sensor scans, it's not even the biggest one we'll be passing as we work our way inward.

The Ships' Graveyard is one of the most massive asteroid belts in the quadrant. It's also ridiculously rich in ores used in constructing warships, which explains the Mega family's major corner on that market. But there are no signs of mining operations in this section of the belt, not even abandoned facilities.

"Captain Farshot," Rose says. "We're picking up transmissions."

I frown as we slide beneath the rocky, lumpy surface of a smaller asteroid. "Transmissions—as in, plural? Are they coming from the blockade?"

"No, Captain Farshot. They're originating from the asteroids."

I look over at Hell Monkey. His hazel eyes are spooked, and he just raises an eyebrow.

"Play it, Rose."

I immediately regret that order. The sounds that fill the *Vagabond* are like something out of a nightmare. A mishmash of static and the fire of laser cannons and broken-up voices and screams. Distress signals. Cries for aid. Calls to evacuate.

"Alyssa." Hell Monkey's voice startles me, and I follow his gaze to the viewscreen as we come around the asteroid and see several more arrayed before us.

They're all bigger, pockmarked with craters and laser-sharp slashes.

And there are ships sticking out of them.

They're not full ships and don't look functional, but they're unmistakably entire sections of old ships fused into the rock and ice of these massive asteroids. There's the prow of a howler; there's the aft section and engine of a gunner. It's not easy to tell where the ships end and the asteroids begin.

"Rose, confirm. Are these transmissions coming from these ships?"

"Affirmative, Captain Farshot."

"That's impossible." Hell Monkey's voice is no louder than a murmur. "These ship designs are centuries old. What the hell even happened here?"

"Rose, cut transmissions." The ship goes quiet. I can't tear my eyes from the horrific fusions of construct and mineral. "History wasn't really my forte. I don't remember everything. Just that there was a major battle here, right, Rose?"

"Correct, Captain Farshot. An inter-system dispute over the rights to the ore in the asteroid belt. There were multiple skirmishes, but this was the site of the final battle. A ship called the *Defiant* implemented an experimental weapon that wiped out itself and all surrounding ships, ally and enemy alike. A truce was reached soon after."

I rub at my sternum. My chest feels really hollow and achy. "Nothing brings us to the negotiating table quite like nearly destroying ourselves, huh."

Hell Monkey drops his eyes down to the conn. "I'm not a big fan of ghost stories. Let's get this done as quickly as possible. We've almost got a lock on the beacon."

I swing out of my jump seat. "I'm going to go suit up. I got a feeling I'm going to need to put boots on one of these asteroids before we're through here."

We've got a locker room toward the aft of the ship—a little room above the aft bay and right next to the escape pods. It's got everything a girl needs to head down to an oxygen-unfriendly planet and not immediately choke and die. Full survival suits. Gravity boots. Harpoons and blasters outfitted to work in all kinds of atmospheric conditions. I'm not sure what to expect on these asteroids, so I put on a full getup and grab a blaster too.

Something about this scenario makes me want a weapon close by. I don't know if you can shoot a ghost—I don't even know if I believe in ghosts—but it doesn't hurt to try.

"Captain?" Hell Monkey calls over the comms. "You'd better come see this."

I book it back to the bridge, and when I get there, the viewscreen is showing the biggest asteroid yet. A few dozen kilometers across at least. Big enough for us and several other worldcruisers to land on. It's not just one ship fused with rock here; there look to be parts from half a dozen ships sticking out from it.

And at the top of it is the outline of an almost fully intact warship. The tip of its prow protrudes from the crystalline minerals spreading like a fungus around it, and you can still read its call sign.

SU7100 Defiant.

"Lemme guess," I say, standing near Hell Monkey's shoulder. "That's where our beacon is."

"Do you even need me to answer that one?"

He doesn't. Because of course it is.

I pull in a deep breath, filling my lungs right up to the brink. Until they stretch and push against the insides of my rib cage. And then I let it all out and spin on my heel, heading for the airlock.

"Park it, H.M. I'm going in."

TWENTY-SIX

Coy meets me on the surface of the asteroid, blaster in hand, camera drone hovering over her shoulder. Her green eyes glitter behind the clear plastic of her helmet, which has been specially designed to accommodate foarian horns, and the smile she gives me has a little more nerves behind it than I usually see in her.

"I'm picking up a static atmosphere inside it," she says, nodding at where the *Defiant* sits underneath layers of rock beneath our feet. "There's an airlock about fifteen meters away from here that we should be able to use to get inside."

Drinn's grumbling voice comes on over her wristband. "Approaching signatures, Captain. Three worldcruisers."

"All three? Already?" Coy sighs. "I thought we'd have a bit more time than that."

"Someone's getting chatty about our coordinates. We'd better get moving." I turn to my own camera drone and poke a gloved finger into its lens. "Come on, Whizzy. Try to keep up."

The airlock is easy enough to find, if a little tricky to get open since it's been forever and a day since it functioned at all. But there are still manual controls, and between Coy and me, we wrench it open. She jumps right in, but I pause for just a second and look back at the *Vagabond*. And Hell Monkey. He's watching me from the bridge—I can feel it—and I give him a little wave. Kinda pathetic, really, but it's all I got.

And then I slide down the ladder after Coy.

We clear the airlock, sealing it shut behind us, and she's right. There's breathable air in here. No gravity, though, so I can take my helmet off, but my boots gotta stay on.

It's dead dark, and I activate the embedded lighting in my survival suit, shedding a halo of illumination all around me. Coy blinks in the sudden brightness; foarians have got pretty sharp vision even in complete darkness, but I don't have that advantage, so she's just going to have to deal. She's taken out a hand scanner, a small device with sensors a bit more powerful than the ones built into our suits, and she moves out ahead of me, swinging the scanner this way and that. I follow slowly on her heels, staring at the scene around me.

If I thought the outside of the *Defiant* was creepy, it's got nothing on the inside. Whatever weapon they set off seems to have frozen half the ship in an instant. A crystalline formation, mixed here and there with the darker ore of the asteroid, crawls up the walls, making the tunnels narrow and hard to navigate, and the air is full of strange ringing notes and echoes.

It's when I spot the first body that I really jump.

"Oh, holy shit!"

"What?" Coy had been moving in the opposite direction, but

she comes scrambling back, pulling up short when she sees what I'm looking at.

The perfectly preserved body of an otari, frozen in crystal, still in his ship's uniform, staring into the darkness.

Coy whispers something under her breath. It sounds like a prayer to the otari war gods. I didn't know she even knew any prayers.

She sees my expression and shrugs. "Seems appropriate here. What the hell even did this?"

I shudder, turning away, and ease my blaster out of its holster. Just in case. "I don't know, but let's make this quick, okay? Which way to the beacon?"

"I'm not sure." She brings her scanner back up. "The signal seems to be shifting a little, and the layout isn't what I expected. It's like the insides got all moved around and nothing is quite where it's supposed to be."

There's a scraping noise over our heads and the sound of voices.

"The airlock." Coy pulls another scanner out of a pocket on her suit and shoves it into my chest. "You go right, I'll go left. First one to find it gives a holler, okay?"

And then she disappears into the darkness before I have time to object.

"No, no, that's fine . . ." I mutter. "I'm fine. This is all fine."

I move off down the corridor, blaster up, fumbling with the hand scanner to try and get a lock on this signal. I'm not one to get wigged, but this place is throwing me off my game. I keep jumping at little noises, and the halls are full of them. Pings and sighs and footfalls and drips—I don't even think there's any damn liquid in this place. What the hell would be dripping? And every now and then I pass another former crew member of the *Defiant*, trapped forever inside a strange ringing crystal.

Hell Monkey's quiet voice comes through on my wristband. "How are you doing, Captain?"

This guy has good timing. "This place is terrible and everything is terrible. How are you?"

He chuckles, and it's like having a little ball of sunlight put inside my chest. "Just watching your ass as always. Mega, Orso, and Roy all made it inside, so keep your eyes peeled."

I ease around a corner and yelp, jumping about a foot in the air.

"What?" Hell Monkey sounds panicked. "What is it?"

I try to catch my breath. "Nothing. I just . . . I thought I saw someone."

"Another crownchaser?"

I frown. "I don't think so. It was just like a shadow or something. I don't even know. This place is throwing me off. I swear I thought I was a lot more chill than this."

He's quiet for a bit, but I can hear his soft breathing so I know the channel is still open. And that helps a little. To have him right there, even if it's just to listen. I steady my hands a bit, settle my pulse and my lungs down, find firmer footing. The hand scanner seems to still be having trouble getting a solid lock on the beacon, but I keep moving around twists and turns in this maze of a crystallized graveyard.

At a four-point intersection, I pause, pressing myself against a wall. I can hear soft footsteps coming from the right corridor, getting closer. So I wait . . .

And then I swing out, blaster up, and find myself barrel to barrel with Faye Orso.

She grins. "This feels familiar."

I relax my shoulders a little, relieved, but I also don't drop my blaster because that'd just be stupid. "Thought you were an asteroid ghost."

Her laugh rings against every facet around us. "They'll make ghosts out of all of us yet."

Heavy boots thud against the ground, and as one, Faye and I swing around to face the sound, weapons up.

Owyn comes around the corner and skids to a stop, his hands up, looking a little rattled. He's got a gun on him, but it's still holstered. "Okay, easy," he says. "None of you win anything by shooting me."

I snort. "Tell that to your parents. Did you seriously call them in for backup out there?"

It's kind of hard to tell in just the lights blazing from our survival suits, but I think he actually blushes. "No, that wasn't me. I swear by the war gods, I don't know who tipped them off or what the hell they think they were doing."

"Sure, Mega," Faye says, and I check the floor to make sure all the sarcasm dripping off her words hasn't made a pool around our feet. "Because it's so unlike your parents to try to butt their way in and make sure you win something."

A noise echoes through the tunnel behind me—maybe

footsteps? Maybe nothing?—and I whip my head around to check. But the tunnel is empty and dark. "We honestly don't know what any of us are capable of anymore." My voice isn't much louder than a mutter, but it carries well enough in this creepy-ass place. "Not with an empire on the line."

This time it's Owyn who jumps, his hand flying to the butt of his blaster. "Did you hear that?"

I didn't, but I'm getting a bad feeling. Bad enough that I'm way more comfortable putting my back to two cutthroat frenemies than leaving it exposed to empty space. Owyn must be sensing the same because pretty soon he's shoulder to shoulder with me.

Faye sniffs. "You two are really skittish," she says, but her voice isn't quite as steady as it was before. She brings her weapon up to her face like she's checking the safety or something, but I catch her peeking over her shoulder.

I pull one hand off my blaster to open another comms channel on my wristband. "Coy?" I say, but I don't say it very loudly. "Nathalia, can you hear me?"

Nothing. Just faint static.

Faye snorts. "Did you lose your pet? That's kind of irresponsible."

"Shut it, Orso. Oh, this is ridiculous." I snatch a disc-shaped object from my belt, activate it, and throw it up. It latches little claws into the ceiling and then the sides of it open up and it blasts light in a ring all around us, illuminating the tunnels for almost twenty meters in each direction.

Mine is empty. I exhale, relieved, right as I hear Faye go, "What the hell . . . ?"

I look over her shoulder. Standing there, just on the edge of the light, is a dark, hooded figure, feet wide apart, hands clutching the biggest damn blaster rifle I've ever seen.

We all stand, frozen, for one heartbeat. Two.

And then everything explodes in a hail of laserfire.

TWENTY-SEVEN

I<small>T</small> <small>TAKES JUST ONE OF THE</small> <small>BOLTS</small> <small>FROM THAT BIG-</small>
ass gun searing past my ear for me to decide I do not want to even
chance getting hit.

Owyn must make the same assessment because he drops low and
rolls to the side, but Faye stands right where she is, blaster out, trigger
going. The look on her face dares you to try to make her move.

I'll take that dare.

I drop my shoulder and plow into her, driving her out of the
open intersection and into the mouth of one of the tunnels. She
curses loudly as she hits the ground, me falling on top of her.

"What the hell, Farshot?!"

I scramble up, offering her a hand. "I'm usually all for laughing in the face of danger, but not this time. Get your ass up, Orso,
come on."

She scowls but still takes it, and we move as a unit to the corner
of the tunnel wall, her going high, me crouching low. Across the
tunnel intersection, Owyn is doing the same thing, and it's kind
of impressive how small he can make himself considering how
massive his frame is. On the ground in between us are the smoking

remains of three camera drones. The hooded figure went for them first. Probably the only reason any of us made it out of the initial flurry unscathed.

I peek around the corner. The person stands there, bold as hell, and lays the hammer down on their rifle, sending these cannon-sized shots at our squishable heads.

"Shit!" I pull back, and then stick my blaster out and send a stream of fire in their general direction. Just holding down the trigger and hoping for the best.

I stop. Faye stops. So does Owyn. Everything is dead quiet. We exchange looks, and then I inch my nose into the open.

BLAM!

I pin myself against the tunnel wall again, my pulse pounding rabbit fast in my throat. I can still feel the heat of the shot across my face. "Lively, that one. We could probably use a few more guns."

Faye growls and leans over me, sticking her arm around the corner to lay down another round of suppressing fire. "Who the hell is it?"

I check the charge in my gun. Eighty-three percent. Gives me a bit of time before it overheats and needs a recharge. "The Megas again, maybe? A backup in case the blockade didn't delay us enough?"

"Could be, but it didn't exactly look like they were trying to miss Owyn. What about Setter? He landed right behind me, but I haven't seen him yet."

I shake my head. "I don't think it's Setter. This isn't really his style."

"You just said none of us know each other anymore in the middle of a crownchase."

"I did. I did say that. Thanks, Faye."

She shrugs and unloads another round of blaster fire.

I rack my brain about Setter, trying to think of everything I know about him, seeing if I can imagine him in any capacity pulling a stunt like this. But it doesn't fit. Setter is a rule follower to a fault, and killing any of us disqualifies him from the chase.

I glance over at Owyn across the way. "Any chance this could be another one of your family's tricks?"

He steps out to get a clearer angle and gets maybe twenty rapid-fire shots off before narrowly dodging a single, massive blast from our mysterious guest. He crouches, panting, and then shakes his head.

"I wanna say no, but I wasn't expecting the blockade either, so . . ."

My wristband beeps, and I hear Hell Monkey's voice very quietly speaking from the other end.

"Alyssa, I'm working at being really calm here, but if you've got a second to let me know why I'm hearing godsdamned blaster fire in there, I would really appreciate it."

Faye laughs out loud, and several shots explode against the corner we're hiding behind.

She clicks her tongue. "Not a fan of laughter apparently . . ."

"I'm here, H.M., I'm here," I say, quickly bringing my wristband closer to my mouth. "There's . . . a third party down here."

"Third party?"

"Not a crownchaser. At least, we don't think so. We don't know who they are. But they're definitely trying to kill us. Listen, you need to warn Coy. She's not with me—I don't know where she is. Warn Setter too, if you can make that happen. I don't know if there are more out there or what, but just in case . . ."

"I'm on it." Hell Monkey pauses and then adds, "You better make it back, Farshot."

The comm cuts off before I can respond, but his words wrap around my chest. I feel them every time I inhale.

I tighten my fingers around my blaster and push onto my feet. I must have *ready to start shit* all over my face because Faye raises her eyebrows at me expectantly.

"On three," I tell her. "One . . ."

Her lips curl into a grin. "Two . . ."

"Three."

We step out together, side by side, barrel to barrel, lighting up that whole tunnel with round after round of blaster fire, and it takes a full three seconds before I realize we're shooting at empty air.

"Hold up! They're gone!"

We let up on our triggers, and the silence that oozes in around us makes my stomach sink. I swing around to put my back against Faye's, scanning everywhere.

The tunnels are empty. The intersection is empty.

Owyn eases out from his hiding spot to join us. His heavy brows lower even farther down on his face. "Where the hell did they go?"

Faye's still pointing her blaster at where the figure used to be, and her free hand taps nervously against the side of her thigh.

"Beating a hasty retreat? Maybe they decided they didn't like the odds?"

I shake my head. "The odds weren't really working against them. I'd say they had the situation pretty well in hand."

We stand together in our little cluster. All I can hear is our breaths hitting the cold air hard and fast. My eyes catch sight of the hand scanner Coy gave me, sitting on the ground where I dropped it in the initial exchange of blaster fire. Its screen blinks green, on and off, on and off, pointing me in the direction of the beacon. I should go over and grab it, but I don't really want to move.

"So . . ." says Owyn. "What now? Do we just . . . get back to it?"

Faye looks back at me. There's a sheen of nervousness to her eyes that you don't usually see in an Orsion pirate. She shakes her head, just slightly. "No one brings a gun like that just to make some fireworks and then bust out of here."

My skin's about to vibrate off my body. Everything has gone ass over tail down here. I tap my wristband to open a channel to Hell Monkey.

"Hey, H.M., feel like doing me a favor?"

"Waiting on your every word, Captain."

"You want to see if *Vagabond*'s scanners can get a look down here? We . . . uh . . . lost our mysterious assassin."

There's a stream of quiet curses and then a "yeah, sure," which has a lot of layers of unsaid stuff underneath it like *are you kidding me* and *what the hell do you mean you lost them* and *you're gonna make me come down there, Farshot.*

Echoes ricochet off the faceted walls. Something passes over us that sounds like a distant moan, and my gaze drifts up the wall to fixate on one of the frozen corpses preserved in crystal. I shiver.

"Give me good news, Hell Monkey. Please."

His sigh fills up the whole comms channel. "Sorry, Captain. Whatever material is in this asteroid, it's not sensor friendly. Everything's bouncing back. It's amazing we got a read off the beacon at all."

And probably why the hand scanners are having trouble pinning down its exact location. Dammit. I'm honestly at a total loss. We're not exactly down here to play nice together, but running off on our own with that shadow guy who-knows-where seems stupid as hell.

Then again, standing around like idiots in the middle of this intersection doesn't seem much better.

I glance up at Owyn, who meets my eyes and then shifts a little closer. His face is pinched and worried, and he starts tapping a message on his wristband. Probably to his companion—Gear—I'm guessing, but I don't want to seem like I'm peeking, so I look away.

Which means I'm half a second late in seeing the air right in front of Owyn ripple.

Half a second late in turning as the hooded figure appears, aglow with the light of the plasma blade held out in front of them.

Half a second late to do something—anything—to stop them as they lunge forward and drive that blade right through the middle of Owyn Mega's chest.

TWENTY-EIGHT

OWYN DOESN'T SCREAM. HE JUST GAPES, HIS FACE stretched with horror and surprise, and then the hooded figure twists the plasma blade and wrenches it free. Owyn collapses in a heap.

The air smells like seared flesh and scorched rock. There's the echo of a scream still ricocheting off the corridor walls. I think it's mine. I think I made that sound. But I can't really remember. I'm having trouble tearing my eyes from Owyn's body and the deep purple otari blood spreading across his back.

Movement in my peripheral vision. I look up right into the barrel of that massive blaster rifle. I bring my own gun up, but I know it's going to be too late. I'm thinking about all those places I never got to see, all the things I never did tell Hell Monkey, and then—

BLAM!

Faye's suddenly beside me, blaster hot, and the figure staggers as their shot goes wide, catching me in the left shoulder.

This time I definitely do scream. That was definitely me. Because holy stars and gods that fucking hurt.

Our mystery guest clutches the wound in their chest, and we

don't even give them a second to realize how screwed they are. I wrench my gun up, and Faye and I blast that bastard with laserfire until they stagger and drop to the ground.

"Stop!" I throw an arm out in front of Faye as the figure crumples, and she lets up on the trigger.

"What are you doing, Farshot? You take it out while it's already down—"

"No, I wanna see it!"

I scramble over to them, kicking away the plasma blade they dropped, snatching the blaster rifle out of their loose fingers. They lie on their back, one leg bent unnaturally underneath them, blood staining their dark clothes. It looks gray. I don't know of any species in our quadrant with gray blood. Their hood has fallen away, but there's a mask covering their entire head.

I rip it off with blood-slicked fingers and immediately jerk backward, falling on my ass.

They have no face.

I've seen a ton of different species. I've met a ton of different races. I've seen humanoids with no mouths or no ears, no noses or no eyes.

But never no face altogether.

They turn their head toward me, but I don't really know if they're looking at me. How do they even see? I glance at their torso, watching for movement, any sign of breathing, but there's nothing. Everything about them is still save for the trickle of their blood.

"Who the hell are you?" My voice comes out in a growl. Like a cornered-animal sound. Which makes sense because I feel pretty cornered right now. I get low, putting my face right up to their empty skin. "Not having a mouth doesn't mean you can't answer, so start talking and I just might have a med patch or two to put on some of these holes you recently acquired. Who sent you? How did you know where we were and why did you . . . did you . . . ?"

I can't finish the words. I want to be intimidating, to scare answers out of them, but my shoulder is on fire with pain and my whole body is starting to shake with adrenaline and shock.

They don't say anything. I don't even know if they can hear me.

Their arm twitches, and I glance up just in time to see them pull a dagger out of nowhere and swing it in a brutal downward arc.

I jerk back—but it was never intended for me. They plunge the blade right into their own temple.

Gray blood sprays across my face. Their body twitches, shudders, and goes limp.

I push away, wiping at my eyes and nose with trembling fingers. Half crawling, half stumbling, I make my way back over to where Faye crouches beside Owyn. She has one of his big, rock-scarred arms in her hands, her thumbs pressed to an otari pulse point along the inside of his elbow. Her luminous gold eyes find me, and she shakes her head.

"Nothing," she says, her voice very quiet.

I don't listen to her. I throw my good shoulder against Owyn's body to roll him flat on his back and fumble with a pocket on my belt. I wasn't lying to the assassin. I do have a couple of med patches, and I struggle to open one up with my shaking hands, one of which is starting to go a little numb as the gunshot wound continues to bleed and bleed.

Faye puts a hand on my arm. "Alyssa, what are you—"

"Just help me with this, would you?"

"He's gone. There's no point—"

"It's one stab wound, Faye. Otari are too tough to go down with one stab wound."

"They put a plasma blade straight through his heart. He's not coming back from that—"

"Faye Orso, would you just godsdamn help me?!"

"Alyssa Farshot, would you just godsdamn listen?!" She grabs my face, pressing it between her hands. "There isn't a med patch anywhere on this rock that's going to put an entire heart back together. It's over. Stop."

I stare at her—at the thin glowing lines curving over her face, at the luminescent cascade of her hair like thousands of fiber optic strands—and then my body gives out and I curl forward until my forehead touches my knees. I don't cry. I just breathe, slow, shaky breaths into the acrid, plasticky smell of my survival suit.

Faye presses a hand against my shoulder. "Honor is calling it in to authorities. They'll come get him. We should go."

I don't say anything.

"There could be more jackasses with big guns about."

"You go," I tell her without raising my head. "I need a minute."

Silence. And then, in a completely disaffected voice like she doesn't even care anymore: "Fine, have it your way."

There's a scrape and a rustle as she gathers her stuff, and then I hear the clomp of her grav boots moving away. I bring my head up, looking around.

Just me and two dead bodies.

And a voice in the darkness. "Alyssa, tell me you're okay."

Hell Monkey.

"I'm here," I tell him, because saying that I'm okay feels like a lie. "I'm . . . I'm here."

"What happened? Are you hurt?"

I look down at my left arm, at the blast wound and the blood dripping down my skin and suit. I probably have less of my own blood on me than I do of Owyn or . . . whatever that person was. "Nothing serious."

I stare down at Owyn. At his face frozen with shock even as his eyes are dead and empty. I remember when he and I were kids and how much bigger he had always been compared to me. How invincible he had seemed. And now . . . This is it. This is all that's left of him.

"Talk to me, Farshot. What are you doing?"

My eyes land on his wristband, and I remember that he'd been typing something. Just before. I grab his hand and pull up the message. I'd guessed right—he'd been trying to send something to Gear.

Just in case I don't make it back up, you should know that I lov

That's it. That's all he'd managed to type. Seeing that word hanging there, unfinished, makes my chest ache. It's not right for it to be frozen, here, on his wristband forever.

"Alyssa?"

I type the last four letters that Owyn couldn't, send it, and then drag myself onto my feet. It takes a second to locate the wreckage of all the camera drones and rifle through the parts, but I manage to find two out of the three memory drives more or less intact. I shove them into my pockets, slap a seal on the torn-up shoulder of my suit, and head back up the tunnel, retracing my steps.

"Get the *Vagabond* prepped, H.M. We're leaving."

TRAGEDY IN THE SHIPS' GRAVEYARD

A hail of gunfire and confusion in the asteroid belt leaves crownchaser Owyn Mega dead

GRIEF, SHOCK, AND ANGER: THE MEGA FAMILY REELS FROM THEIR SUDDEN LOSS

How the loss of their prime heir
will affect the family's future in the empire

WYTHE CALLS FOR CALM IN THE WAKE OF CALAMITY

The steward of the throne vows to convene a committee and review
all available evidence to determine the cause of Mega's death

WHEN COMPETITION TURNS DEADLY

What it means for the empire if it turns out that one of the crownchasers
snapped and made a horrific, bloody decision

WORLDCRUISER S576-034, HYPERLIGHT

"WE FIND THE DRIVE TO MOURN TO BE THE MOST fascinating quirk of biological life," NL7 says as it scans the media feeds. "One thousand and one planets across two hundred systems and hundreds of cultures, and nearly all of you feel the need to mark death of your organic forms in some way. Its ubiquity is quite interesting."

Edgar doesn't stand with the android. He isn't interested in watching the performative mourning by all the prominent political and social leaders and the endless hours of analysis by the *Daily Worlds* as they capitalize on Owyn Mega's death to the tune of trillions of viewers.

He knows the routine. He saw it when he was a boy and his mother—the Great Inventor, the Tech Angel of Voles Enterprises— passed suddenly. So much pontificating. So many empty thoughts and empty prayers.

He'd been overwhelmed by the grief filling his body as a child, but he'd also quickly discovered how much it irritated his father to see him express it. Any glint of tears, any tremble of the shoulders put William Voles on edge, so Edgar had had to isolate it. Put it on separate circuits. He very rarely accesses that part of him, but it is slightly difficult to keep it contained as he watches the other crownchasers react to losing Owyn.

Three of them—Coyenne, Orso, and Roy—appear to still be working on the chase, but even then, they pause in the moments where they think they are clear of the cameras. They visibly grieve.

Faroshti does not seem to be making a move in either direction. She sits in her med bay, alone.

Edgar pauses and enlarges the feed from the *Godsblade*, Owyn Mega's ship. It's already been retrieved from the asteroid belt and is being escorted to Apex, but Owyn's second, Gear Aluma, is still on board. He watches her sit in the bed in Owyn's quarters, wrapped in his sheets, her wings drooping down her back. Artacians don't cry like some species; when they grieve, they shed pinprick-sized spores of light from the ends of their fur.

Owyn's quarters are filled with them.

The back of his throat aches, and he swallows to relax it. To smooth the pain away. But all he does is move it deep inside his chest, where it sits, heavy and sour like guilt. If he'd said something when he'd seen that ship approaching the asteroid belt, if he'd reached out . . .

"What are you watching, Edgar Voles?"

Edgar blinks his eyes clear and swipes the screen away as NL7 approaches. "Just assessing my competitors."

"Do you still wish to proceed with the augmentations to the ship that we recommended?"

He reaches toward the display and flicks a finger at each crownchaser's feed, darkening them one by one. "Of course I do. Our objective is far from complete."

SEVEN YEARS AGO . . .

THE IMPERIAL SCHOOLROOM, THE KINGSHIP, APEX

THE ONLY LIGHT COMES FROM THE HOLOGRAPHIC projection in the middle of the room. I cleared a big space and had the kingship AI fill it with the three-dimensional recording I'd dug out of the archives. It's the fifth time this month I've snuck in after school hours to do this. I can't help it, though. Getting to see her, as tall as she was in life, looking so regal and elegant, her eyes bright with passion as she speaks to a packed crowd on the planet Umbar.

". . . a new shape for our great empire! One that hears and recognizes every voice, every person, without regard for family name! One that doesn't stay mired in what it is, but what it *could be*!"

My mother. Saya Faroshti.

I watch her hologram finish her speech as the crowd goes wild and surges toward her. She steps right down to meet them, and just before she disappears in all the bodies, I say, "Kingship, pause playback."

The image freezes, and I move into the middle of it, imagining if I had actually been there that day, if I had stood here—right *here*—and I could've touched her . . .

I hold my hand just above where hers is. I know if I try, my fingers will go right through her, but just for a second I pretend like they won't. Just for a second, I pretend like I can reach out and pull her to me across time and space. Because I know what happens after this moment.

Saya Faroshti goes to tour an abandoned Umbarian town devastated in the early years of the war. But her security team missed an old land mine hidden in the ruins, still active.

And when the dust settles, my mother is dead.

Something moves in my peripheral vision, and I look up to see Uncle Charlie standing against the wall. His face is soft in the way I've only seen it get when it's just him and me and Uncle Atar.

"She was really something," he says. "She had the gravity of a sun. She pulled everyone to her."

I drop my hand and step out of the projection. My chest feels like it has a weighted ball in it. "If that's true, why did so many people fight to keep her from getting the throne?"

Charlie sighs and puts a hand on my shoulder. "Politics are complicated, Alyssa. There were those who felt the throne should've been theirs. There were those who simply wanted to seize what they saw as a power vacuum. And . . . there were quite a few who were scared of your mother's ideas."

I turn back to the projection, staring at her frozen in the middle, a column of bright sapphire. "She wanted to change the empire."

"She had big ideas. And big ideas often generate big pushback."

Seriously big pushback. As in, twenty-five years of war and she never even made it to her coronation. Seems like overkill to me. "Uncle Atar always tells me how amazing she was, how smart she was. Why didn't he try to do all the things she talked about? He's the one who ended up on the throne—he could've done something."

Charlie's hand tightens on my shoulder, and there's a heavy pause. Then he pulls me around to face him. The strange light of the hologram makes the lines on his face deeper, and his gaze is intense.

"You're too young to understand, Alyssa. Twenty-five years of war. Thousands of cities burned. Millions of lives lost or destroyed. Atar did what he had to do to bring about peace. And that meant he had to make some promises." Charlie's face falls a little. "He and I both had to make promises."

I frown. I can't quite put together all the stuff he's not saying. "What kinds of promises?"

Charlie straightens, the intensity falling away. "Nothing for you to worry about right now." His mouth twitches with a half smile and he touches my cheek for the briefest second. "It's worked out all right in the end. At least, I think so. Come on now. It's just you and me for dinner tonight. Should we get extra dessert and not tell Atar?"

My eyebrows shoot up. "Who are you and what have you done with my uncle Charlie?"

He chuckles a little as he leads me out of the room, but my gaze drifts back to my mother one last time before the door closes tight.

TWENTY-NINE

Stardate: 0.05.22 in the Year 4031

Location: Putting the Ships' Graveyard in our engine backdraft

I SIT IN THE *VAGABOND*'S LITTLE MED BAY, dangling my legs over the side of the bed. I've been doing this for half an hour straight. Just sitting here. Staring down at the ruined survival suit crumpled on the floor, stained with three different types of blood.

My shoulder is all patched up. As soon as my feet hit the ramp, Hell Monkey swept me in to take a look at my wounds and get everything properly fixed so it can heal. He hadn't pressed too many questions on me—must've known I wasn't gonna answer them—and he left a little over an hour ago to hit the bridge and get us the hell out of the asteroid belt.

Good riddance. Need to tell the Society that this place is on my no-go list.

There's the tick-ticking of metal feet outside the med bay doors. JR, pacing, waiting for me to come out so it can interview me. Just the idea of staring into those glowing camera lenses and trying to talk about what happened down there is . . .

I shudder and pull my legs up, press my knees against my chest. I'll just stay here, thanks.

Ta-da. The great and fearless Alyssa Farshot, record-breaking explorer and cruiser jockey. Hiding like a little kid.

Un-fucking-believable.

I tell myself to get it together, give myself the usual tough-love pep talk. But it's still a long stretch before I finally uncurl my body and put boots on the ground.

My legs feel wobbly underneath me. I hate this, I hate this, I hate this. Not feeling strong. Not feeling confident in my own body. Not wanting to leave this stupid little room.

Come on, Farshot. This is the Vagabond Quick. *There isn't a centimeter of this ship you don't know.*

I close my eyes, zip my jumpsuit all the way up, and step outside.

JR is right there, all lenses pointed at me. "Captain Farshot, can you comment on the events that transpired down on the *Defiant?*"

I swallow and try to pull words from somewhere, but my tongue is just too heavy in my mouth. I stare at all of those lens-eyes, and all I can do is shake my head. I leave the mediabot there and amble toward the bridge. My boots drag along the floor. My eyes are open, but they're not really seeing anything. JR tick-ticks after me.

I find Hell Monkey on the bridge, arms crossed over his chest, staring at the media feeds streaming on the wall. When he sees me come through the door, his eyes widen just barely and he reaches out like he's going to turn them all off.

"Don't touch it," I tell him. My voice scrapes against the sides of my throat. "I'm a big girl. I can handle it."

The furrow between his eyebrows says he doesn't believe me. I ignore him. I don't want to be shielded like some fragile shell. I've stared worse things in the eye than this.

Every single news and media feed is filled with Owyn. His face, his life, his family, but especially his death—all the sensational details and exclusive breaking discoveries and a thousand different digital re-creations of what they think *may* have happened based on their position that hour. From what I can tell, none of the other crownchasers has made a statement yet. Wythe has declared they're still looking over the evidence at the scene as part of the ongoing investigation, and Cheery Coyenne and the *Daily Worlds* has led the call for everything to be made public immediately because the people have a Right to Know. If I didn't know Cheery any better, I'd think she really had the public and the truth top of her mind. But it's more likely she's just mad she hasn't had a chance to jump out in front of the story and edit it how *she* wants the narrative to go.

The screen in the bottom left corner catches my eye—buried down there like Hell Monkey thought I wouldn't see it. I wave to pull it up and expand it, spreading it out across the display.

Not a feed from the *Daily Worlds*. From a different media outlet. They've got some pundit on there with the chyron declaring: "CROWNCHASER TURNED MURDERER?"

I swipe the screen to turn up the volume.

". . . truth is crownchaser murdering crownchaser is the only viable explanation," the guy says. "And once you accept that, the question then becomes: Which one pulled the trigger on Owyn Mega? I think there's only one answer to that, and that's Alyssa Farshot. She already threw her cards in with the Coyennes, and who knows how far she's willing to go for that? Her motives and goals are extremely questionable. She hasn't at all demonstrated that she's a worthy successor to our beloved Emperor Atar, may he rest in the light of the—"

I flick a wrist, sending the screen zooming back off to its corner. These jerks can go on all they want, but I don't need to sit here and watch it.

"JR," I say, and the mediabot is right there, ready to record. I pull the memory drives of the camera drones out of my pocket and hold them out. "Take these. Pull everything you can off them. You've got direct access to the news outlets, right? You can transmit to them and not the crownchase officials?"

"That is correct, Captain Farshot."

"Then I've got a comment for you to send them." I turn, squaring my shoulders, and look right down the lenses. "This is Captain Alyssa Farshot with a public message. Mediabot JR426 has the camera drone footage from the *Defiant*. Untouched. Unedited by anyone—not me, not the crownchase officials, not the media. It will be transmitting immediately for everyone to see. I have nothing to hide." I step back. "That's all, JR. The sooner that gets out, the better."

It tilts its head and then clicks its way off the bridge.

My chest felt so empty before, but there's something in there now. Something small and hard and cold. One by one, I turn off every display screen. Everything on my bridge—my bridge—that's hooked into the crownchase, I shut it all down. Methodically. Nothing on my face.

Hell Monkey just watches me for a minute before he says, "Coy sent over a message before she left. About the clue for the next beacon. We left the asteroid without getting it."

"We don't need it." I drop into my jump seat, sinking into the well-worn curves of it. This is the only place I belong. The only place that feels like it fits. What the hell have I been doing out here? I don't even know who I am right now.

Hell Monkey hovers near my shoulder. "You got a look on your face, Alyssa. What's going on?" I can feel the wariness coming off him. Like he's approaching a wild animal.

Alyssa Farshot, wild animal. Alyssa Farshot, erratic and questionable.

Alyssa Farshot, unworthy of her uncle.

"We're not playing their game anymore, H.M." Leaning forward, I tap coordinates into the navcomm dashboard. Coordinates so familiar I could enter them in my sleep. "Time to go home."

THIRTY

Stardate: 0.05.24 in the Year 4031

Location: The only place left for me to go right now

IT'S QUIET ON THE *VAGABOND QUICK.*

It has been for the past two days. As soon as I told JR where we were going and what my plan was, the mediabot established itself in a corner of the bridge and went dormant. All of its lenses dark. No tick-tick of its feet on the floor. Back to being just me and Hell Monkey, which is how I like it.

I mean, I like it better when we're joking around. And screwing around. But nothing about the atmosphere inside the ship right now sets the mood for either of those things. I'm not really talking very much, which—that's weird. And Hell Monkey seems to be reacting to this weirdness by just . . . watching me. Waiting for me to break and spill my guts, I guess.

But I don't have anything to spill. I'm just done.

Rose's steady voice sings out, "Approaching Station Shisso, Captain Farshot."

Something uncoils in my chest hearing those words, and

I stare eagerly at the viewscreen as we glide toward a patchy brown-and-green planet called Eillume. It's a little-known place in a little-known system, and few people give any notice to the rough-looking, cobbled-together space station orbiting above it. Not an official spaceport or big hub or anything like that. Just a collection of old transport ships and citizen stations that have been fused together over the decades into something that looks kind of like a monster on the outside but inside is just a whole bunch of people making a life for themselves without a lot of fuss.

I stumbled upon Station Shisso accidentally on one of my first missions for the Explorers' Society. I was green as hell and running the *Vagabond Quick* by myself after my second engineer told me I had a "death wish" and walked off the job. My ship had gotten hit by rogue debris, and I limped her into one of their ports for repairs. I'd spent a few days there, getting her spaceworthy again, and they hadn't much cared who I was—not my old name or my new name, not who I worked for or where I was born. They'd just fed me, given me a hand with repairs, and sent me on my way.

I came back a few months later when I was in the area. And again after that. And again. Until I became a regular fixture. I started renting quarters in one of the residential spaces. They started reserving a seat for me at the main watering hole.

And two years ago, I'd met a young engineer there with no fear and omni-goggles on his head, and Station Shisso had been cemented in my heart forever.

I'm packed and ready to go as soon as we've stopped, standing by the starboard-side docking seal with my bag over my shoulder and Hell Monkey next to me. I jiggle my legs as I wait for the tunnel to decompress.

Hell Monkey cups my elbow with one of his big hands. "Not that I don't love coming back to Shisso, but you wanna talk to me about what's going on? This is way off course."

I shake my head. "Nope. It's a course correction. We're back right where we need to be."

"Hey. Alyssa. Look at me."

This jerk. He knows exactly how dangerous his eyes are and he's got no qualms about using them. But it feels kind of childish to say no, so I drag my gaze over to his.

"You gotta tell me what page you're on or I won't be able to keep up."

There's a hiss as the decompression is completed and the airlock door slides open. I want to just bolt away down the tunnel, but I owe Hell Monkey something more than that. I turn to him and put a hand on his chest, feeling the pound of his single, human heart underneath the skin and muscle.

"All this time we've been scrambling, trying to walk this line between being in the crownchase and keeping our lives the same as they've always been, and it's . . . it's the stupidest thing, H.M. Why the hell am I running around after a throne I don't even want? Just because my uncle wanted me to? Screw Atar. He's dead." I pull my hand back and hook my thumbs into the straps of my bag. "It doesn't matter who wins. One idiot or another sits on the throne. I just want to go back to doing what we do best, and the easiest way to do that is to not play this game at all."

I walk off down the tunnel, and as soon as I step through the airlock on the other side, I breathe in all the way down to the bottoms of my lungs. All the smells that make up the scent of Shisso—metal, oil, cooking food, synthetic earth. There's a figure waiting for us as we disembark, an older human woman with russet brown skin and silvered hair, dressed in layers of worn, jewel-toned clothes. She moves toward us with a smile and open arms.

I drop my bag and step right up to her. I never turn down a hug offer from Gemi. She gives the best hugs, and I sure as hell need one right now.

Her arms close around me, strong and firm, and she says in a low voice, "Welcome back, Alyssa."

Something about the hug and the warmth in her voice hits a trigger. My breath catches in my chest, and I just about choke on the tears that flood up into my throat. My jaw aches with the effort to hold them back. I feel weeks of grief and guilt fill me up, right to my edges. I don't think there's enough space between my bones to hold it all in.

If I step away right now, would I even be able to keep my shape? Or would I just expand and expand like the universe?

Heavy footsteps behind me. Then the soft touch of a calloused hand between my shoulder blades.

Hell Monkey.

He won't let me float away.

I step back from Gemi's hug and feel him like a wall at my back. Solid enough to lean on. Swiping tears from my vision, I try to smile as Gemi searches my face with a concerned expression.

"There's been a lot of shit happening lately, Gemi," Hell Monkey says.

She nods. "Yes, we have been watching. I'm quite surprised to see you here in the middle of everything." She reaches out, touches my arm and then Hell Monkey's. "You are, of course, always welcome, though. Come."

We don't exactly need an escort around Shisso—I know my way around almost as well as I know my ship—but Gemi is the senior leader on this space station in a lot of ways. So if she wants to walk you to your room, you let her. I expect her to ask questions about the crownchase, about what we're doing showing up on her doorstep, but that's not really giving her a lot of credit. Gemi has seen a lot more of life than either of us, and she knows when not talking is the better option.

We walk through the cargo section of the station, gathered around the most prominent docking ports, though Shisso only engages in some basic trade relationships. The majority of the residential spaces are several levels up, so we get to pass through the engineering section, the market and maker sections, and the agricultural level, all before we get to the quieter floors above. The sun-side sections up here house the school, and you can hear the distant, muffled shouts and laughter of kids out in the corridors. Our quarters are on the other end, planet side, and Gemi walks us to mine first.

She pauses outside the door, puts her hands on my shoulders, and looks me in the eye. "This was always going to be a painful process for you. But you haven't been given any burden too heavy for you to carry."

I'm not sure I really agree with her. This all feels too heavy, and I have some narrow fricking shoulders. But she leaves before I can pull a response out. Which is probably for the best. I just would've said something stupid.

I press my hand against the doorpad, and it unlocks, sliding open with a little beep. I stand frozen in the corridor, staring at the small, cozy quarters that look cold and empty and claustrophobic right now. Like a coffin. The coffin they're lowering Owyn Mega into. The coffin that shot Uncle Atar's body across the stars and into a sun.

Hell Monkey shifts his weight, starting to move off to his own quarters farther down the corridor, but I reach out and grab his hand before he can take half a step.

"I don't . . . don't want to be in there. By myself." I look up into his face. The big hazel eyes. The heavy expressive brows. The scruff all along his jaw. "Can you . . . would you . . ."

"Yeah," he says. He doesn't make me finish, stars love him. His lips quirk up a little as he steps past me. "But I get to be little spoon."

THIRTY-ONE

Stardate: 0.05.27 in the Year 4031
Location: Station Shisso

I SLEEP TEN HOURS THAT FIRST NIGHT, AND IT feels like the first time I've really slept since Uncle Atar died.

Hell Monkey is there when I wake up, crammed in beside me on the bunk, snoring. We've never done this before. Just slept next to each other. I kind of expected not to like it. I've always slept on my own, sprawled out wherever the hell I want. But right now, when I'm worried that the edges of me might bleed outward until I'm nothing, having him here grounds me. Keeps me from scattering into a million pieces.

I nudge him until he flips over on his side, then I curl up against his back. And I sleep again.

Another full day passes as I slip in and out, sometimes deep into dreams, sometimes dozing and half-aware. Hell Monkey isn't always there when I come out of it, but he's usually nearby, moving around the room or reading or fiddling with specs or parts from the *Vagabond* that he's trying to make improvements to.

On the third morning we're on Shisso, Hell Monkey shakes me out of a really good dream, and I scowl at him from just over the covers.

"Excuse me, sir, I'm wallowing here."

He shakes his head, pulling on my arms until I'm sitting upright. "Sorry, but you're going to have to actually function. You've got an incoming message. On a secure channel."

Uh-oh. "Coy?"

"Nope. She's either busy or hasn't tracked us down yet. It's your uncle Charlie."

Well. That's much worse. I pat at my matted, tangled hair and am suddenly very glad that transspace communications don't include smell because I'm definitely a bit on the aromatic side. Slinking across the room, I take a seat at the little desk against the wall and swipe open the blinking message light on my visual display.

Uncle Charlie's face appears immediately, looking a little older, a little more strained, and his shoulders drop visibly when he sees me.

"Alyssa . . ." His voice is heavy with relief. "I'm so glad . . . I wasn't sure . . . It's good to see you."

The sting hits the backs of my eyes, and I blink hard. "Sorry, Uncle Charlie. I didn't mean to worry you."

He presses his mouth into a grim smile. "Well, to be fair, that's hardly a difficult thing to do. It takes very little to worry me. Atar always said—" The next words get stuck in his throat, and he looks away.

Seeing Charlie stumble on his tears triggers my own. The whole world goes a bit blurry as they spill over my eyelashes. "I let him down, Charlie. Uncle Atar—he wanted me to do this, to live up to him and my mother, and I couldn't do it. I don't want it enough. I don't want it at all—"

He waves a hand through the rest of my words. "Your uncle loved you, Alyssa. If he were with me right now, seeing what I'm seeing, he would be proud of you. You've never failed either of us. Do you understand?"

I can't respond. I'm afraid all that will come out are a bunch of ugly sobs. So I swipe at my eyes and nod.

Charlie takes a breath and shoots a quick look over his shoulder. "Alyssa," he says quietly, stepping closer to the display. "I can't tell you the choices you should make. And time is running out before someone catches me talking to a crownchaser. But you should know the stakes for this crownchase are higher than you think. Many are still fighting the old war in their hearts, and this chase is just an extension of it. There's no telling what certain factions might do to win."

A cold feeling trickles down my back. "You're saying—?"

He cuts me off, sweeping another glance around him. "I can't confirm anything, Alyssa. But . . . Nathalia Coyenne has always seemed to be a very good sort of person. She might need friends in this more than it seems."

I'm opening my mouth to respond—though I'm not totally sure with what—when Charlie says quickly, "I have to go. Be safe, Alyssa."

And then the communication goes dead.

I swing around to look at Hell Monkey, who's leaning against the wall with his arms crossed over his chest.

"I'm not sure I like any of what just happened."

He snorts. "What's there to like?"

I scrub at my face, my gaze wandering back to my bunk. I just want to hide again. The blast wound in my shoulder still hurts like hell. I've lost half of what's left of my family. And I've got a sleep deficit that it feels like I'll never catch up on. My only friend is my dear, beloved pillow, which wants absolutely nothing from me.

Hell Monkey catches me before I can disappear under the covers again. "How about we try something new, Farshot? Hear me out. I've got a radical idea called 'shower and food.'"

Actually, now that he mentions it, that doesn't sound half-bad. I'm feeling grimy as hell, and all I've had to eat since we got here are some basic nutrient bars. So I nod, and he steps out into the corridor while I pull myself together.

A half hour later, we're walking together toward Shisso's main restaurant and bar—a place called the Watering Hole. I see several familiar faces as we move down toward the market levels, and they all wave when I wave, say hi when I say hi, and all that. But something is . . . off. They don't always quite meet my eyes. Larg, who's never been tentative in her life, pats me awkwardly on the shoulder when we run into her instead of giving either of us her usual bone-shattering hug.

"What the hell is wrong with everybody?" I mutter to Hell Monkey after Larg shuffles off. "They're all acting weird."

He grimaces, like he's been dreading this question. "Things are different, Alyssa. Before, it didn't matter if you wanted to come here, pretend to be just another station resident. But you're a crown-chaser now. You can't pretend you're just like everyone else—and they can't either."

I stop short, mouth half-open, ready to object—*that's bullshit, I'm the same Alyssa, nothing's changed, nothing has to change*—but there's a ping from my wristband and I hear Gemi's voice.

"Alyssa and Hell Monkey, could you join me up in station control?"

Dammit. No way this could be a good sign.

Station control is a circular structure at the top of Shisso surrounded by windows, giving the people on deck a full view all around them. When we get there, Gemi is standing at a podium on the starboard side of the room, staring outward into the emptiness of space. Or . . . what's usually the emptiness of space.

Instead, I count a dozen ships arrayed in a semicircle around the station. A couple of cruiser-type ships, maybe five or six smaller personal transports, and a handful of hyperlight-capable drones.

I spot the words "THE DAILY WORLDS" emblazoned on one of the cruisers.

Son of a bitch.

Gemi waves me over. Her eyes are very dark and sad. "Alyssa, we seem to have become very popular all of a sudden."

"I see that." I go over to her but wrap my arms tight around my stomach. I'm worried she'll try to hug me or comfort me or something, and I really don't feel like I deserve any of that right now. "I didn't think they'd follow me here. I thought if I was out of the crownchase, they wouldn't care."

She touches my shoulder, very light. "I'm not sure you can count on the benefit of anonymity anymore." Her gaze turns back to all the media circling like vultures. "This is not where we ever wanted Shisso to be. We all came here to build quiet lives away from . . . all of this."

Hell Monkey moves up behind me, and I glance at him. His expression is calm and flat, and I know from experience that's way worse than him looking outright angry. The calmer he gets, the more he's likely to mow someone down.

"Have they contacted you?" he asks Gemi.

"Oh yes," she says, folding wrinkled hands in front of her. "They've all been sending one hail after another. I had to mute them."

"What do they say they want?"

"They want Alyssa." Gemi's eyes land on me again, but I can't meet her gaze. "They want to dock, but we don't have enough ports for half of them, even if I felt inclined to grant their requests. Which I don't."

I take Gemi's hand. "Let me have the podium for a second, okay?" She steps down, and I take her place, using the touch panel in front of me to open a broadband communication. I make sure every ship out there has accepted it before I clear my throat and speak.

"This is Captain Alyssa Farshot of the *Vagabond Quick*. As a fully vested agent of the crownchase, I am ordering you to cease any and all attempts at communicating with or docking at this station.

Disperse immediately and allow Station Shisso to resume its normal trade and transport activities. If you fail to comply with this, I will be lodging a harassment complaint with kingship officials—and you can bet your sweet ass that will not go well for you."

I terminate the channel and step back, heart pounding. Hell Monkey slides over next to me and puts a hand on my back. "You think that'll work?" he asks.

I shrug. "Maybe. I've pulled off worse bluffs than this before."

I have, too. But I don't think this will be one of them. In fact, all I can think right now is how my enormous, beautiful universe—the one that used to be my boundless playground—is starting to get real small, real quick.

THIRTY-TWO

I ESCAPE BACK TO MY QUARTERS.

That's what I'm good at, right? Escaping. Running. That's my best and truest skill. If this crownchase was a race to get *away* from responsibility, I would've had it in the bag on day one.

Stand aside, folks! No one outruns Farshot!

I'm sitting on the bed, elbows propped up on my knees, when the door slides open and Hell Monkey steps in. He pulls a chair over and sits down across from me, mimicking my pose.

I stare down at my feet, tapping the toes of my boots slowly against the alloy floor, one at a time. "Did any of them listen?"

"Some did. Some didn't." His fingers are maybe two or three inches from mine. "Cheery Coyenne's people didn't even flinch. You know there's no way they'll back down."

"I know." I sweep my hands through my tangled hair, yanking on the ends. "We'll have to find somewhere else to ride this out. I've been thinking about some options—"

"I think we need to talk first. Before we go chasing any more options." His voice is soft and serious, and he's got one of those looks leveled at me that means I'm not going anywhere.

"There's nothing to talk about. I left the chase. Decision made."

"Is it? Even after what Charlie told you this morning? Even with Coy still out there with her ass on the line?"

"No one's making her do that." I press my fingertips hard against my eyelids. "You don't understand, Hell Monkey. That throne—it destroys people. And I'm not just talking about Owyn. I'm talking about my uncle. My mother. Pretty much everyone born with the name Faroshti. Our family history is all war and knives in the back and bloodshed and people stepping on each other to sit in one stupid chair."

He nods. "Sure. But then there's also the power and influence and privilege that most people in this quadrant can't even dream of."

Anger licks up my spine like a solar flare. "What the hell is that supposed to mean?"

He doesn't lean away. He meets my glare straight on. "It means you're not the only person in the universe who's lost family, Alyssa. Hell, you're not even the only person in this room. The difference is that when the dust cleared, you were still heir to a godsdamned prime family. And the rest of us had nothing."

I jerk away, scooting backward on my bed until I'm as far away from him as possible. I curl my legs into my chest. Just to put a little more distance between us. My heart ricochets against my rib cage, and the anger and resentment in the back of my throat are starting to get a sour taste. Like maybe I don't have quite the legs to stand on in this argument that I thought I did.

Hell Monkey sighs and leans back in his chair. "Usually when

I make a reference to my past, you just about bust out of your skin wanting to know more."

He's right. Usually I do. But the way this conversation has been going so far, I'm not sure I want to now.

But it's Hell Monkey, and he's waiting for me to respond. So I say, "Tell me about your family, H.M."

His mouth tilts upward in a sad kind of half smile. "They were great. I had three sisters, one brother, and two parents who sang us to sleep every night no matter how tired they were. And I lost them all when I was ten years old."

"Shit." I drop my face onto my knees. Is it possible to feel so awful that the floor would actually open and swallow you up to spare everyone the trouble? "I'm sorry, H.M. I'm so sorry."

There's silence, and I'm terrified to look up. What if he left? What if he decided my self-centered ass wasn't worth it anymore? Then the mattress shifts, and I feel his big body settle in next to me, close enough to touch.

"Nothing for you to be sorry about. You didn't kill them."

I pick my head up off my legs. His profile is almost all shadows, but I can see the shine of his eyes. They're staring at the far wall, but they're not really here. He's not totally here.

"What happened to them?" I ask.

"We lived on the planet Homestead. You probably know it."

I do know it. It's a sister planet to the Voleses' homeworld, Helix. The people on Helix like to refer to Homestead as their "better, simpler half" and their "bread basket," but the truth is that it's where they put all the work they don't want to see. A lot of manufacturing and high-output agriculture and all the factories and refineries that go with it. It's a terraformed planet, so basically Helix custom-built the place to produce all kinds of stuff for themselves and then trucked a bunch of warm bodies over there to do the hard work.

People like Hell Monkey and his folks, apparently.

"We worked on a flower farm," he continues. "Which sounds like it should be all nice and pretty, but there's no such thing as a job like that on Homestead. It was a lot of manure and sweat and bleeding all over from scratches and thorns to grow a ton of flowers that didn't belong there just so someone on Helix had something pretty to stare at in a window for a few days. All my family worked the fields, but I was little for my age and good with a gear wrench, so they had me fixing machines, wedging myself into tiny spaces to grease a cog just so they wouldn't miss a day's production.

"I was half-in, half-out of the wheel well of a combine when the explosion hit." His voice goes rough. Like the memory itself is grating him raw. "The company we worked for had brought in a banned fertilizer—outlawed for being too big of a fire hazard. No one knew, though. Not even the overseers. Not until one of the blades on a gigantic stem stripper machine threw a spark out in the fields and—FWOOM. Whole place went up."

I press myself against his side. "And took everyone with it."

"Just about." His gaze drops to one of my hands, resting on my knee, and he brushes his thumb along my knuckles. "There was a big dustup for, like, a day. An empire official even came and declared there'd be an official investigation. But then the Voleses and the other Helix big shots started passing out credits, and it all went away."

A long silence creeps over us, making me shiver. I don't know what to say. It's not like there's a pithy response to hearing that your closest friend's whole childhood went up in a firestorm. In a seriously literal way. So I say nothing. I just lay my cheek against his arm.

After a few minutes, he looks over at me. He's not off in memory land anymore. He's extremely present.

"I've got no love for the empire, Alyssa. You said you don't want the throne, and I'm there with you. Same page. I'd much rather you be here . . . with me."

Those words are weightier than they seem, and I feel them land in my chest, soft and warm.

"But this kind of running—it's gonna eat you up. You're never gonna be happy unless you see this thing through."

"Happiness is overrated," I grumble.

"No, it's not. You take as much happiness as you can get, wherever you can find it." He scoots away and turns so he can face me, his hands wrapping around my hands. "But right now, you're Alyssa Fucking Farshot. You've got the ship and the skills to get in there, watch Coy's back, and ensure the person who sits on that throne is one who's gonna do right by people. Someone who'll work for planets like Homestead. Planets like Tear. So what are you gonna do?"

Like I even have a chance with him looking at me like that? I mean, seriously. This guy.

"Dammit, Hell Monkey. You're the worst."

ALL CROWNCHASERS CLEARED IN MEGA'S MURDER

Kingship confirms body of unidentified figure captured in the released drone footage was found at the scene

WHO'S BEHIND THE *DEFIANT* ASSAULT

Authorities struggle to uncover any clues
as to the identity of the murderer or what they were
doing in the asteroid belt

KINGSHIP REJECTS
MEGAS PUSH FOR A SPECIAL INQUIRY

The prime family has asked for an independent investigator, but
kingship officials say that everything that can be done is being done

CHEERY COYENNE ANNOUNCES
RELEASE OF "OWYN MEGA: A RETROSPECTIVE"

The executive editor says many of the crownchaser's closest friends
and family contributed to the memorial show

SYSTRIA IX, IN REMOTE ORBIT

THE MEGAS WILL NOT BE SWAYED.

After all the trouble Edgar went to in order to contact them, to make his pitch about backing the Voles family and playing a part in his great victory. He'd appealed to their future, promising them power and wealth beyond what they had even now. He'd appealed to their sense of justice, in helping him put the Coyennes and Faroshtis in their place, in getting to the bottom of Owyn's murder. He'd even tried to appeal to their grief.

And that's when they'd cut the transmission.

He sits in the captain's chair, fingers pressed into his temples, staring into empty space. He'd been certain he could convince them, and now he needs to adjust. It ought to be simple to come up with a different angle. He does this all the time.

But his mind keeps getting stuck. On the twin looks of disdain on the Megas' faces as he talked to them. On everything his father said on his last call.

The family didn't want you . . .

On everything else underneath his father's words.

You'd better not fail, Edgar. Don't disappoint me again, Edgar. I never wanted you, Edgar—

"Edgar Voles," NL7 says suddenly.

He looks up at the android and follows the line of its eyesight back over his shoulder.

There's a figure standing on the bridge.

Edgar jumps sharply to his feet, his breath catching with panic. NL7 steps in front of him, shielding him.

"Who are you?" he snaps. "How did you get on board?"

The figure—tall, hooded, with a mask covering their whole face—doesn't respond. They tilt their head and swipe a gloved hand down, straight through the strategic-operations table.

A hologram. Edgar's shoulders relax a little, but still. The very fact that they were able to project their image onto his ship without permission or notification is exceptional. Edgar moves in front of NL7. He's tempted to adjust his collar, smooth out his shirt, but he knows even those small motions might demonstrate nervousness or weakness and he needs to be in control of this situation. So instead he simply raises his chin higher in the air.

"One of your kind attacked the crownchasers in the asteroid field."

They nod.

"What do you want here?"

They lift their hand and press a button on the sleek cuff wrapped around their forearm. The voice that comes out of it is cold, precise, and completely artificially generated:

WE RECOGNIZE THAT THE VOLES ARE IN PLAY FOR THE SEAL.

WE HAVE A STRONG INTEREST IN YOUR SUCCESS. WE OFFER

OUR ASSISTANCE IN CLEARING YOUR PATH FORWARD.

Edgar hesitates. There is no doubt of the deadly intent behind that offer. Whoever these people are, they've already proven their willingness to spill blood. "How can I trust you? Your . . . affiliate already killed a crownchaser. I'm not interested in being next."

The figure taps out another response.

OUR ALLIES ARE YOUR ALLIES, EDGAR VOLES. BESIDES, YOU ARE RUNNING OUT OF PLANS. AND YOU ARE RUNNING OUT OF TIME.

Edgar's throat tightens, and he turns back to the viewscreen so that the figure can't see him compose himself. "I need a moment," he says over his shoulder, "to confer with my colleague and consider your proposal."

WE WILL RETURN IN FIVE MINUTES. THE OFFER EXPIRES AFTER THAT.

The figure flickers and disappears.

NL7 hovers near his arm. "An ally would be of benefit to us."

It would. He knows it would, and he should jump on an opportunity like this. But something about that figure makes his skin crawl. He keeps thinking about the ragged footage from the asteroid belt of the firefight and Owyn Mega dead on the glass floor. He leans over the conn, bracing his hands on the surface. "This is an entirely unknown element. I don't know . . . I didn't plan for this."

NL7 steps around in front of him. "Do you believe you belong on the throne, Edgar Voles?"

He does. Not just because he wants it, but because he's earned it. None of the others have worked like he has, striven to be the best, to be first, like he has. None of them have even bothered to notice all his struggles and endeavors. He's been aiming himself at this target for half his life, while the other crownchasers have been wasting themselves. It's time for his family to take control of the empire, and he deserves to be the one who leads it.

Edgar takes a slow breath in through his nose. Cool, detached. Voleses don't tremble. Voleses don't fear.

When the figure reappears a few minutes later, he stands tall and ready to meet it.

THE WATERING HOLE, SPACE STATION SHISSO

THE WATERING HOLE IS CROWDED TONIGHT. HALF the station has showed up to shoot drinks and socialize. Some are gathered around the media feed, watching a big speeder race happening over in the Artev system. The rest are lining the bar or crowding the surrounding tables to talk shit and play at dice.

Or lose at dice, if you're me.

I'm out twenty credits in this game, and I've been sitting at the table for only half an hour.

Larg slides me a look, and her species has six eyes, so that's a lot of side-eye. "You actually in this game, Farshot?"

I flick a hand at her. "I'm fine. I'm fine. Just warming up."

Jitka, the foarian who runs the Watering Hole, slides in to drop off a drink and raises their eyebrows at me. "Warming up? That's a new way of putting it."

I push them away. "Hush. It's all part of my diabolical plan."

Across the table from me, Anke laughs out loud and throws out his dice with a dramatic flourish. I groan as the numbers come up and I'm out another ten credits.

"Come off it, Farshot," Anke says. "You're useless tonight. What's the story?"

I toss my hands in the air and lean back. "I just had another engineer walk off the job, that's all."

Larg grunts. "Did you scare the piss out of this one too?"

"No! I mean, maybe a little, but the circumstances—"

Anke shakes his head. "There's always circumstances."

"—the job required a certain amount of risk—"

"There's always a certain amount of risk," Jitka sings out as they bustle by with more drinks.

I scowl at all their smiling faces. "You're terrible. The whole lot of you. Y'know, it really was—"

"Excuse me."

A low voice cuts through our chatter, and I look up at a young guy with big, long-lashed hazel eyes. He's built like a wall—tall, broad-shouldered—and he's got his hands shoved into the pockets of a mechanic's jumpsuit and omni-goggles sitting on his buzzed brown hair.

He's got a cocksure little grin on his face, and he looks me straight in the eye and says, "You're looking for an engineer?"

I give him my most winning smile. "Maybe. Why—you know someone?"

He steps back and winks at me. "Name's Hell Monkey. I'll report for duty in the morning, Captain Farshot."

Then he turns around and disappears into the crowd.

THIRTY-THREE

Stardate: 0.05.28 in the Year 4031
Location: Back on board my baby, but unfortunately not to prepare for an epic run around the Kessell Comet that loops this system

COY IS PRETTY PISSED.

I mean, I expected her to be a little grumpy with me for . . . I dunno . . . dropping out of sight and leaving her high and dry after promising to be her wing-person. But I figured I'd say sorry, promise to buy her three celebratory bottles of Solari whiskey on her coronation day, and that'd be that.

That wasn't that. That wasn't that at all.

"Four," I tell her, smiling as hard as I can at her glowering face on the comms display in my quarters. "Four bottles of Solari whiskey. That's how sorry I am, right?"

She snorts. "I did okay without you, y'know."

"I know! I saw the leaderboard. And I caught up on some of the footage."

Apparently I missed one of the challenges while I was hiding on Shisso. I haven't watched all of it yet—I just skimmed some of the headlines and watched a clip recap reel while I was shoveling down dinner last night. It looks like they'd had to face down a South Art-acian hellbeast—these enormous, wild-dog-looking creatures—and get to the next beacon, all without seriously hurting the animal or any of its cubs. I'm almost a little sorry I missed that one. I dealt with hellbeasts once before while running a mission on Artacia, and it turns out they're suckers for honey. They turn into total softies if you bring some along. Coy apparently had been the only other one who knew the honey trick. Setter had managed to scoop up one of the hellbeast cubs and had essentially used it as leverage to get by safely. Faye had set off a smoke bomb and gotten by in the chaos, but not without a giant gash down the side of her leg.

The performance had given Coy a little jump in the polls, although Faye and Setter weren't far behind. Still doing those prime family names proud, apparently.

My name fell quite a bit. Not below Edgar's, since he's still strangely absent from this whole scuffle, but my approval number definitely isn't great. I guess ducking out and shirking your respon-sibilities to the current favorite doesn't sit well with the general public.

That's okay. I'm not here to be the popular one. I just need to fin-ish what I started. And that begins with some hard-core groveling.

I clear my throat and hold up my hands, palms out. *Yes, hello, here is my gesture of peace.* "Look, I know I screwed you over by ghosting on you, Coy. I didn't . . . handle things well after . . . the *Defiant*. And maybe you don't need me for the rest of this. Maybe you're good. But I did make you a promise. And I'd like to see it through."

Coy stares down at her feet for a moment, sighs, and when she looks up again, the edges of her face have softened. She shakes her head at me. "I'm not mad at you for disappearing, Alyssa."

My eyebrows shoot up. "You're not?"

"Of course not." She waves a hand dismissively. "Are you kidding me? I don't exactly know what happened down there on the *Defiant*, but I can only imagine what it was like to be standing next to poor Owyn when he was killed. I imagine I might've bolted after that my own self. I'm upset because you didn't talk to me."

Oof. I feel that last part. And she's giving me an all-out, hurt-baby-animal look on top of it. Not fair, Coy. Definitely not fair.

"Look, you want to tell everyone in this chase to blow it up their hole, I'm on it," she says. "If you want to throw them two or three or even four middle fingers and run off to Nysus, I will loan you the money and cover your tracks. But you didn't even send me half a comm to let me know what happened. I didn't know if you were okay, if you were hurt, if someone had gotten you. That was unacceptable. Disappear on everyone else, but don't disappear on me. You got that, Farshot?"

"Dammit, Coy. You've got me feeling about one meter tall."

"Well, then, I didn't scold you enough. You should be feeling one *centimeter* tall, if anything."

"Leave off. I get the picture." I drop my hands, wrapping my arms around my stomach. "I'm sorry, Nathalia. I really am. I didn't mean to worry you."

She sniffs. "Well . . . I'll give you a pass this time. That was four Solari whiskey bottles you promised me, right?"

"You bitch. I'm hanging up."

Her laughter rings across the comms and bounces around the walls of my quarters. I love it. If you make Nathalia Coyenne laugh once, you want to do it every time you see her. It's the kind of laugh that just fills you up with gold.

"I saw you remembered the honey trick with those hellbeasts," I tell her as her laughter dies down. "Nice work."

"Can you believe it? Who knew that would come in handy in this of all things?" She drops down onto her bed on the far side of her room and groans. "I wonder how many more of these ridiculous challenges we're going to have to do. Three more? Ten more? What's the acceptable number of hoops to jump through to prove yourself as the leader of an empire?"

"Maybe it's a chase of attrition. Last one still running around is the one who gets it."

"If that's true, then I'm rightly screwed because there's no way that Setter Roy is giving up for anything short of death. Maybe not even then."

She's not wrong. He's always been pretty tenacious, even as a kid, but it seems to have gotten exponentially more intense since then. Not in a bad way, necessarily. But almost definitely in a way that's gonna give him a heart attack at a young age if he doesn't learn to unclench a bit.

"So . . . again, not that you need me or anything, but . . . how are you doing with your next clue?"

"Ah yes. That." She sighs and gets to her feet, coming over to the display panel. I can see her typing at something just to the side of the screen. "Well, I'm sure I'll have it figured out in a jiffy—you know how clever I am—but I suppose I won't say no to a little extra perspective on this."

There's a little beep from the comms that confirms a file was just received, and Coy gives me a devilish grin. "Have fun with this one, Farshot."

Welp. That's a bad sign.

I accept the file and pull it up, displaying it as a projection in the middle of my room:

An enormous string of numbers: 04371922516236092955257095087050.

And below that, one simple phrase: From the crown, I see it.

THIRTY-FOUR

"THAT IS A LOT OF EFFING NUMBERS."

Hell Monkey stands next to me, hands on his hips, staring at the three-dimensional projection of the clue Coy sent me. I called him pretty much immediately. If you're gonna unpack thirty-two non-sequential numbers and a mysterious phrase, you probably want every brain on board involved in it.

I catch myself gnawing on a thumbnail and quickly cross my arms over my chest. "Any ideas?"

"That *was* my idea. That this is a lot of effing numbers. That's it. That's the end of it."

I jam an elbow into his side. "Great. That isn't at all helpful."

"What did you expect?" He rubs at the sore spot, his big shoulders lifting in a shrug. "I'm good with numbers, but I like them in context, where they're related to something. Not just floating around all willy-nilly. What does Coy have so far?"

"Nothing. If she had any leads, why would she be needing us to look at it?" I step into the middle of the room, bringing my hands out in front of me. "Rose, give me full manual control of the image, please."

"Manual control initiated, Captain Farshot."

"Thanks, Rose, you're a peach."

"Has Coy done *anything* with it so far?" Hell Monkey asks, circling around the edge of the room. "Basic record searches?"

"Yes, she did. And it was totally simple and we're just trying to see if we can solve it again for funsies."

Hell Monkey glowers at me. I just give him a shrug and start manipulating the three-dimensional numbers in the air in front of me. Bringing them up to eye level, splitting them into groups and then into pairs and then combining them again.

"Rose," I call, and she chirrups a little note of acknowledgment. "I'm betting on you being a better ship's AI than Coyenne's shabby hunk of metal. You can kick the *Gun*'s ass, right?"

"I do not understand your query, Captain Farshot."

"We'll work on it. Just tell me: Can you find anything that might correspond with a string like this of thirty-two numbers? Something that could conceivably be applied to the crownchase. Like, not thirty-two numbers that's the high score of some person's bagautchi game or something."

"You never know. It could be pointing to a bagautchi score." Hell Monkey crouches in the corner, fingers threaded in front of him. He's still glowering at me. "Maybe it's the key to the universe."

I match his expression. "Maybe your face is."

"Inspiring words. Truly you are meant to sit on a throne of royalty."

Rose's voice cuts through our squabbling. "Captain Farshot, I can find nothing that fits your specifications."

"What about dividing it up?" H.M. asks. He pushes back onto his feet and walks right up behind me, reaching over my shoulder to fiddle with the number string. He splits it in two, sending one to either side of the room, and then he starts fussing with the latter half, dividing sixteen into two eights and then the eights into four sets of four and rearranging them and flipping around. "Rose, any leads if we divide it up more like this?"

I drift toward the rest of the string, the first set of sixteen numbers, as the AI responds overhead.

"Searching for potential combinations for numerical groups—sixteen sets of two, eight sets of four, four sets of eight, two sets of sixteen, and variations therein—as they could relate to a point or points connected to the crownchase . . ."

0437192251623609. Something about it bothers me. Like it's poking at the edge of my brain, saying, *You should know this, Alyssa, wake up.*

"There are five hundred seventy-three potential solutions to your query."

Hell Monkey growls. "Well, damn. What's the word, Captain? Should we make a list? Divide it up with Coy?"

"Yeah, okay," I say, half listening. "Call Coy. We've got work to do."

As soon as we get a response from the *Gilded Gun*, we start processing through the metric ton of options that Rose provided to us. Combinations that refer to manufacturing numbers and market codes, transactions and ship keys—we look at each one, try to plug in the numbers we have, see what it pulls up, and then cross it out when it's nonsense or set it to the side when it holds a scrap of possibility.

It's mind-numbing. I'm not a great student, to be honest, and I wander off a few times, going back to the display of the numerical string. Gods, I know there is *something* about this that I should recognize. It's like when you wake up and you're trying to remember the dream you were having and the feeling of it is still there, on the tips of your fingers, but you can't grab it all up before it slips away.

We're two hours in when Hell Monkey shouts, "LATITUDE!"

On the expanded display, Coy leans back in her chair, boots up on the desk, one eyebrow raised. "I'm sorry—are you having a fit?"

Hell Monkey makes a gesture at her. Not a nice one.

"Longitude and latitude, Coyenne. If you take out all the divisions and put the numbers together, they're sixteen numbers."

Oh shit. I jump up from where I've been sitting on my bed and wade into the middle of the projection again, spreading the numbers out in front of me at eye level. I'm staring at them so hard my eyes are burning, but I can feel it. The impression of something coming into focus.

"So, that could explain half of the numbers," Coy says, bringing her feet down to the floor.

I swipe aside everything except the first sixteen numbers, the ones that have been nagging at me for hours now, and I start to break them into pieces.

Drinn grumbles, rising to his considerable vilkjing height. "Need a planet or they're useless. Random longitude and latitude— could apply to anywhere."

Hell Monkey sighs. "Okay, that's true, but it's more of a start than we had five minutes ago so—ah!"

He jumps as I grab him suddenly by the shirtsleeve, bouncing a little on my toes. "I've got the rest of it," I say, my voice tight with excitement. "The last half is where you look on the planet, but the first half"—I bring the number string up so everyone can see—"is the planet you're going to. They're celestial coordinates, just like the Society gives us when we're headed someplace new. They're just stripped of all the spaces and labels and stuff. See?" I swipe my hands around, dividing up the projection again and bringing each part up one at a time. "0437—that's 4:37 a.m., the time of day to orient you. 192251—the right ascension: 19 hours, 22 minutes, 51 seconds. And the last part, 623609—that's the declination: +62 degrees, 36' 09". TA-DA!"

Drinn stares at the screen for a few seconds, then grunts and nods, which I choose to take as a celebratory hug. Hell Monkey whistles his appreciation, but then he holds up a finger.

"One problem, boss. Celestial coordinates need a point of origin. Without that, we don't know if we're aiming at the right planet."

Coy finally gets up, flinging an arm around Drinn's shoulder, and there's a broad grin on her face. "Now it's my turn to be clever. Because they've already told us where our point of origin is." With her free hand, she gestures at the screen, bringing up that phrase that I'd almost forgotten about. "'From the crown, I see it.' It's the kingship, darlings. We're starting at Apex."

THIRTY-FIVE

Stardate: 0.05.30 in the Year 4031
Location: Face-first in a cup of coffee. Also, hyperlight.

WE DON'T ACTUALLY HAVE TO FLY TO APEX.

I mean, I guess we could've, but it's way easier and less time-consuming to just have Rose calculate where the celestial coordinates are pointing based off the kingship's location. Beats adding several days of hyperlight to our trip.

It turns out the numbers line up with the planet Deoni, the fourth planet from the sun in the Roros system. Definitely a few days' journey by hyperlight—hello, vastness of space—which is fine because I'm not in a hurry to see what's planned for us once we get there.

That's not a knock on Deoni. The people of Deoni are almost universally great. I've been there for a couple different missions for the Society, and everyone I've met there has zero pretension. It's refreshing as hell. The climate of their planet, though, can be a little . . . let's call it challenging. It's dry, it's prone to massive dust storms, and almost everything that grows there is either spiky, bony, poisonous, or some combination of those three.

Basically it's an ideal setting for whatever the crownchase has cooked up next.

We've had some time to rattle around inside the *Vagabond Quick*. Try to figure out what to expect for the next round. I wake the mediabot up because I feel a little bad seeing it propped up in the corner of the bridge, thinking it's got no other point on here. Good ol' JR comes out swinging with the questions, and I give it one super-short interview about why I'm back before shooing it away to wander the ship and try to entertain itself. Hell Monkey spends most of his time fiddling around on the bridge, tweaking the controls on the conn, messing with the settings on all the different displays and viewscreens. I even catch him cleaning—he really hates being bored.

And me? I go find Uncle Atar.

It's occurred to me recently how little time I've spent—sober—dealing with his absence. Truly, seriously dealing with it.

Staring grief in the face isn't my forte. It requires cruising into uncharted stars with no shields, no guns, and comms channels fully open. That's not something I generally do.

But hey, I'm trying something new these days. Why not.

I keep to my quarters, and I start flipping through all the things I have left to connect me to Uncle Atar. His life, his work, our life together on the kingship for all those years.

There aren't a lot of actual physical mementos. I didn't take much when I left. I had just wanted to be shed of everything, but I'm kind of regretting it now. I wish I had something more tangible in the narrow little closet of stuff in my quarters. I unearth just about everything in there, dumping it out on the bed and the floor, wading through clothes and shoes and old plaques of commendation that I always meant to hang up somewhere but then never got around to it because who really wants to spend an afternoon trying to mount frames totally straight.

At the very back, in a dark, dusty corner, I finally find it: a box only about thirty centimeters long and fifteen centimeters wide. In it are a handful of childhood keepsakes. Proof that I hadn't been completely heartless when I'd set off for the stars. I'd stuck it back here and forgotten about it over the years.

On the very top is Gamgee, a stuffed blue-and-gray leviathan plushy, well-worn and faded from years of snuggles. He had been my favorite friend and sleeping buddy for most of my life, even after I had gotten too old to play with those kinds of things. I cradle him in my lap, running my thumbs over the patchy fur on his face. Gamgee had been here with me during my first nights on the *Vagabond Quick*, when the bigness of the universe had seemed ready to eat me up. But then I'd taken on my first engineer, and I'd gone from "girl by herself on a ship" to "captain." Captains needed to be adult and serious. They shouldn't be cuddling stuffed animals. So I'd stowed him away.

"Sorry, Gamgee," I whisper, giving his cartoonish face a kiss.

I tuck him underneath my arm and sort through the other items in the box.

A raw golden stone from the moons around Ysev—Charlie had gotten it for me. Ysev had seemed so far away back then, so exotic. I'd worn some of the jagged edges smooth from handling it over and over and over again. Picturing myself out here.

A few keepsakes Atar had given me that had been favorites of my mother's—a vial of perfumed oil from Nysus, a hallüdraen ceremonial knife passed down from my great-grandmother, a bangled armband made from dark blue iridescent metal found on Dalis. I'd had other things of hers, but these had been the ones I came back to again and again.

A handful of holodiscs, each holding images and recordings I had made or other people had made. One is of Atar and Charlie and me. One is of my mother that Uncle Atar had put together from his own images and recordings. One is of me and Coy and a few of the other prime family kids that Coy had given me as a gift for my fourteenth birthday.

And one is a holodisc that Uncle Atar had given me on the day I left. *A special message,* he'd told me. *For once you're up there in the stars.*

I hadn't watched it. I'd been afraid it would make me feel bad for jetting away, so I'd set it aside.

Better late than never.

I clear a space on my messy floor and set the disc down, sinking back onto my bed as a life-sized image of Emperor Atar Faroshti, ruler of the United Sovereign Empire, fills the space.

It hits me in the chest like a blaster shot. To see him there as he was a few years ago, looking tall and healthy and not gaunt and half–wasted away like he'd been the last time I saw him. The blue of his eyes is so bright, his face full and handsome instead of sunken in like a skeleton. He looks so real in this moment that I ache to hug him, to feel him put his arms around me and hold me and tell me that it's going to be okay, that I'm doing things right, that I'm still and always will be his little Birdie.

Tears spill out of the corners of my eyes as the holographic Atar smiles gently and starts to speak.

"Hello, Birdie. Or I suppose I should call you Captain Faroshti now. I'm glad you're listening to this. I was worried you wouldn't." I half laugh, half sob, squeezing Gamgee against my chest. "I know you've been itching to leave the kingship for a while now, and I can't blame you. Not when there is so much to see in this universe. I got to see it once, when I was young, before the war. Your mother and I traveled the stars, and it shaped so much of what she and I dreamed of for this empire. They are some of my fondest memories of Saya—crisscrossing the quadrant, staying up late and talking about our visions for the future. She was . . . such a brilliant fixed point in my world. I wish you could have known her." Holographic Atar pauses, a few tears slipping over his high cheekbones. "As much as those years meant to me, this has meant even more—raising you, seeing you grow and develop and reach for the edges of the horizon. It has been everything to me, Birdie. More than a thousand empires. Charlie and I will miss you very much. Please come back and visit sometimes. We love you."

The holodisc goes dark. But I don't notice. I pour every tear in my body into Gamgee's soft, tiny body.

I'm still crying, curled on my bed, when Hell Monkey comes to find me two hours later. He takes me in with one look and lies down next to me without saying a word. His big arms wrap around me, anchoring me to him, and he's my only source of gravity for the rest of the night.

THIRTY-SIX

Stardate: 0.05.31 in the Year 4031

Location: Approaching the planet Deoni with clean hair and clean pants—it's a miracle

WHEN ROSE'S VOICE SINGS OUT THE NEXT DAY TO say we're dropping out of hyperlight, I step onto the bridge clear-eyed, cleaned-up, showered and everything. I'm not even wearing my typical jumpsuit. I've put on my mother's favorite armband, wrapped around my right bicep, and I found a new coat when I was stuffing all my clothes back in my closet—Charlie's parting gift from when I first left Apex. Tunic-length, high-collared, sleeveless, fitted, in a deep blue fabric with etchings in faint gold. Its design is hallüdraen, made up for nobility and the house colors of Faroshti. It's the first time I've ever worn it, and it feels like armor somehow.

Hell Monkey raises an eyebrow when he sees me, and there's the ghost of a smile on his lips.

"Captain," he says, and the layers of meaning he manages to put into that one word make my heart flutter a little.

I grin at him and waggle my eyebrows. Ever the professional. "What's the situation? I was busy primping."

"Approaching the planet Deoni. I've already laid in coordinates to move us into orbit."

I step up next to him. My eyes are fixed on the sandy-brown planet in our viewscreen, but I barely see it. My mind is one hundred percent focused on the engineer beside me. "What would I do without you?" I say, but it's not a light, teasing question. It's an honest-as-hell question.

He doesn't answer. He just gives me a playful nudge with his elbow.

"Proximity alert," Rose calls.

I shoot a look at Hell Monkey, who shrugs. "Probably Coyenne just got here before us."

"Probably. Put it on the viewscreen, Rose. Identify."

There's a beat, and then Rose says, "Identification: Worldcruiser S576-034. No name on record. Currently registered to crownchaser Edgar Marius Tycho Voles."

My eyebrows shoot up so high they probably hit my hairline. "Well, that's a first." I slide into my jump seat, working the touch screens on the conn to do a sensor sweep of the other ship. I'm not sure what I'm expecting to find, exactly. I only get the basics: it's a worldcruiser, there's a person on board who's probably Edgar Voles–shaped, and there isn't any other biological life-form with him.

It's surprising to see him here, to say the least. There's no rule that says you have to perform the challenges that have been set out—otherwise I would've been disqualified the moment I ran for Shisso. The only real goal is to find the seal, however you choose to go about doing that. You can try to hang back and watch, ride people's tails, but the galaxy is a big-ass place and you can't track someone once they hop into a hyperlight lane. Which means the challenges are often your best bet to find the seal, so the less you participate in them, the less likely it is you'll be the first person to the finish line.

That's the theory anyway.

But here's Edgar, who hasn't shown his face anywhere near the crownchase for weeks, three steps ahead of us. That's not just odd—that's almost impossible. Unless he's got insider information. Or unless . . . he's had eyes on us this whole time. Something stealthy enough to evade all our internal sensors . . .

"Hell Monkey, start scanning the planet surface. There should be four different points that match the latitude-longitude coordinates you figured out, so we just need to sort out which one it is."

"On it, Captain."

I bend over my own section of the conn, using my body to try to hide the series of intensive commands I type into the dash. I could just tell Rose what to do, but my gut says I should go for subtle and secret here instead of shouting about it out loud.

Rose's voice breaks in. "Proximity alert. The Gilded Gun is dropping out of hyperlight."

"Coy knows the dance steps at this point. Rose, hail Worldcruiser S576-034 on a public channel."

She beeps in acknowledgment and half a second later comes back with, "There is no response, Captain Farshot."

"Send them a communication: Edgar Voles, this is Alyssa

Farshot. Nice to see your face finally. I wasn't sure you were going to come out and play with us."

I wait. I can hear the conn beeping as Hell Monkey's quick-moving fingers work on the planetary scans, and there's also the tick-tick and whirring sounds I'm getting used to associating with the mediabot. It's likely hovering around behind our seats, and I'm not really sure when it showed up on the bridge, but it doesn't matter at this point. I keep my eyes fixed on Voles's worldcruiser orbiting ahead of us, like if I stare hard enough, I can bore a hole in its alloy shell and see inside.

I've got that bad flutter in my stomach.

"Your communication to Worldcruiser S576-034 was received, Captain Farshot. There is no response. They have blocked additional incoming transmissions."

Ooookay. Not feeling friendly at all apparently. Fine.

The dash in front of me beeps as results scroll onto the screen, and I bite my tongue to keep from cursing out loud. That little asshole dumped some kind of mobile spy device onto our ship. A really clever one too, if it's managed to avoid detection this long. I should've suspected shit like this from a godsdamned Voles.

I kick Hell Monkey under the conn and tap at my screen to draw his attention to it. I watch as his eyes widen with realization. He looks at me, a question on his face, and at my nod, he slides out of his chair. I take over the planetary scan, one ear on Hell Monkey as he moves to the back of the bridge and climbs oh-so-quietly on top of the strategic-ops table. There's the pop of a ceiling panel coming free, a racket of scrambling and cursing, and then the thud of boots crashing down onto the floor.

"Hell Monkey?" I call over my shoulder. "Did you win?"

He reappears next to me, face a little flushed, holding a little mechanical device in his big hands. Several of its filament legs are gone, and its body is half-crushed. "Victory is mine."

"My hero," I say, fluttering my eyelashes at him. "Voles can suck it if he thinks he's gonna get to spy on us anymore."

He drops back into his seat. "How about Deoni? How's that looking?"

"Substantially less good. I can't pick up anything down there." I sit back a little, my gaze switching to the planet filling almost the entire background of the screen. "Rose, what's the current date down on Deoni?"

"It is currently the sixth day of the month of Cadon."

"Dammit!" I slam a hand down on the armrest of my jump seat, and Hell Monkey shoots me a side-eye.

"Something you want to share with the class, Captain?"

I gesture grumpily at the sandy swirls all over the planet atmosphere. "It's the middle of their high season. They've got sandstorms all over the place. No way we're getting a read on anything from up here. There's going to be atmospheric interference over eighty percent of the planet."

Hell Monkey sighs. "That explains why Voles is sitting up here. He's probably having trouble pinpointing where the beacon is too."

"Maybe." I chew on the inside of my cheek, staring at the world-cruiser and then at Deoni and then back again. "H.M., is one of the corresponding coordinates near Voles's orbital location?"

He checks the readout again. "Near-ish. Latitude 29.552570, longitude -95.087050. A ton of interference in that location. Can't tell if that's because of a sandstorm or something else. I can put together a work-around, but it's going to take time. A few hours probably."

"We don't have a few hours." I type in a quick message to Coy to let her know what I'm thinking, and her response is immediate: *Are you bloody well kidding me, Farshot?*

"Get yourself strapped in, Hell Monkey," I say, buckling my harness on and cracking my knuckles. "Edgar Voles is absurdly smart, but we've got one distinct advantage over him."

Hell Monkey sighs, but he's got a grin starting to stretch across his face. "And what's that, Captain?"

I wrap my hands around the *Vagabond*'s manual controls. "No godsdamned sense of self-preservation."

And then I rev the engines and punch it for the storm-covered surface.

CROWNCHASERS CONVERGE ON DEONI

Latest development marks the return of Farshot and a growing lead in the polls for Coyenne

VOLES VISIBLE FOR THE FIRST TIME SINCE THE CHASE BEGAN

Ardent crownchase watchers spotted signs of his worldcruiser in Deoni orbit hours before other chasers arrived

JENNA MEGA: "WHERE IS OUR JUSTICE?"

The Mega family matriarch releases an impassioned statement as the investigation into her son's death seemingly goes dark

ROY FAMILY REACTS TO HEIR'S STEADY SUCCESS

Insiders say the family sees Setter's position at the top of the polls as a good sign that public opinion on the Roys has shifted since the end of the Twenty-Five-Year War

DEONI, STANDARD ORBIT

IF ONLY EVERY CLUE TO THE CROWNCHASE HAD BEEN like the latest one.

As soon as Edgar Voles saw the string of numbers via the spider implanted on Nathalia Coyenne's ship, he and NL7 had processed possibilities, narrowed them down, and figured it all out. Well before any of the others. Which only served to reinforce what he already knew: he was better equipped than they were for the throne. He deserved to hold the seal. He ought to be at the top of any leaderboard.

But that's okay. All the clues and challenges are unnecessary noise. What matters is who is standing at the end, holding the seal. That is the fixed point that Edgar keeps his eyes on.

He'd been in orbit around Deoni for several hours before Faroshti had arrived. Never able to make a quiet entrance, that one. She had blared across his comms, completely distracting, especially when he was concentrating so hard on completing the last stage of his plans. Then the other one—Coyenne—had shown up, and logic dictated that the remaining two were sure to follow in short order. It was all very abrasive to have his space invaded by these new parties when he'd had all this quiet time to work.

They've arrived too late to be a true disruption, though. He's put what he wants into place already, an added challenge for the remaining contestants who are so eager to run every tightrope set in front of them. There is, after all, no rule against laying additional impediments in the paths of your fellow competitors. Something to trip them up. Maybe make them stumble.

He needs to wait on only one more result from the planet surface before he can leave orbit and put everyone behind him.

NL7 monitors the display. "The final probe is approaching the perimeter. Estimated time to interaction: four minutes, fifty-four seconds."

"Thank you, NL7. Prepare to jump to hyperlight on my mark." Edgar sends a secure transmission to his new ally and then leans back in his chair.

Such a small amount of time to wait in the grand scheme of things. . . .

VOLES ENTERPRISES HEADQUARTERS, HELIX

IT TAKES THIRTY STEPS FOR ME TO WALK ACROSS this lobby. About a hundred steps to walk all the way around the edges. And only about five minutes of pacing before I start to irritate the receptionist.

That's fine. We can both be irritated together.

Hell Monkey and I are supposed to be well on our way to Rhydin IV, but I got an urgent request from Dr. Wesley to make a quick stop here and pick up an item that William Voles had contacted her about. Some sort of family artifact he's requesting be analyzed in exchange for a big research donation. H.M. refused to set foot anywhere near Helix, so I'm here on my own, waiting and waiting for the senior Voles to acknowledge my presence.

I'm on my twenty-sixth circuit of the lobby space when the main doors whoosh open and in walks Edgar Voles, with his favorite android companion right beside him. He stops short when he sees me, visibly surprised.

I wave at him. It's very suave. "Hey, Edgar. How's it hanging?"

He flicks a glance at the android and then straightens his shoulders. "Alyssa. It's been a while."

Three years at least. I can't quite remember when it was that his father stopped bringing him to the kingship for quarter-council weeks. The fact is, even when William Voles had brought Edgar along, he hadn't let his son run around with the rest of us prime family kids. He'd always kept Edgar confined to their quarters or had him escorted around by strictly programmed nanny droids. And you don't start anything with a nanny droid.

"What are you doing here, Alyssa?" Edgar asks. The question is about as friendly as it sounds.

"Explorers' Society business. Your dad apparently wants our science folks to look at some heirloom? I'm just the messenger."

"Oh." Edgar's demeanor gets a bit less bristly. "Of course. Father is conducting business off-site, but I can get the item for you. Follow me."

I fall into step behind him and the android, and they lead me onto the high-speed lifts. Voles Enterprises is one of the tallest buildings on Helix, which is already known for its skyscrapers. William Voles's office is on the very top floor, surrounded by soaring windows, and I swear I can see the curve of the planet from this high up.

While Edgar goes to a safe concealed behind a bookshelf in the far corner, I wander over to a wall of display screens, trying to occupy myself so it doesn't look like I'm snooping for the combination or anything. The screens all have various shots of design schematics and diagrams for an android model I haven't seen before.

"New project you're working on?" I call over my shoulder.

There's a pause, and then Edgar says, "Oh, yes. That. Public suppression droids. They're extremely promising."

I'm not sure promising is the word I'd use for it. Judging by the specs, these things would be built like tanks and tricked out with all kinds of gas canisters and electroshock attachments and other "nonlethal" weapons that can still do a hell of a lot of damage. "They look kinda brutal."

The safe door shuts, and I turn to see Edgar carrying a long, flat metal box over to his father's desk. "They are designed to be quick and effective, yes," he says dismissively. "For the containment and dispersal of unruly mobs. My father's idea primarily, although he's letting me assist in the refinement of the prototype."

The note of pride in his voice at that last part is hard to miss. "Working your way up, huh?"

"Yes," he says, and the cold intensity in his voice sends a little shiver down my spine. "That is the plan."

He punches a complex code into a panel on the metal box, and it pops open. He raises the lid just enough to stick his hand in and extract a smaller box, square this time, with the same kind of number pad on the top of it. "Here you are. My father already packaged it to prevent any unauthorized tampering."

He's giving me a Very Significant Look, so I put on my biggest, most disarming smile. "Don't worry about me. I don't mess with the dusty relics—I just move them from point A to point B."

He doesn't smile back. He just stares at me and then the door and then me again, and says, "I trust you can see yourself out."

"Yup, sure can." I back away, shooting him a thumbs-up. "Great catching up, Edgar. Been a blast."

I can't get out of the building fast enough.

THIRTY-SEVEN

Stardate: 0.05.31 in the Year 4031
Location: Getting my ass handed to me by a bunch of spinning sand clouds

ABOUT TWO SECONDS AFTER THE INITIAL DESCENT, we hit the roiling wall of a sandstorm.

About two seconds after that, I'm regretting my whole decision. I mean, seriously, what was I thinking? I'd rather ride another flame tsunami any day. At least that gives you some good visuals—liquid flames curling around and in front of you, all orange and red and white and blue. Riding a Deoni sandstorm is just as precarious, but instead you're staring out at swirling, endless dark beige. My jaw throbs from clenching it so hard, and my arms and hands ache with the effort of trying to hold the *Vagabond Quick* on course.

The wind roars over us. So many grains of sand pound into the ship's outer hull that it sounds like we're trapped in a tunnel of white noise.

"Definitely got a signal now," Hell Monkey calls over the barrage. "Beacon is dead ahead of us. Just hold it steady."

"Yeah, sure," I growl. "No problem. This is easy stuff."

A gust of wind hits us hard on the port side, and we whirl, spinning aft to stern. I scramble to right us again, cursing loudly. Hell Monkey works frantically at the comms, trying to reset our course. Our sensors are freaking out all over the place, and I almost miss the big dark shape heading straight toward us in the murk. I jam the controls forward, swooping us down and out of the way at the last possible second as a massive creature drifts over us, keening as it rides the currents with apparently little concern for the violent winds.

"Holy shit, Hell Monkey, it's a storm whale! I've never seen—"

"Any other time, Alyssa! Literally, any. Other. Time."

I wrench the *Vagabond* around, getting her nose pointed in the right direction again, angling northeast, trying to zigzag her bulk through this mess so we're not bucking the winds the whole time.

The ship shudders in a very disconcerting way.

"Captain Farshot," Rose says, her calm voice really at odds with the shit we're dealing with here. "The thrusters are reaching critical energy expenditure. They can maintain the current output for only two more minutes."

Because that's what I want. To be stuck in the middle of a Deoni sandstorm with no engine power left. That's a quick way to get yourself spun like a top and then slammed into something big and immovable.

"Hell Monkey, gun the sublight engines."

He shoots me a look. "It's considered bad manners to flash your sublights in atmo."

"We're kilometers above the surface, and everyone on the

surface is bunkered down anyway. The *Vagabond* can take it. Give me one quick pulse, see if we can get clear of this mess."

"You're the boss." He hits the gas (so to speak), and we're both rocked backward as the ship takes a sudden leap forward, a blaze of radiant energy coming off her engines.

"Three-second hold!" I yell . . . and then I pray.

One . . . It's all whirling storm in front of us.

Two . . . Still violent. Still sandy.

Thre—

We spin out into clear air, and Hell Monkey drops us back to thrusters immediately. There's open sky above us, a slight haze over the sun but nothing else. Below is the brown, dynamic landscape of Deoni, being carved into new shapes by the storm activity, and behind us, a dark, swirling wall of sand.

But it's what's ahead of us that'll really knock your pants off.

Hovering in the air are thousands of large oval-shaped devices, constructed of some kind of matte black alloy, each almost five meters in diameter. There are no lights on them, no sign of a power source save for thin interlocking beams of red light that connect them all together into an enormous, spherical laser web. The spaces between them look big enough to drive a worldcruiser through. Maybe even two side by side. It's hard to tell.

"What. The. Hell."

Hell Monkey works the touch screens on the conn, running sensor sweeps and frowning and shaking his head at the readout. "This is definitely where the beacon is. I'm getting a reading on it, but it's somewhere inside all that."

I rub at the furrow that feels like it's permanently imbedding into my forehead. "Why didn't we pick up any of this—whatever this is? There's so many of them and the storm is clear here. We should've picked up something."

"It's not the storm blocking signals in there. It's . . . whatever the hell is inside it," Hell Monkey grumbles. "I don't know. These readings don't make any sense."

Rose beeps a proximity alert, and Coy is on the comms a moment later. "Are you seeing this, Farshot?"

"I'm seeing it," I tell her. "And that's about all I got. If you're feeling inspired, I'm open to it."

I can hear Drinn's rolling-boulders voice overhead. "Captain, there's something moving inside the field."

"Can you identify it?" Coy asks.

"Oblong, about two meters in length—about the same size and shape of a standard-sized probe. It's approaching the massive energy signature in the center of the sphere."

"I see it too," Hell Monkey confirms. "It's weird. Got some kind of modified exterior. Like a crystalline structure. I'm not getting much more than that. It—" He sits back. "It's gone. Hit that big energy field in the middle and just disappeared."

Drinn speaks up again. "Captain, I just got a notification from our orbital sensor. Edgar Voles is leaving orbit and preparing for hyperlight. And two new worldcruiser signatures are being detected approaching the system."

"Orso and Roy." Coy sighs. "Our head start is quickly disappearing."

I scowl at the sphere filling our windows. "We never had a head start on this one. Edgar Voles was way ahead of us."

Hell Monkey raises his eyebrows. "You think he did this?"

Yes, I do. But that's entirely a gut instinct and not something I have solid evidence for. It seems impossible that someone would be able to construct something like this and not have it take days, but I wouldn't put it past a Voles. Not for a second.

"I think he's been off the radar for a while, and he's smart as hell." I pull up our specs, inputting coordinates as I type. "Rose, prep two of our standard probes and launch them toward the center of that sphere."

"Understood, Captain Farshot. Launching in three . . . two . . . one . . ."

They shoot forward, twin trails of green light streaking through the gloomy sky. For just a moment, as they close in on the perimeter of the sphere, I think maybe I'm wrong, that it isn't what it looks like.

And then two of the devices wobble, break off from the web, and fly toward the probes.

They explode. Two mini balls of fire, raining half-melted metal parts on the ground below.

"This isn't a challenge," I growl. "Edgar built a minefield."

THIRTY-EIGHT

THE STRATEGIC-OPS AREA OF THE BRIDGE IS JUST one big projected image right now.

Hell Monkey made several in-depth sensor sweeps, and Rose reconstructed a three-dimensional layout of the maze. I'm crouching in front of the glowing picture right now, staring up at it, rocking onto my toes and back to my heels again and again. Just . . . trying to think our way out of this.

The whole sphere is several thousand cubic kilometers around, made up of thousands of these devices that—charmingly—seem to be magnetically drawn to things like probes and the outer hull of worldcruisers and other things I wouldn't want to be inside when they hit. About ten kilometers in, it looks like the bombs stop and there's an open core. We can't see much more than that from the viewscreen because there's some kind of fog cloud filling it. And all Hell Monkey has been able to pick up is "massive energy signature, definitely not normal," and then it's a lot of shrugging and grumbling.

"Proximity alert," Rose calls out, and I don't wait for the rest of it because I've been expecting this one. I leap over to the dash and slam on the conn, opening a communication channel to the two worldcruisers dropping in to join the party.

"Faye, Setter, this is Alyssa—do not approach that sphere. Do you copy? Those things are bombs with a magnetic propulsion bonus. Don't get near it."

I wait, my heart slamming against my sternum in the silence, all my nerves vibrating. And then:

"Very generous sharing, Farshot," Faye croons. "Are we just supposed to take your word for it?"

I throw my hands in the air. Not that they can even see me— we're on audio only—but still. "You think we're sitting around back here just for giggles? Ask Coy. She saw it too."

Setter's deep, serious voice comes across next. "That's a bit pointless given that you and Nathalia are working together. She would obviously corroborate your account."

"It's all right," Coy says, joining the conversation in one of her more affected drawls. "Let them throw themselves at that thing. It only serves to make my life easier."

"Nobody is throwing themselves at an—UGH!" I wave my hands at the *Vagabond* viewscreen. "Rose, initiate visual communications on-screen. Everybody show their damn faces, okay?"

Coy responds immediately, appearing as she prefers people to see her: leaning back in her chair, boots up on the dash, like this is a dice table and not a crownchase. Setter is next, sitting in his jump seat just as proper as I would expect, elbows on his armrests, hands folded in his lap. Faye finally appears on-screen, and she's . . . cleaning her blasters.

I cross my arms over my chest. "Really, Faye? Don't you think that's a little obvious?"

"I don't know what you're talking about, Alyssa." She points one at the screen, making a show of pretending to ensure the barrel is clear, and then she flashes a big grin. "I'm just performing regular maintenance on my firearm, as is recommended."

"Okay, yahoos." I drop into my own seat and tap a few buttons on the conn so the projected scan of the sphere floats in front of me. "We have a magnetized minefield and a beacon with a mysterious something-or-other inside it, and it's all looking a bit dicey, to be honest."

Setter raises his eyebrows at me. "You want us to all work together on this? That's not really the spirit of the crownchase."

I shrug. "A momentary pause where we combine our resources, and then we go right back to punching each other in the face over a tiny hunk of metal that we may or may not find. That's feasible, right?"

"I don't see what the big deal is," says Faye, flipping a hand at the projection. "It's just another challenge, like the others, so there's probably a way out or through or whatever."

Hell Monkey leans over the back of my chair. "Except we don't think this trap was laid by the crownchase."

Setter doesn't say anything, that stoic expression not even wavering. I swear to the stars he's secretly an otari. Faye drops her blaster, leaning forward on her elbows.

"No? Another party, then? Not"—her eyes slice over to me—"not someone like that person from the *Defiant*?"

That sends a little shiver down my spine, but I shake my head.

"No. Not that. Edgar Voles was in orbit when Coy and I got here, and we found some surveillance toys of his creeping around our ship."

"If you believe my mother's little birds," Coy chimes in, "he was lurking around here for quite some time." She flicks a wrist, brings an image into the air—a headline from the *Daily Worlds*—and reads it aloud. "'Ardent crownchase watchers spotted signs of his worldcruiser in Deoni orbit hours before other chasers arrived.' Very promising."

Setter tilts his chin up, sucking in a breath through his teeth. "That is something I do not like. I was hoping Voles would fail to make any significant move until it was too late."

Coy laughs. "That sounds downright impractical of you, Setter. Are you feeling all right?"

In the viewscreen, Honor Winger slides onto the armrest next to Faye and murmurs something I can't hear. But it doesn't matter because a second later, Faye bursts out, "That's a good point— you're all saying he just sat in orbit and that's it? He didn't come down here to the beacon at all?"

"Not that we saw." I sigh, rubbing hard at the bridge of my nose. I think I'm getting a migraine. I've never had a migraine before, but I might be on the cusp of a brand-new pain window. "He took off just before you two dropped out of hyperlight, right after . . . Gah!" I sit up suddenly and grab Hell Monkey by the shirtsleeve. The look on his face is very alarmed. If I were anyone else but me, he'd probably slug me. "He left right after that weird thingy disappeared into all that stuff in the middle."

Setter shifts to the edge of his seat. "A thingy?"

The word sounds so weird coming out of his mouth that I almost laugh. Very loudly. But instead I nudge Hell Monkey, who says, "Drinn picked it up. Probe-shaped, but it had some kind of outer casing that was weird—"

"Send me your sensor readouts. Both of you." Setter's already fixated on the conn, fingers moving across the dash, but he pauses and shakes his head. "I mean . . . I'm sorry . . . I think I have an idea. Something I read about recently. Prototype ship modifications. Just . . . send me those. Please. If you can. I—yes."

Faye snorts. "Nice out, Roy."

Hell Monkey drops down into his jump seat and transmits the information. And then there are several quiet, awkward moments as we wait for who-the-hell-knows. Whatever Setter is figuring. Probably something important. I hope.

Faye whistles a few notes. "Anyone want to play Triple Dares?"

"Ooh!" Coy pulls her feet off the dash, her face lighting up, but I cut her off quickly.

"I'd like to point out that there are no med facilities open anywhere near here and I'm not flying anybody to one, so put a cork in it, Coy."

Grumbling, she slouches down in her chair again.

"I think I have it," Setter says at last, saving all of us from more thumb twiddling. "I think I have a way for us to get through the minefield."

THIRTY-NINE

WE HAVE THREE HOURS.

That's our best estimate as to when the area we're in is gonna get slammed by a new sandstorm, so that's our window to get this situation handled. I don't want to fly into that minefield half-cocked under calm conditions, and I definitely don't want to do it with gale-force winds and a blanket of swirling sand screaming across the *Vagabond*'s prow.

Setter says that probe thingy Edgar sent through had been wrapped in some kind of superconductor material so it wasn't magnetic like usual. He thinks we can all modify our worldcruiser shields to do something similar—put off a super-unattractive vibe to the mines—but the problem is that, individually, it would take seven or eight hours for one of our ship AIs to calculate and make the adjustments needed.

We don't have that time. Which is why I suggested networking. We could link all our AIs together, and it would cut the processing time to two hours. Hell Monkey said he has a few tricks to shave another half an hour off that, at least.

So—and I gotta say, I never saw this moment coming when this chase started—we used docking cables to pull our ships into a tight little diamond-shaped cluster and got our computers all talking to each other. We even combined our abilities to root out the rest of Edgar's spiders from everyone's ships before we networked, so he has zero eyes on any of us anymore. Like, hey, that's some team-work, right? Not bad for a bunch of politicians' kids. But I guess when one person spies on you and lays a minefield between you and the biggest prize in the universe, it really inspires you to lay aside your differences.

That was almost an hour ago. The engineers—Hell Monkey, Drinn, Honor, and Sabela—are off somewhere, I think on the *Gilded Gun*, making the modifications to help the AIs along. I swear they're all like kids at a Ballarian candy market, crawling around, half in and half out of panels, giving each other shit about how poorly the other worldcruisers are being maintained. I got the distinct impression that I was more in the way than not, so I retreated to the galley and a strong pot of coffee. Rose is off-line right now, all power diverted to the shield modifications, but I need something to do and I'm not totally devoid of cooking skills. So I make a BEC. I'm not hungover, but my stomach kind of feels that way. Jittery, unsettled. Like I got the Eastern Sea sloshing around in there.

You gotta tamp that crap down with bacon grease.

I'm sliding the sandwich onto a plate when I hear a voice behind me.

"That smells positively sinful."

I smile, but I don't turn around. Just pull out another plate and some more eggs. "Welcome aboard the *Vagabond*, Coy. You get bored over there?"

She snorts. "Like you aren't climbing the walls here? I tried to help, but Drinn told me to go away. I get the feeling they're rather in their groove."

"Same. I hope they can wrap it up soon. I've been watching sensors, and there's definitely a storm starting to develop to the northeast."

I turn, one plate in either hand, and catch sight of a figure hovering around the galley door, arms crossed over her chest. "Hey, Faye."

She sighs and steps forward, dropping her hands to her hips. "Honor said it sounded like you two were over here. She suggested I . . . socialize."

A quick glance at Coy, who looks amused as hell, and then I hold out the plates. "Well . . . make yourself useful, then."

She takes them, though she makes sure to give me a look like it's the biggest inconvenience of her life. Faye always gonna be Faye. I dig back into our food supply, coming up with more sandwich ingredients, and I'm halfway through another one when suddenly there is a person just there, practically right up on my elbow. I yelp and jump about six feet.

"Holy hell, Setter! Don't do that!"

He shrugs. "I wasn't being particularly stealthy in my approach."

"I saw him come in," Coy calls from the table with a mouth half-full of food.

"Thanks, Coy." I poke Setter in the chest and put two more eggs on to cook. "Stuff like this is why I didn't like to play with you when we were kids."

He huffs a little laugh. "You didn't like to play with me, Alyssa, because I always pointed out when you were breaking the rules."

"Well, that too. It's not like we were committing murder or anything. A little rule breaking is healthy for kids."

"For kids like you and Coy, maybe. Not for me." There's no trace of any kind of laugh now in his quiet voice. "I had—*have*—to walk a very fine line in the Roy family."

That stops me, and I glance at him. His expression is stoic. But his eyes are sad. I wish I had something I could say, but my mind has gone blank. So I just shove a plated sandwich into his hands and say, "Go eat something. Take a load off."

It strikes me a few minutes later, as we're all sitting there eating (with JR lurking around and getting a shot of all this heartwarming action), that this is one of the weirdest moments of the crownchase by far. It's been a bit since so many of us were in the same room. The last time was probably at Coy's party on Yasha. And even then, we'd still been missing Faye.

Like we're missing Owyn now.

"You broke the rules once," Faye says suddenly, cutting through the silence. Her eyes are on Setter, who bolts down the food in his mouth before saying, "I'm sorry?"

"I remember. You did break the rules." A grin is growing on her face. "When we were racing on that empty storage deck on the kingship."

As soon as she says it, the memory floods back to me, and I laugh, tipping my head back. "Oh gods, she's right. What were we—nine, ten?"

"You were nine," says Coy with a wink. "The rest of us were ten.

Owyn was eleven and just hit a growth spurt and would *not* shut up about how fast he could run. 'I beat every otari in my recruitment class—*twice!*'"

"'While I was sick!'" adds Faye.

"'And carrying a bag of lost puppies!'" crows Coy.

I'm still laughing and now Coy is laughing. Setter shakes his head down at his plate. But I'm sitting next to him and I can see the little ghost of a smile creeping across his mouth.

"And we all called bullshit on him and challenged him to race us," says Faye.

"Of course we did," I say, turning to Setter. "And he flattened all of us—except you. You asked him the specific parameters of the race, what exactly constituted a win. And Owyn said, 'First one around the deck.' That was it. So he took off running, and you . . . went over, broke the lock on a hovercart, and zoomed past him like he was standing still."

Faye has started giggling now. "He was so mad. Fire-coming-off-his-head mad. I think it's the only time I ever saw him like that."

Setter sits up and shrugs, his grin obvious now. "He didn't say it had to be on foot. He should've been more specific."

Coy snorts, which makes the rest of us laugh harder, and for a moment, I'd swear we were all kids again.

Setter carefully brushes crumbs off the table and onto his plate as the laughter starts to die down. "I still owe you one," he says, nodding at me. "For taking the blame for the broken lock."

I wave his words away. "Eh. They never would've believed it was you anyway. They were used to me doing stupid crap like that."

Setter's wristband beeps an alert, and he frowns down at it, then swipes it up to project a visual display so the whole table can see it.

It's a *Daily Worlds* breaking-news bulletin. A correspondent stands on the kingship, talking urgently to the camera drone hovering in front of them.

". . . all those just joining us, spokespeople from the kingship announcing that they're suspending all ongoing investigations surrounding the death of crownchaser and prime family heir Owyn Mega and the unknown assailant that invaded the crownchase, citing concerns about internal security violations. This comes after days of silence regarding Mega's murder and public outcries for justice—"

Faye reaches over and smacks Setter's wristband, cutting off the feed. "I'm full up on bullshit right now, thanks."

Setter shakes his head. "I just don't understand. This is a threat to the crownchase—to all of us. Why wouldn't the kingship want to complete their investigation?"

I snort into my mug. "Maybe they don't consider it a threat. Maybe it's a bonus."

Faye slumps back, crossing her arms. "They won't be able to put it off forever. Not with the Megas. Jenna will light their asses up."

"You'd be surprised what they can do," Coy says, her voice quiet. "Whoever controls the kingship holds a lot of keys to a lot of doors."

I scan each of their faces—all the laughter gone, replaced by hollowness (Setter), sharpness (Faye), or a little of both (Coy). I tap the table, drawing their eyes.

"They won't hold the kingship forever. One of us will. So let's decide now: whoever wins this thing will find out who killed Owyn and make them pay. Agreed?"

I wait as Setter nods, then Faye. Coy nods as well and pulls a little metal flask out of the back of her belt. She pours a bit of what's inside into her coffee and then does the same for us. Then she holds her mug in the air and says, "To Owyn Mega. May he ride with the war gods forever."

"To Owyn Mega," the rest of us echo.

Tears sting the backs of my eyes. I swallow them down with the bitter taste of coffee and the burn of alcohol.

The clomping of boots fills the corridor, and a moment later, Hell Monkey leans in the galley doorway. He nods at the others, but his eyes find mine immediately.

"I know that look," I say, swinging my legs out of my seat. "That's your *there's good news and bad news* look."

He laughs a little, rubbing at his shaved head. "Well, the good news is that the shield modifications are complete. The bad news"—he looks around me to the other three—"is we're about to have to take this truce to a whole new level."

FORTY

"WE'RE STUCK TOGETHER," HELL MONKEY TELLS US as soon as the other engineers have joined us. "We managed to network the ships and fix the shields so they'll repulse those mines, but it's a hard manual override."

"We had to do some of this rewiring with actual, physical wires," adds Sabela, shifting her weight forward in her hoverchair. "And if we drop those so we can spread out—poof. It's all gone."

Okay . . . Okay, this is gonna be . . . different. I pace the room, tapping my hands against my legs, trying to process. "Can we fly like this? Like, in the formation we're in now?"

Hell Monkey shrugs. "If we put some extra clamps on the cables, one or two worldcruisers could probably tow the others."

"One," grumbles Drinn. "In that minefield, you want one set of coordinates, one trajectory, one person's hands on the wheel."

Sabela nods. "It's a good point. Don't try to stick two threads through one eye."

Honor shakes her head, sighing. "You and your sewing metaphors."

Sabela turns her head and winks. "It's called having a hobby,

Winger. You should try it."

"I don't like this," says Faye. "Four worldcruisers stuck together—that's a four-times-bigger target to hit."

"But one with shields working for it rather than against it," points out Coy.

Setter tents his fingers together, frowning. "Will we have access to our ship AIs?"

"Limited capacity only," says Sabela. "What we're asking them to do right now is taking a lot of their . . . concentration, so to speak. They'll be able to maintain some basic ship functions, but much more than that and it'd be like trying to cook a meal and juggle at the same time."

Honor's mouth quirks in a wry grin. "So if you were hoping for any help plotting a course through the enormous laser web, you're out of luck. All trajectories and coordinates will have to be done by hand."

Coy whistles, long and low. "Now that's bad news. You should've led with *that*. I haven't manually navigated a course in ages. I'm not even sure I remember how."

"I do." I don't say it very loud, but those two words cut through the chatter. All eyes turn to me, and I hold my chin a little higher. Because I can't network a ship's computer or reprogram a shield generator or even process my own basic emotions, but this? This I can do. "I know how to chart a course, and I can get us to the other side. Get back to your ships. Get your cannons warmed up just in case. If this goes south, we're going out swinging. And if we make it through, we'll part ways on the other side. Got it?"

I sweep a look at everyone—crownchasers and engineers—and I'm not sure for a second who is going to listen and who is going to give me the finger. But one by one, starting with Coy, they nod and disperse, and pretty soon it's just me and Hell Monkey again.

He cracks half a smile, but I can see it takes work. "Commanding always looks good on you, Farshot."

Shrugging, I stride past him and head for the bridge. "Let's see how long I can hold on to it. By the time we get into the middle of this thing, they might seriously regret falling in behind me."

Hell Monkey is right on my heels, almost bumping into me when I stop by the strategic-ops table. "Do you know?" he asks in a low voice. "What's at the center of the minefield?"

I pull up a projection of the navigational chart for the surrounding area and then sweep a look around, checking to ensure our resident mediabot isn't close enough to hear me. It's on the bridge, but not right on top of us, so I angle my head away from it and drop my voice.

"I have an idea. But"—I exhale and sag a little—"it's ridiculous, H.M. Like it shouldn't be anywhere on my sensors because it's not actually possible, but . . ."

He nods. "But Voles's probe went in there and disappeared, so where did it go?"

I straighten and grab a tablet from a holder on the wall, pulling up the formulas I'll need to plot a safe(ish) course. "This could all be a real big mistake."

"We could do what Voles did. Just send a probe. It'll just . . . take a few more hours to modify one."

I shake my head, scribbling on the tablet surface with my fingertip. "We're already behind. Time to get bold. And a little stupid."

Hell Monkey grins. "Aye, Captain."

By the time the other crownchasers report in over the open comms channel ten minutes later, I'm ready. Sitting in my jump seat, harness buckled, hands on the controls. I know she's "just" an AI, but it's weird and somehow extra quiet without Rose's voice. Not like she's talking at us all the time, but she's usually always there when we call out. Like an incorporeal aunt or something.

I take a deep breath, flex my fingers, and then propel the *Vagabond* forward.

Stars and gods, she feels different like this, towing three other ships behind her. It takes a minute for me to adjust to the weight and the drag and the awkward size. Which is a minute too long because it throws my course off and we almost hit one of those lasers right off the bat and blow our asses sky-high. Hell Monkey sucks in a breath as we come . . . this . . . close . . .

And then we're past. Only, like, twenty more of those to go. No big.

The laser lines cast weird slices of red light across the bridge as I ease our bulky shape past the next set of mines. It's so quiet that I swear I can hear the other chasers breathing.

Faye's voice blurts out over the comms, making me jump. "It's like walking through a damn cemetery."

"Faye!" I snap. "That scared the living hell out of me!"

Coy jumps in immediately because of course she does. "I thought we'd all agreed not to talk. Is that not true? Are we talking now? Because I would feel much better—"

"This is an extremely delicate situation," Setter says, sounding like a disapproving teacher. "It would be better to maintain a level of quiet—"

"Oh, boo on you, Roy, you'd have us all as quiet as Carnoghlian monks all the time—"

Faye pipes in with a comment that I only half hear because I'm trying to keep from clipping a laser with the *Gilded Gun*'s keel, but the sound of their bickering actually relaxes me. Which might be kind of weird. But it helps take a little of the pressure off my mind. Like putting on white noise or something to help you zone out.

We're about halfway across when Hell Monkey says, very quietly, "Not to be that guy, but can you go any faster?"

I give him one hell of a side-eye. "Yes, this definitely seems like something I should rush."

"I just got a ping off our sensors. Our good luck is running out. There's a sandstorm moving in fast."

Shiiiiiiiiiiiiit. I put a little more oomph in our thrusters. Just a little. Going much faster than this would put us at risk. The four of us all clumped together means it's a much tighter squeeze than one alone, but hey. At least there aren't any mines flying at us yet.

"How far away is the edge of the storm?"

"Seven and a half minutes. I don't think we'll get much more time than that."

"So much for that three-hour window." It's gonna be close. It took us about ten minutes to make it halfway through, and it's gonna get even tighter before we break clear. Hell Monkey puts a countdown clock in the upper corner of the viewscreen and I keep an eye on it as we get closer . . . and closer . . .

At a minute and a half left, I put a call out over the channel. "Coy. Faye. Setter. Your cannons all ready to go?"

"Of course," Coy says. "Why? Are you worried?"

"Check your sensors. Take a peek north." I glide the ships to a stop, taking a deep breath, wiggling my fingers to loosen some of the tension that's been building in them. Next to me, Hell Monkey pulls up the *Vagabond*'s gun controls.

Faye lets out a string of curses across the channel, and Coy joins her on some of the more colorful ones.

"That's an enormous storm," Setter says, very calmly. "Sabela, how far away—"

"Five hundred meters. It's gonna be on us in twenty-five seconds."

There are two rings of bombs and a hundred meters between us and the center of this minefield. I don't know what's inside it— there's some kind of cloud or fog concealing the core—but I know that if I lean on the thrusters, even dragging three other ships, I can get us clear in ten seconds.

As long as we don't get exploded to death.

"Weapons hot, folks. Shoot those things down before they hit us."

I don't wait for feedback. As soon as I see Hell Monkey nod, I floor it.

I clip a laser line almost immediately out of the gate. I mean, it's not like our current configuration is set up for dexterity, especially not when we're going for speed. The ships twist a little with the sudden change of speed and—bam. The port side of the *Deadshot* runs through part of the web and this horrible wailing siren fills the air.

"LIGHT IT UP!" Faye hollers, and then all I hear is the thud of cannon fire and the roar of an explosion. The shock wave slaps against the side of us, knocking us farther offtrack, and I slam down on the thrusters, pushing them to accelerate faster.

Yelling from Coy and Setter. More alarms and wailing and cannons.

Two more mines explode, rocking us around on violent air currents.

We're fifty meters away, but it feels like we're standing still. Faster, dammit. FASTER.

Hell Monkey curses and scrambles at the gun controls, catching a mine dropping straight down on us at the last second and blasting it into nothing. The concussive force slams hard into the *Vagabond*'s dorsal—sparks flying, metal groaning. The red emergency lights start to flash.

Ignore it, Farshot. Almost there. Almost there . . .

The viewscreen goes white for a second as we hit the edge of that cloud-like something or other, and then . . . we're through.

The space around us is open air, clear of mines or laser webs or anything else except two things, both about fifty meters away.

A floating beacon.

And a wormhole.

"I don't fucking believe it," breathes Hell Monkey in awe, his eyes practically bugging out of his head.

I don't either. Suspecting it is one thing, but seeing it is a whole other. I check the sensors, but they're telling me exactly what my eyes are. Someone or something managed to defy every law of physics I know and construct the entrance to an artificial wormhole inside the atmosphere of Deoni. It's bordered by these intermittent metal globes, like maybe that's what's projecting it? Or just containing it? I don't honestly know and I don't really have time to find out because there's ten seconds left before that sandstorm hits and according to our sensors, half a dozen of the mines we triggered are still flying toward us.

The other crownchasers are filling up the comms, yelling—about the bombs, about the storm, about the actual real-life wormhole dead in front of us—but I don't hear any of it. I hear the distant boom of more cannons blasting into the minefield and see the numbers ticking down on the viewscreen.

Very smoothly, very deliberately, I reach over and flip on the sublight engines.

As we're burning across the open space, a whole world of chaos closing in on us, I hear Setter yell, "ALYSSA FARSHOT, ARE YOU TRYING TO GET US ALL KILLED?"

And then we hit the entrance of the wormhole. And it's all just darkness and silence.

IS THE END IN SIGHT?
As the polls tighten, experts say the crownchase may be entering its final stages

WHAT IS HAPPENING ON DEONI?
With four crownchasers now down on the storm-riddled planet, we analyze what outcome viewers should expect to see

"JUSTICE FOR OWYN" PETITION ROCKETS TO 3 BILLION
The kingship responds with a statement declaring that "policy will be dictated by the needs of the empire, not the will of a mob"

WEAPONS MANUFACTURER MISSING ITEMS, POSSIBLE THEFT
Reports say that at least one ship and an array of other potentially dangerous devices have disappeared from a Mega facility on Rava VI

WORLDCRUISER S576-034, IN HYPERLIGHT

EDGAR HAD CONSIDERED GOING THROUGH THE WORM-hole himself. After he'd done the requisite reconnaissance, of course, and ensured not only that the structure was stable but that it led to the same location each time. He'd sent three probes in over several hours while he'd implemented the minefield his new allies had procured for him. The first two had taken an hour after passing the perimeter before they started transmitting—both from the same set of coordinates—but he'd wanted a third data point to make sure. Wormhole travel was tricky at best, and he couldn't afford a misstep. Especially not now. Not when he'd lost his biggest advantage in the chase so far.

Edgar paces in front of the monitors that used to be linked to his spiders. They're all dark now. He hadn't noticed Alyssa finding the first one—he'd been distracted trying to finish the minefield—but he'd watched as the rest of the crownchasers had rooted them out of their ships and destroyed them one by one, working together like a cohesive team. The thought puts an unpleasant, bitter taste on the back of his tongue that he can't quite swallow away.

He has no need for sour memories from childhood. It doesn't matter now.

"Incoming transmission, Edgar Voles," says NL7. "The third probe."

Finally. "Do the coordinates match?" he asks as he joins the android at the strategic-operations table.

"It does. It seems to have exited in the same proximity as the other two."

He sucks in a deep breath, not sure whether he feels elated or frustrated. On the one hand, he knows for certain where the wormhole leads. On the other hand, it will take him around six hours at hyperlight to reach that system. It could potentially put him far behind the other crownchasers, if they are able to make it past the minefield he'd left.

But then again, it's not as if he doesn't have a contingency plan.

"NL7, initiate hyperlight. Maximum possible speed." He sits down in his chair and taps out a message.

Coordinates confirmed. I will meet you in that system in six hours and thirty-seven minutes. The others are in pursuit. Be prepared to encounter any and all of them.

The response is swift and abrupt.

WE WILL CLEAR THE WAY FOR YOU.

NORTHWEST RECEPTION ROOMS, THE KINGSHIP, APEX

"ALYSSA FAROSHTI, YOU'RE GOING TO GET US ALL in trouble," Setter grumbles in my ear.

I shoot him a glare over my shoulder. "No one asked you to come, Setter."

We're crammed into a narrow service passage, peeking into the crowded reception rooms where most of the elite of the empire are mingling and drinking and being boring. My uncles are in there somewhere too, but I'm not looking for them. Actively trying to avoid them is more like it.

"Seriously, Setter, it's Triple Dares." Faye moves up from the back, squeezing past Owyn and Coy so she can get a look at the room. "If you're not here for some trouble, why are you playing?"

She presses close beside me as she scans the people, and my heart flutters. It's been doing that a lot lately when Faye is near. I look back at Coy, who winks at me and gives me a double thumbs-up. I'm tempted to strangle her.

"Over there," Faye says, pointing to a table in a corner by the windows. There are rows of delicate flute glasses sitting on top of it, and behind them, three buckets full of ice with a bottle of

Systrian champagne chilling in each one.

Faye had dared me to go steal one.

"Your move, Faroshti," she whispers in my ear, and I shiver as her breath hits my neck.

I sweep a quick look at the closest partygoers and dart toward another table situated close to the service passage. This one has hors d'oeuvre trays all over it, and I sweep one up and prop it up on my shoulder, blocking full view of my face as I work my way along the wall. When I get to the champagne table, I turn my back to it and grope with my free hand, fingers finally closing on the neck of one of the bottles. I slip it up under my jacket and jam it in the back waistband of my pants, then speed walk toward the service passage. I can see Coy and Faye and Owyn and Setter just inside it, urging me on—

—and then there's a body in front of me. I tilt my head up to see William Voles, his dark hair slicked back, his face all sharp angles, his eyes narrow and cold.

"Primor Voles." I swallow. The freezing-cold condensation of the champagne bottle is soaking through my shirt. I lift my tray right up under his nose. "Canapé?"

A slight sneer twists his mouth, and he pushes the tray back down. "You really are such a testament to your uncle."

I hear people say that a lot in different ways. All of them implying that I'm an embarrassment or a disappointment to the great and beloved Atar Faroshti. Honestly, I'm over it. It doesn't even bother me anymore.

I grin up at him. "You mean charming and destined for greatness?"

"A once great and powerful family . . ." He plucks one of the hors d'oeuvres off the tray and pops the whole thing in his mouth, looking down his nose at me as he chews and swallows. "Quite frankly, I don't expect the new reign of the Faroshti to last all that long."

Uncle Charlie says I'm too impulsive. That I don't stop and think enough. That whenever I get an idea in my head, I should take a deep breath and count to ten before I act on it.

So I take a deep breath. I count to ten.

Then I dump the whole tray of canapés on William Voles's fancy clothes, spin away from him, and make a break for my friends.

We race back down the service passage, laughing, and we don't stop running until we're all the way on the other side of the kingship.

FORTY-ONE

Stardate: 0.05.32 in the Year 4031
Location: Riding impossible wormholes halfway across the quadrant. It's okay. Jealousy is totally natural.

I BLINK.

And all I see are stars, filling up my eyes.

I blink.

And I pour into them and spread out and out into nothingness.

I blink—

—and the *Vagabond*'s emergency lights flicker on all over the bridge, angry and red. Giving me shape again. My body floats upward, held down only by the harness wrapped around my torso. I look over at Hell Monkey, and he's blinking, slow, disoriented, like he's just waking up.

The rest of the power surges back on, lights come up, and I drop forward, my chest slamming into the buckles of the harness.

I grunt, flailing for the controls. "Hell Monkey—"

"Working on it." He stretches his arm, just managing to brush fingertips across the right buttons on the conn so the *Vagabond* starts to slowly tilt back into place. "Regaining appropriate altitude."

It's pretty ungraceful with the shifting gravity, but I manage to scramble my ass back into my seat and hit the comms channel, still open and connected to the other three ships.

"Hey, sound off. Everyone make it through okay?"

Coy's laughter rings out over the space, and my breath rushes out of me in relief. "Well. If that wasn't something for the history books."

"Everything accounted for over here," Faye chimes in. "Honor lost her goggles, but otherwise we're good."

Setter's voice, when he responds, sounds definitely less pleased than the other two. "We are . . . fine. I'm almost positive there was a less risky way to have approached all of this."

"Hey, you're the one who started everything up with your plan for shield modifications," I point out. "Which, speaking of . . ."

Hell Monkey is already one step ahead of me. "Networking connections got broken on the ride—cables too. We're four separate ships again."

Good. I mean, not that I didn't like the group effort, but I like the *Vagabond* as is. My quick, nimble, sixty-two-meter-long baby.

"Rose?" I call out. "You there again?"

"Good evening, Captain Farshot." I grin at the sound of her automated voice. "Your heart rate appears severely elevated. Do you require assistance?"

"I love you too, Rose." Tension leaves my body in little waves. First from my stomach, then from my back, then my neck. I pull my arms across my body, trying to stretch out the muscles in my shoulders and wrists. "Okay . . . anyone's ship in bad shape after all that? We got any bearings yet?"

"Still working on where we ended up," says Hell Monkey. "Gonna take a few more minutes before the sensors get calibrated to give us more than 'Hey, we're in space.'"

"The *Gun* got rattled a little in that ride," Coy calls over the channel, "but she's pretty intact."

"Same for the *Wynlari*," says Setter. "Some minor damage to the hull on our starboard side, but that's the extent of it."

Silence falls. We all wait for the Orso crew to sound off. And we wait . . .

"Faye?" asks Coy after a minute. "You still there?"

Faye snorts. "It's not sharing hour, pretties. As far as you're all concerned, the *Deadshot* is in perfect condition."

Can't really fault her for that one. We're not exactly all on the same side here. Not anymore. Which is why when I get the results from a full scan of the *Vagabond*, I downplay it with, "Our ass got a little singed, but we're flying pretty still."

That's not entirely true. One of our engines shows signs of damage. Nothing that's gonna have us falling out of the sky in the next few hours or so, but the kind of damage that could get a little more serious if we don't take a look at it soon. But I'm not sure how much of it even Hell Monkey can fix without docking somewhere for a day or two.

I mute our end of the channel and look over at my engineer. When he catches my eyes, he shakes his head. "Just guessing off the scans, but I think I'm gonna have to suit up and go outside to do repairs. And I'd have to reroute a lot of Rose's bandwidth to help me out."

"Dammit." I take a slow breath and let it out to a seven-count. "Okay, let's just hold off for right now. Maybe we can catch a break—"

Coy's voice cuts across the bridge. "Farshot, check your short-range sensors—are you seeing them?"

I unmute immediately. "What is it? Rose, put whatever the hell she's talking about on-screen."

The viewscreen flips over to show three probes, all outfitted with a weird, rocklike shield around them, drifting in a little cluster about a hundred meters off our keel.

"They're transmitting their coordinates," says Setter quietly. "Long-distance."

Coy sighs. "I guess we can expect Edgar to join us soon."

Faye doesn't say anything. But a second later, I hear the distant boom-boom-boom of the *Deadshot's* cannons going off, and one by one the probes go up in little balls of flame and shattered metal and circuitry.

"He'll still have the coordinates," I tell her. "I mean, not to be a dick. Just pointing it out."

"Doesn't matter." Her voice sounds distant. Like she's leaning back away from the comms to show just how little she's caring about all this. "He tried to blow us up, so I get to take away some of his toys."

"In all fairness," says Setter, "he didn't do anything against any of the rules. We're allowed to try to impede each other, throw up obstacles, and so forth. After all, Faye and Alyssa, you got in a blaster fight—"

"Oh . . . I . . ." I stutter. Damn, that Setter can put you on the spot. "I mean, just a little one . . ."

"—and Faye, you locked Alyssa in a room—"

Faye clears her throat. "I had no doubt she could get out easily."

"—so just because Edgar worked on a much larger and much more effective scale doesn't mean he is in the wrong—"

Hell Monkey shoots a hand out and mutes our end again. "Long-range sensors are up again, Captain." His voice is tight and urgent, his fingers working quickly across the dash as he processes the incoming information. "We're in the middle of the Emoa system."

The name sounds vaguely familiar. "Emoa . . . That puts us on the outer edge of the quadrant, I'm pretty sure. One of the newer additions to the empire and relatively uncharted. Seven planets total. Two categorized as terrestrial."

"Viola and Calm," says Hell Monkey, nodding. And then he shoots me a look. Like, a *look*. "And I'm picking up a beacon on Calm."

FORTY-TWO

The channel between the four worldcruisers goes dead.

Coy goes dark first, and the *Gilded Gun* shoots off toward Calm, burning engines hot at top sublight speed. Setter and Faye take off right on her tail, and I grab the controls to follow, cursing my slow reflexes.

And then more cursing as it quickly becomes clear that that engine damage is going to put us at a disadvantage in a race right now.

"Rose, redirect any auxiliary power to sublight engines." I flick a glance over at Hell Monkey. "What do we have in our arsenal that can help us out here? Anything nonlethal we can detonate? EMP pulses or something?"

No answer. I raise my eyebrows at him, one eye still on the worldcruisers pulling away ahead of us. He's half folded over the conn, frowning at the readout.

"Hey, H.M., did you feel like participating in this situation?" I ask, waving around the bridge. "Or were you just gonna sit this one out?"

He straightens. "Rose, show me our starboard on the viewscreen—forty degrees to a hundred forty degrees, wide scan."

The lights of the worldcruiser engines disappear, and instead the screen is filled with a wide expanse of stars.

And something very small, but moving very quickly toward us. It's almost hard to pick out by the naked eye, and our sensors are showing not much more than a blip.

This doesn't look like a blip. This looks a hell of a lot bigger than a blip.

Dread settles heavy and ice-cold in my stomach. "What is that?"

This time Rose is the one who answers. "Incoming warship signature. Matches known configurations for the starkiller stealth classification. Only known registration and manufacturer: the Mega Shipping Conglomerate."

I frown at the screen. "A Mega ship? What the hell is a Mega ship doing way out here? Do they have any bases in this system?"

H.M. inputs the query into the conn and then shakes his head at the results. "Nothing. Closest base is two systems away."

"Excuse me, Captain Faroshti." JR appears behind my chair, and I crane my neck around to see it. "Media reports that the Megas were recently victims of a burglary at one of their weapons facilities. Including the theft of at least one stealth-capable ship. Is it possible that's relevant in this instance?"

Yeah. Yeah, I'd say that's pretty damn relevant. A stolen ship means just about anybody could be at the helm over there. On a ship called a *starkiller*. Very comforting. If Rose thought my pulse was fast before, she's going to be super concerned now because I can feel my heart hammering the hell out of my rib cage. I swing back around to the conn.

"Rose, analyze that ship's trajectory and give me a time to intercept. Hell Monkey, try to hail Coy."

I jam the controls forward, trying to will the *Vagabond* to go faster, even with the damage dragging her down. Come on, baby . . . come on, baby . . .

"Captain Farshot, the warship is on an intercept course with the worldcruiser the *Gilded Gun*. Maximum sublight speed. Time to engagement is six minutes."

So on top of being a stolen starkiller ship, it's also in a serious hurry. This is not getting better. "And how long until we can get there?"

"Seven minutes and thirty-two seconds."

I pull the *Vagabond*'s nose starboard several degrees, hoping I can maybe angle it so we can get in between the warship and the crownchasers. "H.M., anything from Coy?"

"Nothing. She's not responding to hails."

"The others?"

"Not them either." His voice sounds strangled. Like the rising anxiety on the bridge is wrapping itself around his throat. "They're all running hot, redirecting everything to engine power to try to beat each other to that planet. Extraneous systems are deprioritized."

Extraneous systems—like long-range sensors, like communications. Which means none of them are going to pick up that warship until it's right on top of them. If it even bothers to get that close. A warship like that has a lot more weapons than the cannons on these cruisers—and it can shoot from a lot farther away too.

I can feel the worry building, and I'm having trouble swallowing it back down. Instead it's just flooding my chest, scrabbling around like a rabid Tiraxian badger, making it hard for me to think, to figure out a plan, because I can't breathe, there's not enough room between my ribs, and it's too tight in here, it's too much, it's too—it's too—

Warm hands wrap around my arms and spin me in my chair. Hell Monkey crouches in front of me. His grip is solid and heavy on my wrists, anchoring me in place, but that's the only part of him touching me. He holds the rest of himself away to give me space. So I have full access to all the oxygen floating around me.

I suck in a shaky breath.

"Who are you?" he asks in a quiet voice.

I stare down into his face, take one more breath, and grit my jaw. "I'm Captain Alyssa Fucking Farshot."

He grins. "You're godsdamn right. So what do you need me to do?"

"Get to the engine room," I tell him, straightening. "Whatever you can get out of our engines, I want it." He nods and is off the bridge in half a moment.

I spin in my chair and sit forward onto the edge, straightening the collar of my coat, raising that hard Faroshti jawline and those cheekbones that people always told me came from my mother.

"Rose, keep us on an intercept trajectory. Maximum sublight speed."

And then I hail the warship, video and audio, looking right into the viewscreen with my best *come on, try me* look.

"Mega warship, this is Captain Alyssa Farshot of the *Vagabond Quick*. You're looking a little lost here, kitten. This is crownchasers business."

Silence.

Stars and gods, Coy, please check your sensors.

I try again. "This is all coming off very aggressive, starkiller, and I'd hate to have to run my boot right up your ass. Very unpleasant for both of us. Why don't you come back here and talk this out with me?"

My viewscreen flickers, and then an image fills the space.

A masked figure in a hooded cloak.

The blood freezes in my body, and for a second, I'm not on the bridge of the *Vagabond* anymore. I'm down in the haunted crystal tunnels of the *Defiant*. I'm pinned against the wall. I'm watching Owyn fall. I'm covered in blood. . . .

I blink. And I'm back on the *Vagabond*. Where I belong. Where I'm in control. I let that fear trying to bubble up harden into something cold and sharp. "Oh, look. There's more than one of you. How delightful."

Its hands move over the controls, and a mechanical voice transmits over the comms.

WE ARE MANY MORE. WE ARE HERE TO CLEAR THE WAY.

"Oh hell, no. I have unfinished business with you assholes that we can take care of right here and now. Come on—my ship is damaged, we're limping along. . . . I'm a prime target. Come take your shot. I won't run."

The voice laughs, harsh and unnatural. The sound of it is unnerving as hell.

WE HAVE MORE THAN ENOUGH FIREPOWER FOR ALL OF YOU.

WAIT YOUR TURN.

The channel cuts off, and I watch, helplessly, as the warship races past the point where the *Vagabond* had been hoping to intercept it. I light up the cannons, but by the time I get them warmed up and ready, it's already leaving us in the dust. Which means I'm right back where I was, scrambling desperately to close the distance. Farther ahead, I can see Setter's and Faye's ships nearing the gray-green planet Calm, and beyond that is Coy, starting to slow as she angles to enter orbit.

The ship jumps a little underneath me, and I steady myself as Hell Monkey races back onto the bridge, panting.

"I managed to get us a boost. Not much—maybe ten thousand kilometers or so—and it'll only last a few minutes, but it could help. . . ."

He trails off when he sees me already shaking my head, and his slow, heavy footsteps draw near the back of my chair.

"It's too late. They're already out of range. I—"

"Weapons alert," calls Rose. "Detecting dual missile launch from the Mega warship. Target: the *Gilded Gun*."

I don't mean to gasp, but it slips out of my mouth. Hell Monkey reaches down for my hand, and I grab on to his fingers furiously, leaning into his arm. Watching on the viewscreen as two bright red missiles cut across the stars toward Coy. Listening as Rose's voice coolly counts down to disaster.

"Impact estimated in four . . ."

Come on, Coy. Do something.

". . . three . . ."

Swerve. Deploy countermeasures. *Something.*

". . . two . . ."

It's not supposed to go like this. Please, gods, don't let it go like this.

". . . one . . ."

FORTY-THREE

At the last possible second, I see the *Gilded Gun* swerve. A bloom of fire bursts and then Rose again:

"Impact detected. Successful hit."

This weird strangled noise comes out of my mouth. For a moment, I feel like I'm in a bubble and everything else has stopped and I'm just staring as Coy's ship spins and falls, dragged into Calm's gravity well, trailing flames and smoke. Setter's and Faye's ships pull up, turn toward the threat they didn't know was coming—but slow, so slow, and the warship bears down on them.

We're too far away; our sublight engines are too jacked up.

Time to get a little wild.

"Hell Monkey, strap in. Get the cannons warmed up."

He obeys immediately as I lay in the riskiest course I've ever plotted in my life. Hyperlight engines are not really meant for short sprints into the middle of a bunch of ship traffic, but you know . . . desperate times and stuff.

"Captain Farshot, this is not a recommended course of action given current parameters—"

"Save it, Rose."

Hell Monkey raises a nervous eyebrow. "Are you actually planning what I think you're planning?"

"More or less. Just be ready to fire as soon as we're out." I check the trajectory angle one more time—*deep breath, Farshot*—and then I hit it.

A burst of diffused light. A streak of stars.

And then we're there, right above the stolen warship, and I yell, "NOW!"

Hell Monkey doesn't hesitate. He hauls down on the cannons, launching rounds from all of them. They hit—boom, boom, boom, boom—peppering the hull as we sail past. I push the *Vagabond* until we're close to the other two worldcruisers and then swing around so we're facing the warship, sitting directly in its path.

"Doesn't look like we did much damage," Hell Monkey mutters. "We're gonna run out of cannon charges way before they start feeling the hurt."

On the edge of the viewscreen, I can see the curve of the planet—its atmosphere a pall of gray-green clouds and flashes of lightning. I can't see where Coy fell. If she cracked against the solid ground. If she broke up in the storms.

I flip a signal on the comms, sending a ping to the other two worldcruisers, and they respond immediately.

"On your starboard," Setter says as soon as the channel is open.

"Off your port side." Faye's voice sounds hard and angry. "I've got all our cannons hot and probably five or six rounds left."

"Use whatever you've got." I tighten my grip on the controls. "I'm going to try to draw their fire."

"You're not as quick as usual," Setter points out. "Are you sure—"

"Proximity alert," says Rose. "Warship approaching with weapons live."

"I'll just have to be squirrelly, Setter. Worry less about us and focus on trying to punch a hole in that ship."

I slam down on the controls, shooting the *Vagabond* forward, right at the warship's nose. As soon as it fires, I dive, throwing us into a roll. The guns follow and I'm having to react quick as hell to keep from getting clipped by them as we swoop underneath the keel and come up on the aft.

"Missiles launched!" Hell Monkey calls. "Deploying countermeasures!"

I curse vividly. Peel us off to the right, trying to get clear as one, two, three of the warship's missiles collide with our decoys and explode, rattling our hull. I keep the *Vagabond* close to the warship, weaving a pattern around the big bulk of her. She's got serious armor and shields and weapons every which way, but world-cruisers are lighter, quicker. We've got to be able to use that to our advantage.

As we get close to the prow, I nod at Hell Monkey, and he opens up another spread from our cannons. I haul up on the *Vagabond*'s nose to avoid the blowback.

"Direct hits," he says. "Their forward shielding has definitely taken a beating."

I arc a sharp U-turn to come about. "How about our shielding?"

"Looking weak, Captain. That missile shock wave put a hurt on our aft shields in particular."

I ping the channel again. "Faye, Setter—how are you holding up?"

"We've landed some serious blows," says Faye, her voice tight and bright with adrenaline. "But not doing the kind of damage we need."

"Similar situation over here." I see Setter's worldcruiser on the viewscreen darting over the warship's dorsal, cannons blazing. "I'm getting low on ammo charges."

I punch the *Vagabond*'s engines, coming back in for another sweep, and that's when I see a bright flash from one of the warship's starboard-side guns. A heartbeat—and then one of the *Wynlari*'s engines disappears in fire and smoke.

"SETTER!" My voice sounds shrill as hell over the comms channel, but I don't care. I plow the *Vagabond* toward the warship, cutting in between her and the *Wynlari*, and Hell Monkey doesn't even need a word from me to launch every cannon we have. They land in barrage, and the warship's shields waver, that starboard gun bursting into pieces that drift gently away.

I spin the *Vagabond* away in a sharp arc, six g's of force flattening me into my seat as we come about near the *Wynlari*. She looks pretty banged up, her engines smoking in a not-good way and at least two of her cannons gone. But I can't see any plumes that would signal she's venting oxygen or otherwise breathable air.

The *Deadshot* darts overhead, unloading cannon fire as Faye calls over the channel, "Roy, you'd better sound off quick before your mothers sense you missing and burn half the system down!"

"I'm here." His voice is a little rough, but at least he's up and he can speak. "I've got a few minor lacerations. Sabela's hurt—she needs medical attention." I can hear her in the background, protesting loudly that she's fine.

"There's a facility on Viola," Hell Monkey says, already pulling up the specs of the neighboring planet. Always three steps ahead, that one. "We can cover your ass."

Yes, we absolutely can. As soon as the *Wynlari* starts to move off, I put the *Vagabond* to work, throwing her into big, spiraling loops around the warship, scattering spreads of shining red decoys in our wake like fireworks to draw the signals of any missiles this guy might try to launch at Setter's retreat. It's kind of like a rollercoaster ride with six times as much danger.

A little giggle rises in the back of my throat. I clamp down on it. I don't think it's a good sign.

I think I might be standing on that raggedy edge here.

Pulling out of the spiral, I slice the *Vagabond* right over the top of the warship, back to front, Hell Monkey firing at will. And as a nice change of pace, I actually hear him let out an appreciative whistle.

"Hell yeah. Now that finally hurt them a little," he says.

I throw a fist in the air, crowing for our small triumph, as I swing the *Vagabond*'s nose back around—

—just in time to see a missile streak toward the *Deadshot* and explode in a ball of fire.

FORTY-FOUR

Faye releases a stream of decoys a second too late, and the explosion sends her ship spinning and smoking out toward the void of space.

"FAYE!" The scream tears my throat raw. "Faye! Honor! Respond!"

Precious, silent seconds, and then Honor, coughing hard as she replies, "Faye is down! She got hit in the head, and there's blood . . . I . . . I'm not . . ."

"The warship is turning around," Hell Monkey mutters to me through gritted teeth. "They smell a kill shot."

I lean so close to the comms my lips are practically touching it, like I can convey the urgency just by body angle. "Honor, get your ass in that jump seat and fly. Do you hear me? Fly that ship out of here now or you're both dead."

I don't wait for her to respond. I flip to a new channel and sing out to the warship, "Hey, new best friend! You're not leaving, are you? Because I'm still having a ton of fun over here."

I flick a glance over to Hell Monkey, but he shakes his head. "Still turning . . ."

"Fire everything we've got left. Their starboard side is weak anyway, and they're an idiot to flash it at us."

"My pleasure, Captain," he growls, and squeezes the cannon triggers.

The successive booms—one, two, three, four . . . eight of them in all—thud in my chest, and I watch with a violent pleasure as they impact the warship in bursts of flames and metal pieces.

"Now that made them stop," says Hell Monkey. "Status of the *Deadshot*: she's crawling away. Slow going, but she's making progress."

Honor needs a distraction, she needs time to make her retreat. And us? I'm not sure how we get out of this one with no more ammo and a damaged ship that's only getting more beat up with all this tight flying.

Actually, I do. I have an idea. I just don't like it.

But there aren't any other options left that I can see.

I press my hands against the conn, feeling it hum like a living thing. I look over at Hell Monkey, who's glaring at the warship slowly swinging back around toward us. I can see it on his face—he'd take the stand with me right now. The two of us. Going down in a blaze of glory together, just like I promised. And maybe we will someday.

But not today.

I mute the channel. "H.M., I need you to prep two survival suits. And three pods."

It takes him half a second to put it together, and his eyes widen. "You can't be serious, Alyssa—"

"I'm deadly serious," I say, cutting him off. "This is an order. From your captain."

"There isn't much of a charge on the suits—"

"I know. It'll be enough. Go."

He races off, and I look over at the mediabot, hovering and unsure. "Go with him. Do what he says. Move fast."

It tick-tick-ticks off down the corridor, and I pull my shoulders back and face the viewscreen.

"Rose," I call, my fingers moving across the touch screens in front of me. I can do it without hardly even looking. That's how well I know this stupid, exquisite ship.

"Yes, Captain Farshot."

Her cool voice hits me in the gut, but I push it down. "Redirect all available power to the forward shields and the sublight engines."

"Yes, Captain Farshot."

There's a question blinking at me right now on the comms display:

⟫⟫⟫ Confirm initiate self-destruct?

Yes. I think I'm gonna be sick, but I confirm.

⟫⟫⟫ Submit identity confirmation.

I press my left hand firmly against the panel for it to scan.

⟫⟫⟫ Match confirmed. Self-destruct initiated.

I set a one-minute timer and then say, "Rose, I need a burst from the engines at their top speed on my mark. Got that?"

"Understood, Captain Farshot."

The *Vagabond* shakes violently as a barrage from the warship slams into our forward shields. I grab the back of my jump seat to steady myself and then unmute the channel to the warship, switching to visual this time so the hooded figure on the other side can see my face.

The blank nothingness of its mask fills the screen, and its voice blares over the comms link.

THERE WILL BE NO QUARTER OFFERED, CROWNCHASER.

I shrug. "Wouldn't take it anyway, numbnuts. I was actually calling to see if *you* wanted to surrender to me. Y'know, show a little survival instinct. Live to fight another day."

The figure leans in and tilts its head.

DESTROYING YOU WILL BE VERY SATISFYING.

"Can't say I didn't try. Die in a fire, asshole." I flip him two middle fingers and then cut the feed.

Warning lights flare up all over the dash—incoming fire—but I shut it out, taking three seconds, three precious seconds, to look at the bridge of the *Vagabond Quick*. My baby. My home. I memorize her as she is now—the worn cushions of the jump seats, the scuffs on the panels, the layout of every screen, and the smooth feel of the conn underneath my fingertips. Every bump, every scratch, every sign that for three amazing years, I lived here and found myself here.

Bending down, I press my lips against the dashboard, an ache from suppressed tears building in my throat.

Stars guide you, *Vagabond Quick*.

And then I bolt, sprinting down the corridor and skidding into my quarters. Wasting a few precious heartbeats to grab the holo-discs from my uncle, the mementos of my mother. And then I make a break for it to the aft bay, where Hell Monkey is already suited up and wrestling a very confused mediabot into an escape pod. The ship rattles as shots crash against our shields somewhere near the prow.

I snatch my own survival suit and awkwardly stumble into it as I yell, "IN! NOW! LET'S GO!"

Hell Monkey closes JR in and moves toward his own, pausing to sweep a sad look at the walls all around us. Then he steps into the pod and the door slides shut.

I'm still wriggling my gear on as I get in and seal the pod doors. I double-check the communication link with the main ship.

"Rose? What's the time left on the self-destruct?"

"Eleven seconds, Captain Farshot."

I sigh as I fumble with the release valve. I can hear the muffled thud and hiss off to my right as Hell Monkey's escape pod disengages and shoots off toward the planet.

"You've been an absolute peach, Rose." My throat tightens around the words. I almost can't get them out. "You know that?"

"Of course, Captain Farshot." She doesn't have a mouth, so it's not like she can smile, but I swear I feel like she's smiling. In an AI way, I guess. "Eight seconds remaining."

Time to go. "Hit the engines, Rose."

And then I yank on the release valve.

. . . five . . .

. . . four . . .

. . . three . . .

. . . two . . .

. . . one . . .

By some twist of fate, I watch it all happen through the window on the door of my pod. I see the *Vagabond Quick* shoot toward the warship like an arrow a second after I disembark. I see her crash into it, nose to nose, as it tries—too late—to move out of the way.

And then I see my beautiful ship go up in a torrent of flames and shattered pieces, taking the warship with her.

CHAOS OVER CALM

**At least two crownchaser ships appear to go down
in a fierce firefight in the remote Emoa system**

ATTACKING WARSHIP FLOWN
BY UNIDENTIFIED PILOT

The Mega facility on Rava VI confirms the warship
matches the one recently stolen, but authorities have
no clues as to who flew it

WYTHE ISSUES BLISTERING
CONDEMNATION

The steward denounced the violence reported near Calm,
but refrained from drawing further conclusions
as to what sparked the firefight

WHAT HAPPENS IF NO ONE WINS THE CHASE?

Crownchasers have died trying to find the seal before,
but experts say there is no precedent for a full competitor wipeout

EMOA SYSTEM, APPROACHING THE PLANET CALM

Edgar stares at the viewscreen, at the wreckage of the warship and the worldcruiser mingling together, big chunks of the debris getting gradually pulled into the planet's gravitation. He sighs, very slowly, out his nose. His teeth grit hard against each other.

He and NL7 had dropped out of hyperlight in time to see the *Vagabond Quick* ram into the warship and explode. In time to spot three escape pods streaking down toward the planet where the next beacon is. In time to realize that his strategy hadn't been quite as successful as he'd planned. The figure had certainly sewn chaos, but Edgar's way forward isn't quite as a clear as they had promised.

He either overestimated his ally or underestimated the other crownchasers, and he isn't quite sure which one it is.

"We found the others, Edgar Voles," says NL7.

He steps over to the jump seat where the android sits, utilizing the conn to perform long-range sensor sweeps. "All of the others?"

"All remaining worldcruisers, correct." It swipes at the screen to put a map of their current coordinates on display. Two small lights are moving around and away from Calm, heading for the more well-known and developed planet of Viola. "Signatures identify these two as the *Wynlari* and the *Deadshot*. Both ships show significant damage, and the *Deadshot* is running a medical alert message. A Viola hospital has already launched an emergency liftship to assist them."

So that put Setter Roy and Faye Orso out of the game. At least temporarily. "What about these two?" Edgar asks, motioning to the other two indicators.

"This one located inside the planet's thermosphere must be what remains of Faroshti's ship," says NL7. "Which means that, logically, this one coming from the planet itself must be Nathalia Coyenne's ship, the *Gilded Gun*."

Edgar raises his eyebrows. "You don't know for sure?"

NL7 tilts its head. "The atmosphere is in constant turmoil. Riddled with acidic rainstorms. More complete information is difficult to procure, but we can tell you that it is a signature compatible with the worldcruiser classification."

He frowns at that little glowing light. "Could it be wreckage? Like the *Vagabond*?"

"Possible," says NL7, "but not probable."

"Why not?"

"Because it is moving."

Edgar steps back, folding his arms over his chest. Someone with a flight-capable worldcruiser made it down onto the planet. Not just anyone-someone—that Coyenne girl. So ambitious and affected and careless. So unlike what the empire ought to have on the throne. And after everything he set into motion to prevent it. It is . . . infuriating. He feels the emotion flood hot over his skin.

He knows if he looked now, he'd be flushed, that his eyes would be fever bright.

He stuffs his hands into his pockets and curls them into fists, squeezing them tight to keep the anger quelled.

"Do you wish to go down onto Calm, Edgar Voles?" asks NL7.

He shakes his head and points to a spot on the map projection. "Take us there. Keep close track of that worldcruiser signature down on the planet, but power down all other extraneous systems. Anything that might be easily picked up by a passing ship. I want us to stay in the dark for a little while longer."

Edgar breathes, slow, in and out, until he feels the blood start to drain from his face again.

There is time still. The race isn't yet over.

EASTERN HANGAR BAY, THE KINGSHIP, APEX

UNCLE ATAR'S HANDS ARE FIRM ON MY SHOULDERS as he steers me off the internal transport. There's a blindfold wrapped around my eyes so I can't see where we've stopped, but it's not hard for me to guess. All the scents in the air are familiar—ship exhaust; engine oil; cold, fresh air slapping into us; the sharpness and salt of the ocean.

It's the hangar bay. Probably on the east side judging by the angle of the air flow. I've spent enough time down here over the years to have it memorized.

"Have you guessed yet, Birdie?" I can hear the grin in Uncle Atar's voice. He's getting a huge kick out of this whole deal.

"You got me my own waveskimmer?" It's not a great guess. I honestly don't think my uncles would be going through all this subterfuge stuff just for a waveskimmer. But anything more than that seems . . . too much to hope, I guess.

I feel Uncle Charlie put his hand on top of Atar's and squeeze. "Just show her. You've teased her long enough."

Gentle fingers pull the blindfold away and I blink in the bright light of the hangar, trying to clear the spots from my vision.

And then I see it.

A worldcruiser.

An actual worldcruiser with a tiny red bow on the prow.

I whirl around to Atar and Charlie, who stand, arms around each other, grinning at me. I'm having a hard time catching my breath. "That's . . . ?"

Charlie nods. "Yes."

"And it's . . . ?"

"Yours," says Atar. "It's not the latest model, mind you. It's a few years old and been around the quadrant a bit—"

I don't wait for him to finish. I hug him, hard. And then I hug Charlie, and then I hug them both again. I bury my face in their shoulders to hide the fact that there are tears welling in my eyes, and that shit is just embarrassing.

I finally step away, clearing my throat and wiping awkwardly at my face as I turn back to the ship.

My ship.

Walking around it, I reach out and put my hand on the silvered alloy of her hull. It's warm to the touch and almost feels like she's humming just for me. I don't care how old she is or how many times she's been around the sun—she's beautiful.

I come around to the prow and stare up at her and that little red bow my uncles put on her.

Atar steps up behind me. "She needs a name."

Oh man, I have a name. I have entire files filled with all the potential names I've thought up over the years. I never settled on one in particular because I always thought I'd know the right one when I met the ship.

And it's true. I do.

"I'm gonna call her the *Vagabond Quick*."

FORTY-FIVE

Stardate: 0.05.32 in the Year 4031
Location: Crash-landing on Calm and I'd really like to punch which-ever idiot thought he was being so cute when he named this planet

I PASS OUT AT SOME POINT AS THE ESCAPE POD rattles through the stratosphere. Which is kind of fine because it's not like I can do much on this ride except hold on and wait. World-cruiser escape pods are graded for planetary reentry only in the technical sense. It'll get you down to the surface, but if you're look-ing for a cushy ride, you're gonna be disappointed.

I felt blood oozing out of my nose before everything went dark. I'm just saying.

When I come to, everything hurts. Even my fingernails. I feel like I went nine rounds with a vilkjing.

But the pod's stopped moving.

The window is covered with grime and spots of liquid, and I can't make out much beyond the vague shadowy shapes of rocks. There's a lot of wind howling around out there. Distant thunder too. I start double-checking my suit, making sure the helmet is on tight, all the seals are locked up. No leaks, no holes, oxygen charged and functioning. You do not want to be on an unknown planet with a run in your survival suit stockings.

It's tight quarters, but I manage to wriggle my arm up so I can access the radial sensors on the reinforced wristband built into the suit. Their feedback is that it's nasty as hell outside and that Calm won't be making any vacation lists for the foreseeable future. But the conditions shouldn't be a problem as long as I keep my suit on. They also pick up two other escape pods within 150 meters of me, which means that at least the homing coordinates on these things worked correctly.

I tap the communications on. "Hell Monkey, you all right?"

I wait, expecting to hear his voice come right back to me. But the silence stretches. And then it stretches some more.

"H.M.? You getting this?"

Nothing.

Panic kicks me in the chest like an adrenaline shot. I yank the door lever and boot it open, sending it flying as I rush out. The pod landed at an odd angle on a mound of broken black rock, and I tumble down it in a heap, scrambling too fast to get my feet under me. The ground shifts as I haul myself upright—centimeters and centimeters of rough dark gravel moving around under my boots—but I plow through it toward the closest pod, feeling like I'm wading ankle-deep in the worst ocean ever.

Escape Pod 002 lies flat and peaceful, like someone placed it there. I suck in a breath as I pop the door open.

JR the mediabot looks up at me, camera lenses glowing like it must've been recording the whole way down.

"Captain Farshot," it says immediately. "Would you care to comment on the destruction of your ship?"

I sigh. "Cheery Coyenne should promote you." And then I turn and slog off, running as hard as I can. I call out to Hell Monkey a few more times as I work my way over the terrain, thinking maybe he just didn't hear me before or maybe the distance messed up his reception. But still no response.

By the time I reach Escape Pod 001, wedged between two big boulders, my heart pounds against my ribs and my breath sounds fast and ragged in my own ears. I haul myself up the pockmarked rock faces and drag the pod door open.

Hell Monkey lies inside, eyes closed inside his helmet. Very still. Very pale.

It feels like a black hole woke up and sucked away my lungs and my heart and left only my broken ribs. I reach out and put a shaking hand on Hell Monkey's chest.

His eyes flicker open.

All my breath comes back to me in a rush. Tears flood my vision. This son of a bitch. If I wasn't so happy to see him alive, I'd straight up murder him.

"Hey, boss." His voice is a soft rasp. I can see the pain in the lines of his face. "You weren't worried about me, were you?"

I laugh. My hand comes up to wipe tears from my face before I remember I have a stupid helmet on. "Damn you to every star, Hell Monkey. Are you hurt? You sound hurt."

He ticks his chin up in a tight nod. "Right arm. Right side of my chest. Got banged up pretty good on landing."

Yeah, it looks like it. I pull up his left arm and check the vitals on his wristband. Slightly elevated heart rate, blood pressure—kind of to be expected at the moment. I run my hand very gently along his injured arm and the side of his body, but it's hard to tell with the suits and the gloves and all that stuff. It doesn't feel like any bone is poking out. That's about all I got.

"Captain Farshot?"

I stick my head back out of the pod and look down at JR, shifting nervously on the ground. "I'm not doing interviews right now!"

"There's an incoming rainband." The mediabot points over its shoulder. A wall of heavy clouds—underneath the already turbulent cloud cover—sweeps toward us over the rocks, liquid streaming from its belly. "Estimated to be highly acidic," it adds. "It might be advisable to find extra cover."

Dammit. I don't want to move Hell Monkey without knowing how badly he's injured, but I don't know how caustic the acid rain is on this planet. Survival suits can take a lot, but you don't just want to assume they'll hold up fine when the other option is "sky-water slowly dissolves you into a pile of viscera."

"Scout us a decent spot," I tell JR, and then turn back to Hell Monkey. "We've gotta move."

"Awesome, great. Here I go." He closes his eyes, jaw tight. "Am I moving yet?"

"Very funny. Put your good arm around me. We'll just take this one step at a time."

It's slow and painful—mostly for Hell Monkey—and I keep checking over my shoulder to see that rainband getting closer and closer. But I manage to get him out of the pod and down to the ground with minimal jostling. Most of his weight is draped over my shoulders, and with the ground basically a mire, it takes everything I've got to haul both of us away from the boulders and in the direction of our forever-friend, the mediabot. JR found an overhang in a nearby cliff face. It's not far, really, but by the time I manage to get both of us there, I'm pouring sweat and sucking air like I'm brand-new to this exploring stuff. Hell Monkey's face looks a little green inside his helmet, and he lets out a pained groan as I lower him gently onto the ground, situating him as close to the cliff as possible.

I straighten, trying to catch my breath, getting a look at the half-ass cave. It's not so much that I'd want to spend an extended period of time here, but it should be enough shelter for a bit while I send up some emergency subspace beacons. See if I can get ahold of someone out there with a working ship who wants to take on passengers.

Hell Monkey coughs, and I turn to see him trying to pull himself up into a sitting position. I drop down to my knees beside him to help.

"Is this absolutely necessary right this second?" I ask as I get a shoulder underneath his arm and scoot him up.

He leans back against the rock. His breath comes too tight and too short. "I forgot to tell you something," he says. "Before we left."

I play back the last moments on the *Vagabond*, trying to think what it might be, but I've got nothing. "What is it?"

He rolls his head to the side to look straight at me. His hazel eyes are darker than usual, and the twist of his mouth is a little bit wry and a little bit sad. "I only had time to fully charge the air supply on one suit. So I charged yours. I only have about ten minutes of oxygen left."

FORTY-SIX

I STARE AT HELL MONKEY, ABSOLUTELY FROZEN, for probably five or six seconds. My brain plows through every possible response and every option I have to fix this because I'm gonna have to do something. As far as I can remember, there were no other ships around Calm, and Setter and Faye are headed to Viola on injured cruisers (and, in Faye's case, with an injured captain). They could pick up a subspace beacon. So could the people on Viola. But I don't think any of them can make it down here in ten minutes.

Probably closer to nine and a half minutes now.

I blink, refocusing on Hell Monkey's face, his skin tinged grayish, sweat beading along his forehead. But his eyes are still locked on me, solid and steady. There's this solar flare of bright, sharp energy inside of me. Like fear, maybe. And anger. And love.

I set my jaw against it and glare at Hell Monkey. "Welp, now instead of getting to cuddle while I whisper sweet nothings in your ear, you're gonna have to sit over there all cold and lonely while I try to figure out how to redistribute my oxygen supply to supplement yours."

I roll to my feet and head to the edge of the overhang. The bands of acid rain are almost on us. I grab the short tube off the belt of my survival suit and set it up with a clear shot up at the sky, driving it into the loose ground to give it decent purchase. It shoots one, two, three bright red bolts and they go up and up and disappear beyond the clouds.

I'm not the praying type. But I kind of wish I had someone to pray to right now.

I retreat deeper under the overhang. Rain follows soon after, pattering and hissing across the rocks and gravel. Hell Monkey leans against the cliff, watching it come down, and I crouch next to him, trying to get an angle on the oxygen storage tank on his back. I don't want to jostle him too much. I'm not sure dragging him over here like dead weight did him much good.

"You can't get mad at me, Alyssa," he says. "You would've done the exact same thing."

I hate how ragged his voice sounds. It makes my lungs feel too tight. "That's obviously not true. I would've kept all the air to myself and left you to twist."

He chuckles, but it's kind of halfway a cough. "Sure, sure . . ."

I frown at the tank configuration on his back. There's not an obvious, easy way to give him some of the oxygen from mine. Usually, you charge them in an environment with fully breathable air all around, and there doesn't seem to be a sealed input device. I can't even take off my own tank to try to get a better look at this whole mess. Not without, y'know, instantly starting to suffocate.

I check my wristband. My breathable air is sitting at eighty-three percent. Gives me a few hours easily, maybe more if I keep it chill and relax instead of doing laps around the planet.

I kneel down in front of him so I can keep one eye on how he's doing and start laying everything I have out in front of me. Emptying every single pocket and compartment and clip on my belt. There's gotta be something that I can use.

And what if you can't, Farshot? What if this is how the you-and–Hell Monkey adventure ends?

Godsdammit, I do not want to have that thought. It's making tears flood the backs of my eyes, and I need my vision clear.

I clear my throat hard. "You know what sucks?"

He drags his gaze away from the rain streaming in sizzling ropes across the overhang. His eyebrows raise sky-high. "Just the one thing?"

"We're going to cork it on this terrible fucking planet, and I don't even know your real name. Two years flying together—I've never known your name."

The words come out in a tumble, and I can't bring myself to look at him. (The great and powerful Alyssa Farshot, folks. She's so brave she can't look at a boy.) But it feels like it might be too much, to ask this. Like I'm trying to dig up something buried. Which I kind of am. I should take it back. I should tell him to forget it and—

"Eliot," he says just as I'm about to open my mouth. "I was named Eliot, after my grandfather."

"Eliot." I try out the name, see how it feels on my tongue, and a smile stretches across his face. Not wry or joking, but an all-the-way, soul-deep kind of smile.

"That sounds good. You saying my name. I could get used to that."

The way he's looking at me—I think I could tell him right then. That he's light-years more than just my buddy or my engineer or my copilot. That I think I might love him and I've maybe loved him for a while now. But the words get stuck in my throat.

"My mom called me Hell Monkey," he says, his gaze going a little distant. "As a nickname. Because I was always running around, getting into trouble. Not, like, bad trouble. Just kid stuff." He shrugs and then winces when it pulls at his injury. "When I left home, after the fire, I didn't want to hand people my real name, so I started telling people to call me Hell Monkey. It's weird, but it felt like a way I could have her with me."

I understand and I also kind of don't. Because I walked away from my family and shed my name, and I didn't hold on to it. I don't always feel very good about that.

I think about that last message Uncle Atar recorded for me, asking me to come back sometimes, to keep one foot on Apex with him and Charlie. I didn't. I didn't realize—not until he was gone.

I shift so I'm sitting next to Hell Monkey and I put my gloved hand over his, trying to squeeze his fingers through the thick material. "My uncle always called me Birdie."

He nods and says, totally deadpan, "That makes sense. You do have a really big nose."

A bark of laughter bursts out of me and I nudge him in the leg. "Shut up. We should really stop talking. Save your oxygen charge."

He shakes his head. "Nah. What's the point in that? I don't want to go quietly."

I wrap my hand tighter around his. "I don't want you to go at all," I whisper, but I say it to the rain.

The minutes tick by, and I can't sit still and watch them count down. I need to move or do something. I go through the survival suit items again. I call JR over and see what it can offer. I manage to jury-rig a piece that plugs between my tank and his tank and pulls maybe five extra minutes of breathable air over to him before it breaks because it was shoddy even under the best conditions. I try but I can't put it back together.

I scream with frustration, and all I can see is a blur because the tears won't stay down anymore.

Hell Monkey's stopped talking. His eyes are closed and his breathing is getting shallow. And I can't do anything.

I. Can't. Do. Anything. Except cry.

JR hovers nearby, its camera lenses constantly glowing. "Captain Farshot—"

I put a hand up in its face. "Not a good time, buddy. Seriously. Read the room."

"I apologize, Captain Farshot, but you're getting an incoming communication."

It points down at my wristband, where a little blue light is blinking. My breath catches in my throat, and I fumble to hit the button.

The voice of Nathalia Coyenne comes blasting across the frequency: "Alyssa Charlemagne Farshot, if you somehow managed to get yourself killed on this planet, I'm absolutely never speaking to you again."

FORTY-SEVEN

IT'S THE MOST BEAUTIFUL THING I'VE EVER SEEN. The *Gilded Gun* descending onto this godsforsaken planet in the middle of acid fricking rain.

I can't believe she's here and . . . relatively intact. Her starboard engine looks in bad shape and there are swaths of scorch marks on her hull. But she's flying. And certainly more functional than my poor *Vagabond*.

The bay doors open, and a tall, lithe figure, fully suited up, comes running down the ramp. I practically tackle Coy in a hug as she reaches the overhang, squeezing her tight. My rib cage feels like it's so full it's gonna burst in every direction, and I keep laughing.

I'm definitely going to need to get off this emotional roller coaster soon. I don't think I can take too much more. I'm built way more for liquid intake than for all this teary output.

I pull back after only a hot second and grab her by the arm, dragging her over to Hell Monkey. "His oxygen tanks are low and he's hurt. We need to get him inside quick."

She sweeps down without a word and gets a shoulder under him. I lift him on the other side. I thought it was hard hauling him around before, but he's so much more limp and heavy now that it's a struggle even with two of us. I start to panic again, throat closing up as my boots slip in the thick gravel.

And then Drinn sweeps down the ramp, says, "Sorry. Helmet got stuck," and he takes up Hell Monkey like he's not much bigger than a child and runs him into the ship. I stand there for a moment, suddenly unsure what to do with my empty arms, rain hissing as it hits my survival suit. Coy rushes by me with JR wrapped in a protective covering, ushering it up and out of the rainstorm, and I follow on their heels, closing the aft bay doors behind us.

As soon as the bay seals up, I pop my helmet off and race after Drinn and Hell Monkey. The *Gilded Gun*'s layout isn't quite the same as the *Vagabond*'s, but I manage to find the med bay with only min-imal scrambling. And that's probably because I've only got half my head on straight and a survival suit hanging off my hips.

By the time I catch up to them, Drinn has Hell Monkey out of his suit and propped up on an inclined bed. The vilkjing is fitting diagnostic-treatment cuffs around his arm and torso, and he's still passed out, his skin looking gray under the harsh artificial lights.

Drinn must hear me shuffling around because he says without looking over at me, "He's alive. Gave him a sedative." He motions at the equipment wrapped around him. "This is probably gonna hurt. Better if he's out."

Makes sense. It does. My guess is that he's got broken bones in his arm and ribs, and that's the best-case scenario. It's gonna be painful once the "treatment" aspect of the diagnostic-treatment cuffs starts to kick in and knit cells back together. But I still wish I could see him move, open his eyes, something.

Drinn straightens and stretches an arm out, nudging me toward the door. "Get your suit off. Go find Coy. There's still work to do."

I go. Dragging my feet a little on the way out. And it's only really the fact that there is a lot of explaining I need to hear from Coy that I put any hustle in my steps on the way down the corridor. I drop the slightly acid-scarred pieces of my survival suit off in an alcove and head to the bridge. Coy is already there, perched in the captain's chair. The *Gilded Gun* rumbles to life under my boots as she lifts back up through the turbulent air and above the storm clouds. I watch Coy check a three-dimensional planetary map, locate a specific spot, and then kick up the speed, zooming us off to some location. I can't really make out where or how far away it is because I don't even know where our escape pods landed.

I take a second to look at her—she's got ashy smudges in a few places on metal-gray skin, a bandage wrapped around her upper right arm, but otherwise . . . she's Coy. Alive and well and not blown up.

I move up on quiet feet and drop a kiss on the top of her head, right between her spiraled horns, before I plop down into the co-pilot seat.

She raises an eyebrow at me, a wry smile curling her mouth. "And what was that for?"

I shake my head. "It's just good to see you, Coyenne."

"Alive, you mean?" She laughs. "I imagine from your position it didn't look like good news for your oldest and loveliest friend ever."

"I mean . . . you were on fire and spiraling toward an unfriendly planet, so . . ."

Her expression sobers a bit. "It was dodgy for a minute. But Drinn is a magician and he works quick, thank the stars. He got us stabilized, I kept us from crashing, and we managed to keep her together." Coy flicks a look at me. "Our sensors picked up a pretty big explosion up there. Was it . . . ?"

"The *Vagabond*." Her name is bittersweet on my tongue. "And the warship with it. Setter and Faye got clear."

Coy reaches for my hand and squeezes it. "I'm sorry, Alyssa. Really. She was a good ship. One of the best."

I open my mouth to reply, but the *Gun*'s AI breaks in: "Approaching designated coordinates, Captain Coyenne."

"Thank you, Nova. Initiate landing sequence as programmed." Coy swings her chair around and waggles her eyebrows at me. "Go get a new suit, Farshot. We've got time for one more walk before we leave."

The beacon.

Hand to the stars, I'd almost forgotten about the stupid beacon. The one thing we were all scrambling for in the first place. I'd lost track of it somewhere between the exploding ships and watching Hell Monkey slowly suffocate.

Coy didn't, though. Girl knows how to get herself a throne.

It takes us only two or three minutes to pull on fresh survival suits and head back into Calm's balmy, hospitable landscape. It's raining here too. Poisonous and corrosive. Really delightful. The ship is perched on the edge of a steep canyon of slick, eroded black rock. It's hard to see the bottom—it's so dark down there—and the only thing I can hear besides the rain is the wind. Howling like a wild beast. It basically sounds like a black hole looks.

We've got all the equipment a worldcruiser can offer, but even with full rappelling gear and self-adhering grips, it's slow going. More than once, Coy and I slip and are jerked out of a death fall by our protective gear. When we finally reach the bottom, our boots sink—a dozen centimeters at least—into sludge and mud. I can't wait to get back to the Explorers' Society and tell them I'll quit if they ever ask me to come back here. This planet is the worst.

Coy checks her wristband, scanning the surrounding area, and then points down a narrow crawl space between two cliff faces.

This beacon better be worth it.

Coy goes first, bracing herself between the slippery rocks, and I follow right behind her, dropping onto much firmer, drier ground. It's sheltered down here by the overhanging rock above and the curves of the cliff face below, shutting out the worst of the storm outside.

I'm still looking around, taking stock, when Coy seizes my arm in a fierce grip.

"Ow! Hey, what the hell—"

"Alyssa!" Her voice is tight with excitement. "It's here."

I turn, following her gaze to the back of the overhang. There's a pile of rocks, set up almost like a short podium or an altar, and there, at the top, is something metallic and gleaming. A disc, a little smaller than my hand.

The seal. The royal seal of the United Sovereign Empire.

"Holy shit." I don't mean to say it out loud. It just slips out.

Coy crashes into me, crushing me in a hug and squealing.

Actually squealing like a little kid. It's the unshielded, unfettered Coy that no one ever really sees.

"Alyssa, we did it! We actually did it!"

I squeeze her back and then extract myself, taking her helmet in my hands. "We're going to step carefully, though, yes? Just in case. Stay behind me. Let me look at things."

She's practically vibrating with the desire to bolt over and grab it, but she listens and waits while I bring my wristband up and use the sensors on it to scan the seal and the space around it.

The signature that bounces back makes the readout go wild, filling with information too fast for me to process all at once. I have to stare at it, Coy craning to see over my shoulder, for probably a full minute, and while I still don't understand it necessarily, it's familiar.

"I've seen this before," I murmur. "On the *Vagabond*. You know when we'd get shut down for not being the first one to get the next clue? This signature started appearing in our systems."

"Okay . . ." She's trying to be patient. I can hear the strain in her voice. "It's tied to the crownchase. That makes sense. Is there anything else around it to worry about, though?"

I'm not picking up anything physical around us except the disc, but the energy coming from it is so complex, so responsive, so . . . aware.

I stare at that small, innocuous seal gleaming in the faint light. "It's alive, Coy."

"What do you mean, 'alive'? It's basically a piece of jewelry, isn't it?"

I shake my head. "That's not what I'm picking up now. It's, like, a ship AI or something. It's active, and it *knows*."

The seal starts to glow, pinpricks of light rising to its surface connected by geodesic lines. The symbol of the empire. And then, in the air just above it:

⟫⟫ **Welcome, crownchaser. Return to the kingship and claim your throne.**

Coy's eyebrows rise up and up, and she shoots me a slightly weirded-out look.

I shrug. "Well? You don't want to keep the sentient royal emblem waiting. That's rude."

She steps forward, hand outstretched, but just a few centimeters short of taking the seal, she stops. Turns. And looks at me.

"Do you want it?"

My mouth falls open. I gape at her for one second, two seconds. Then: "Are you high, Coy?"

She steps forward and takes my hands in hers. "I didn't get here all by myself. I'm here because of you. You earned this as much as I did. It's only fair to ask—do you want to take the seal?"

I study her face very carefully. I know her masks very well. I can almost always spot the edges. But there are no edges to her now. There's no scheme in the corners of her mouth or false bottoms to her eyes. Her earnestness is real. She couldn't have surprised me more if she'd stabbed me in the gut.

My gaze drifts from Coy's face to the royal seal. Just sitting there. The fate of a thousand and one worlds compressed in a fifteen-centimeter disc. Do I want it? I know it's what Uncle Atar was hoping for, but I can't choose this path based on someone else's wants. It's gotta be what I want. We're talking trillions of people and their lives and their hopes resting in the hands of the empress, and they deserve someone who's more than lukewarm to the whole concept of ruling. They need passion and politics, and I'm neither.

I don't want to be, either.

I look up into Coy's green eyes. "No. I want you to take it, but I want you to promise me you'll do better. Better than our parents. Better than their parents. I want you to swear you're gonna listen to all those people who aren't getting heard right now."

She nods, her mouth set in a solemn line. "Like on Tear. Like you were telling me about."

And here I hadn't thought she was even listening to me. I guess I should know better than to underestimate Nathalia Coyenne. "Yeah, Tear would probably be a good place to start. But, Coy, hand to the stars, if you show even the slightest sign of becoming a dickbag with that crown, I will personally assassinate you, and I won't feel bad about it."

Coy grins and leans forward, pressing her helmet to mine. "I know you will, Alyssa. I won't fail you."

Then she turns, steps over to the rocks, and picks up the seal.

Breath rushes out of me in a wave of relief. The crownchase is over.

FORTY-EIGHT

I'M THERE WHEN HELL MONKEY WAKES UP. THE sedative Drinn gave him was short-acting, and by the time we get back on board with the royal seal and point the *Gilded Gun* up at the stars, he's already stirring. He doesn't fully come around, though, until about two or three minutes after we break atmo and start to put some distance between us and Calm. I'm sitting on the edge of his bed, holding his hand, and it feels a little cheesy but completely worth it when his eyes finally open and a tired grin creeps across his face.

"I thought Drinn would be the one snuggling me when I came to."

I pat his arm. "We flipped for it. I lost, so you're stuck with me."

"I'll manage, I guess." He shifts a little, trying out his arm. His face squishes up with pain, but he's got movement in it at least.

"How is it feeling?"

"Stiff. A little achy. Nothing that'll keep me down for very long." He levers himself up on the bed so he can get a better look at my face. "What's the status? Where are we?"

I don't know how to answer that.

We're at the end.

We're at the beginning.

But instead I just let this simmering bright ball of light burst across my face in the form of a big grin. I take his face between my hands and tell him, "It's over."

And then I kiss him. And I'm not drunk or out of sorts or otherwise incapacitated. I have no excuse for it except that I just want to. I want to taste the warmth of his mouth and feel that exchange that kisses provide. Where I take a little of him and he takes a little of me, and if they're the right sort of person, like Hell Monkey is, they won't just take the good parts and leave the bad. They'll take a little bit of all of you and leave a little bit of all of them, and you'll step back a bit different and a bit more than you were before.

I kiss him and I keep kissing him, and he wraps his one good arm around my back to press me harder against his chest.

I know I had reasons, once, to keep him at arm's length. To avoid this. But hand to the stars, I can't remember what they ever were now.

I pull back after a minute, and Hell Monkey looks at me with this half-delighted, half-dazed expression.

"Were we talking about something?" His voice rumbles down my spine. "I can't remember."

I laugh and pat him on the cheek. "Only about our sudden and amazing freedom. No big deal."

"Oh, sure, that." He keeps his arm around me, like he thinks if he breaks contact, the whole scene will dissolve. "You said it's over—are you meaning like . . . this whole mess? The actual crownchase is over?"

"Coy and I found the seal. Down on Calm. We tracked that last beacon, and—ta-da—there it was."

His eyes grow probably three sizes. "Holy crap. What happened? What'd you do?"

"I didn't do anything. Coy went up and took it, and that's that. She's on the bridge now with the Gun's mediabot, giving a winner's interview. She wants to get it transmitted to the media feeds before we jump to hyperlight and head to Apex. Show the quadrant their new empress."

Empress Nathalia Coyenne. I get a vision of her, all decked out in royal finery, sitting on the throne, surrounded by the Coyenne family colors. That's actually going to be a thing. I'm going to have to, like, bow and call her "Your Highness" or some shit like that. That's weird to try to wrap my brain around.

Hell Monkey's smile splits his whole face. "I can't believe it. We actually did it, Farshot. We're out. You're out."

I can't keep it cool like I want. I grin like an idiot right with him. I even bounce a little on the edge of my seat. It's very mature. "We can find a new ship, maybe one with an upgraded six-fusion engine. . . ."

"That's the kind of sexy talk I like," he says, waggling his eyebrows. "What else you got, Farshot?"

"And Drago VIII is still sitting out there, just waiting to be circumnavigated. . . ."

"Oof, take it easy on me. I'm still kinda injured, y'know."

We can pick up right where we left off, I think. And then, as Hell Monkey leans in to kiss me again, *Well, maybe not right where we left off. Maybe a little better than that.*

The lights in the med bay flicker. And then go dark.

I push away from Hell Monkey. My boots hit the floor as the emergency lighting comes up, casting a red glow over everything.

"What the hell? What's happening?" he mutters.

I shake my head and cast a glance back at him, at the stabilizing wraps encasing his torso. I put a hand on his chest and press him back onto the bed. "Stay here." He starts to protest, and I cut him off. "You're still healing. I'm sure it's all fine. I'm just going to go make sure everything is okay."

I slip out into the corridor, moving a little slower than normal to keep my boots from clomping on the metal floors. Goose bumps are creeping up my skin, and I'm getting that bad-fluttery feeling in my stomach. The one that says, *Listen, Farshot, I don't know if you've had enough coffee to deal with this.* Every part of me strains to listen, to see if I can catch any unfamiliar sounds over the hum of the sublight engines.

Or wait . . . no . . . No humming. No sublight engines. We're not moving.

A distant shout, coming from the bridge. I can't tell what the shout was, but it doesn't sound like anything good.

Screw stealthy. I break into a sprint, storming down the halls, almost running over JR the mediabot as it wanders from the galley, looking confused.

"Captain Farshot, is this a planned—"

I plow by without answering.

About midway down the port-side corridor, I spot a hole in the ceiling and skid to a stop, staring up at it.

Someone has cut through the hull of the *Gilded Gun* and jammed an illegal docking seal around it.

We've been boarded. Oh gods. Nathalia.

I haul ass for the bridge, arms and legs pumping, my heart ramming against my sternum. Tension twists like a fist in my chest, and my brain jumps from *who could've possibly* to *please let her be okay* to *I'm going to fucking murder someone.*

I round a corner and the doorway to the bridge is ahead of me, wide open. I sprint through it, full-out—

—and slam into an invisible wall.

I crumple to the ground, all the breath knocked out of me. My face throbs, and the front of my body aches from the impact. I taste copper on my tongue. Something warm and wet oozes from one side of my nose, and my right ankle feels like someone twisted it around the wrong way. Groaning, I roll onto my side, scrambling to get my arms and legs under me and take stock of what the hell is happening.

I'm just inside the *Gilded Gun's* bridge, but the air in front of me doesn't look quite right. It's got a wavy, slightly foggy quality to it—possible to see through, but when I try to put a hand through it, it might as well be steel.

A godsdamned force field.

Just beyond it, I can see Coy, straight-shouldered, chin up. Putting on her full haughtier-than-thou look. She's standing over the smashed, twisted remains of the *Gun's* assigned mediabot. At her back is what looks like another mediabot, but it's been augmented, pieces added to its gear. It's holding Coy's blaster pressed to her back.

And in front of her, receiving one hundred percent of her glare, is Edgar Voles.

I can't hear anything through the field, but I can see him talking to her, one hand out, the other clutching a blaster of his own while he gestures decisively. Coy doesn't look impressed with whatever he's saying. Her mouth twists, and she laughs in his face. A bright red flush rises in his cheeks.

"HEY!" I scream, pounding my fists on the force field. I limp up and down as far as I can get, waving wildly, trying to draw attention. "HEY, VOLES! OVER HERE!"

They all look. Edgar and his robot give me a quick once-over and then turn away from me. Coy quirks a smile and gives me a little wave. I don't like the look in her eyes. There's a dangerous edge in it that puts a cold, dark lump in the back of my throat.

JR peeks its head around the corner. "Captain Farshot . . ."

I shoot out a hand and drag the mediabot forward, right up to the edge of the field. "Film that," I bark at it, and then scramble around, looking for something, anything, I can use.

For what, Farshot? What the hell do you think you're going to do?

I don't know, but stars and gods, I've got to try something.

Edgar is mad now. I don't know when I've seen him so obviously and visibly mad. He's in Coy's face, yelling something, and she rises to meet him, yelling back. And that bot with Edgar takes half a step back, points its blaster, and shoots Coy in the leg.

I can see the pain and the scream cross her face, and my ribs are a vise crushing my lungs. I can't breathe, my pulse fills my ears, and like a wild, cornered thing, I dig my nails into a wall panel and rip it off, using it like a bat to hit the force field over and over.

This seems to catch Edgar's eye. He pauses to look at me for just a second—and Coy makes her move. She leaps up, kicks the robot's blaster from its grip, and then runs at Edgar.

I don't see exactly what happens next. There's a flurry of movement—Edgar and Coy twine together in a violent twist of limbs—and then, in the middle of their bodies, three bright flashes.

Blaster fire.

The panel falls from my scratched and bleeding fingers, and I wait, holding my breath, for Edgar to fall to the ground.

But he doesn't. Coy does.

My Coy. My Nathalia. She drops to her knees, her chest a mess of scorched flesh and dark green blood, spreading through her clothes and pouring down her body. She wavers; her eyes find mine. And she collapses.

I scream. I scream from my stomach, from my soul. I scream loud enough and long enough that it sinks into the walls and floors of the ship. I throw every part of me against the force field, bruising my legs and my arms and my shoulders.

Edgar's robot picks up a half-meter-long baton device and clanks over toward me.

I'm ready. I'm seething and tasting spit and blood. "COME ON, YOU METAL SON OF A BITCH! I'LL RIP OUT YOUR CIRCUITS AND FORCE FEED THEM TO YOU!"

I don't see how it brings the force field down. All I know is that it disappears, and the robot immediately shoves that baton into my stomach. My muscles seize up. Bright, sharp pain lances through my brain. And then the last thing I remember is the metal floor rushing toward my face.

HAS THE SEAL BEEN FOUND?
Experts say there's cause to think the crownchase has ended, but a winner has yet to emerge

WYTHE: "WE WILL NOT RECOGNIZE A FALSE CLAIMANT"
The steward of the throne releases a statement vowing to fully verify any declared winner before ceding the power of the throne

WILLIAM VOLES CALLS EMERGENCY IMPERIAL COUNCIL MEETING
Prime family patriarch says, given the multiple interferences in the crownchase, they must convene to discuss viable paths forward

ORSO, ROY REPORTED AT A VIOLA HOSPITAL
The two crownchasers are both said to be stable and healing from injuries sustained in the mysterious firefight over Calm

A HYPERLIGHT LANE, HEADING FOR APEX

Edgar once read that close to ninety percent of all recognized species in the empire have blood or a blood-like substance as part of their biological makeup. It's such a common thing to so many life-forms that there really should be nothing significant about it. It's a simple organic output. That's all.

Edgar tells himself this as he strips off his ruined clothes and throws them in the incinerator.

He tells himself this as he washes Nathalia Coyenne's blood off his hands.

And then he washes them again. And again.

He tells himself this as he walks, shoulders back, onto the bridge of Worldcruiser S576-034, with those same hands jammed into his pockets to keep them from shaking.

NL7 stands at the strategic-operations table. The royal seal sits in the middle of it, and the android moves its hands through the air as it assesses the diagnostic readouts being projected above it. Edgar steps up next to it, but he doesn't look at the display. His eyes are fixed on the royal seal. It's so small really, its surface completely blank and clean at the moment.

It certainly doesn't look worth killing for.

That hadn't been the plan. NL7 had proposed that as his first move, but he'd balked at the suggestion. Killing a fellow crown-chaser would disqualify him from the throne. And in any case, he'd thought he could reason with Nathalia. That in the precarious situation she'd been backed into, she'd be amenable to negotiation. He'd even offered her significant power under his rule.

She'd laughed at him. Anger had flooded every part of him. He hadn't even been able to see straight.

But he still hadn't shot her. Not until she'd tackled him and grabbed for the blaster and his grip had slipped in the struggle. . . .

There'd been so much blood. Maybe he should go wash his hands again.

"Very curious," says NL7. "There's an intelligence in this, Edgar Voles."

He drags his eyes up to the readouts but hardly sees them. "In what? In the seal?"

"Correct. Highly sophisticated. A central sentience within the disc controlling billions of microscopic nanoids. It is plausible that the seal itself was coordinating the crownchase this entire time. That would certainly be a way to ensure impartiality—"

Edgar shakes his head. His chest is filled with a heavy ache, and his skin crawls with guilt. With grief even, maybe. He can't seem to collect his emotions right now and shove them back into the box he built for them. He can still feel the warmth of blood soaking into his shirt. And see Nathalia's shocked face as she slipped to the ground.

He's glad his father isn't here to see this. All of this. The abject failure of his too soft, too emotional son. The great family disap-pointment.

Edgar stuffs his hand back in his pocket. "It's not important. I'm no longer a candidate to claim the throne."

NL7 looks over at him, tilting its head. "How so, Edgar Voles?"

"I broke one of the explicit rules. I killed a fellow crownchaser. That's automatic disqualification."

NL7 turns back to the projection and wipes it clean, pulling up two different files. One is the list of crownchase rules and regulations. One is the complete history of imperial crownchases.

"In 2297, two years after a crownchase won by the Coyenne prime family, the former crownchaser of the Megas killed the former crownchaser of the Roys in a personal skirmish. The Roys used the laws as written at that time to disqualify the Mega prime family from the next chase for the throne. They won their case on this technicality, but after that, a new phrase was introduced into the canon."

NL7 zooms in on one of the article lines:

. . . *crownchaser who kills a fellow crownchaser before the royal seal has been found* . . .

Edgar stares at those last seven words, weighing them in his head. *Before the royal seal has been found.* It's slow to dawn, an unusual phenomenon in and of itself for someone as smart as him, but it pushes its way past the pall of emotions clogging his brain.

He killed Nathalia Coyenne, but it wasn't until *after* the seal had been retrieved. He hadn't violated the rules as written. He can still sit on the throne. Where he belongs.

He reaches out and picks up the royal seal for the first time since they came back from the *Gilded Gun*, testing the feel of the smooth, cool metal in his palm. Cupping it in front of him, he walks over and sits in the captain's chair, spinning to face NL7. "You still have the mediabot's ability to record and transmit, yes?"

"Of course, Edgar Voles."

"Good. Begin." He waits until the lenses on NL7's stolen body glow with blue light, and then he takes a deep breath and says, "This is Edgar Marius Tycho Voles. I have claimed the royal seal of the United Sovereign Empire. I am your new emperor."

CHEERY COYENNE'S LUXURY STAR-YACHT, APEX ORBIT

I KNOW I SHOULD BE AT THE PARTY DOWNSTAIRS. That's the whole reason why I'm even up here instead of down on the planet like usual.

But I found the observation deck and I can't make myself leave.

I've never been this close to the stars before.

I've seen them from the windows of the kingship. I've seen them in the on-board planetarium.

But this is different. They're *right here*. I could almost touch them. I could fall right off the edge of this ship and into the middle of them and watch them ripple around me like water.

I don't know how Uncle Atar was ever able to drag himself away from them.

It's probably been an hour since I snuck out. Or close to that. My uncles are going to start getting worried about where I am. Ms. Coyenne and her husband might notice soon too and be offended that the emperor's niece bailed on them.

And Nat—

"Found you!" Someone half tackles me, and I yelp in surprise. I recognize Nathalia's tall, gangly figure and big green eyes a second later, and I relax as she slings an arm over my shoulders. "Should've guessed you'd be up here."

I scratch at the back of my head. "I was coming right back down, I swear, I—"

"No, you weren't, liar." She hip checks me and spins around to sprawl on one of the long, low couches scattered around the room. "It's fine. It's a party for my parents, really. My birthday is just a convenient excuse for them to trap everyone on board and play mind games with them."

I sit down next to her and pull my knees into my chest. "Do you think that's going to be us someday? Like, we won't be able to trust anything the other person is saying and we'll always be trying to get an angle on people. . . ."

Nathalia screws her face up, thinking for a long minute. "Honestly? Maybe. I mean, eventually we're all going to have to take over whatever it is all our parents do, and then . . . ?"

She shrugs, like it's no big deal, and I feel my face fall. My eyes drift back to the stars.

She sits forward and grabs my hand, squeezing it tight. "Not us, though, Alyssa. Everyone else can turn on each other and play their stupid games, but you and me—we have each other's backs. We'll always be there for one another, right?"

I look back at her, and my heart swells. "Always. I promise."

Nathalia smiles, bright, like a supernova. "Me too."

I hold on to her hand so tight and so long that my fingers start to ache. But I don't let go.

Because I made a promise.

FORTY-NINE

I WAKE UP GASPING.

Lightning is wrapped around my body. A thousand Puorvian wasps are trapped inside my skin. I surge upward—I don't even know where I think I'm going—but strong hands clamp down on my arms and hold me in place.

I try to focus on the person in front of me. My eyes feel jumpy. My ears are full of buzzing.

"Alyssa!"

I know that voice. That's Hell Monkey's voice. I squeeze my eyes shut and then snap them open again, and this time they land securely on his face. He reaches down and plucks something from my chest, just over my heart.

A syringe. An empty syringe.

Now I know why I'm feeling the strong urge to lift tables and see how far I can throw them. "You gave me an adrenaline shot."

"I'm sorry." He puts one hand on my cheek, his thumb along my jaw to keep me framed on him. My jittery brain keeps trying to drift. "I'm so sorry, but I need you up. They left a hull breach in the port-side corridor and they set the self-destruct on the ship and we—"

I scramble onto my feet, grabbing Hell Monkey's uninjured shoulder to heave myself up. My body feels weird. Like the insides of me are all hollow but the outsides are lit up with angry energy. It makes me feel only half-here, half in control of what I'm doing. I register the sight of JR nearby, its body smashed all to hell.

I register the sight of Coy too, but I can't . . .

I can't.

"Find Drinn," I tell Hell Monkey. "We're gonna need him."

I don't think he wants to leave me. I can feel him hover around near my shoulder for a few seconds too long, but then he takes off, door sliding closed behind him. I steady myself on the table and lurch across the bridge, falling into the captain's chair.

The conn swims in front of my eyes. I'm not sure exactly what that robot hit me with, but I think I might've needed a little while longer to sleep it off. My head doesn't seem quite connected to the rest of me. I scrub at my face and focus.

The self-destruct clock is ticking down. Forty-two seconds and counting.

Hands vibrating, I move my fingers as quickly as I can over the dash. I don't have the initial codes or commands Edgar Voles used—or maybe his fucking robot used—so I have to settle for work-arounds. Overrides and back doors that I've learned from driving a worldcruiser class starship for the past three years. It takes longer than it would if I had proper authorization, but if I can move quickly enough, if I can type quickly enough—

⟫⟫ Self-destruct cancellation request received.

Good.

⟫⟫ Submit captain identity confirmation.

Oh.

It means Coy.

My gaze drifts down to her, a crumpled, blood-covered heap on the floor. The thought of using her body so callously, like she's just a tool, churns my stomach. But there's only fifteen seconds left to self-destruct. And a dead hero can't avenge anyone.

I vault out of the chair and haul her right arm out from under her. Her skin is already too cool, too clammy; the feel of it sends a shudder down my body. She's not close enough to reach the panel from here, so I have to scoop my arms underneath her shoulders and drag her body a few meters. But it's awkward because she is—was—a lot taller than me and exhaustion is starting to creep back into my limbs. At one point, I actually slip in her blood and fall on my ass and I think I might laugh or maybe cry or maybe scream down the godsdamned stars. I grit my teeth and dig in my heels and pull the dead weight of her body until I can stretch her arm up to the conn and press her lifeless hand against the screen.

Five seconds left.

The ship scans her fingers and palm, processes them.

Four seconds left. Three seconds . . .

))) **Identity confirmed. Self-destruct canceled.**

I let Coy's arm fall, and I fall with it, collapsing on the floor beside her body.

Her *body*.

I look at her—really look at her—for the first time, sprawled right in front of me. Her legs twisted at odd angles. Her chest a mass of blasted flesh and congealed blood. And her face . . . Empty. Completely empty. Eyes staring at nothing. All spark, all essence, all of what made her Nathalia Coyenne—evaporated. Just like that.

She was here—she was *right here*. Bold and vibrant and devilish, even with blasters pointed at her.

And now . . . nothing. Now all that sits here is a broken ex-cruiser jockey and the husk of the girl who should've been empress.

I wait for the tears to come. I can feel them pressing against the backs of my eyes. But they don't fall. I wait and wait, the lower half of me going numb from being in the same position on the cold bridge floor. But they just sit there. Building up in my chest.

The port-side door slides open and Hell Monkey rushes in. He stops short when he sees me curled up on the ground with Nathalia's blood all over my arms and chest and neck. He moves forward slowly and carefully. Like the whole room is made of glass. Or maybe just I am.

He crouches down next to me and reaches a hand out, but I shake my head. I don't want him to touch me right now. I don't want anyone to touch me right now. I can still feel Coy's cold skin on my fingertips and I hate it and cherish it at the same time.

"Drinn?" I ask.

"I found him," Hell Monkey says. "They shot him, but he's alive. Critical, but alive. I got him back to the med bay and got treatment cuffs on him. Hopefully that fixes him up all right."

I nod and then cut a glance over at him. "How about you? How's your arm?"

There's a beat where he cocks his head at me—like, *are you really* asking about a minor broken arm after this?—and then he realizes what I'm really asking and a fierceness drops over his expression. "Strong enough, Captain."

"Good. Help me up. We've got work to do."

FIFTY

Stardate: 0.06.01 in the Year 4031, under the reign of the Never-Crowned Empress, Nathalia Matilda Coyenne, long may she rest in glory

Location: Preparing to take a hyperlight lane straight up Edgar Voles's ass

IT'S BEEN SEVENTEEN HOURS SINCE COY DIED HERE on her own bridge. Seventeen hours, three minutes, and forty-three seconds.

Not that I'm counting.

I still haven't cried at all. My tears have gone dormant. Like they've buried themselves deep underneath my skin. Probably somewhere beneath all these brand-new layers of simmering violence.

That's fine. I don't have time for tears anyway.

I rock back on my heels, taking another look at the circuit board I'm reconfiguring. It taps directly into the conn, and Hell Monkey says a few easy changes will help us optimize screen controls. Just enough to shave a few seconds off our reaction times. I'll take it—I'll take any advantage we can get—but I need Hell Monkey in the engine room, trying to repair whatever damage he can without us taking time to dock somewhere. So he walked me through how to switch the circuitry around. Three times. I think the last time stuck, though. Scanning it now, I think it looks about how Hell Monkey had described it.

I roll my aching shoulders—who knew fiddly circuit work could make your arms hurt so much?—and feel the iridescent metal of my mother's armband tighten around my bicep.

I brush my fingertips along the feathered etchings.

Count up another body that hit the ground for the throne. It's been eating people up my whole life.

I pick up the wall panel from the ground and shove it back into place, wiping my hands on a towel as I cross back over to the captain's chair. Spots of Coy's blood still stain my skin, now mixed with the blue-tinged oil that lubricates the inside workings of the ship. Her body isn't here any longer, though, and I scrubbed the blood from the floor myself, the old-fashioned way, with a brush and solvent and all of my grief while Hell Monkey sealed up the hull breach in the corridor. Afterward, he helped me wrap her in a big cloth of the Coyenne family colors that we found hung up in her quarters. We placed her in a stasis chamber, to keep her body preserved.

Until I can bring her to her mother.

Cheery Coyenne is going to kill everyone for this.

But only if I don't do it first.

Heavy boots cross the bridge, and I feel Hell Monkey at my

back. He doesn't touch me—he hasn't even tried since he found me with Coy's body on the bridge. He's just been hovering nearby, quiet, steady. Waiting on me.

"I checked in on Drinn," he says, holding out a flask of water. "He's sleeping, but the worst of it seems to have passed."

I nod, take the water, and then lean back against him. Not very much, but it's still nice to let someone else take some of the weight I'm dragging. Even just for a moment.

"I'm gonna rename her," I say, gesturing at the navcomm area.

He slips a hand around my waist. "New captain, new name. Makes sense to me. What'd you have in mind?"

"The *Nathalia*. She's gonna be named the *Nathalia*."

He doesn't say anything. Just nods and holds me a little tighter. I squeeze his fingers and then step out of his arms, slipping into the captain's chair. It's not my seat. It's not my ship. Coy should be the one sitting here right now, and instead of pushing that thought aside, I let it stay, let it turn to a bright, hot pool of lava in my stomach. Reaching forward, I swipe my fingers across one of the screens on the dash, calling up the ship's AI.

"What can I do for you, Alyssa Farshot?" The AI's voice is a little deeper than Rose's, but still with that cool, mechanical quality. It takes me a second to remember the name Coy had given them.

I sit up straighter, fix the collar on my Faroshti coat. There might be blood on me still, but I'm kind of okay with that. "Nova, I need you to broadcast a message. Broadband and public. Any and all open channels and media feeds."

"Understood. Transmission initiated. Speak when ready."

I stare straight into the viewscreen. "This is Alyssa Farshot, heir to the Faroshti prime family, captain of the worldcruiser *Nathalia*. Nathalia Coyenne, heir to the Coyenne prime family, was the rightful winner of the crownchase and your true empress. Edgar Voles is a traitor and a murderer. Any claim he makes on the throne is illegitimate, and I call upon the kingship officials to arrest and detain him on sight."

I lean forward, letting all that rage light up my eyes and harden my jaw. "And Edgar? If you're seeing this, you'd better run. Because I'm coming for you."

Acknowledgments

When I was much younger, my idea of being a professional author meant holing up in a cabin in the mountains, typing up all my stories on paper, and mailing them off to a publisher in New York City to be made into a book. It was only as an adult that I realized it actually takes a big, wonderful community to make a book, and I feel incredibly blessed by all of those who have helped me make this one possible.

To Lara Perkins: I couldn't ask for a better advocate or a better partner in publishing. Thank you for believing in my stories. To Greg Ferguson and Tara Weikum: thank you for supporting my vision for Alyssa Farshot and all the characters in this sprawling space empire. Thanks to the entire team at Harper for all the hard work and long hours you put in to transform this book into its final form: to Sarah Homer, Jon Howard, and Stephanie Evans for honing the fine details and reining in my penchant for italics; to Doaly for the amazing cover art that brought Alyssa to life and to Chris Kwon and Jenna Stempel for the incredible design work; to Allison Brown for everything you do to transform my digital words into a real, actual book; to Anna Bernard and Sabrina Abballe and

Shannon Cox for supporting *Crownchasers* and helping bring it to libraries, bookstores, and homes all over the country; to Marieke Nijkamp, Alechia Dow, and Michelle Vardanian for your careful eyes, thoughtful critiques, and honest opinions.

I'm extremely lucky to be surrounded by so many talented friends and colleagues who've been there over the years whenever I needed support, advice, or just a chance to vent. To Natalie Parker and Tessa Gratton: I'm so glad I came to Lawrence that day for a casual writers' meetup. I had no idea how important it would be. To Megan Bannen, Amanda Sellet, and Sarah Henning, for fielding all my texts—the desperate ones, the grumpy ones, and the excited ones. To all of the Kansas City-Lawrence writers—Adib Khorram, Christie O. Hall, Dot Hutchinson, Bethany Hagen, L. L. McKinney, Jennifer Mendez, Meghan Stigge, Natasha Hanova: you all are the best freaking group. To Marieke, Dahlia Adler, and Chessie Zappia: for being there with me since way back on the 2012 pitch contest circuit. And to all the Roaring 20s debuts: thank you for being a sounding board and a place to commiserate.

I save my family for last because they have been with me on this writing journey for so long. To all the extended Klemans and Coffindaffers—my grandma and grandpa, all my aunts and uncles and cousins—thank you for every time you patiently listened while I rambled about the story I was working on. To Kathleen and Julie, who prove that family is as much about soul as it is about blood. To all my friends who've cheerleaded me and my stories, whether they were on the page or being told over a *Dungeons & Dragons* table.

To Shauna and Tess, my sisters, my constant support team.

To Mom and Dad, who always knew I would get here someday.

To Miriam and Evelyn, my bright, beautiful souls who had to be patient during all those times I had to work.

And to Dave. My rock. My big damn hero. I love you always.